P9-EMM-986

DARTH BANE
PATH OF DESTRUCTION

STAR WARS

DARTH BANE
PATH OF DESTRUCTION

A NOVEL OF THE OLD REPUBLIC

Drew Karpyshyn

LUCAS BOOKS

DEL REY BALLANTINE BOOKS
NEW YORK

Published in the United States by Del Rey Books, an imprint of The Random House Publishing Group, a division of Random House, Inc., New York.

DEL REY is a registered trademark and the
Del Rey colophon is a trademark of Random House, Inc.

ISBN-10 0-345-47736-7
ISBN-13 978-0-345-47736-1

Printed in the United States of America on acid-free paper

www.starwars.com
www.delreybooks.com

2 4 6 8 9 7 5 3 1

First Edition

To Jen, who makes everything possible.

————

ACKNOWLEDGMENTS

This novel couldn't have come together without the help of many people.

I'd like to thank my editors Shelly Shapiro and Sue Rostoni for giving me this chance and for sticking with me through all my rewrites and revisions. I shudder to think what I would have ended up with had it not been for their valuable comments and ideas.

Anyone who has read the Jedi vs. Sith series will see the creative debt I owe to Dark Horse Comics, but I'd also like to point out the contributions of my friends and coworkers at BioWare. Much of the groundwork and background material for this novel evolved out of our research and work together on KOTOR, especially Dave Gaider, Luke Kristjanson, Peter Thomas, and James Ohlen.

Thanks for everything, guys.

Drew

In the last days of the Old Republic, the Sith—followers of the Force's dark side and ancient enemies of the Jedi order—numbered only two: one Master and one apprentice. Yet it was not always so. A thousand years before the Republic's collapse and Emperor Palpatine's rise to power, the Sith were legion . . .

————

Lord Kaan, Sith Master and founder of the Brotherhood of Darkness, strode through the gore of the battlefield, a tall shadow in the night's gloom. Thousands of Republic troops and nearly a hundred Jedi had given their lives trying to defend this world against his army—and they had lost. He relished their suffering and despair; even now he could sense it rising up like the stench from the broken corpses scattered about the valley.

In the distance a storm was brewing. As each flash of lightning illuminated the sky, Korriban's great Sith temple was momentarily visible in the distance, a stark silhouette towering over the barren horizon.

A pair of figures waited in the center of the slaughter, one human and the other Twi'lek. He recognized them despite the darkness: Qordis and Kopecz, two of the more powerful Sith Lords. Once they had been bitter rivals, but now they served together in Kaan's Brotherhood. He approached them quickly, smiling.

Qordis, tall and so lean as to appear almost skeletal, smiled back. "This is a great victory, Lord Kaan. It has been far too long since the Sith have had an academy on Korriban."

"I sense you are eager to begin training the new apprentices here," Kaan replied. "I expect you will provide me with many more powerful—and loyal—Sith adepts and Masters in the coming years."

"Provide *you*?" Kopecz asked pointedly. "Don't you mean provide *us*? Are we not all part of the Brotherhood of Darkness?"

His question was met with an easy laugh. "Of course, Kopecz. A mere slip of the tongue."

"Kopecz refuses to celebrate in our triumph," Qordis noted. "He has been like this all night."

Kaan clasped a hand on the hefty Twi'lek's shoulder. "This is a great victory for us," he said. "Korriban is more than just another world: it is a symbol. The birthplace of the Sith. This victory sends a message to the Republic and the Jedi. Now they will truly know and fear the Brotherhood."

Kopecz shrugged free of Kaan's hand and turned away with a flick of the tips of the long lekku wound around his neck. "Celebrate if you wish," he called over his shoulder as he walked away. "But the real war has only just begun."

PART ONE

Three Years Later

1

Dessel was lost in the suffering of his job, barely even aware of his surroundings. His arms ached from the endless pounding of the hydraulic jack. Small bits of rock skipped off the cavern wall as he bored through, ricocheting off his protective goggles and stinging his exposed face and hands. Clouds of atomized dust filled the air, obscuring his vision, and the screeching whine of the jack filled the cavern, drowning out all other sounds as it burrowed centimeter by agonizing centimeter into the thick vein of cortosis woven into the rock before him.

Impervious to both heat and energy, cortosis was prized in the construction of armor and shielding by both commercial and military interests, especially with the galaxy at war. Highly resistant to blaster bolts, cortosis alloys supposedly could withstand even the blade of a lightsaber. Unfortunately, the very properties that made it so valuable also made it extremely difficult to mine. Plasma torches were virtually useless; it would take days to burn away even a small section of cortosis-laced rock. The only effective way to mine it was through the brute force of hydraulic jacks pounding relentlessly away at a vein, chipping the cortosis free bit by bit.

Cortosis was one of the hardest materials in the galaxy. The force of the pounding quickly wore down the head of a jack, blunting it until it became almost useless. The dust clogged the hydraulic pistons, making them jam. Mining cortosis was hard on the equipment . . . and even harder on the miners.

Des had been hammering away for nearly six standard hours. The jack weighed more than thirty kilos, and the strain of keeping it raised and pressed against the rock face was taking its toll. His arms were trembling from the exertion. His lungs were gasping for air and choking on the clouds of fine mineral dust thrown up from the jack's head. Even his teeth hurt: the rattling vibration felt as if it were shaking them loose from his gums.

But the miners on Apatros were paid based on how much cortosis they brought back. If he quit now, another miner would jump in and start working the vein, taking a share of the profits. Des didn't like to share.

The whine of the jack's motor took on a higher pitch, becoming a keening wail Des was all too familiar with. At twenty thousand rpm, the motor sucked in dust like a thirsty bantha sucking up water after a long desert crossing. The only way to combat it was by regular cleaning and servicing, and the Outer Rim Oreworks Company preferred to buy cheap equipment and replace it, rather than sinking credits into maintenance. Des knew exactly what was going to happen next—and a second later, it did. The motor blew.

The hydraulics seized with a horrible crunch, and a cloud of black smoke spit out the rear of the jack. Cursing ORO and its corporate policies, Des released his cramped finger from the trigger and tossed the spent piece of equipment to the floor.

"Move aside, kid," a voice said.

Gerd, one of the other miners, stepped up and tried to shoulder Des out of the way so he could work the vein with his own jack. Gerd had been working the mines for nearly twenty standard years, and it had turned his body into a mass of hard, knotted muscle. But Des had been working the mines for ten years himself, ever since he was a teenager, and he was just as solid as the older man—and a little bigger. He didn't budge.

"I'm not done here," he said. "Jack died, that's all. Hand me yours and I'll keep at it for a while."

"You know the rules, kid. You stop working and someone else is allowed to move in."

Technically, Gerd was right. But nobody ever jumped another miner's claim over an equipment malfunction. Not unless he was trying to pick a fight.

Des took a quick look around. The chamber was empty except for the two of them, standing less than half a meter apart. Not a surprise; Des usually chose caverns far off the main tunnel network. It had to be more than mere coincidence that Gerd was here.

Des had known Gerd for as long as he could remember. The middle-aged man had been friends with Hurst, Des's father. Back when Des first started working the mines at thirteen, he had taken a lot of abuse from the bigger miners. His father had been the worst tormentor, but Gerd had been one of the main instigators, dishing out more than his fair share of teasing, insults, and the occasional cuff on the ear.

Their harassments had ended shortly after Des's father died of a massive heart attack. It wasn't because the miners felt sorry for the orphaned young man, though. By the time Hurst died, the tall, skinny teenager they loved to bully had become a mountain of muscle with heavy hands and a fierce temper. Mining was a tough job; it was the closest thing to hard labor outside a Republic prison colony. Whoever worked the mines on Apatros got big—and Des just happened to become the biggest of them all. Half a dozen black eyes, countless bloody noses, and one broken jaw in the space of a month was all it took for Hurst's old friends to decide they'd be happier if they left Des alone.

Yet it was almost as if they blamed him for Hurst's death, and every few months one of them tried again. Gerd had always been smart enough to keep his distance—until now.

"I don't see any of your friends here with you, old man," Des said. "So back off my claim, and nobody gets hurt."

Gerd spat on the ground at Des's feet. "You don't even know what day it is, do you, boy? Kriffing disgrace is what you are!"

They were standing close enough to each other that Des could smell the sour Corellian whiskey on Gerd's breath. The man was drunk. Drunk enough to come looking for a fight, but still sober enough to hold his own.

"Five years ago today," Gerd said, shaking his head sadly. "Five years ago today your own father died, and you don't even remember!"

Des rarely even thought about his father anymore. He hadn't been sorry to see him go. His earliest memories were of his father smacking him. He didn't even remember the reason; Hurst rarely needed one.

"Can't say I miss Hurst the same way you do, Gerd."

"Hurst?" Gerd snorted. "He raised you by himself after your mama died, and you don't even have the respect to call him *Dad*? You ungrateful son-of-a-Kath-hound!"

Des glared down menacingly at Gerd, but the shorter man was too full of drink and self-righteous indignation to be intimidated.

"Should've expected this from a mudcrutch whelp like you," Gerd continued. "Hurst always said you were no good. He knew there was something wrong with you . . . Bane."

Des narrowed his eyes, but didn't rise to the bait. Hurst had called him by that name when he was drunk. *Bane.* He had blamed his son for his wife's death. Blamed him for being stuck on Apatros. He considered his only child to be the bane of his existence, a fact he'd tended to spit out at Des in his drunken rages.

Bane. It represented everything spiteful, petty, and mean about his father. It struck at the innermost fears of every child: fear of disappointment, fear of abandonment, fear of violence. As a kid, that name had hurt more than all the smacks from his father's heavy fists. But Des wasn't a kid anymore. Over time he'd learned to ignore it, along with all the rest of the hateful bile that spilled from his father's mouth.

"I don't have time for this," he muttered. "I've got work to do."

With one hand he grabbed the hydraulic jack from Gerd's grasp. He put the other hand on Gerd's shoulder and shoved him away. Stumbling back, the inebriated man caught his heel on a rock and fell roughly to the ground.

He stood up with a snarl, his hands balling into fists. "Guess your daddy's been gone too long, boy. You need someone to beat the sense back into you!"

Gerd was drunk, but he was no fool, Des realized. Des was bigger, stronger, younger . . . but he'd spent the last six hours working a hydraulic jack. He was covered in grime and the sweat was dripping off his face. His shirt was drenched. Gerd's uniform, on the other hand, was still relatively clean: no dust, no sweat stains. He must have been planning this all day, taking it easy and sitting back while Des wore himself out.

But Des wasn't about to back down from a fight. Throwing Gerd's jack to the ground, he dropped into a crouch, feet wide and arms held out in front of him.

Gerd charged forward, swinging his right fist in a vicious uppercut. Des reached out and caught the punch with the open palm of his left hand, absorbing the force of the blow. His right hand snapped forward and grabbed the underside of Gerd's right wrist; as he pulled the older man forward, Des ducked down and turned, driving his shoulder into Gerd's chest. Using his opponent's own momentum against him, Des straightened up and yanked hard on Gerd's wrist, flipping him up and over so that he crashed to the ground on his back.

The fight should have ended right then; Des had a split second where he could have dropped his knee onto his opponent, driving the breath from his lungs and pinning him to the ground while he pounded Gerd with his fists. But it didn't happen. His back, exhausted from hours of hefting the thirty-kilo jack, spasmed.

The pain was agonizing; instinctively Des straightened up, clutching at the knotted lumbar muscles. It gave Gerd a chance to roll out of the way and get back to his feet.

Somehow Des managed to drop into his fighting crouch again. His back howled in protest, and he grimaced as red-hot daggers of pain shot through his body. Gerd saw the grimace and laughed.

"Cramping up there, boy? You should know better than to try and fight after a six-hour shift in the mines."

Gerd charged forward again. This time his hands weren't fists, but claws grasping and grabbing at anything they could find, trying to nullify the younger man's height and reach by getting in close. Des tried to scramble out of the way, but his legs were too stiff and sore to get him clear. One hand grabbed his shirt, the other got hold of his belt as Gerd pulled both of them to the ground.

They grappled together, wrestling on the hard, uneven stone of the cavern floor. Gerd had his face buried against Dessel's chest to protect it, keeping Des from landing a solid elbow or head-butt. He still had a grip on Des's belt, but now his other hand was free and punching blindly up to where he guessed Des's face would be. Des was forced to wrap his arms in and around Gerd's own, interlocking them so neither man could throw a punch.

With their limbs pinned, strategy and technique meant little. The fight had become a test of strength and endurance, with the two combatants slowly wearing each other down. Dessel tried to roll Gerd over onto his back, but his weary body betrayed him. His limbs were heavy and soft; he couldn't get the leverage he needed. Instead it was Gerd who was able to twist and turn, wrenching one of his hands free while still keeping his face pressed tight against Des's chest so it wouldn't be exposed.

Des wasn't so lucky . . . his face was open and vulnerable. Gerd struck a blow with his free hand, but he didn't hit with a closed fist. Instead he drove his thumb hard into Des's cheek, only a few centimeters from his real target. He struck again with the thumb, looking to gouge out one of his opponent's eyes and leave him blind and writhing in pain.

It took Des a second to realize what was happening; his tired mind had become as slow and clumsy as his body. He turned his face away just as the second blow landed, the thumb jamming painfully into the cartilage of his upper ear.

Dark rage exploded inside Des: a burst of fiery passion that burned away the exhaustion and fatigue. Suddenly his mind was clear, and his body felt strong and rejuvenated. He knew what he was going to do next. More importantly, he knew with absolute certainty what Gerd would do next, too.

He couldn't explain how he knew; sometimes he could just anticipate an opponent's next move. Instinct, some might have said. Des felt it was something more. It was too detailed—too specific—to be simple instinct. It was more like a vision, a brief glimpse into the future. And whenever it happened, Des always knew what to do, as if something was guiding and directing his actions.

When the next blow came, Des was more than ready for it. He could picture it perfectly in his mind. He knew exactly when it was coming and precisely where it would strike. This time he turned his head in the opposite direction, exposing his face to the incoming blow—and opening his mouth. He bit down hard, his timing perfect, and his teeth sank deep into the dirty flesh of Gerd's probing thumb.

Gerd screamed as Des clamped his jaw shut, severing the tendons and striking bone. He wondered if he could bite clean through and then—as if the very thought made it happen—he severed Gerd's thumb.

The screams became shrieks as Gerd released his grasp and rolled away, clasping his maimed hand with his whole one. Crimson blood welled up through the fingers trying to stanch the flow from his stump.

Standing up slowly, Des spat the thumb out onto the ground. The taste of blood was hot in his mouth. His body felt strong and reenergized, as if some great power surged through his veins. All the fight had been taken out of his opponent; Des could do anything he wanted to Gerd now.

The older man rolled back and forth on the floor, his hand clutched to his chest. He was moaning and sobbing, begging for mercy, pleading for help.

Des shook his head in disgust; Gerd had brought this on himself. It had started as a simple fistfight. The loser would have ended up with a black eye and some bruises, but nothing more. Then the older man had taken things to another level by trying to blind him, and he'd responded in kind. Des had learned long ago not to escalate a fight unless he was willing to pay the price of losing. Now Gerd had learned that lesson, too.

Des had a temper, but he wasn't the kind to keep beating on a helpless opponent. Without looking back at his defeated foe, he left the cavern and headed back up the tunnel to tell one of the foremen what had happened so someone could come tend to Gerd's injury.

He wasn't worried about the consequences. The medics could reattach Gerd's thumb, so at worst Des would be fined a day or two's wages. The corporation didn't really care what its employees did, as long as they kept coming back to mine the cortosis. Fights were common among the miners, and ORO almost always turned a blind eye, though this particular fight had been more vicious than most—savage and short, with a brutal end.

Just like life on Apatros.

2

Sitting in the back of the land cruiser used to transport miners between Apatros's only colony and the mines, Des felt exhausted. All he wanted was to get back to his bunk in the barracks and sleep. The adrenaline had drained out of him, leaving him hyperaware of the stiffness and soreness of his body. He slumped down in his seat and gazed around the interior of the cruiser.

Normally, there would have been twenty other miners crammed into the speeder with him, but this one was empty except for him and the pilot. After the fight with Gerd, the foreman had suspended Des without pay, effective immediately, and had ordered the transport to take him back to the colony.

"This kind of thing is getting old, Des," the foreman had said with a frown. "We've got to make an example of you this time. You can't work the mines until Gerd is healed up and back on the job."

What he really meant was, *You can't earn any credits until Gerd comes back.* He'd still be charged room and board, of course. Every day that he sat around doing nothing would go onto his tab, adding to the debt he was working so desperately to pay off.

Des figured it would be four or five days until Gerd was able to handle a hydraulic jack again. The on-site medic had reattached the severed thumb using a vibroscalpel and synthflesh. A few days of kolto injections and some cheap meds to dull the pain, and Gerd would be back at it. Bacta therapy could have him back in a day; but bacta was expensive, and ORO wouldn't spring for it unless Gerd had miner's insurance . . . which Des highly doubted.

Most miners never bothered with the company-sponsored insurance program. It was expensive, for one thing. What with room, board, and the fees covering the cost of transport to and from the mines, most thought they gave ORO more than enough of their hard-earned pay without adding insurance premiums onto the stack.

It wasn't just the cost, though. It was almost as if the men and women who worked the cortosis mines were in denial, refusing to admit the potential dangers and hazards they encountered every day. Getting insurance would force them to take a look at the cold, hard facts.

Few miners ever reached their golden years. The tunnels claimed many, burying bodies in cave-ins or incinerating them when somebody tapped into a pocket of explosive gases trapped in the rock. Even those who made it out of the mines tended not to survive long into their retirement. The mines took their toll. Sixty-year-old men were left with bodies that looked and felt like they were ninety, broken shells worn down by decades of hard physical labor and exposure to airborne contaminants that slipped through the substandard ORO filters.

When Des's father died—with no insurance, of course—all Des got out of it was the privilege of taking on his father's accumulated debt. Hurst had spent more time drinking and gambling than mining. To pay for his monthly room and board he'd often had to borrow credits from ORO at an interest rate that would be criminal anywhere but in the Outer Rim. The debt kept piling up, month to month and year to year, but Hurst didn't seem to care. He was a single parent with a son he resented, trapped in a brutal job he despised; he had given up any hope of escaping Apatros long before the heart attack claimed him.

The Hutt spawn probably would have been glad to know his son had gotten stuck with his bill.

The transport sped above the barren rocks of the small planet's flatlands with no sound but the endless drone of the engines. The featureless wastes flew by in a blur, until the view out the window was nothing but a curtain of shapeless gray. The effect was hypnotic: Des could feel his tired mind and body eager to drift into deep and dreamless sleep.

This was how they got you. Work you to exhaustion, dull your senses, numb your will into submission . . . until you accepted your lot and wasted your entire life in the grit and grime of the cortosis mines. All in the relentless service of the Outer Rim Oreworks Company. It was a surprisingly effective trap; it worked on men like Gerd and Hurst. But it wasn't going to work on Des.

Even with his father's crushing debt, Des knew he'd pay ORO off someday and leave this life behind. He was destined for something greater than this small, insignificant existence. He knew this with absolute certainty, and it was this knowledge that gave him the strength to carry on in the face of the relentless, sometimes hopeless grind. It gave him the strength to fight, even when part of him felt like giving up.

He was suspended, unable to work the mines, but there were other ways to earn credits. With a great effort he forced himself to stand up. The floor swayed under his feet as the speeder made constant adjustments to maintain its programmed cruising altitude of half a meter above ground level. He took a second to get used to the rolling rhythm of the transport, then half walked, half staggered up the aisle between the seats to the pilot at the front. He didn't recognize the man, but they all tended to look the same anyway: grim, unsmiling features, dull eyes, and always wearing an expression as if they were on the verge of a blinding headache.

"Hey," Des said, trying to sound nonchalant, "any ships come in to the spaceport today?"

There was no reason for the pilot to keep his attention fixed on the path ahead. The forty-minute trip between the mines and the colony was a straight line across an empty plain; some of the pilots even stole naps along the route. Yet this one refused to turn and look at Des as he answered.

"Cargo ship touched down a few hours ago," he said in a bored voice. "Military. Republic cargo ship."

Des smiled. "They staying for a while?"

The pilot didn't answer; he only snorted and shook his head at the stupidity of the question. Des nodded and stumbled back toward his seat at the rear of the transport. He knew the answer, too.

Cortosis was used in the hulls of everything from fighters to capital ships, as well as being woven into the body armor of the troops. And as the war against the Sith dragged on, the Republic's need for cortosis kept increasing. Every few weeks a Republic freighter would touch down on Apatros. The next day it would leave again, its cargo bays filled with the valuable mineral. Until then the crew—officers and enlisted soldiers alike—would have nothing to do but wait. From past experience, Des knew that whenever Republic soldiers had a few hours to kill they liked to play cards. And wherever people played cards, there was money to be made.

Lowering himself back onto his seat at the rear of the speeder, Des decided that maybe he wasn't quite ready to hit his bunk after all.

By the time the transport stopped on the edges of the colony, Des's body was tingling with anticipation. He hopped out and sauntered toward his barracks at a leisurely pace, fighting his own eagerness and the urge to run. Even now, he imagined, the Republic soldiers and their credits would be sitting at the gaming tables in the colony's only cantina.

Still, there was no point in rushing over there. It was late afternoon, the sun just beginning its descent beyond the horizon to the north. By now most of the miners from the night shift would be awake. Many of them would already be at the cantina, whiling away the time until they had to make the journey out to the mines to start their shift. For the next two hours Des knew he'd be lucky to find a place to sit down in the cantina, never mind finding an empty seat at a pazaak or sabacc table. Meanwhile, it would be another few hours before the men working the day shift climbed onto the waiting transports to head back to their homes; he'd get to the cantina long before any of them.

Back at his barracks, he stripped off his grime-stained coveralls and climbed into the deserted communal showers, scouring the sweat and fine rock dust from his body. Then he changed into some clean clothes and sauntered out into the street, making his way slowly toward the cantina on the far side of town.

The cantina didn't have a name; it didn't need one. Nobody ever had any trouble finding it. Apatros was a small world, barely more than a moon with an atmosphere and some indigenous plant life. There were precious few places to go: the mines, the colony, or the barren wastes in between. The mines were a massive complex encompassing the caves and tunnels dug by ORO, as well as the refining and processing branches of ORO's operations.

The spaceports were located there, too. Freighters left daily with shipments of cortosis bound for some wealthier world closer to Coruscant and the Galactic Core, and incoming vessels bringing equipment and supplies to keep the mines running arrived every other day. Employees who weren't strong enough to mine cortosis worked in the refining plants or the spaceport. The pay wasn't as good, but they tended to live longer.

But no matter where people worked, they all came home to the same place at the end of their shifts. The colony was nothing more than a ramshackle town of temporary barracks thrown together by ORO to house the few hundred workers expected to keep the mines running. Like the world itself, the colony was officially known as Apatros. To those who lived there, it was more commonly referred to as "the muck-huts." Every building was the same shade of dingy gray durasteel, the exterior weathered and worn. The insides of the buildings were virtually identical, temporary workers' barracks that had become all too permanent. Each structure housed four small private rooms meant for two people, but often holding three or more. Sometimes entire families shared one of those rooms, unless they could find the credits for the outrageous rents ORO charged for more space. Each room had bunks built into the walls and a single door that opened onto a narrow hall; a communal bathroom and shower were located at the end. The doors tended to squeak on illfitting hinges that were never tended to; the roofs were a patchwork of quick fixes to seal up the leaks that inevitably sprang whenever it rained. Broken windows were taped against the wind and cold, but never replaced. A thin layer of dust accumulated over everything, but few of the residents ever bothered to sweep out their domiciles.

The entire colony was less than a kilometer on each square side, making it possible to walk from any given building to any of the other identical structures in less than twenty standard minutes. Despite the unrelenting

similarity of the architecture, navigating the colony was easy. The barracks had been placed in straight rows and columns, forming a grid of
utilitarian streets between the uniformly spaced domiciles. The streets
couldn't exactly be called clean, though they were hardly festering with
garbage. ORO cleared trash and refuse just often enough to keep conditions sanitary, since an outbreak of diseases bred by filth would ad-
versely affect the mine's production. However, the company didn't seem
to mind the cluttered junk that inevitably accumulated throughout the
town. Broken-down generators, rusted-out machinery, corroded scraps of
metal, and discarded, worn-out tools crowded the narrow streets between
the barracks.

There were only two structures in the colony that were in any way dis-
tinguished from the rest. One was the ORO market, the only store on-
world. It had once been a barracks, but the bunks had been replaced with
shelves, and the communal shower area was now a secure storage room.
A small black-and-white sign had been fastened to the wall outside, listing the hours of operation. There were no displays to lure shoppers in,
and no advertising. The market stocked only the most basic items, all at
scandelous markups. Credit was gladly advanced against future wages at
ORO's typically high interest rate, guaranteeing that buyers would spend
even more hours in the mine working off their purchases.

The other dissimilar building was the cantina itself, a magnificent triumph of beauty and design when compared with the dismal homogeny
of the rest of the colony. The cantina was built a few hundred meters beyond the edge of the town, set well apart from the gray grid of barracks.
It stood only three stories high, but because every other structure was
limited to a single floor it dominated the landscape. Not that it needed to
be that tall. Inside the cantina everything was located on the ground
floor; the upper stories were merely a façade constructed for show by
Groshik, the Neimoidian owner and bartender. Above the first-floor ceiling, the second and third floors didn't really exist—there were only the
rising walls and a dome made of tinted violet glass, illuminated from
within. Matching violet lights covered the pale blue exterior walls. On almost any world the effect would have been ostentatious and tacky, but
amid the gray of Apatros it was doubly so. Groshik often proclaimed that

he had intentionally made his cantina as garish as possible, simply to offend the ORO powers-that-be. The sentiment made him popular with the miners, but Des doubted if ORO really cared one way or the other. Groshik could paint his cantina any color he wanted, as long as he gave the corporation its cut of the profits each week.

The twenty-standard-hour day of Apatros was split evenly between the two shifts of miners. Des and the rest of the early crew worked from 0800 to 1800; his counterparts worked from 1800 to 0800. Groshik, in an effort to maximize profits, opened each afternoon at 1300 and didn't close for ten straight hours. This allowed him to serve the night-crew workers before they started and catch the day crew when that shift was over. He'd close at 0300, clean for two hours, sleep for six, then get up at 1100 and start the process all over again. His routine was well known to all the miners; the Neimoidian was as regular as the rising and setting of Apatros's pale orange sun.

As Des crossed the distance between the edge of the colony proper and the cantina's welcoming door, he could already hear the sounds coming from inside: loud music, laughter, chatter, clinking glasses. It was almost 1600 now. The day shift had two hours to go before quitting time, but the cantina was still packed with night-shift workers looking to have a drink or something to eat before they boarded the shuttles that would take them to the mines.

Des didn't recognize any faces: the day and night crews rarely crossed paths. The patrons were mostly humans, with a few Twi'leks, Sullustans, and Cereans filling out the crowd. Des was surprised to notice a Rodian, too. Apparently the night crew were more tolerant of other species than the day shift. There were no waitresses, servers, or dancers; the only employee in the cantina was Groshik himself. Anyone who wanted a drink had to come up to the large bar built into the back wall and order it.

Des pushed his way through the crowd. Groshik saw him coming and momentarily dipped out of sight behind the bar, reappearing with a mug of Gizer ale just as Des reached the counter.

"You're here early today," Groshik said as he set the drink down with a heavy thud. His low, gravelly voice was difficult to hear above the din of the crowd. His words always had a guttural quality, as if he were speaking from the very back of his throat.

The Neimoidian liked him, though Des wasn't sure why. Maybe it was because he'd watched Des grow up from a young kid to a man; maybe he just felt sorry Des had been stuck with such a rankweed for a father. Whatever the reason, there was a standing arrangement between the two: Des never had to pay for a drink if it was poured without being asked for. Des gratefully accepted the gift and downed it in one long draft, then slammed the empty mug back down onto the table.

"Ran into a bit of trouble with Gerd," he replied, wiping his mouth. "I bit his thumb off, so they let me go home early."

Groshik tilted his head to one side and fixed his enormous red eyes on Des. The sour expression on his amphibian-like face didn't change, but his body shook ever so slightly. Des knew him well enough to realize the Neimoidian was laughing.

"Seems like a fair trade," Groshik croaked, refilling the mug.

Des didn't guzzle the second drink as he had the first. Groshik rarely gave him more than one on the house, and he didn't want to abuse the bartender's generosity.

He turned his attention to the crowd. The Republic visitors were easy to spot. Four humans—two men, two women—and a male Ithorian in crisp navy uniforms. It wasn't just their clothes that made them stand out, though. They all stood straight and tall, whereas most of the miners tended to hunch forward, as if carrying a great weight on their backs.

On one side of the main room, a smaller section was roped off from the rest of the cantina. It was the only part of the place Groshik had nothing to do with. The ORO Company allowed gambling on Apatros, but only if it was in charge of the tables. Officially this was to keep anyone from cheating, but everyone knew ORO's real concern was keeping the wagers in check. It didn't want one of its employees to win big and pay off all his or her debts in one lucky night. By keeping the maximum limits low, ORO made sure it was more profitable to work the mines than the tables.

In the gaming section were four more naval soldiers wearing the uniform of the Republic fleet, along with a dozen or so miners. A Twi'lek woman with the rank of petty officer on her lapel was playing pazaak. A young ensign was sitting at the sabacc table, talking loudly to everyone around him, though nobody seemed to be listening to him. Two more officers—both human, one male, one female—also sat at the sabacc table. The woman was a lieutenant; the man bore the insignia of a full commander. Des assumed they were the senior officers in charge of the mission to receive the cortosis shipment.

"I see you've noticed our recruiters," Groshik muttered.

The war against the Sith—officially nothing more than a series of protracted military engagements, even though the whole galaxy knew it was a war—required a steady stream of young and eager cadets for the front lines. And for some reason the Republic always expected the citizens on the Outer Rim worlds to jump at the chance to join them. Whenever a Republic military crew passed through Apatros, the officers tried to round up new recruits. They'd buy a round of drinks, then use it as an excuse to start up a conversation, usually about the glorious and heroic life of being a soldier. Sometimes they'd play up the brutality of the Sith. Other times they'd spin promises of a better life in the Republic military—all the while pretending to be friendly and sympathetic to the locals, hoping a few would join their cause.

Des suspected they received some kind of bonus for any new recruit they conned into signing up. Unfortunately for them, they weren't going to find too many takers on Apatros. The Republic wasn't too popular on the Rim; people here, including Des, knew the Core Worlds exploited small, remote planets like Apatros for their own gain. The Sith found a lot of anti-Republic sympathizers out here on the fringes of civilized space; that was one of the reasons their numbers kept growing as the war dragged on.

Despite their dissatisfaction with the Core Worlds, people still might have signed up with the recruiters if the Republic wasn't so concerned with following the absolute letter of the law. Anyone hoping to escape Apatros and the clutches of the mining corporation was in for a rude shock: debts to ORO still had to be paid, even by recruits protecting the galaxy against the rising Sith threat. If someone owed money to a legitimate corporation, the Republic fleet would garnish his or her wages until those debts were paid. Not too many miners were excited about the prospect of joining a war only to have the privilege of not getting paid.

Some of the miners resented the senior officers and their constant push to lure naïve young men and women into joining their cause. It didn't bother Des, though. He'd listen to them prattle on all night, as long as they kept playing cards. He figured it was a small price to pay for getting his hands on their credits.

His eagerness must have shown, at least to Groshik. "Any chance you heard a Republic crew was stopping by and then picked a fight with Gerd just so you could get here early?"

Des shook his head. "No. Just a happy coincidence, is all. What angle are they working this time? Glory of the Republic?"

"Trying to warn us about the horrors of the Brotherhood of Darkness" was the carefully neutral reply. "Not going over too well."

The cantina owner kept his real opinions to himself when it came to matters of politics. His customers were free to talk about any subject they wanted, but no matter how heated their arguments became, he always refused to take sides.

"Bad for business," he had explained once. "Agree with someone and they'll be your friend for the rest of the night. Cross them and they might hate you for weeks." Neimoidians were known for their shrewd business sense, and Groshik was no exception.

A miner pushed his way up to the bar and demanded a drink. When Groshik went to fill the order, Des turned to study the gaming area. There weren't any free seats at the sabacc table, so for the time being he was forced into the role of spectator. For well over an hour he studied the plays and the wagers of the newcomers, paying particular attention to the senior officers. They tended to be better players than the enlisted troops, probably because they had more credits to lose.

The game on Apatros followed a modified version of the Bespin Standard rules. The basics of the game were simple: make a hand as close to twenty-three as possible without going over. Each round, a player had to either bet to stay in the hand, or fold. Any player who chose to stay in could draw a new card, discard a card, or place a card into the interference field to lock in its value. At the end of any round a player could come up, revealing his or her hand and forcing all other players to show their cards, as well. Best hand at the table won the hand pot. Any score over twenty-three, or below negative twenty-three, was a bomb-out that required the player to pay a penalty. And if a player had a hand that totaled exactly twenty-three—a pure sabacc—he or she won the sabacc pot as a bonus. But what with random shifts that could unexpectedly change the value of cards from round to round, and other players coming up early, a pure sabacc was a lot harder to achieve than it sounded.

Sabacc was more than a game of luck. It was about strategy and style, knowing when to bluff and when to back down, knowing how to adapt to the ever-changing cards. Some players were too cautious, never betting more than the minimum raise even when they had a good hand. Others were too aggressive, trying to bully the rest of the table with outrageous bets even when they had nothing. A player's natural tendencies showed through if you knew what to look for.

The ensign, for example, was clearly new to the game. He kept staying in with weak hands instead of folding his cards. He was a chaser, not satisfied with cards good enough to collect the hand pot. He was always looking for the perfect hand, hoping to win big and collect the sabacc pot that kept on growing until it was won. As a result, he kept getting caught with bomb-out hands and having to pay a penalty. It didn't seem to slow his betting, though. He was one of those players with more credits than sense, which suited Des just fine.

To be an expert sabacc player, you had to know how to control the table. It didn't take Des many hands to realize the Republic commander was doing just that. He knew how to bet big and make other players fold winning hands. He knew when to bet small to lure others into playing hands they should have folded. He didn't worry much about his own cards; he knew that the secret to sabacc was figuring out what everyone else was holding . . . and then letting them think they knew what cards *he* was holding. It was only when all the hands were revealed and he was raking in the chips that his opponents would realize how wrong they'd been.

He was good, Des had to admit. Better than most of the Republic players who passed through. Despite his pleasant appearance, he was ruthless in scooping up pot after pot. But Des had a good feeling; sometimes he just knew he couldn't lose. He was going to win tonight . . . and win big.

There was a groan from one of the miners at the table. "Another round and that sabacc pot was mine!" he said, shaking his head. "You're lucky you came up when you did," he added, speaking to the commander.

Des knew it wasn't luck. The miner had been so excited, he was twitching in his seat. Anyone with half a brain could see he was working toward a powerful hand. The commander had seen it and made his move, cutting the hand short and chopping the other gambler's hopes off at the knees.

"That's it," the miner said, pushing away from the table. "I'm tapped out."

"Looks like now's your chance," Groshik whispered under his breath as he swept past to pour another drink. "Good luck."

I don't need luck tonight, Des thought. He crossed the floor of the cantina and stepped over the nanosilk rope into the ORO-controlled gaming room.

3

Des approached the sabacc table and nodded to the Beta-4 CardShark dealing out the hands. ORO preferred automated droids to organic dealers: no salary to pay, and there was no chance a wily gambler could convince a droid to cheat.

"I'm in," he declared, taking the empty seat.

The ensign was sitting directly across from him. He let out a long, loud whistle. "Blast, you're a big boy," he shouted boisterously. "How tall are you—one ninety? One ninety-five?"

"Two meters even," Des replied without looking at him. He swiped his ORO account card through the reader built into the table and punched in his security code. The buy-in for the table was added to the total already owing on his ORO account, and the CardShark obediently pushed a stack of chips across the table toward him.

"Good luck, sir," it said.

The ensign continued to size Des up, taking another long drink from his mug. Then he brayed out a laugh. "Wow, they grow you fellas big out here on the Rim. You sure you ain't really a Wookiee somebody shaved for a joke?"

A few of the other players laughed, but quickly stopped when they saw Des clench his jaw. The man smelled of Corellian ale. Same as Gerd had when he'd picked a fight with Des just a few hours earlier. Des's muscles tightened, and he leaned forward in his chair. The smaller man let out a short, nervous breath.

"Come on now, son," the commander said to Des in a calming voice, stepping in to control the situation the same way he'd been controlling the table all game long. He had an air of quiet authority, a patriarch presiding over a family squabble at the dinner table. "It's just a joke. Can't you take a joke?"

Turning to face the only player at the table good enough to give him a real challenge, Des flashed a grin and let the tension slip from his coiled muscles. "Sure, I can take a joke. But I'd rather take your credits."

There was a brief pause, and then it was as if everyone had sighed in relief. The officer chuckled and returned the smile. "Fair enough. Let's play some cards."

Des started slow, playing conservatively and folding often. The limits on the table were low; the maximum value of any given hand was capped at one hundred credits. Between the five-credit ante and the two-credit "administration fee" ORO charged players each time they started a new round, the hand pots would barely cover the cost of sitting down at the table, even for a solid player. The trick was to win just enough hand pots to be able to stick around long enough for a chance at the sabacc pot that continued to build with each hand.

When he first started playing, one of the soldiers tried to make small talk. "I notice most of the human miners here shave their heads," he said, nodding out at the crowd. "Why is that?"

"We don't shave. Our hair falls out," Des replied. "Comes from working too many shifts in the mines."

"Working the mines? I don't get it."

"The filters don't remove all the impurities from the air. You work ten-hour shifts day in and day out, and the contaminants build up in your system." He spoke in a flat, neutral voice. There was no bitterness; for him and the rest of the miners it was just a fact of life. "It has side effects. We get sick a lot; our hair falls out. We're supposed to take a few days off now and again, but ever since ORO signed those Republic military contracts the mines never shut down. Basically, we're being slowly poisoned to make sure your cargo hold's full when you leave."

That was enough to kill any other attempts at conversation, and they continued the hands in relative silence. After half an hour Des was about even for the night, but he was just getting warmed up. He pushed in his ante and the ORO cut, as did the other seven players at the table. The dealer flipped two cards out to each of them, and another hand began. The first two players peeked at their cards and folded. The Republic ensign glanced at his cards and threw in enough chips to stay in the hand. Des wasn't surprised—he hardly ever folded his cards, even when he had nothing.

The ensign quickly pushed one of his cards into the interference field. Each turn, a player could move one of the electronic chip-cards into the interference field, locking in its value to protect it from changing if there was a shift at the end of the round.

Des shook his head. Locking in cards was a fool's play. You couldn't discard a locked-in card; Des usually preferred to keep all his options open. The ensign, however, was thinking in the short term, not planning ahead. That probably explained why he was down several hundred credits on the night.

Glancing at his own hand, Des chose to stay in. All the rest of the players dropped, leaving just the two of them.

The CardShark dealt out another round of cards. Des glanced down and saw he had drawn Endurance, a face card with a value of negative eight. He was sitting at a total of six, an incredibly weak hand.

The smart move was to fold; unless there was a shift, he was dead. But Des knew there was going to be a shift. He knew it as surely as he had known where and when Gerd's thumb was going to be when he bit down on it. These brief glimpses into the future didn't happen often, but when they did he knew enough to listen to them. He pushed in his credits. The ensign matched the bet.

The droid scooped the chips to the center of the table, and the marker in front of him began to pulse with rapidly changing colors. Blue meant no shift; all the cards would stay the same. Red meant a shift: an impulse would be sent out from the marker, and one electronic card from each player would randomly reset and change its value. The marker flickered back and forth between red and blue, gaining speed until it was pulsing so quickly the colors blurred into a single violet hue. Then the flashing began to slow down and it became possible to tell the individual colors apart again: blue, red, blue, red, blue . . . It stopped on red.

"Blast!" the ensign swore. "It always shifts when I have a good hand!"

Des knew that wasn't true. The chances of shifting were fifty–fifty: completely random. There was no way to predict whether a shift was coming . . . unless you had a gift like Des occasionally did.

The cards flickered as they reset, and Des scooped up his hand one more time. Endurance was gone, replaced by a seven. He was sitting at twenty-one. Not a sabacc, but a solid hand. Before the next round could begin, Des flipped his cards over, exposing his hand to the table. "Coming up on twenty-one," he said.

The ensign threw his cards to the table in disgust. "Blasted bomb-out."

Des collected the small stack of chips that were the hand pot, while the other man grudgingly paid his penalty into the sabacc pot. Des guessed it was closing in on five hundred credits by now.

One of the miners at the table stood up. "Come on, we got to go," he said. "Last speeder leaves in twenty minutes."

With grumbles and complaints, the other miners got up from their seats and trudged off to start their shift. The ensign watched them go, then turned curiously to Des.

"You ain't going with them, big fella? I thought you were complaining about never getting a day off earlier."

"I work the day shift," Des said shortly. "Those guys are the night shift."

"Where's the rest of your crew?" the lieutenant asked. Des clearly recognized her interest as an attempt to keep the ensign from saying something to further antagonize the big miner. "The crowd's become awfully thin." She waved her hand around at the cantina, now virtually empty except for the Republic naval soldiers. Seeing the open seats at the sabacc table, a few of them were wandering over to join their comrades in the game.

"They'll be along soon enough," Des said. "I just ended my shift a bit early today."

"Really?" Her tone implied that she knew of only one reason a miner's shift might end early.

"Lieutenant," one of the newly arrived soldiers said politely as they reached the table. "Commander," he added, addressing the other officer. "Mind if we join in, sir?"

The commander looked over at Des. "I don't want this young man to think the Republic is ganging up on him. If we take all the seats, where are his friends going to sit when they show up? He says they'll be along any minute."

"They're not here now," Des said. "And they're not my friends. You might as well sit down." He didn't add that most of the day-shift miners probably wouldn't play, anyway. When Des showed up at the table they tended to call it a night; he won too often for their liking.

The empty seats were quickly filled up.

"So how are the cards treating you, Ensign?" a young woman asked the man Des had bested in the last hand. She sat down beside him and placed a full mug of Corellian ale on the table in front of him.

"Not so good," he admitted, flashing a grin and exchanging his empty mug for the full one. "I might have to owe you for this drink. I can't seem to catch a break tonight." He nodded his head in Des's direction. "Watch out for this one. He's as good as the commander. Either that, or he cheats."

He smiled quickly to show it was just another of his mildly offensive jokes. Des ignored him; it wasn't the first time he'd been called a cheat. He was aware that his precognition gave him an advantage over the other players. Maybe it was an unfair advantage, but he didn't consider it cheating. It wasn't as if he knew what was going to happen on every hand; he couldn't control it. He was just smart enough to make the most of it when it happened.

The CardShark began passing out chips to the newcomers, wishing each of them a perfunctory "Good luck" as it did so.

"So it seems you don't really get on well with the other miners," the lieutenant said, keying on Des's earlier comments. "Have you ever thought about changing careers?"

Des groaned inwardly. By the time he had joined the table the officers had given up their recruiting spiel and stuck mostly to playing cards. Now he'd given her an opening to bring it up again.

"I'm not interested in becoming a soldier," he said, anteing up for the next hand.

"Don't be so hasty," she said, her voice slipping into a soothing, gentle patter. "Being a soldier for the Republic has its rewards. I suspect it's better than working the mines, at least."

"There's a whole galaxy out there, son," the commander added. "Worlds a lot more attractive than this one, if you don't mind me saying."

Don't I know it, Des thought. Out loud he said, "I don't plan to spend my whole life here. But when I do get off this rock, I don't want to spend my days dodging Sith blasters on the front lines."

"We won't be fighting the Sith for much longer, son. We've got them on the run now." The commander spoke with such calm assurance, Des was half tempted to believe him.

"That's not how I hear it," Des said. "Rumor is the Brotherhood of Darkness has been winning more than its share of the battles. I heard it's got more than a dozen regions under its control now."

"That was before General Hoth," one of the other soldiers chimed in.

Des had heard of Hoth on the HoloNet; he was a bona-fide hero of the Republic. Victorious in half a dozen major confrontations, he was a brilliant strategist who knew how to snatch victory from the jaws of defeat. Not surprising, given his background.

"Hoth?" he asked innocently, glancing down at his cards. Garbage. He folded his hand. "Isn't he a Jedi?"

"He is," the commander replied, peeking at his own cards. He pushed in a small wager. "A Jedi Master, to be more accurate. And a fine soldier, too. You couldn't ask for a better man to lead the Republic war effort."

"The Sith are more than just soldiers, you know," the drunken ensign said earnestly, his voice even louder than before. "Some of them can use the Force, just like the Jedi! You can't beat them with blasters alone."

Des had heard plenty of wild tales of Jedi performing extraordinary feats through the mystical power of the Force, but he figured they were legends and myth. Or at least exaggerations. He knew there were powers that transcended the physical world: his own premonitions were evidence of that. But the stories of what the Jedi could do were just too impossible to believe. If the Force was really such a powerful weapon, why was this war taking so long?

"The idea of answering to a Jedi Master doesn't really appeal to me," he said. "I've heard some strange things about what they believe in: no passion, no emotion. Sounds like they want to turn us all into droids."

Another round of cards was dealt out to the remaining players.

"The Jedi are guided by wisdom," the commander explained. "They don't let things like desire or anger cloud their judgment."

"Anger has its uses," Des pointed out. "It's gotten me out of some nasty spots."

"I think the trick is not to get into those spots in the first place," the lieutenant countered in her gentle voice.

The hand ended a few turns later. The young woman who had bought the ensign his drink came up on twenty—not a great hand, but not a bad one, either. She looked over at the commander as he flipped up his cards, and smiled when he had only nineteen. Her smile faded when the drunken ensign showed his twenty-one. When he scooped up the pot, she cut his laugh short with a friendly elbow to his ribs.

Everyone anted and the dealer flicked out another pair of cards to each player.

"The Jedi are the defenders of the Republic," the lieutenant went on earnestly. "Their ways can seem strange to ordinary citizens, but they're on our side. All they want is peace."

"Really?" Des said, glancing at his cards and pushing in his chips. "I thought they wanted to wipe out the Sith."

"The Sith are an illegal organization," the lieutenant explained. She folded her cards after a moment of careful deliberation. "The Senate passed a bill outlawing them nearly three thousand years ago, shortly after Revan and Malak brought destruction to the entire galaxy."

"I always heard Revan saved the Republic," he said.

The commander jumped back into the conversation. "Revan's story is complicated," he said. "But the fact remains, the Sith and their teachings were banned by the Senate. Their very existence is a violation of Republic law—and with good reason. The Jedi understand the threat the Sith represent. That's why they've joined the fleet. For the good of the galaxy, the Sith must be wiped out once and for all."

The drunken ensign won the hand again, his second in a row. Sometimes it was better to be lucky than good.

"So the Republic says the Sith must be wiped out," Des said as he anted up for the next hand. "If the Sith were the ones in charge, I bet they'd say the same thing about the Jedi."

"You wouldn't say that if you knew what the Sith were really like," one of the other soldiers said. "I've fought against them: they're bloodthirsty killers!"

Des laughed. "Yeah, how dare they try to kill you in the middle of a war? Don't they know you're busy trying to kill them? How rude!"

"You bloody Kath-mutt!" the soldier snapped, rising up from his seat.

"Sit down, deckman!" the commander barked. The soldier did as he was told, but Des could feel the tension in the air. Everyone else at the table—with the possible exception of the two officers—was glaring at him.

Good. The last thing on their minds now was cards. Angry people didn't make good sabacc players.

The commander sensed things were bad, too. He did his best to defuse the situation.

"The Sith follow the teachings of the dark side, son," he said to Des. "If you saw the kinds of things they've done during this war . . . and not just to other soldiers. They don't care if innocent civilians suffer."

Only half listening, Des glanced at his cards and placed a wager.

"I'm not stupid, Commander," he said then. "Whether the Republic officially acknowledges it or not, you're at war with the Brotherhood of Darkness. And bad things happen during a war, on both sides. So don't try to convince me the Sith are monsters. They're people, just like you and me."

Of all the players at the table, only the commander folded his cards. Des knew that at least a few of the soldiers were playing bad hands simply for the chance to take him down.

The commander sighed. "You're right, to a point. The ordinary troopers—who serve in the army because they don't know what the Sith

Masters and the Brotherhood of Darkness are really like—are just people. But you have to look at the ideals behind this war. You have to understand what each side really stands for."

"Enlighten me, Commander." Des put just a hint of condescension in his voice and casually tossed in some more chips, knowing it would rile up the table even more. He was glad to see that nobody folded; he was playing them like a Bith musician trilling out a tune on a sabriquet.

"The Jedi seek to preserve peace," the commander reiterated. "They serve the cause of justice. Whenever possible, they use their power to aid those in need. They seek to serve, not to rule. They believe that all beings, regardless of species or gender, are created equal. Surely you can understand that."

It was more a statement than a question, but Des answered anyway. "But all beings aren't really equal, are they? I mean, some are smarter, or stronger . . . or better at cards."

He drew a small smile from the commander with the last comment, though everyone else at the table scowled.

"True enough, son. But isn't it the duty of the strong to help the weak?"

Des shrugged. He didn't believe much in equality. Working to make everybody equal didn't leave much chance for anyone to achieve greatness. "So what about the Brotherhood of Darkness?" he asked. "What do they believe in?"

"They follow the teachings of the dark side. The only thing they seek is power; they believe the natural order of the galaxy is for the weak to serve the strong."

"Sounds pretty good if you're one of the strong." Des flipped his cards up, then scooped up the pot, relishing the grumbling and curses muttered under the breath of the losers.

Des flashed a nasty grin around the table. "For the sake of the Republic, I hope you guys are better soldiers than you are sabacc players."

"You mudcrutch, rankweed coward!" the ensign shouted, jumping up and spilling his drink onto the floor. "If it wasn't for us, the Sith would be all over this pit of a world!"

Another miner would have taken a swing at Des, but the ensign—even more than slightly drunk—had enough military discipline to keep his fists at his sides. A stern glare from the commander made him sit down and mumble an apology. Des was impressed. And a little disappointed.

"We all know why the Republic cares about Apatros," he said, stacking his chips and trying to appear nonchalant. In fact, he was scanning the table to see if anyone else was getting ready to make a move on him.

"You use cortosis in the hulls of your ships, you use it in your weapons casings, you even use it in your body armor. Without us, you wouldn't stand a chance in this war. So don't pretend you're doing any favors here: you need us as much as we need you."

Nobody had anted yet; all eyes were drawn to the drama unfolding among the players. The CardShark hesitated, its limited programming uncertain how to handle the situation. Des knew Groshik was watching from the far side of the cantina, his hand near the stun blaster he kept stashed behind the bar. He doubted the Neimoidian would need it, though.

"True enough," the commander conceded, pushing his ante in. The others, including Des, followed suit. "But at least we pay you for the cortosis we use. The Sith would just take it from you."

"No," Des corrected, studying his cards, "you pay ORO for the cortosis. Those credits don't make it all the way down to a guy like me." He folded his hand but didn't stop talking. "See, that's the problem with the Republic. In the Core everything's great: people are healthy, wealthy, and happy. But out here on the Rim things aren't so easy.

"I've been working the mines almost as long as I can remember, in one way or another, and I still owe ORO enough credits to fill a freighter hull. But I don't see any Jedi coming to save me from that little bit of injustice."

Nobody had an answer for him this time, not even the commander. Des decided they'd talked enough politics; he wanted to focus on winning the two thousand credits that had built up in the sabacc pot. He went in for the kill.

"Don't try to sell me on your Jedi and your Republic, because that's exactly what it is: *your* Republic. You say the Sith only respect strength? Well, that's pretty much the way things are out here on the Rim, too. You look out for yourself, because nobody else will. *That's* why the Sith keep finding new recruits willing to join them out here. People with nothing feel like they've got nothing to lose. And if the Republic doesn't figure that out pretty soon, the Brotherhood of Darkness is going to win this war no matter how many Jedi you have leading your army."

"Maybe we should just stick to cards," the lieutenant suggested after a long, uncomfortable silence.

"That works for me," Des said. "No hard feelings?"

"No hard feelings," the commander said, forcing a smile.

A few of the other soldiers murmured assent, but Des knew the hard feelings were still there. He'd done everything he could to make sure they ran deep.

4

The hours ticked by. Other miners began to arrive, the day shift coming in to replace the night crew that had left. The CardShark kept dealing, and the players kept betting. Des's stack of chips was growing steadily larger, and the sabacc pot kept on growing: three thousand credits, four thousand, five . . . None of the players seemed to be having fun anymore; Des figured his scorching rant had burned off all the pleasure from the game.

Des didn't care. He didn't play sabacc for fun. It was a job, same as working the mines. A way to earn credits and pay off ORO so he could leave Apatros behind forever.

Two of the soldiers pushed away from the table, their credits cleaned out. Their seats were soon filled by miners from the day shift. The lure of the massive sabacc pot was enough to draw them in, despite their reluctance to go up against Des.

Another hour passed and the senior officers—the lieutenant and the commander—finally packed it in. They, too, were replaced by miners with visions of hitting one good hand and cashing in the unclaimed sabacc pot. The Republic soldiers who stuck around, like the ensign who had first challenged Des, must have had deep, deep pockets.

With the constant influx of new players and new money, Des was forced to change his strategy. He was up several hundred credits; he had enough of a cushion built up that he could afford to lose a few hands if he had to. Now his only concern was protecting the sabacc pot. If he didn't have a hand he thought he could win with, he'd come up in the first few turns. He wasn't going to give anyone else a chance to build up a hand of twenty-three. He stopped folding, even when he had weak cards. Sitting out a hand gave the other players too much of a chance to win.

Some lucky shifts and some poor choices by his opponents made sure his strategy worked, though not without a cost. His efforts to protect the sabacc pot began to eat into his profits. His stack of winnings shrank quickly, but it would all be worth it if he won the sabacc pot.

Through hand after agonizing hand players continued to come and go. One by one the soldiers gave up their seats, forced out when they ran out of chips and couldn't afford more. Of the original group, only Des and the ensign remained. The ensign's pile was growing. A few of the soldiers stayed to watch, rooting for their man to beat the miner with the big mouth.

Other spectators came and went. Some were just waiting for a player to drop so they could swoop in and take the seat. Others were drawn by the intensity of the table and the size of the pots. After another hour the sabacc pot hit ten thousand chips, the maximum limit. Any credits paid into the sabacc pot now were wasted: they went straight into the ORO accounts. But nobody complained. Not with the chance to win a small fortune on the table.

Des glanced up at the chrono on the wall. The cantina would be closing in less than an hour. When he'd first sat down at the table, he'd felt certain he was going to win big. For a while he had been ahead. But the last few hours had drained his chips. Working to protect the sabacc pot was crippling him: he'd gone through all his profits and had to re-buy-in twice. He'd fallen into the classic gambler's trap, becoming so obsessed with winning the big pot that he'd lost sight of how much he was losing. He'd let the game get personal.

His shirt was hot and sticky with sweat. His legs were numb from sitting so long, and his back was aching from hunching forward expectantly to study his cards.

He was down almost a thousand credits on the night, but none of the other players had been able to cash in on his misfortune. With the Sabacc pot capped all the antes and penalties went straight to ORO. He'd have to work a month of grueling shifts in the mines if he ever wanted to see any of those credits again. But it was too late to turn back now. His only consolation was that the Republic ensign was down at least twice as much as he was. Yet each time the man ran out of chips, he'd just reach into his pocket and pull out another stack of credits, as if he had unlimited funds. Or as if he just didn't care.

The CardShark fired out another hand. As he peeked at his cards, Des began to feel the first real hints of self-doubt. What if his feeling was wrong this time? What if this wasn't his night to win? He couldn't remember a moment in the past when his gift had betrayed him, but that didn't mean it couldn't happen.

He pushed his chips in with a weak hand, defying every instinct that told him to fold. He'd have to come up at the start of the next turn, no matter how weak his cards were. Any longer and someone else might steal the sabacc pot he was working so hard to collect.

The marker flickered and the cards shifted. Des didn't bother to look; he simply flipped over his cards and muttered, "Coming up."

When he saw his hand he felt like he'd been slapped. He was sitting at negative twenty-three exactly, a bomb-out. The penalty cleaned out his stack of chips.

"Whoa, big fella," the ensign mocked drunkenly, "you must be lum-soaked to come up on that. What the brix were you thinking?"

"Maybe he doesn't understand the difference between plus twenty-three and minus twenty-three," said one of the soldiers watching the match, grinning like a manka cat.

Des tried to ignore them as he paid the penalty. He felt empty. Hollow.

"You don't talk so much when you're losing, huh?" the ensign sneered.

Hate. Des didn't feel anything else at first. Pure, white-hot hatred consumed every thought, every motion, and every ounce of reason in his brain. Suddenly he didn't care about the pot, didn't care about how many credits he had already lost. All he wanted was to wipe the smug expression from the ensign's face. And there was only one way he could do it.

He shot a savage glare in the ensign's direction, but the man was too drunk to be intimidated. Without taking his eyes off his enemy, Des swiped his ORO account card into the reader and rang up another buy-in, ignoring the logical part of his mind that tried to talk him out of it.

The CardShark, its circuits and wires oblivious to what was really going on, pushed a stack of chips toward him and uttered its typically cheery, "Good luck."

Des opened with the Ace and two of sabers. He was at seventeen, a dangerous hand. Lots of potential to go too high on his next card and bomb out. He hesitated, knowing that the smart move was to fold.

"Having second thoughts?" the ensign chided.

Acting on an impulse he couldn't even explain, Des moved his two into the interference field, then pushed his chips into the pot. He was letting his emotions guide him, but he no longer cared. And when the next card came up as a three, he knew what he had to do. He shoved his three into the interference field beside the two that was already there. Then he bet the maximum wager and waited for the switch.

There were actually two ways to win the sabacc pot. One was to get a hand that totaled twenty-three exactly, a pure sabacc. But there was an even better hand: the idiot's array. In modified Bespin rules, if you had a hand of two and three in the same suit and drew the face card known as the Idiot, which had no value at all, you had an idiot's array . . . 23 in the literal sense. It was the rarest hand possible, and it was worth more than even a pure sabacc.

Des was two-thirds of the way there. All he needed now was a switch to take his ten and replace it with the Idiot. Of course, that meant there had to be a switch. And even then he'd have to draw the Idiot off it . . . and there were only two Idiots in the entire seventy-six-card deck. It was a ridiculously long shot.

The marker came up red; the cards shifted. Des didn't even have to look at his hand: he *knew*.

He stared right into the ensign's eyes. "Coming up."

The ensign looked down at his own hand to see what the switch had given him and began to laugh so hard he could barely show his hand. He had the two of flasks, the three of flasks . . . and the Idiot!

There were gasps of surprise and murmurs of disbelief from the crowd. "How do you like that one, boys?" he cackled. "Idiot's array on the switch!"

He stood up, reaching out for the stack of chips on the small pedestal that sat in the center of the table representing the sabacc pot.

Des whipped his hand out and snagged the young man's wrist in a grip as cold and hard as durasteel, then flipped over his own cards. The entire cantina became silent as a tomb; the ensign's laughter died in his throat. A second later he pulled his hand free and sat back down, dumbfounded. From the far edge of the table somebody let out a long, low whistle of amazement. The rest of the crowd burst into noise.

"... never in my life ..."

"... can't believe ..."

"... statistically impossible ..."

"*Two* idiot's arrays in the same hand?"

The CardShark summarized the result in the purest analytical fashion. "We have two players with hands of equal value. The hand will be determined by a sudden demise."

The ensign didn't react with the same kind of calm. "You stupid mudcrutch!" he spat out, his voice strangled with rage. "Now nobody's going to get that sabacc pot!" His eyes bulged out wildly; a vein was pulsing on his forehead. One of his fellow soldiers had placed a hand on his shoulder, as if afraid his friend might leap across the table to try to choke the life out of the miner on the other side.

The ensign was right: neither of them would be collecting the sabacc pot on this hand. In a sudden demise each player was dealt one more card, and the value of the hands was recalculated. If you had the better hand, you'd win ... but you wouldn't get the sabacc pot unless you scored twenty-three exactly. That, however, seemed impossible: there were no more Idiots to deal out to preserve an idiot's array, and no single card had a value higher than the Ace's fifteen.

Not that Des cared. It was enough to have destroyed his opponent's will; to have crushed his hopes and robbed him of his victory. He could feel the ensign's hate, and he responded to it. It was like a living being ... an entity he could draw strength from, fueling his own raging inferno. But Des didn't put his emotions out on display for the rest of the crowd to see. The hate burning in him was his own private store, a power raging inside him so fierce he felt it could crack the world if he let it escape.

The dealer flicked out two cards faceup for everyone to see. They were both nines. Before anyone even had time to react the droid had recalculated the hand, determined that the two players were still tied, and fired out another card to each of them. The ensign took an eight, but Des got another nine. Idiot, two, three, nine, nine . . . twenty-three!

He reached out slowly and tapped his cards, whispering a single word to his opponent: "Sabacc."

The soldier went ballistic. He leapt up, grabbed the underside of the table with both hands, and gave a mighty heave. Only the weight of the table and the built-in stabilizers kept it from flipping over, though it rocked and slammed back into the ground with a deafening crash. All the drinks on it spilled over; ale and lum washed across the electronic cards, causing them to spark and short out.

"Sir, please don't touch the table," the CardShark implored in a pitiful voice.

"Shut up, you hunk of rusted scrap metal!" The ensign grabbed one of the overturned mugs from the table and hurled it at the droid. It connected with a ringing thud. The droid stumbled back and fell over.

The ensign thrust a finger at Des. "You cheated! Nobody gets sabacc on a sudden demise! Not unless he cheats!"

Des didn't say anything; he didn't even stand up. But his muscles were braced in case the soldier made a move.

The ensign turned back to the droid as it rose shakily to its feet. "You're in on it!" He threw another mug at it, connecting again and dropping the droid a second time. Two of the other soldiers tried to restrain him, but he shook free of their grip. He spun around, waving his arms at the crowd. "You're all in on it! Dirty, Sith-loving scum! You hate the Republic! You hate us. We know you do. *We know!*"

The miners pushed in closer, grumbling angrily. The ensign's insults weren't far off the mark; there were a lot of bad feelings toward the Republic on Apatros. And if he didn't watch his mouth, somebody was going to show him just how strong those feelings were.

"We give our lives to protect you, but you don't give a wobber! Any chance to humiliate us, you take it!"

His friends had grabbed him again, trying to wrestle him out the door. But there was no way they could get through the crowd now. From the looks on their faces, the soldiers were terrified. With good reason, Des thought. None of them was armed; their blasters were back on their ship. Now they were trapped in the center of a hostile crush of heavily muscled miners who'd been drinking all night. And their friend wouldn't shut up.

"You should get down on your knees and thank us each and every time we land on this ball of bantha sweat you call a planet! But you're too stupid to know how lucky you are to have us on your side! You're nothing but a bunch of filthy, illiterate—"

A lum bottle hurled anonymously from the crowd struck him hard in the side of his head, cutting his words short. He dropped to the floor, dragging his friends down with him. Des stood motionless as a mass of angry miners surged.

The sound of a blaster caused everyone to freeze. Groshik had climbed up onto the top of the bar, his stunner already charging up to fire again. But everybody knew the next shot wouldn't be aimed at the ceiling.

"We're closed," he croaked as loud as his raspy voice could manage. "Everybody get out of my cantina!"

The miners began to back off, and the soldiers stood up warily. The ensign swayed, the cut on his forehead bleeding into his eye.

"You three first," the Neimoidian said to the ensign and the soldiers who supported him. He waved the barrel of his weapon menacingly around the room. "Clear a path. Get them out of here."

Everyone but the soldiers remained frozen. This wasn't the first time Groshik had whipped out the stunner. The BlasTech CS-33 Firespray stun rifle was one of the finest nonlethal crowd-control devices on the market, capable of incapacitating multiple targets with a single shot. More than a few of the miners had felt the brutal force of its wide-beam blast rendering them unconscious. From personal experience Des could attest to the fact that it wasn't a pain anyone was likely to forget.

Once the Republic crew vanished into the night, the rest of the crowd began to move slowly toward the door. Des fell into step with the masses, but as he passed the bar Groshik pointed the blaster right at him.

"Not you. You stay put."

Des didn't move a millimeter until all the others were gone. He wasn't scared; he didn't think Groshik would really fire. Still, he saw no advantage in giving him a reason to.

Only after the last patron had left and closed the door did Groshik lower his arm. He clambered down awkwardly from the bar and set the rifle on the table, then turned to Des.

"I figured it was safer to keep you here with me for a bit," he explained. "Those soldiers were pretty mad. They might be waiting for you on the walk home."

Des smiled. "I didn't figure you were mad at me," he said.

Groshik snorted. "Oh, I'm mad at you. That's why you're going to help me clean up this mess."

Des sighed and shook his head in mock exasperation. "You saw what happened, Groshik. I was just an innocent bystander."

Groshik wasn't in any mood to hear it. "Just start picking up the chairs," he muttered.

With the help of the CardShark—at least it was good for something besides dealing, Des thought—they finished cleaning up in just over an hour. When they were done the droid waddled out on shaky legs, heading toward the maintenance facilities for repairs. Before it left, Des made sure his sabacc winnings had been credited to his account.

Now that it was just the two of them, Groshik motioned Des over to the bar, grabbed a couple of glasses, and took a bottle down from the shelf.

"Cortyg brandy," he said, pouring them each half a glass. "Direct from Kashyyyk. Not the hard stuff the Wookiees drink, though. Milder. Smoother. More tame."

Des took a sip and nearly choked as the fiery liquid burned its way down his throat. "This is tame? I'd hate to see what the Wookiees drink!"

Groshik shrugged. "What do you expect? They're Wookiees."

With his second sip, Des was more careful. He let it roll across his tongue, savoring the rich flavor. "This is good, Groshik. And expensive, I bet. What's the occasion?"

"You had quite a day. I thought you could use it."

Des drained his glass. Groshik filled him up halfway, then corked the bottle and set it back on the shelf.

"I'm worried about you," the Neimoidian rasped. "Worried about what happened in the fight with Gerd."

"He didn't give me much choice."

The Neimodian nodded. "I know, I know. Still . . . you bit off his thumb. And tonight you nearly started a riot in my bar."

"Hey, I just wanted to play cards," Des protested. "It's not my fault things got out of hand."

"Maybe, maybe not. I saw you tonight. You were goading that soldier, playing him like you play everyone who sits down against you. You push them, twist them, make them dance like puppets on a string. But this time you never let up. Even when you had the advantage, you kept pushing. You *wanted* him to go off like that."

"Are you saying I planned this whole thing?" Des laughed. "Come on, Groshik. It was the cards that set him off. You know I wasn't cheating— it's just not possible. How could I control what cards were dealt?"

"It was more than the cards, Des," Groshik said, his gravelly voice dropping so low that Des had to lean in close to hear. "You were angry, Des. More angry than I've ever seen you before. I could feel it from all the way across the room, like something in the air. We could all feel it.

"The crowd turned ugly in a hurry, Des. It was like they were feeding off your rage and your hate. You were projecting waves of emotion, a storm of anger and fury. Everyone else just kind of got swept up in it: the crowd, that soldier . . . everybody. Even me. It was all I could do to aim that first shot from my blaster at the ceiling. Every instinct in my body was telling me to fire it into the crowd. I wanted to take them all down and leave them writhing in pain."

Des couldn't believe his ears. "Listen to what you're saying, Groshik. It's crazy. You know I wouldn't do that. I *couldn't* do that. Nobody could."

Groshik reached up a long , thin hand and patted Des on the shoulder. "I know you'd never do it on purpose, Des. And I know how crazy it sounds. But there was something different about you tonight. You gave in to your emotions, and it unleashed something . . . strange. Something dangerous."

Groshik tossed his head back and drained the last of his cortyg, shuddering as it went down. "Just watch yourself, Des. Please. I've got a bad feeling."

"Be careful, Groshik," Des replied with another laugh. "Neimoidians aren't known for relying on their feelings. It's not good for business."

Groshik studied him carefully for a moment, then nodded wearily. "True. Maybe I'm just tired. I should get some sleep. And so should you."

They shook hands, and Des left the cantina.

5

The streets of Apatros were dark. ORO charged such high rates for power that everyone turned off all their lights when they went to bed, and tonight the moon was only the barest sliver in the sky. There wasn't even the cantina's glow to guide him: Groshik had shut off the lights on its walls and dome until he opened the next day. Des stayed in the middle of the street, trying to avoid barking his shins on the debris hidden in the darker shadows along the edges.

Yet somehow, despite the near-absolute darkness, he saw them coming.

It was a split second before it happened, a sense that danger was coming . . . and where it was coming from. Three silhouettes leapt at him, two coming head-on and another attacking from behind. He ducked forward just in time, feeling the metal pipe that would have cracked his skull and knocked him cold swiping through the air a hairbreadth above him. He popped back up as it passed and lashed out with a fist, driving into the featureless head of the nearest figure. He was rewarded with the sick crunch of cartilage and bone.

He ducked again, this time to the side, and the pipe that would have brained him square between the eyes thumped down hard across his left shoulder. He staggered to the side, driven by the force of the blow. But in the darkness it took a moment for his opponents to locate him, and by then he had regained his balance.

Through the gloom he could just make out the vague outlines of his at-tackers. The one he'd punched was slowly standing up; the other two stood wary and ready. He didn't have to see their faces to know who they were: the ensign and the two soldiers who'd half carried the man from the cantina. Des could smell the reek of Corellian ale wafting up at him, con-firming their identities. They must have waited outside the cantina and followed him until they thought they could get the jump on him. That was good: it meant they hadn't gone back to their ship to get their blasters.

They came at him again, rushing him all at once. They had the num-bers and months of military hand-to-hand combat training on their side; Des had strength, size, and years of bare-knuckle brawling on his. But in the darkness, none of that really mattered.

Des met their charge head-on, and all four combatants tumbled to the ground. Punches and kicks landed without any thought given to target or strategy: the blind fighting the blind. Each blow he landed brought a sat-isfying grunt or groan from his opponents, but his enjoyment was limited by the pummeling his own body was enduring.

It didn't matter if his eyes were open or closed, he couldn't see a thing. He reacted on instinct; aches and pains were washed away in the darkness by the adrenaline pumping through his veins.

And then suddenly he saw something. Someone had drawn a vibro-blade. It was still black as the heart of the mines during a cave-in, yet Des could see the blade clearly, as if it glowed with an inner fire. It stabbed toward him and he grabbed the wrist of the wielder, twisting it back and driving it toward the dark mass from which it had appeared. There was a sharp cry and then a choking gurgle, and suddenly the burning blade in his vision winked out, the threat extinguished.

The mass of bodies entwined with his quickly untangled, two of them scampering clear. The third was motionless. A second later he heard the click of a luma switching on, and he was momentarily blinded by its beam of light. Eyes squeezed shut, he heard a gasp.

"He's dead!" one of the soldiers exclaimed. "You killed him!"

Shading his eyes against the illumination, Des glanced down to see ex-actly what he'd expected: the ensign lying on his back, the vibroblade plunged deep into his chest.

The luma flicked off, and Des braced himself for another assault. Instead he heard the sounds of footsteps fleeing in the night, heading toward the docking pads.

Des looked down at the body, planning to grab the glowing blade and use its light to guide him through the darkness. But the blade wasn't glowing now. In fact, he realized, it had never really glowed at all. It couldn't have: vibroblades weren't energy weapons. Their blades were simple metal.

There were more pressing concerns than how he had seen the vibroblade in the darkness, however. As soon as they reached their ship, the soldiers would report to their commander, who would report the incident to the ORO authorities. ORO would turn the planet upside down looking for him. Des didn't like his chances. It would be the word of a miner—one with a history of brawls and violence, at that—against two Republic naval soldiers. No one would believe it had been an act of self-defense.

And had it been, really? He had seen the blade coming. Could he have disarmed his opponent without killing him? Des shook his head. He didn't have time for guilt or regrets. Not now. He had to find somewhere safe to hide out.

He couldn't go back to his barracks: that was the first place they'd look. He'd never reach the mines on foot before daybreak, and there was nowhere on the open wastes he could hide once the sun came up. There was only one option, one hope. Eventually they'd go looking for him there, too. But he had nowhere else to go.

————

Groshik must have still been awake, because he answered the door only seconds after Des began pounding on it. The Neimoidian took one look at the blood on the young man's hands and shirt and grabbed him by the sleeve.

"Get in here!" he croaked, yanking Des through the door and slamming it shut behind him. "Are you hurt?"

Des shook his head. "I don't think so. The blood isn't mine."

Taking a step back, the Neimoidian looked him up and down. "There's a lot of it. Too much. Smells human."

When Des didn't reply, Groshik ventured a guess. "Gerd's?"

Another shake of the head. "The ensign," Des said.

Groshik dropped his head and swore under his breath. "Who knows? Are the authorities after you?"

"Not yet. Soon." Then, as if trying to justify his actions, he added, "There were three of them, Groshik. Only one's dead."

His old friend nodded sympathetically. "I'm sure he had it coming. Just like Gerd. But that doesn't change the facts. A Republic soldier is dead . . . and you're the one who's going to take the blame."

The cantina owner led Des over to the bar and brought down the bottle of cortyg brandy. Without saying a word, he poured them each a drink. This time he didn't stop at half glasses.

"I'm sorry I came here," Des said, desperate to break the uncomfortable silence. "I didn't mean to get you mixed up in this."

"Getting mixed up in things doesn't bother me," Groshik reassured him with a comforting pat on his arm. "I'm just trying to figure a way to get us out of this now. Let me think."

They downed their glasses. It was all Des could do to keep from panicking; with each passing second he expected a dozen men in ORO body armor to crash down the cantina's door. After what seemed like hours, but was probably only a minute or two, Groshik began to talk. He spoke softly, and Des wasn't sure if the Neimoidian was addressing him or merely talking out loud to help himself think.

"You can't stay here. ORO can't afford to lose their Republic contracts. They'll turn the whole colony upside down to find you. We have to get you offworld." He paused. "But by morning, your picture will be on every vidscreen in Republic space. Changing your looks won't help much. Even with a wig or facial prosthetics you tend to stand out in a crowd. So that means we have to get you out of Republic space. And that means . . ." Groshik trailed off.

Des waited expectantly.

"Those things you said tonight," Groshik ventured, "about the Sith and the Republic. Did you mean it? Did you *really* mean it?"

"I don't know. I guess so."

There was another long pause, as if the bartender was gathering himself. "How would you feel about joining the Sith?" he suddenly blurted out.

Des was caught completely off guard. "*What?*"

"I know . . . people. I can get you offworld. Tonight. But these people aren't looking for passengers: the Sith need soldiers. They're always recruiting, just like those Republic officers tonight."

Des shook his head. "I don't believe this. You work for the Sith? You always said never to take sides!"

"I don't work for the Sith," Groshik snapped. "I just know people who do. I know people who work for the Republic, too. But they're not going to be much help in this situation. So I need to know, Des. Is this something you want?"

"I don't have a lot of other options," Des mumbled in reply.

"Maybe, maybe not. If you stay here, the ORO authorities are sure to find you. This wasn't a cold-blooded murder. The judiciary probably won't let you get off by pleading self-defense, but they'll have to admit there were extenuating circumstances. You'll serve time on one of the penal colonies—five, maybe six years—and then you're a free man."

"Or I join the Sith."

Groshik nodded. "Or you join the Sith. But if I'm going to help you do this, I want to be sure you know what you're getting into."

Des thought about it, but not for long. "I've spent my entire life trying to get off this hunk of rock," he said slowly. "If I go to a prison world, I'm trading one barren, blasted planet for another. No different than staying right here.

"If I join the Sith, at least I'm out from under ORO's thumb. And you heard what that Republic commander said about them. The Sith respect strength. I think I'll be able to hold my own."

"I don't doubt that," Groshik conceded. "But don't dismiss everything else that commander said. He was right about the Brotherhood of Darkness. They can be ruthless and cruel. They bring out the worst in some people. I don't want you to fall into that trap."

"First you tell me to join the Sith," Des said, "now you're warning me against joining them. What's going on?"

The Neimoidian gave a long, gurgling sigh. "You're right, Des. The decision is made. Grim fate and ill fortune have conspired against you. It's not like sabacc; you can't fold a bad hand. In life you just play the cards you're dealt." He turned away, heading for the small stairs at the back of the cantina. "Come on. In a few hours, after they've searched the housing units in the colony, they'll start searching the starport for you. We have to hurry if we want to get you safely hidden away on one of the freight cruisers before then."

Des reached out across the bar and grabbed Groshik's shoulder. Groshik turned to face him, and Des clasped the Neimoidian's long, slender forearm.

"Thank you, old friend. I won't forget this."

"I know you won't, Des." Though the words were kind, there was an unmistakable sorrow in the gravelly voice.

Des released his grip, feeling awkward, ashamed, scared, grateful, and excited all at the same time. He felt like he needed to say something else, so he added, "I'll make this up to you somehow. The next time we meet—"

"Your life here is over, Des," Groshik said, cutting him off. "There won't be a next time. Not for us."

The Neimoidian shook his head. "I don't know what's ahead of you, but I get the feeling it isn't going to be easy. Don't count on others for help. In the end each of us is in this alone. The survivors are those who know how to look out for themselves."

With that he turned away, his feet shuffling briskly across the cantina's floor as he headed to the back exit. Des hesitated a moment, Groshik's words burning into his mind, then rushed off to follow.

————

Huddled in the hold of the ship, Des tried to get comfortable. He'd been crammed into the small smuggler's hatch for nearly an hour. It was a tight fit for a man of his size.

Twenty minutes earlier he had heard an ORO patrol come to inspect the ship. They had made a cursory search; not finding the fugitive they were seeking, they had left. A few seconds later the captain, a Rodian pilot, had rapped hard on the panel keeping Des hidden.

"You stay until engines go," he had called in passable galactic Basic. "We take off, you come out. Not before."

Des hadn't recognized him when he'd climbed aboard; he had looked like any other Rodian he'd ever seen. Just another independent freighter captain picking up a load of cortosis, hoping to sell it on some other world for enough profit to keep his ship flying another few months.

If ORO had offered a reward for Des's capture, the captain probably would have sold him out. That meant the ORO managers hadn't put a price on his head. They were more worried about paying out a bounty than letting a fugitive escape Republic justice. It wasn't important that they found him, as long as they could show the Republic they had tried. Groshik must have realized all this when he made the arrangements to smuggle Des aboard.

The high-pitched whine of the engines powering up caused Des to brace himself against the walls of his close quarters. A few seconds later the whine became a deafening roar, and the ship lurched beneath him. The repulsors fired, counterbalancing the vessel, and Des felt the press of the g's as the ship took to the sky.

He kicked at the panel once, knocking it free, and untangled himself from the hidey-hole. The captain and crew weren't around; they would all be at their stations for liftoff.

Des didn't know their destination. All he knew was that at the end of the trip a human woman was waiting to sign him up for the Sith army. As before, the thought filled him with a mix of emotions. Fear and excitement dominated all the others.

There was a slight jostling of the ship as it broke atmosphere and began to speed away from the tiny mining world. A few seconds later Des felt an unfamiliar but unmistakable surge as they jumped to hyperspace.

A sudden sense of liberation filled his spirit. He was free. For the first time in his life, he was beyond the grasping reach of ORO and its cortosis mines. Groshik had said that grim fate and ill fortune were conspiring against him, but Des wasn't so sure now. Things hadn't worked out quite the way he'd planned—he was a fugitive with the blood of a Republic soldier on his hands—but he had finally escaped Apatros.

Maybe the cards he'd been dealt weren't so bad, after all. In the end he'd gotten the one thing he wanted most. And when you came right down to it, wasn't that the only thing that really mattered?

6

Phaseera's yellow sun was directly overhead, beaming down across the lush valley and over the jungle camp where Des and his fellow Sith troopers waited. Beneath the shelter of a cydera tree, Des ran a quick system check on his TC-22 blaster rifle to pass the time. The power pack was fully charged, good for fifty shots. His backup power pack checked out, too. The aim was off just slightly, a common problem with all TC models. They had good range and power, but over time their scopes could lose precise calibration. A quick adjustment brought it back into line.

His hands moved with a quick confidence born of a thousand repetitions. Over the past twelve months he'd gone through the routine so many times he barely even had to think about it anymore. A pre-battle weapons check wasn't standard practice in the Sith militia, but it was a habit he'd gotten into—one that had saved his life on several occasions. The Sith army was growing so fast that supply couldn't keep up with demand. The best equipment was reserved for veterans and officers, while new recruits were forced to make do with whatever was available.

Now that he was a sergeant he could have requested a better model, but the TC-22 was the first weapon he'd learned to fire and he'd become pretty good with it. Des figured a little routine maintenance was a better option than learning to master the subtle nuances of another weapon.

His blaster pistol, however, was top of the line. Not all Sith troopers were given pistols: for most soldiers a medium-range, semi-repeating rifle was weapon enough. They'd probably be dead long before they ever got close enough to their enemy to use a pistol. But in the past year Des had proven a dozen times over that he was more than just turret fodder. Soldiers good enough to survive the initial rush and get in tight to the enemy ranks needed a weapon more suited to close-quarters fighting.

For Des that weapon was the GSI-21D: the finest disruptor pistol manufactured by Galactic Solutions Industries. Optimum range was only twenty meters, but within that distance it was capable of disintegrating armor, flesh, and droid plating with equal efficiency. The 21D was illegal in most Republic-controlled sectors of the galaxy, a testament to its awesome destructive potential. The disruptor's power pack carried only enough charge for a dozen shots, but when he was eye-to-eye with an opponent it rarely took more than one.

He slid the pistol into the holster clipped to his belt, checked the vibroblade in his boot, and turned his attention to his troops. All around him the men and women of his unit were following his lead, making similar inspections of their own equipment as they waited for the orders. He couldn't help but smile; he'd trained them well.

He'd joined the Sith armies as a way to escape both prison and Apatros itself. But it hadn't taken him long to actually grow fond of the soldier's life. There was a camaraderie among the men and women who fought at his side, a bond that quickly extended to include Des himself. He'd never felt any connection to the miners on Apatros and indeed had always considered himself something of a loner. But in the military he'd found his true place. He belonged here with the troops. *His* troops.

Senior Trooper Adanar noticed his gaze and responded by thumping a closed fist lightly against his chest twice, just over his heart. It was a gesture known only to members of the unit: a private sign for loyalty and fidelity, a symbol of the bond they all shared.

Des returned the gesture. He and Adanar had been in the same unit since day one of their military careers. The recruiter had signed them up together and assigned them both to the Gloom Walkers, Lieutenant Ulabore's unit.

Adanar picked up his rifle and sauntered over to where his friend was sitting. "You figure we're going to need that disruptor pistol of yours any-time soon, Sarge?"

"No harm in being prepared," Des replied, whipping out the disruptor and giving it a spinning flourish before returning it to its holster.

"I wish they'd give us the go-ahead already," Adanar grumbled. "We've been in position for two days now. How long are they going to wait?"

Des shrugged. "We can't go until they're ready to move in with the main force. We go too early and the plan falls apart."

The Gloom Walkers had earned quite a reputation over the past year. They'd been in scores of battles on half a dozen worlds, and they'd tasted far more than their share of victories. They'd gone from being one of a thousand expendable front-line units to elite troops reserved for critical missions. Right now they were the key to capturing the manufacturing world of Phaseera—if someone would just give them the order to go. Until then they were stuck in this jungle camp an hour's march away from their objective. They'd been here only a couple of days, but it was already beginning to take its toll.

Adanar began to pace. Des sat calmly in the shade, watching him march back and forth.

"Don't wear yourself out," he said after a minute. "We're not going anywhere until nightfall at the earliest. You might as well get comfort-able."

Adanar stopped pacing, but he didn't sit down. "Lieutenant says this is going to be easy as a spicerun," he said, trying to keep his voice casual. "You figure he's right?"

Lieutenant Ulabore had received many accolades for the success of his troops, but everyone in the unit knew who was really in charge when the blaster bolts started flying.

That fact had become painfully clear nearly a year before back on Kashyyyk, where Des and Adanar had seen their first action. The Brother-hood of Darkness had tried to secure a foothold in the Mid Rim by in-vading the system, sending in wave after wave of troops to capture the resource-rich homeworld of the Wookiees. But the planet was a Republic stronghold and they weren't about to retreat, no matter how badly out-numbered.

When the Sith fleet first landed, their enemies simply vanished into the forest. The invasion turned into a war of attrition, a long, drawn-out campaign fought among the branches of the wroshyr trees high above the planet's surface. The Sith troopers weren't used to fighting in the treetops, and the thick foliage and kshyy vines of the forest canopy provided perfect cover for the Republic soldiers and their Wookiee guides to launch ambushes and guerrilla raids. Thousands upon thousands of the invaders were wiped out, most dying without even seeing the opponent who had fired the fatal shot . . . but the Sith Masters just kept sending more troops in.

The Gloom Walkers were part of the second wave of reinforcements. During their first battle they were separated from the main lines, cut off from the rest of the army. Alone and surrounded by enemies, Lieutenant Ulabore panicked. Without direct orders, he had no idea what to do to keep his unit alive. Fortunately, Des was there to step in and save their hides.

For starters, he could sense the enemy even when he couldn't see them. Somehow he just *knew* where they were. He couldn't explain it, but he'd stopped trying to explain his unique talents long ago. Now he just tried to use them to his best advantage. With Des as their guide, the Gloom Walkers were able to avoid the traps and ambushes as they slowly worked their way back to rejoin the main force. It took three days and nights, countless brief but deadly battles, and a seemingly endless march through enemy territory, but they made it. Through all the fighting, the unit lost only a handful of soldiers, and the troops who made it back knew they owed their lives to Des.

The story of the Gloom Walkers became a rallying point for the rest of the Sith army, raising morale that had become dangerously low. If a single unit could survive for three days on its own, they reasoned, then surely a thousand units could win the war. In the end it took almost two thousand units, but Kashyyyk finally fell.

As leader of the heroic Gloom Walkers, Lieutenant Ulabore was given a special commendation. He never bothered to mention that Des was really the one responsible. Still, he'd been smart enough to promote Des to sergeant. And he knew enough to stay out of the way when things got hot.

"So?" Adanar repeated. "What's the word, Des? When they finally give us the go, is this mission going to be a spicerun?"

"The lieutenant's just saying what he thinks we all want to hear."

"I know that, Des. That's why I'm talking to you. I want to know what we're really in for."

Des thought about it for a few moments. They were holed up in the jungle on the edge of a narrow valley—the only route into Phaseera's capital city, where the Republic army had set up its base camp. On a nearby hill overlooking the valley was a Republic outpost. If the Sith tried to move troops through the valley, even at night, the outpost was sure to spot them. They'd signal ahead to the base camp so their defenses would be up and fully operational long before the enemy ever reached them.

The Gloom Walkers' mission was simple: eliminate the outpost so the rest of the army could launch a surprise attack on the Republic base camp. They had interference boxes—short-range jamming equipment they could use to keep the outpost from transmitting a signal to warn the main camp—but they'd have to hit them fast. The outpost reported each day at dawn, and if the Gloom Walkers struck too soon, the Republic would realize something was wrong when the daily report didn't come in.

The timing was critical. They'd have to take them out just before the main force entered the area. That would leave a few hours to cross the valley and catch the base camp unprepared. It was doable, but only if everything was coordinated perfectly. The Gloom Walkers were in place, but the main force wasn't ready to make its move yet . . . and so they waited.

"I'm worried," Des finally conceded. "Taking that outpost won't be easy. Once we get the go-ahead there's no margin for error. We have to be perfect. If they've got any surprises waiting for us, we could be in trouble."

Adanar spit on the ground. "I knew it! You've got a bad feeling, don't you? This is Hsskhor all over again!"

Hsskhor had been a disaster. After Kashyyyk fell, the surviving Republic soldiers fled to the neighboring world of Trandosha. Twenty units of Sith troopers, including the Gloom Walkers, were sent in pursuit. They caught up to the Republic survivors on the desert plains outside the city of Hsskhor.

A day of savage fighting left many dead on both sides, but no definitive victor. Des had been uneasy throughout the battle, though at the time he hadn't been able to say why. His unease had grown as night fell and both

sides retreated to opposite ends of the battlefield to regroup. The Trandoshans had struck a few hours later.

The pitch-black night wasn't a problem for the reptilian Trandoshans: they could see into the infrared spectrum. They seemed to come out of nowhere, materializing from the darkness like a nightmare given substance.

Unlike the Wookiees, the Trandoshans weren't allied with either side in the galactic civil war. The bounty hunters and mercenaries of Hsskhor cut a swath of destruction through the ranks of Republic and Sith alike, not caring whom they fought just as long as they came away with trophies from their kills.

Details of the massacre were never officially released. Des had been at the very center of the carnage, and even he could barely piece together what had happened. The attack caught the Gloom Walkers, like every other unit, completely off guard. By the time the sun rose nearly half the Sith troops had been cut down. Des lost a lot of friends in the slaughter ... friends he might have saved if he had paid more attention to the dark premonition he'd felt when he first set foot on that forsaken desert world. And he vowed he'd never let the Gloom Walkers get caught in a slaughter like that again.

In the end Hsskhor paid a heavy price for the ambush. Reinforcements were sent in from Kashyyyk to overwhelm both the Republic forces and the Trandoshans. It took less than a week for the Sith to claim victory, and the once proud city was sacked and razed to the ground. Many of the Trandoshans simply gave up the fight to defend their homes and offered their services to their conquerors. They were bounty hunters and mercenaries by trade, and hunters by nature. They didn't care whom they were working for, as long as there was a chance to do some more killing. Needless to say, the Sith had welcomed them with open arms.

"This isn't going to be a repeat of Hsskhor," Des assured his nervous companion. It was true he had an uneasy feeling once again. But this time it was different. Something big was going to happen, but Des couldn't say for sure whether it would be good or bad.

"Come on, Des," Adanar pressed. "Go talk to Ulabore. He listens to you sometimes."

"And tell him what?"

Adanar threw his hands up in exasperation. "I don't know! Tell him about your bad feeling. Make him get on the comm to HQ and tell them to pull us back. Or convince them to send us in! Just don't leave us sitting out here like a bunch of dead womp rats rotting in the sun!"

Before Des could answer, one of the junior troopers, a young woman named Lucia, ran up and snapped off a crisp salute. "Sergeant! Lieutenant Ulabore wants you to assemble the troops by his tent. He'll address them in thirty minutes," she said, her voice earnest and excited.

Des flashed a smile at his friend. "I think we've finally got our orders."

———————

The soldiers stood at attention as the lieutenant and Des reviewed the troops. As it always did, the inspection consisted of Ulabore moving up and down the ranks, nodding and giving half-muttered approvals. It was mostly for show, a chance for Ulabore to feel as if he had something to do with the success of a mission.

Once they were done, the lieutenant marched to the front of the column and turned to face the troops. Des stood alone in front of the unit, his back to them so he could be face-to-face with his superior officer.

"Everyone here is familiar with our mission objective," Ulabore began, his voice unusually high-pitched and loud. Des guessed he was trying to sound authoritative, but it came across as shrill.

"I'll leave the specifics of the mission to the sergeant here," he continued. "Our task is not an easy one, but the days of the Gloom Walkers getting easy jobs are long gone.

"I don't have much else to say; I know you're all as eager as I am to end this pointless waiting. That's why I'm happy to inform you that we've been given the order to move out. We hit the Republic outpost in one hour!"

Horrified gasps and loud whispers of disbelief rose up from the ranks. Ulabore stepped back as if he'd been slapped. He'd obviously been expecting cheers and exultation, and was rattled by the sudden anger and lack of discipline.

"Gloom Walkers, hold!" Des barked. He stepped up to the lieutenant

and lowered his voice. "Sir, are you certain those were the orders? Move in one hour? Are you certain they didn't mean one hour after nightfall?"

"Are you questioning me, Sergeant?" Ulabore snapped, making no attempt to keep his own voice down.

"No, sir. It's just that if we leave in one hour it'll still be light out. They'll see us coming."

"By the time they see us we'll already be close enough to jam their transmitters," the lieutenant countered. "They won't be able to signal back to the base camp."

"It's not that, sir. It's the gunships. They've got three repulsorcraft equipped with heavy-repeating flash cannons. If we try to take the outpost during the day, those things will mow us down from the sky."

"It's a suicide mission!" someone shouted out from the ranks.

Ulabore's eyes became narrow slits, and his face turned red. "The main army is moving out at dusk, Sergeant," he said through tightly clenched teeth. "They want to cross the valley in darkness and hit the Republic base camp at first light."

"Then there's no reason for us to move so soon," Des replied, struggling to remain calm. "If they start at dusk, it's going to take at least three hours before they reach the valley from their current position. That gives us plenty of time to take the outpost down before they get here, even if we wait until after dark."

"It's obvious you don't understand what's really going on, Sergeant." Ulabore spoke as if arguing with a stubborn child. "The main force isn't going to start moving until *after* we report our mission is complete. That's why we have to move now."

It made sense: the generals wouldn't want to risk the main force until they knew for certain the valley was secure. But sending them in during the light of day guaranteed that the Gloom Walkers' casualty rate would increase fivefold.

"You have to comm back to HQ and explain the situation to them," Des said. "We can't take on those gunships in the air. We have to wait till they ground them for the night. You have to make them understand what we're up against."

The lieutenant acted as if he hadn't even heard him. "The generals give the orders to me, and I give them to you," he snapped. "Not the other way around! The army is moving out at dusk, and that's not going to change to fit your schedule, Sergeant!"

"They won't have to change their plans," Des insisted. "If we leave as soon as it gets dark, we'll still have that outpost down by the time they reach the valley. But sending us in now is just—"

"Enough!" the lieutenant snapped. "Quit braying like a bantha cut off from its herd! You have your orders, now follow them! Or do you want to see what happens to soldiers who defy their superior officers?"

Suddenly it was clear to Des what was really going on. Ulabore knew the order was a mistake, but he was too scared to do anything about it. The order must have come directly from one of the Dark Lords. Ulabore would rather lead his troops into a slaughter than face the wrath of a Sith Master. But Des wasn't about to let him drive the Gloom Walkers to their doom. This wasn't going to become a repeat of Hsskhor. He hesitated for only a second before slamming his fist into his lieutenant's chin, knocking him cold.

There was stunned silence from the rest of the troops as Ulabore slumped to the ground. Des quickly took away the fallen officer's weapons, then turned and pointed at a pair of the newest recruits.

"You two, keep an eye on the lieutenant. Make sure he's comfortable if he wakes up, but don't let him anywhere near the comm."

To the communications officer he said, "Just before dusk send a message back to HQ telling them our mission is complete so they can start moving the main force into the valley. That will give us two hours to achieve our objective before they get here."

Turning to address the rest of the troops, he paused to let the gravity of his next words sink in. "What I've done here is mutiny," he said slowly. "There's a chance anyone who follows me from here on in will face a court-martial when this is over. If any of you feel you can't follow my orders after what I've done here today, speak up now and I'll surrender command to Senior Trooper Adanar for the rest of the mission."

He gazed out across the soldiers. For a second nobody spoke; then as one they all raised their fists and gave two light raps on their chest, just above the heart.

Overwhelmed with pride, Des had to swallow hard before he could give his final order to the troops . . . *his* troops. "Gloom Walkers, dismissed!"

The ranks dispersed in groups of twos and threes, the soldiers whispering quietly to one another. Adanar broke away from the rest and came up to Des.

"Ulabore's not going to forget this," he said quietly. "What are you going to do about him?"

"After we take that outpost they'll want to pin a medal on our commanding officer," Des replied. "I'm betting he'd rather shut up and accept it than let anyone know what really happened."

Adanar grunted. "Guess you got it all worked out."

"Not quite," Des admitted. "I'm still not sure how we're going to take down that outpost."

7

The outpost was located in a clearing on the top of a plateau overlooking the valley. Under the cover of night, the Gloom Walkers had moved silently through the jungle until they had it surrounded. Des had broken the unit up into four squads, each approaching from a different side. Each squad carried an interference box with it.

They had set up and activated the i-boxes once they'd closed to within half a kilometer of the base, jamming all transmissions within their perimeter. The squads had continued on to the edges of the clearing then stopped, waiting for Des to give them the signal to move in. With no communication among the squads—the i-boxes jammed their own equipment as well—the most reliable signal was the sound of blasterfire.

As he stared across the clearing at the three repulsorcraft sitting on the landing pad atop the outpost's roof, Des felt a familiar feeling in the pit of his stomach. All soldiers felt the same thing going into battle, whether they admitted it or not: fear. Fear of failure, fear of dying, fear of watching their friends die, fear of being wounded and living out the rest of their days crippled or maimed. The fear was always there, and it would devour you if you let it.

Des knew how to turn that fear to his own advantage. *Take what makes you weak and turn it into something that makes you strong.* Transform the fear into anger and hate: hatred of the enemy; hatred of the Republic and the Jedi. The hate gave him strength, and the strength brought him victory.

For Des the transformation came easily once the fighting started. Thanks to his abusive father, he'd been turning fear into anger and hate ever since he was a child. Maybe that was why he was such a good soldier. Maybe that was why the others looked to him for leadership.

They were waiting on his signal even now, waiting for him to take the first shot. As soon as he did, they'd charge the outpost. The Gloom Walkers were outnumbered nearly two to one; they'd need the advantage of surprise to even out the odds. But those gunships were a problem Des hadn't anticipated.

The clearing was surrounded by bright lights that illuminated everything within a hundred meters of the outpost itself. And even though the repulsorcraft were grounded, there was a soldier stationed in the open flatbed at the rear of each vehicle, operating the turrets. The armored walls of the flatbed rose to waist height to give the gunner some cover, and the turret itself was heavily shielded to protect it from enemy fire.

From the landing pad on the roof, the gunners had a clear view of the surrounding area. If he fired that first shot, the other units would charge out into the clearing and right into a storm of heavy-repeating blasterfire. They'd be torn apart like zucca tossed into a rancor pit.

"What's the matter, Sarge?" one of the soldiers in his squad asked. It was Lucia, the junior trooper who'd delivered Ulabore's orders to him earlier. "What are we waiting for?"

It was too late to call off the mission. The main army was already on the move; by the time Des got back to camp to warn them, they'd be halfway through the valley.

He glanced down at the young recruit and noticed the scope on her weapon. Lucia was carrying a TC-17 long-range blaster rifle. Her knuckles were white from gripping her weapon too tightly in fear and anticipation. She'd seen only minor combat duty before being assigned to the Gloom Walkers, but Des knew she was one of the best shots in the unit. The TC-17 was only good for a dozen shots before the power cell had to be switched out, but it had a range well over three hundred meters.

Each of the four squads had a sniper assigned to it. When the fighting began, their job was to watch the perimeter of the battle and make sure none of the Republic soldiers escaped to warn their main camp.

"See those soldiers standing in the rear of the gunships? The ones working the flash cannons?" he asked her.

She nodded.

"If we don't get rid of them somehow, they're going to turn our squads into turret fodder about ten seconds after this battle begins."

She nodded again, her eyes wide and scared. Des tried to keep his voice even and professional to calm her down.

"I want you to think about this very carefully now, trooper. How fast do you think you could take them out from here?"

She hesitated. "I . . . I don't even know if I could, Sarge. Not all of them. Not from this angle. I could get a line on the first one, but as soon as he goes down, I doubt the others will stand still long enough for me to take aim. They'll probably duck down in the flatbed for cover. And even if I take the gunners out, there's half a dozen more soldiers on that roof who would jump in to take their places. I can't drop nine targets that fast by myself, Sarge. Nobody can."

Des bit his lip and tried to figure out an answer to the problem. There were only three gunships. If he could somehow get a message to the sniper in each squad and have them fire at exactly the same time, they might be able to take out the unsuspecting gunners . . . though they'd still have to stop the other six soldiers from replacing them.

He cut off his own line of thought with a silent curse. It would never work. Because of the i-boxes there was no way to get a message to the other squads in time.

Taking the sniper rifle from Lucia's hands, he brought the weapon up and set his eye to the scope to get a better look at the situation. He scanned the roof quickly from side to side, noting the position of every Republic soldier. With the magnification of the scope he could make out their features clear enough to see their lips moving as they spoke.

The situation was practically hopeless. The outpost was the key to taking Phaseera, and the turrets on the roof were the key to taking the outpost. But Des was out of options and almost out of time.

He felt the fear stronger than ever and took a deep breath to focus his mind. Adrenaline began to pump through his veins as he redirected the fear to give him strength and power. He lined the blaster's scope up on one of the gunners, and a red veil fell across his vision. And then he fired.

He acted on instinct, moving too quickly to let his conscious thoughts get in the way. He didn't even see the first soldier drop; the scope was already moving to his next target. The second gunner had just enough time to open his eyes wide in surprise before Des fired and moved on to the third. But she'd seen the first gunner go down and had already dropped down behind the armored walls of the gunship's flatbed for cover.

Des resisted the impulse to fire wildly and moved the scope in a tight circle, looking in vain for a clean shot. The sound of blasterfire exploded in the night, along with shouts and pounding feet as the Gloom Walkers burst from their cover and rushed the outpost. They'd followed their orders to the letter, charging out at the sound of the first shot. Des knew he had only a few seconds before the turrets opened up on them and turned the clearing into a killing field, but he couldn't see the shot to take out the third gunner.

He whipped the rifle around in desperation, looking for a new target on the roof. He set his sights on a soldier crouched down low beside a small canister. The soldier wasn't moving, and he'd covered his face with his hands as if shielding his vision. The blast from Des's weapon hit him square in the chest just as the device at the soldier's feet detonated.

"Flash canister!" Lucia screamed, but her warning came too late. The view through the scope vanished in a brilliant white flare, temporarily blinding Des.

But with his vision gone, he could suddenly see everything clearly. He knew the position of every soldier even as they all scrambled for cover; he could track exactly where they were and where they were going.

The soldier in the third turret was training the cannons on the incoming wave of troopers. In the excitement she'd popped her head up just slightly above the walls of the flatbed, leaving the smallest of targets exposed. Des took her with a single shot, the bolt going in cleanly through one ear hole on her helmet and out the other.

It was as if time had slowed down. Moving with a calm and deadly precision, he trained his rifle on the next target, taking her through the heart; barely a moment later he got the soldier beside her right between his cold blue eyes. Des took one man in the back as he ran for the nearest gunship. Another was halfway up one of the flatbed's ladders when a bolt sliced through his thigh, knocking him off balance. He fell from the ladder, and Des put another shot through his chest before he hit the ground.

It had taken less than three seconds to wipe out eight of the nine soldiers. The last one made a run for the edge, hoping to escape by diving off the roof on the far side of the building. Des let him run. He could feel the terror coming in waves off his doomed prey; he savored it for as long as he could. The soldier leapt from the rooftop and seemed to hang in midair for a second; Des fired his last three shots into his body, draining the weapon's power cell.

He handed the weapon back to Lucia, blinking rapidly at the tears welling up as his eyes tried to soothe their damaged retinas. The effects of the flash canister were only temporary; his vision was already beginning to return. And the miraculous second sight he'd experienced was slipping away.

Rubbing his eyes, he knew now was not the time to think about what had just happened. He'd eliminated the gunners, but his troops were still outnumbered. They needed him down in the hot zone, not here on the edges of the battle.

"Keep an eye on that roof," he ordered Lucia. "If any of those Republic mudcrutches appear on top, take them out before they get to the gunships."

She didn't reply; her mouth was hanging open in amazement at what she'd just witnessed.

Des grabbed her by the shoulder and gave her a rough shake. "Snap out of it, trooper! You've got a job to do!"

She shook her head to gather her senses and nodded, then loaded another energy cell into her weapon. Satisfied, Des pulled out the 21D and charged across the clearing, eager to join in the battle.

————

Three hours later it was all over. The mission had been a complete success: the outpost was theirs, and the Republic had no idea that thousands of Sith troopers were marching through the valley to attack them at first light. The battle itself had been short but bloody: forty-six Republic soldiers dead, and nine of Des's own. Every time a Gloom Walker went down, part of Des felt he'd failed somehow, but given the nature of their mission, keeping the casualties under double digits was more than he could have reasonably hoped for.

Once their objective was secured he'd left Adanar and a small contingent to hold the outpost. With Des in the lead, the rest of the unit marched back to its base camp.

Along the way he tried to ignore the hushed whispers and furtive looks the rest of the company was giving him. Lucia had spread the word of his amazing shooting, and it was the talk of the unit. None of them was brave enough to say anything to his face, but he could hear snippets of conversation from the ranks behind him.

Honestly, he couldn't blame them. Looking back, even he wasn't sure what had happened. Des was a good marksman, but he was no sniper. Yet somehow he'd managed to pull off a dozen impossible shots with a weapon he'd never fired before . . . most of them after being blinded by a flash canister. It was beyond unbelievable. It was as if, when he'd lost his vision, some mysterious power had taken over and guided his actions. It was exhilarating, but at the same time it was terrifying. Where had this power come from? And why couldn't he control it?

He was so wrapped up in his thoughts that at first he didn't even notice the strangers waiting at their base camp. It was only after they stepped up and slapped the stun cuffs on his wrists that he realized what was going on.

"Welcome back, Sergeant." Ulabore's voice was filled with bile.

Des glanced around. A dozen enforcers—the military security of the Sith army—were standing with weapons drawn. Ulabore stood behind them, a deep bruise on his face where Des had struck him. In the background Des could see the two junior recruits he'd left in charge of Ulabore. They were staring down at the ground, embarrassed and ashamed.

"Did you really think those raw recruits would keep their commanding officer trussed up like some kind of prisoner?" Ulabore taunted him from behind the protective wall of armed guards. "Did you really believe they would follow you in your madness?"

"That madness saved our lives!" Lucia shouted. Des held up his shackled hands to silence her: this situation could get out of hand far too easily.

When nothing else happened, the lieutenant seemed to gain some courage. He stepped out from behind the protective wall of enforcers and over to Des.

"I warned you about disobeying orders," he sneered. "Now you get to see firsthand how the Brotherhood of Darkness deals with mutinous soldiers!"

A few of the Gloom Walkers began to reach slowly for their weapons, but Des shook his head and they froze. The enforcers already had their blasters drawn and weren't afraid to use them. The troopers wouldn't manage to get off even a single shot.

"What's the matter, Sergeant?" Ulabore pressed, drawing closer to his defeated enemy. Too close. "Nothing to say?"

Des knew he could kill the lieutenant with one quick move. The enforcers would take him out, but at least Ulabore would go with him. Every fiber of his being wanted to lash out and end both their lives in an orgy of blood and blasterfire. But he managed to fight the impulse. There was no point in throwing his life away. A court-martial would likely end in a death sentence, but at least if he went to trial he'd have a chance.

Ulabore stepped up and slapped him once across the face, then spit on his boots and stepped back. "Take him away," he said to the enforcers, turning his back on Des.

As Des was taken away he couldn't help but see the look in the eyes of Lucia and the troopers whose lives he'd saved only hours ago. He had a feeling the next time the unit went into combat, Ulabore would suffer an unfortunate—and fatal—accident.

That realization brought the hint of a smile to his lips.

———

The enforcers marched him through the jungle for hours, weapons drawn and trained on him the entire time. They only lowered them when they reached the sentries on the perimeter of the main Sith camp.

"Prisoner for a court-martial," one of the enforcers said flatly. "Go tell Lord Kopecz." One of the sentries saluted and ran off.

They marched Des through the camp toward the brig. He saw recognition in the eyes of many of the soldiers. With his height and bald head he was an imposing figure, and many of the troops had heard of his exploits. Seeing a formerly ideal soldier being brought before a court-martial was sure to leave an impression.

They reached the camp's makeshift prison, a small containment field over a three-by-three-by-three-meter pit that served as a holding area for captured spies and POWs. The enforcers had relieved him of his weapons when they first took him into custody; now they did a more thorough search and stripped him of all other personal effects. Then they shut down the containment field and roughly tossed him in, not even bothering to release his cuffs. He landed awkwardly on the hard ground at the bottom of the hole. As he struggled to his feet he heard an unmistakable hum as the field was activated once again, sealing him in.

The pit was empty, other than Des himself. The Sith didn't tend to keep prisoners around for long. He began to wonder if he'd made a serious mistake. He'd hoped his past service might buy him some leniency at his trial, but now he realized his reputation might actually work against him. The Sith Masters weren't known for their tolerance or their mercy. He'd defied a direct order: there was a good chance they'd decide to make a harsh example of him.

He couldn't say how long they'd left him at the bottom of the pit. After a while he fell asleep, exhausted by the battle and the forced march. He slipped in and out of consciousness; at one point it was light outside his prison and he knew day must have come. The next time he came to it was dark again.

They hadn't fed him yet; his stomach was growling in protest as it gnawed away at itself. His throat was parched and dry; his tongue felt as if it had swollen up large enough to choke him. Despite this, there was a slowly increasing pressure on his bladder, but he didn't want to relieve himself. The pit stank enough already.

Maybe they were just going to leave him here to die a slow and lonely death. Given the rumors he'd heard of Sith torture, he almost hoped that was the case. But he hadn't given up. Not yet.

When he heard the sound of approaching footsteps he scrambled to his feet and stood straight and tall, even though his hands were still cuffed in front of him. Through the containment field he could just make out the blurred forms of several guards standing on the edge of the pit, along with another figure wearing a heavy, dark cloak.

"Take him to my ship," the cloaked figure said in a deep, rasping voice. "I will deal with this one on Korriban."

8

Des never got a clear look at the man who'd ordered his transfer. By the time they'd gotten him out of the pit, the cloaked figure had vanished. They gave him food and water, then let him clean and refresh himself. Though he was freed from the cuffs, he was still under heavy guard as he boarded a small transport ship heading for Korriban.

Nobody spoke to him on the trip, and Des didn't know what was going on. At least he wasn't cuffed anymore. He chose to take that as a good sign.

They arrived in the middle of the day. He had expected them to touch down at Dreshdae, the only city on the dark and forbidding world. Instead the ship landed at a starport built atop an ancient temple overlooking a desolate valley. A chill wind blew across the landing pad as he disembarked, but it didn't bother Des. After the stale air of the pit, any breeze felt good. He felt a shiver go down his spine as his foot touched Korriban's surface. He'd heard that this had once been a place of great power, though now only the merest shadows remained. There was an undercurrent of malice here; he'd felt it as soon as the transport had entered the bleak planet's atmosphere.

From this vantage point he could make out other temples scattered across the world's desert surface. Even at this distance he could perceive the eroded rock and crumbling stone of the once grand entrances. Beyond the valley, the city of Dreshdae was a mere speck on the horizon.

He was met on the landing pad by a hooded figure. He could tell right away this wasn't the same one who had come to him in the pit. This person had neither the size nor the impressive bearing of his liberator; even through the containment field Des had been able to sense his commanding presence.

This figure, which Des now thought to be female, motioned for him to follow. Silently she led him down a flight of stone steps and into the temple itself. They crossed a landing and descended another set of stairs, then repeated the pattern, working their way level by level down from the temple's apex to the ground below. There were doors and passages leading off from each landing, and Des could hear snippets of sound and conversation echoing from them, though he could never quite tell what was being said.

She didn't speak, and Des knew better than to break the silence himself. Technically, he was still a prisoner. For all he knew, she was leading him to his court-martial. He wasn't about to make things worse by asking foolish questions.

When they reached the bottom of the building, she led him to a stone archway with yet another flight of stairs. These were different, however: they were narrow and dark, and wound their way down until they vanished from sight deep in the bowels of the ground. Without a word his guide handed him a torch she had taken from a bracket on the wall and then stepped aside.

Wondering what was going on, Des made his way carefully down the steep staircase. He couldn't say how much deeper he went; it was difficult to maintain any perspective in the narrow confines of the stairwell. After several minutes he reached the bottom, only to find a long hallway stretching out before him. At the end of the hallway he encountered a single room.

The room was dark and filled with shadow. Only a few torches sputtered on the stone wall, their dying flames barely able to pierce the gloom.

Des paused at the threshold, letting his eyes adjust. He could just make out a dim figure inside. It beckoned to him.

"Come forward."

He felt a chill, though the room was far from cold. The air itself was electric, filled with a power he could actually feel. He was surprised that he didn't feel afraid. He recognized what he felt as the chill of anticipation.

As Des moved deeper into the room the features of the shrouded figure became clear, revealing himself to be a Twi'lek. Even under the loose-fitting robe he wore, Des could see he was thick and heavyset. He stood nearly two meters tall, easily the largest Twi'lek Des had ever met . . . though not quite as large as Des himself.

His lekku wound down his broad chest and wrapped back up around his muscular neck and shoulders; his eyes glowed orange beneath his brow, mirroring the flickering torches. He smiled, revealing the sharp, pointed teeth common to his species.

"I am Lord Kopecz of the Sith," he said. At that moment, Des knew without a doubt this was the cloaked one who had come to him in the pit, and he gave a slight bow of his head in acknowledgment.

"I am to be your inquisitor," Lord Kopecz explained, his voice showing no emotion. "I alone will determine your fate. Rest assured my judgment will be final."

Des nodded again.

The Twi'lek fixed his burning orange eyes on Des. "You are no friend of the Jedi or their Republic."

It wasn't a question, but Des felt compelled to answer anyway. "What have they ever done for me?"

"Exactly," Kopecz said with a cruel smile. "I understand you have fought many battles against the Republic forces. Your fellow troopers speak highly of you. The Sith have need of men like you if we are to win this war." He paused. "You were a model soldier . . . until you disobeyed a direct order."

"The order was a mistake," Des said. His throat had grown so dry and tight that he had trouble getting the words out.

"Why did you refuse to attack the outpost during the day? Are you a coward?"

"A coward wouldn't have completed the mission," Des replied sharply, stung by the accusation.

Kopecz tilted his head to the side and waited.

"Attacking in the daylight was a tactical mistake," Des continued, trying to press his point. "Ulabore should have relayed that information back to command, but he was too scared. Ulabore was the coward, not me. He would rather risk death at the hands of the Republic than face the Brotherhood of Darkness. I prefer not to throw my life away needlessly."

"I can see that from your service record," Kopecz said. "Kashyyyk, Trandosha, Phaseera . . . if these reports are accurate, you have performed incredible feats during your time with the Gloom Walkers. Feats some would claim to be impossible."

Des bristled at the implication. "The reports are accurate," he replied.

"I have no doubt that they are." Kopecz either hadn't noticed or didn't care about the tone of Des's reply. "Do you know why I brought you to Korriban?"

Des was beginning to realize that this wasn't really a court-martial after all. It was some kind of test, though for what he still wasn't sure.

"I feel I've been chosen for something."

Kopecz gave him another sinister smile. "Good. Your mind works quickly. What do you know of the Force?"

"Not much," Des admitted with a shrug. "It's something the Jedi believe in: some great power that's supposed to be just floating out there in the universe somewhere."

"And what do you know of the Jedi?"

"I know they believe themselves to be guardians of the Republic," Des replied, making no attempt to hide his contempt. "I know they wield great influence in the Senate. I know many believe they have mystical powers."

"And the Brotherhood of Darkness?"

Des considered his words more carefully this time. "You are the leaders of our army and the sworn enemy of the Jedi. Many believe that you, like them, have unnatural abilities."

"But you do not?"

Des hesitated, struggling to come up with the answer he thought Kopecz wanted to hear. In the end he couldn't figure out what his inquisitor was looking for, so he simply told the truth. "I believe most of the stories are greatly exaggerated."

Kopecz nodded. "A common enough belief. Those who do not understand the ways of the Force regard such tales as myth or legend. But the Force is real, and those who wield it have power you can't even imagine.

"You have seen many battles but you have not experienced the real war. While troops vie for control of worlds and moons, the Jedi and Sith Masters seek to destroy each other. We are being driven toward an inevitable and final confrontation. The faction that survives, Sith or Jedi, will determine the fate of the galaxy for the next thousand years.

"True victory in this war will not come through armies, but through the Brotherhood of Darkness. Our greatest weapon is the Force, and those individuals who have the power to command it. Individuals like you."

He paused to let his words sink in before continuing. "You are special, Des. You have many remarkable talents. These talents are manifestations of the Force, and they have served you well as a soldier. But you have only scratched the surface of your gift. The Force is real; it exists all around us. You can feel the power of it in this room. Can you sense it?"

Des hesitated only a moment before nodding. "I feel it. Hot. Like a fire waiting to explode."

"The power of the dark side. The heat of passion and emotion. I can feel it in you, as well. Burning beneath the surface. Burning like your anger. It makes you strong."

Kopecz closed his eyes and tilted his head back, as if basking in the heat. The tips of his head-tails twitched ever so slightly. The only sound was the faint crackle of flame from the torches. A bead of sweat rolled down the crown of Des's bare scalp and along the back of his neck. He didn't wipe it away, though he did shift his feet uncomfortably as it trickled its way between his shoulder blades. The slight movement seemed to snap the Twi'lek out of his trance.

He didn't speak again for several seconds, but he studied Des intently with his piercing gaze. "You have touched the Force in the past, but your abilities are an insignificant speck beside the power of a true Sith Master," he finally said. "There is great potential in you. If you stay here on Kor- riban, we can teach you to unleash it."

Des was speechless.

"You would no longer be a trooper on the front lines," Kopecz contin- ued. "If you accept my offer, that part of your life is over. You will be trained in the ways of the dark side. You will become one of the Brother- hood of Darkness. And you will not return to the Gloom Walkers."

Des felt his heart pounding, his head swimming. As long as he could remember, he'd known he was special because of his unique talents. And now he was being told that his abilities were nothing compared with what he could really accomplish.

Still, part of him balked at the idea of leaving his unit without even hav- ing a chance to say good-bye. He considered Adanar, Lucia, and the oth- ers as more than just fellow soldiers; they were his friends. Could he really abandon them like this, even for the chance to join the Sith Masters?

He recalled one of the last things Groshik had ever said to him: *Don't count on others for help. In the end each of us is in this alone. The survivors are those who know how to look out for themselves.*

Everything he'd had, he'd given to his unit. He'd saved their lives too many times to count. And in the end, when the enforcers had come to take him away, they'd been powerless to save him. They would have tried if he'd let them, but they would have failed. Des realized the truth: his unit—his friends—could do nothing for him now.

He could rely only on himself, like always. He'd be a fool to turn this opportunity down.

"I am honored, Master Kopecz, and I gratefully accept your offer."

"The way of the Sith is not for the weak," the big Twi'lek warned. "Those who falter will be . . . left behind." There was something ominous in his tone.

"I won't be left behind," Des replied, unfazed.

"That remains to be seen," Kopecz noted. Then he added, "This is a new beginning for you, Des. A new life. Many of the students who come here take a new name for themselves. They leave their old life behind."

Des had no desire to hang on to any part of his old life. An abusive fa- ther, the brutality of working the mines on Apatros; he had been seeking a new life for as long as he could remember. The Gloom Walkers had offered an escape, but it had been a temporary one. Now he had a chance to leave his past behind forever. All he had to do was embrace the Brotherhood of Darkness and its teachings. And yet, for reasons he couldn't explain, he felt the cold grip of fear closing in on him. The fear made him hesitate.

"Do you wish to choose a new name for yourself, Des?" Kopecz asked, possibly sensing his reluctance. "Do you wish to be reborn?"

Des nodded.

Kopecz smiled once more. "And by what name shall we call you now?"

The fear would not stop him; he would seize the fear, transform it, and make it his own. He would take what had once made him weak and use it to make himself strong.

"My name is Bane. Bane of the Sith."

———

Lord Qordis, exalted Master of the Sith Academy on Korriban, scratched gently at his chin with long, talon-like fingers.

"This student you have brought me—this Bane—has never been trained in the ways of the Force?"

Kopecz shook his head and twitched his lekku ever so slightly in annoyance. "As I told you before, Qordis, he grew up on Apatros, a world controlled by the ORO Company."

"Yet you managed to find this young man and bring him here to the Academy. It seems almost too convenient."

The heavyset Twi'lek snarled. "This is not a plot against you, Qordis. That is no longer our way. We are a Brotherhood now, remember? You are too suspicious."

Qordis laughed. "Not suspicious; cautious. It has helped me to maintain my position here among so many powerful and ambitious young Sith."

"He is as powerful as any of them," Kopecz insisted.

"But he is also older. We prefer to find our students when they are younger and more . . . malleable."

"Now you sound like a Jedi," Kopecz sneered. "They seek younger and younger pupils, hoping to find them pure and innocent. In time they will refuse any who are not infants. We must be quick to pluck those they leave behind. Besides," he continued, "Bane is too strong to simply pass over, even for the Jedi. We are lucky we found him before they did."

"Yes, lucky," Qordis echoed, his voice dripping with sarcasm. "His arrival here seems to be an incredible turn of many fortuitous events. Quite lucky indeed."

"Some might see it that way," Kopecz admitted. "Others might see it as something more. Destiny, perhaps."

There was silence while Qordis considered his longtime rival's words. "The other acolytes have been training for many years. He will be far behind," he said at last.

"He will catch up, if given the chance," Kopecz insisted.

"And I wonder . . . will the others give him that chance? Not if they are smart. I'm afraid we may simply be throwing away one of Lord Kaan's best troopers."

"We both know the Jedi won't be defeated by soldiers," Kopecz snapped. "I'd gladly trade a thousand of our best troopers for even one Sith Master."

Qordis seemed taken aback by his passionate reaction. "He is that strong, is he? This Bane?"

Kopecz nodded. "I think he might be the one we've been searching for. He could be the Sith'ari."

"Before he can claim that title," Qordis said with a cunning smile, "he'll have to survive his training."

PART TWO

9

Peace is a lie. There is only passion.
Through passion, I gain strength.
Through strength, I gain power.
Through power, I gain victory.
Through victory my chains are broken.

Kopecz was gone, rejoining Kaan's army and the war being waged against the Jedi and the Republic. Bane had remained behind at the Sith Academy on Korriban to learn the ways of the Sith. His first lesson began the next morning, at the feet of Lord Qordis himself.

"The tenets of the Sith are more than just words to be memorized," the Master of the Academy explained to his newest apprentice. "Learn them, understand them. They will lead you to the true power of the Force: the power of the dark side."

Qordis was taller than Kopecz. Taller even than Bane. He was very thin and clad in a black, loose-fitting robe, with the hood drawn back to fall across his shoulders. He might have been human, but something about his appearance seemed off. His skin was an unnatural, chalky hue, made even more obvious by the glittering gems encrusting the many rings on his long fingers. His eyes were dark and sunken. His teeth were sharp and pointed, and his fingernails were curved and wicked talons.

Bane knelt before him, similarly clad in a dark robe with the hood drawn back. Earlier this morning he had heard the Code of the Sith for the first time, and the words were still fresh and mysterious. They swirled through the undercurrents of his mind, occasionally bubbling up into his conscious thoughts as he tried to absorb the deeper meaning behind them.

Peace is a lie. There is only passion. He knew the first tenet to be true, at least. His entire life was proof of that.

"Kopecz tells me you come to us as a raw apprentice," Qordis noted. "He says you have never been trained in the ways of the Force."

"I'm a quick learner," Bane assured him.

"Yes . . . and strong in the power of the dark side. But the same can be said of all who come here."

Not sure how to respond, Bane decided the wisest course of action was to stay silent.

"What do you know of this Academy?" Qordis finally asked.

"The students here are taught to use the Force. They are taught the secrets of the dark side by you and the other Sith Lords." After a brief hesitation he added, "And I know there are many other academies like this one."

"No," Qordis corrected. "Not like this one. It is true we have other training facilities spread across our ever-growing empire, places where individuals with promise are taught to control and use their power. But each facility is unique, and where individual students are sent depends on how much potential we see in them.

"Those with a noticeable but limited ability are sent to Honoghr, Gentes, or Gamorr to become Sith Warriors or Marauders. There they are taught to channel their emotions into mindless rage and battle fury. The power of the dark side transforms them into ravaging beasts of death and destruction to be unleashed against our enemies."

Through passion I gain strength, Bane thought. But when he spoke he said, "Brute strength alone is not enough to bring down the Republic."

"True," Qordis agreed. From the tone of his voice Bane knew he had said what his Master wanted to hear.

"Those with greater ability are sent to worlds that have allied with our cause to destroy the Republic: Ryloth, Umbara, Nar Shadaa. These students become creatures of shadow, learning to use the dark side for secrecy, deception, and manipulation. Those who survive the training became unstoppable assassins, capable of drawing on the dark side to kill their targets without ever moving a muscle."

"Yet even they are no match for the Jedi," Bane added, thinking he understood the direction the lesson was taking.

"Precisely," his Master agreed. "The academies on Dathomir and Iridonia are most similar to the one here. There apprentices study under Sith Masters. Those who succeed in their training become the adepts and acolytes who swell the ranks of our armies. They are the counterparts to the Jedi Knights who stand in the way of our ultimate conquest.

"But even as the Jedi Knights must answer to the Jedi Masters, so must the adepts and acolytes answer to the Sith Lords. And those with the potential to become Sith Lords—and only those with such potential—are trained here on Korriban."

Bane felt a shiver of excitement. *Through strength I gain power.*

"Korriban was the ancestral home of the Sith," Qordis explained. "This planet is a place of great power; the dark side lives and breathes in the very core of this world."

He paused and slowly extended his skeletal hand, palm upward. It almost seemed as if he was cradling something unseen—something precious and invaluable—in his claw-like fingers.

"This temple we stand in was built many thousands of years ago to collect and focus that power. Here you can feel the dark side at its strongest." He closed his fist so tightly that his long fingernails cut into his palm, drawing blood. "You have been chosen because you have great potential," he whispered. "Great things are expected of the apprentices here on Korriban. The training is difficult, but the rewards are great for those who succeed."

Through power I gain victory.

Qordis reached out and placed his wounded palm on the crown of Bane's bare scalp, anointing him with the blood of a Sith Lord. Bane had seen plenty of blood as a soldier, yet for some reason this ceremonial act of self-mutilation revolted him more than any battlefield gore. It was all he could do not to pull away.

"You have the potential to become one of us—one of the Brotherhood of Darkness. Together we can cast off the shackles of the Republic."

Through victory my chains are broken.

"But even those with potential can fail," Qordis finished. "I trust you will not disappoint us."

Bane had no intention of doing that.

The next few weeks passed quickly as Bane threw himself into his studies. To his surprise, he discovered that his inexperience with the Force was the exception rather than the rule. Many of the students had trained for months or years before they had been accepted at the Academy on Korriban.

At first Bane found this troubling. He had just started his training and he was already behind. In such a competitive, ruthless environment he would be an easy target for every other student. But as he mulled it over, he began to realize he might not be as vulnerable as he'd thought.

He alone, of all the apprentices at the Academy, had been able to manifest the power of the dark side without any training at all. He'd used it so often he'd come to take it for granted. It had given him advantages over his opponents in cards and brawling. In war it had warned him of danger and brought him victory in otherwise impossible circumstances.

And he'd done it all on instinct, with no training, without even any conscious idea of what he was doing. Now, for the first time, he was being taught to truly use his abilities. He didn't have to worry about any of the other students . . . if anything, they should be worrying about him. When he completed his training, none of the others would be his equal.

Most of his learning came at the feet of Qordis and the other Masters: Kas'im, Orilltha, Shenayag, Hezzoran, and Borthis. There were group training sessions at the Academy, but they were few and far between. The weak and the slow could not be allowed to hold back the strong and ambitious. Students learned at their own pace, driven by their desire and hunger for power. There were, however, nearly six students for every Master, and the apprentices had to prove their worth before one of the instructors would spend valuable time teaching them the secrets of the Sith.

Though he was a neophyte, Bane found it easy to garner the attention of the Sith Lords, particularly Qordis. He knew the extra attention would inevitably breed animosity in the other students, but he forced himself not to think about that. In time the additional instruction he got from the Masters would allow him to catch up to and pass the other apprentices, and once he did he wouldn't need to worry about their petty jealousies.

Until then he was careful to stay out of the way and not draw attention to himself.

When he wasn't learning from the Masters, he was in the library studying the ancient records. As the Jedi kept their archives at their Temple on Coruscant, so the Sith had begun to collect and store information in the archives of Korriban's temple. However, unlike the Jedi library—where most of the data was stored in electronic, hologrammic, and Holocron formats—the Sith collection was limited to scrolls, tomes, and manuals. In the three thousand standard years since Darth Revan had nearly destroyed the Republic, the Jedi had waged a tireless war to eradicate the teaching tools of the dark side. All known Sith Holocrons had been either destroyed or spirited away to the Jedi Temple on Coruscant for safekeeping. There were many rumors of undiscovered Sith Holocrons—either hidden away on remote worlds, or covetously hoarded by one of the dark Masters eager to keep its secret knowledge for himself. But all efforts by the Brotherhood to find these lost treasures had proved futile, forcing them to rely on the primitive technologies of parchment and flimsiplast.

And because the collection was constantly being added to, the indexes and references were hopelessly out of date. Searching the archives was often an exercise in futility or frustration, and most of the students felt their time was better spent trying to learn from or impress the Masters.

Perhaps it was because he was older than most of the others, or maybe because his years of mining had taught him patience—whatever the explanation, Bane spent several hours each day studying the ancient records. He found them fascinating. Many of the scrolls were historical records recounting ancient battles or glorifying the deeds of ancient Sith Lords. By itself the information had little practical use, but he could see each individual work for what it actually represented: a tiny piece of a much larger puzzle, a clue to a much greater understanding.

The archives supplemented what he learned from the Masters. It gave context to abstract lessons. Bane felt that, in time, the ancient knowledge would be the key to unlocking his full potential. And so his understanding of the Force slowly took shape.

Mystical and unexplainable, the Force was also natural and essential: a fundamental energy binding the universe and connecting all living things within it. This energy, this power, could be harnessed. It could be manipulated and controlled. And through the teachings of the dark side, Bane was learning to seize hold of it. He practiced his meditations and exercises daily, often under the watchful eye of Qordis. After only a few weeks he learned to move small objects simply by thinking about it—something he would have thought impossible only a short time before.

Yet now he understood that this was only the beginning. He was starting to grasp a great truth on a deep, fundamental level: that the strength to survive must come from within. Others will always fail you. Friends, family, fellow soldiers . . . in the end, each person must stand alone. When in need, look to the self.

The dark side nurtured the power of the individual. The teachings of the Sith Masters would make him strong. In pleasing them, he could unlock his full potential and one day sit among them.

————

When the first wave of the attack came, the Republic fleet orbiting the skies of Ruusan was caught completely unprepared. A small and politically insignificant planet, the heavily forested world had been used as a base to stage devastating hit-and-run attacks against the Sith forces stationed in the nearby Kashyyyk system. Now the enemy had turned that same strategy against them.

The Sith struck without warning, materializing en masse from hyperspace: an almost suicidal maneuver for such a massive fleet. Before an alarm could even be sounded, the Republic ships found themselves being bombarded by three Dreadnaught cruisers, two corsair battleships, dozens of interceptors, and a score of Buzzard fighters. And at the head of the attack was the flagship of the Brotherhood of Darkness, the Sith Destroyer *Nightfall*.

In his meditation sphere aboard *Nightfall*, Lord Kaan was directing the assault. From inside the chamber he could communicate with any of the other ships, issuing his orders with the knowledge they would be instantly and completely obeyed. The chamber was alive with light and sound: glowing monitors and flashing screens beeped incessantly to alert him to the constantly changing updates on the status of the battle.

The Dark Lord, however, never even glanced at the screens. His perception extended far beyond the meditation sphere, far beyond the data spit out by the electronic readouts. He knew the location of each vessel engaged in the conflict: his own and those of the enemy. He could sense every volley fired, every evasive turn and roll, every move and countermove made by every ship. Often he could sense them even before they happened.

His brow was knotted in intense concentration; his breath came in long, ragged gasps. Beads of perspiration rolled down his trembling body. The strain was enormous, yet with the aid of the meditation sphere he maintained his mental focus, drawing on the dark side of the Force to influence the outcome of the conflict despite his physical exhaustion.

The art of battle meditation—a weapon passed down from the ancient Sith sorcerers—threw the enemy ranks into chaos, feeding their fear and hopelessness, crushing their hearts and spirits with bleak despair. Every false move by the opponent was magnified, every hesitation was transformed into a cascade of errors and mistakes that overwhelmed even the most disciplined troops. The battle had only just begun, and it was already all but over.

The Republic fleet was in complete disarray. Two of its four *Hammerhead*-class capital ships had lost primary shields in the first strafing run of the Buzzards. Now the Sith Dreadnaughts were moving in, targeting the suddenly vulnerable Hammerheads with their devastating forward-mounted laser cannons. On the verge of being crippled and left utterly helpless, they were just now managing to scramble their own fighters to ward off the rapidly closing enemy cruisers.

The other two capital ships were being ravaged by *Rage* and *Fury*, the Sith battleships. The ponderous Republic Hammerheads relied on support ships to establish a defensive line to hold off enemy attackers while they positioned themselves to bring their heavy guns to bear. Without these defensive lines they were all but helpless against the much quicker and more nimble corsairs. *Rage* and *Fury* cut in along a vector that minimized the number of cannons the Hammerheads could target them with, then swept across their bows, firing all guns. When the Hammerheads tried to change direction to bring more guns to bear, the corsairs would pivot and double back for another pass along a different vector, inflicting even more damage. The savage maneuver was known as *slashing the deck,* and without the support of fighters or battleships of their own, the capital ships couldn't withstand it for long.

Aid from the Republic battleships, however, was not likely to come. The one on point patrol was already a charred and lifeless hull, obliterated in the first seconds of the attack by a direct hit from *Nightfall's* guns before it could raise its shields. The other two were being swarmed by interceptors and pounded by *Nightfall's* broadside laser artillery, and didn't figure to last much longer than the first.

Kaan could feel it: panic had set in among the Republic troops and commanders. His attack was pure offense; his strategy maximized damage but left his own ships exposed and vulnerable to a well-organized counterattack. But no such response was forthcoming. The Republic captains were unable to coordinate their efforts, unable to establish their lines of defense. They couldn't even organize a proper retreat . . . escape was impossible. Victory was his!

And then suddenly *Fury* was gone, snuffed out by an explosion that ripped the corsair apart. It had happened so quickly that Kaan—even with the precognitive awareness of his battle meditation—hadn't sensed it coming. The two Hammerheads had turned at tangential angles, both somehow locking in on *Fury's* path simultaneously. One had opened up with its forward cannons to take down *Fury's* shields, while the other had unleashed a barrage of laserfire at the exact same spot, causing a massive detonation that destroyed the battleship in the blink of an eye. It was a brilliant maneuver: two different ships perfectly coordinating their efforts while under relentless assault to wipe out a common foe. It was also impossible.

Kaan ordered *Rage* into evasive action; the corsair peeled off its attack run just as the Hammerheads opened fire, narrowly avoiding the fate of its sister ship. The Dreadnaughts closing in on the crippled Hammerheads were also forced to break off their attack run as four full squads of Republic fighters burst forth from the cargo bays of their supposedly defenseless prey. Even under ideal conditions it would have been hard to scramble the fighters so quickly; in this situation it was unthinkable. Yet

Kaan could feel them: nearly fifty Aurek fighters flying in tight formation, pressing the attack on the Dreadnaughts while all four Hammerheads pulled back. They were establishing a defensive line!

Drawing on the power of the dark side, Lord Kaan pushed out with his will to touch the minds of the enemy. They were grim, but not desperate. Some were afraid, but none panicked. All he felt was discipline, purpose, and resolve. And then he felt something else. Another presence in the battle.

It was subtle, but he was certain it hadn't been there at all in the first few minutes of the attack. Someone was using the Force to bolster the morale of the Republic troops. Someone was using the light side to counter the effects of Kaan's battle meditation and turn the tide. Only a Jedi Master would have the strength to oppose the will of a Sith Lord.

Kopecz felt it, too. Strapped into the seat of his interceptor, he was spinning and swerving through the Hammerhead's barrage of antifighter turret blasts when the presence of the Jedi Master crashed over him like a wave. It caught him off guard, causing him to lose his focus for a split second. For any other pilot, that would have been enough to end his life, but Kopecz was no ordinary pilot.

Reacting with a quickness born of instinct, honed by training, and bolstered by the power of the dark side, he slammed the throttle back and pushed hard on the stick. The interceptor lurched down and forward into a sharp dive, narrowly ducking beneath three successive blasts of the Hammerhead's ion cannons. Pulling out of the dive, he banked into a wide roll and circled back toward the largest of the four Republic cruisers. The Jedi was there. He could sense him: the Force was emanating from the ship like a beacon. Now Kopecz was going to kill him.

Back on *Nightfall,* Kaan was also locked in mortal combat with the Jedi Master, though theirs was a battle waged through the ships and pilots of their respective fleets. The Republic had more ships with greater firepower; Kaan had been relying on the element of surprise, and his battle meditation to give the Sith the advantage. Now, however, both of those advantages had been nullified. Despite his strength, the Dark Lord was no expert in the rare art of battle meditation. It was one of many talents, and he had worked to develop them all equally. The opposing Jedi, however, had likely been trained from birth for just such a confrontation. The tide of the battle was slowly turning, and the Dark Lord was becoming desperate.

He gathered his will and lashed out with a sudden surge of dark side power, a desperate gambit to swing the engagement back under his control. Spurred on by adrenaline, bloodlust, and the irresistible compulsion of their leader, a pair of buzzard pilots tried to ram their ships into the nearest Aurek squadron, determined to break their formation with a suicide attack. But the Republic pilots didn't panic or break ranks trying to avoid his reckless charge. Instead they met the assault head-on, firing their weapons and vaporizing the enemy before any harm could be done.

On the other side of the battle, Kopecz's interceptor knifed through the defensive perimeter established around the capital ship and its precious Jedi cargo, too quick and nimble for either the Aurek fighters or the turrets to get a lock. Penetrating the Republic lines, Kopecz flew his ship into the heart of the main hangar; the blast doors closed a fraction of a second too late. He opened fire as his ship spun and skidded across the docking bay's floor, wiping out most of the soldiers unfortunate enough to be caught inside.

As the ship slowed to a halt, he popped open the hatch and flipped out of his seat. Nimbly landing on his feet, he drew and ignited his lightsaber in one smooth motion. The first sweeping arc of the crimson blade caught the blasterfire of the two troopers who had survived the initial assault, deflecting it harmlessly away. Another flip closed the six-meter distance between the Twi'lek and his attackers; another arc of the blade ended their lives.

Kopecz paused to assess the situation. Mangled bodies and shattered machinery were all that remained of the crew and equipment that maintained the Republic fighters. Smiling, he crossed over to the hatch leading into the interior of the capital ship.

He strode quickly and confidently through the halls, guided by the power emanating from the Jedi Master like a tuk'ata drawn by the scent of a squellbug. A security team intercepted him in one of the hallways. The red badges on their sleeves marked them as an elite squad of specially trained soldiers: the best bodyguards the Republic military had to offer.

Kopecz knew they must have been good . . . one actually managed to fire her weapon twice before the entire unit fell to his lightsaber.

He entered a large chamber with a single door at the back. His prey was beyond that door, but in the center of the room a pair of Selkath— amphibious beings from the world of Manaan—barred his way with lightsabers drawn. These were mere Padawans, however, servants of the Jedi Master. Kopecz didn't even bother engaging them in lightsaber combat: it would have been beneath him. Instead he thrust a meaty fist forward and used the Force to hurl them across the room. The first Padawan was stunned by the impact. By the time he struggled uncertainly to his feet, his companion was already dead, the life choked out of her by the power of the dark side.

The surviving Padawan retreated as Kopecz slowly advanced; the Sith Lord crossed the room with measured strides as he gathered his power. He unleashed it in a storm of electricity, bolts of blue-violet lightning ripping through the flesh of his unfortunate victim. The Selkath's body danced in convulsions of agony until his smoking corpse finally collapsed to the floor.

Reaching the door at the rear of the room, Kopecz opened it and stepped into the small meditation chamber beyond. An elderly Cerean female, clad in the simple brown robes of a Jedi Master, was seated crosslegged on the floor. Her creased and wrinkled face was bathed in sweat from the strain of using her battle meditation against Kaan and the Sith.

Exhausted, drained, she was no match for the Sith Lord who loomed above her. Yet she made no move to flee or even defend herself. With certain death only seconds away, she kept her mind and power focused entirely on the fleet battle.

Kopecz couldn't help but admire her courage even as he methodically cut her down. Her calm acceptance robbed his victory of any joy. "Peace is a lie," he muttered to himself as he stalked back through the halls toward the docking bay and his waiting ship, anxious to leave before *Nightfall* or one of the other ships blew the Hammerhead to bits.

The death of the Jedi Master turned the tide once more. Resistance crumbled; the battle became a Sith rout, and then a slaughter. No longer protected by the power of the light side of the Force, the Republic soldiers were completely demoralized by the terror and despair Kaan spawned in their minds. Those who were strong-willed gave up all hope save that of escaping the battle alive. The weak-willed were left so despondent, they could only hope for a quick and merciful death. The former didn't get what they wanted, but the latter did.

Strapped into the hatch of his interceptor, Lord Kopecz launched his craft from the hangar mere seconds before the capital ship was destroyed in a glorious and cataclysmic explosion.

The Sith losses that day were heavier than expected, but their victory was absolute. Not a single Republic ship, pilot, or soldier escaped the First Battle of Ruusan alive.

10

Bane's power was growing. In only a few months of training he had
learned much about the Force and the power of the dark side. Physically,
he felt stronger than ever before. In morning training runs he could
sprint at nearly full speed for five kilometers before he even began breathing heavily. His reflexes were quicker, his mind and senses were sharper
than he possibly could have imagined.

When necessary he could channel the Force through his body, giving
him bursts of energy that allowed him to do seemingly impossible feats:
perform full flips from a standing position; survive falls from incredible
heights uninjured; leap vertically ten meters or more.

He was completely aware of his surroundings at all times, sensing the
presence of others. Sometimes he could even get a feel of their intentions,
vague impressions of their very thoughts. He was able to levitate larger
objects now, and for longer periods. With each lesson his power grew. It
became easier and easier to command the Force and bend it to his will.
And with each week, Bane realized he had surpassed another of the apprentices who had once been ahead of him.

Less and less of his time was spent in the archives studying the ancient
scrolls. His initial fascination with them had faded, swept away by the intensity of Academy life. Absorbing the knowledge of Masters long dead
was a cold and sterile pleasure. Historical records were no competition

for the feeling of exhilaration and power he felt when actually using the Force. Bane was part of the Academy and the Brotherhood of the Darkness. He was part of the now, not the ancient past.

He began to spend more time mingling with the other students. Already he could sense that some of them were jealous, though none dared to act against him. Competition among the students was encouraged, and the Masters allowed the rivalry to drift into the animosity and hatred that fueled the dark side. But there were harsh penalties for any apprentice caught interfering with or disrupting the training of another student.

Of course, all the apprentices understood that the punishment was actually for the crime of being careless enough to get caught. Treachery was tacitly accepted, as long as it was done with enough cunning to avoid the notice of the instructors. Bane's phenomenal progress protected him from the machinations of his fellow students; no one could move against him without drawing the attention of Qordis or the other Sith Lords.

Unfortunately, the extra attention made it difficult for Bane himself to use treachery, manipulation, or similar techniques to attain greater status within the Academy.

There was, however, one sanctioned way students could bring a rival down: lightsaber combat. The chosen weapon of both the Jedi and the Sith, the lightsaber was more than just a blade of energy capable of cutting through almost every material in the known galaxy. The lightsaber was an extension of the user and his or her command of the Force. Only those with strict mental discipline and total physical mastery could use the weapon effectively . . . or so Bane and the others had been taught.

Few of the students actually possessed lightsabers yet; they still had to prove themselves worthy in the eyes of Qordis and the others. Yet that didn't keep Lord Kas'im, the Twi'lek Blademaster, from instructing them in the styles and techniques they would use once they had finally earned their weapons. Each morning the apprentices would gather on the wide, open roof of the temple to practice their drills and routines under his watchful eye, struggling to learn the exotic maneuvers that would bring them victory on the battlefield.

———

Perspiration was already running down the crown of Bane's head and into his eyes as he put his body through its paces. He blinked away the stinging sweat and redoubled his exertions, carving the air before him again and again and again with his training saber. All around him other apprentices were doing the same; each was struggling to conquer his or her own physical limitations and become more than just a warrior with a weapon. The goal was to become an extension of the dark side itself.

Bane had begun by learning the basic techniques common to all seven traditional lightsaber forms. His first weeks had been spent in endless repetitions of defensive postures, overhand strikes, parries, and counter-strikes. By observing the natural tendencies of his students as they learned the basics, Lord Kas'im determined which form would best match their style. For Bane he chose Djem So, Form V. The fifth form emphasized strength and power, allowing Bane to use his size and muscles to his best advantage. Only after he was able to perform each of the moves of Djem So to the satisfaction of Kas'im was he allowed to begin the real training.

Now, along with the other students at the Academy, he spent the better part of an hour each morning practicing his techniques with his training saber under the Blademaster's watchful eye. Made of durasteel with blunted edges, the training sabers were crafted specifically so that their balance and heft mimicked the energy beams projected by real lightsabers. A solid blow could inflict serious damage, but since a lightsaber did not work that way, each training blade was also covered with millions of toxin-filled barbs too small to see, fashioned from the microscopic ridge spines of the deadly pelko bug—a rare insect found only deep beneath the desert sands of the Valley of the Dark Lords on Korriban itself. With a direct hit, the minuscule barbs could pierce the weave of any fabric; the pelko venom would cause the flesh immediately to burn and blister. Temporary paralysis set in instantly at the point of infection, leaving any limb struck all but useless. This provided an excellent way to mimic the effects of losing a hand, arm, or leg to a lightsaber blade.

The morning was filled with the grunts of the apprentices and the *swish-swish-swish* as their blades sliced the air. In some ways it reminded Bane of his military training: a group of soldiers united in the repetition of drills until the moves became instinctive.

But there was no sense of camaraderie at the Academy. The apprentices were rivals, plain and simple. In many ways it wasn't that different from his days on Apatros. Now, however, the isolation was worth it. Here they were teaching him the secrets of the dark side.

"Wrong!" Kas'im suddenly barked. He had been walking up and down the ranks of apprentices as they trained, but had now stopped right beside ·Bane. "Strike with malice and precision!" He reached out and seized Bane's wrist, turning it roughly and changing the angle of the training blade. "You're coming in too high!" he snapped. "There is no room for error!"

He stayed at Bane's side for several seconds, watching to ensure the lesson had been properly learned. After several hard thrusts by Bane with the altered grip, the Blademaster nodded in approval and continued his rounds.

Bane repeated the single move over and over, careful to maintain the height and angle of the blade exactly as Kas'im had shown him, teaching his muscles through countless repetitions until they could replicate it flawlessly each and every time. Only then would he move on to incorporating it into more complicated maneuvers.

Soon he was breathing heavily from his exertions. Physically Kas'im's training sessions couldn't measure up to hammering a cortosis vein with a hydraulic jack for hours at a time. But they were far more exhausting in other ways. They demanded intense mental focus, an attention to detail that went far beyond what was visible to the naked eye. True mastery of the blade required a combination of both body and mind.

When two Masters engaged in lightsaber combat, the action happened too quickly for the eye to see or the mind to react. Everything had to be done on instinct; the body had to be trained to move and respond without conscious thought. To accomplish this, Kas'im made his students practice *sequences*, carefully choreographed series of multiple strikes and parries drawn from their chosen style. The sequences were designed by the Blademaster himself so that each maneuver flowed smoothly into the next, maximizing attack efficiency while minimizing defensive exposure.

Using a sequence in combat allowed the students to free their minds from thought as their bodies automatically continued through the moves.

Using sequences was more efficient and much quicker than considering and initiating each strike or block on its own, providing an enormous advantage over an opponent unfamiliar with the technique.

However, ingraining a new sequence so it could be properly executed was a long and laborious process. For many it would take two to three weeks of training and drills—longer if the sequence was derived from a style the student was still struggling to master. And even the tiniest mistake in the smallest of moves could render the entire sequence worthless.

Kas'im had spotted a potentially fatal flaw in Bane's technique. Now Bane was determined to fix it, even if it meant hours of practice on his own time. Bane was relentless in his pursuit of perfection—not just in his combat training, but in all his studies. He was a man on a mission.

"Enough," Kas'im's voice called out. At that single command all the students stopped what they were doing and turned their attention to the Blademaster. He was standing at the head of the assemblage, facing them.

"You may rest for ten minutes," he told them. "Then the challenges will begin."

Bane, along with most of the others, lowered himself into a meditative position, legs crossed and folded beneath him. Laying his training saber on the ground beside him, he closed his eyes and slipped into a light trance, drawing on the dark side to rejuvenate his aching muscles and refresh his tired mind.

He let the power flow through him, let his mind drift. As it often did, it drifted back to the first time he'd touched the dark side. Not the fumbling brushes he'd had back on Apatros or during his days as a soldier, but a true recognition of the Force.

It had been his third day here at the Academy. He'd been applying the meditation techniques he'd learned the day before when suddenly he felt it. It was like the bursting of a dam, a raging river flooding through him, sweeping away all his failings: his weakness, his fear, his self-doubt. In that instant he'd understood why he was here. At that moment his transformation from Des to Bane, from mere mortal to one of the Sith, had truly begun.

Through power, I gain victory.
Through victory my chains are broken.

Bane knew all about chains. Some were obvious: an abusive, uncaring father; grueling shifts in the mines; debts owed to a faceless, ruthless corporation. Others were more subtle: the Republic and its idealistic promises of a better life that never materialized; the Jedi and their vow to rid the galaxy of injustice. Even his friends in the Gloom Walkers had been a kind of chain. He'd cared for them, been responsible for them. Yet in the end, what use had they been when he'd needed them most?

He understood now that personal attachments could only hold him back. Friends were a burden. He had to rely on himself. He had to develop his own potential. His own power. In the end, that was what it really came down to. Power. And, above all else, the dark side promised power.

He heard the sounds of movement around him; the soft shuffle of robes as the other apprentices rose from their meditations and made their way toward the challenge ring. He grabbed his training saber with one hand and sprang to his feet to join them.

At the end of each session the class would gather in a wide, irregular circle at the top of the temple. Any student could step into the circle and issue a challenge to another. Kas'im would observe the duels closely, and once it was over he would analyze the action for the class. Those who won would be praised for their performance, and their status in the informal hierarchy of the Academy would rise. Those who lost would be chastised for their failings, as well as suffering a blow to their prestige.

When Bane had first begun his training, many of the students had eagerly called him out. They knew he was a neophyte in the Force and they were eager to take down the heavily muscled giant in front of their classmates. At first he had declined the challenges. He knew they were the quickest way to gain prestige at the Academy, but he wasn't foolish enough to be drawn into a battle he was guaranteed to lose.

In the past months, however, he had worked hard to learn his style and refine his technique. He learned new sequences quickly, and when Kas'im himself had commented on his progress, Bane had felt confident enough to begin accepting the challenges. He wasn't victorious every time, but he was winning far more duels than he was losing, slowly climbing his way to the top of the ladder. Today he felt ready to take another step.

The apprentices were standing three rows deep, forming a ring of bodies around a clearing in the center roughly ten meters in diameter. Kas'im stepped into the middle. He didn't speak, but merely tilted his head—a sign that it was time for the challenges to begin. Bane stepped into the center before anyone else could make a move.

"I challenge Fohargh," he announced in ringing tones.

"I accept" came the reply from somewhere in the crowd on the opposite side. The apprentices parted to let the one challenged pass. Kas'im gave a slight bow to each combatant and stepped to the clearing's edge to give them room.

Fohargh was a Makurth. In many ways he reminded Bane of the Trandoshans he had fought in his days with the Gloom Walkers. Both species were bipedal saurians—lizardlike humanoids covered in leathery green scales—but the Makurths had four curved horns growing from the top of their heads.

Early in Bane's training, he had fought Fohargh—and he had lost. Badly.

The Makurth was nocturnal by nature. Like the miners of the night shift on Apatros, however, he had grown accustomed to an unnatural schedule in order to train with the rest of the apprentices at the Academy. During their first duel Bane had underestimated Fohargh, expecting him to be sluggish and slow during the daylight hours. He wouldn't make that mistake twice.

As Kas'im and the apprentices watched in silence, the two combatants circled each other in the ring, training sabers held out before them in standard ready stances. The Makurth's breath came in grunts and growls from his flaring nostrils as he tried to intimidate his human opponent. From time to time he'd give a short bellow and shake his four-horned lizard's head while flashing his savage teeth. The last time he'd faced the green-scaled, snorting demon of an apprentice, Bane had been intimidated by Fohargh's act. Now he simply ignored the posturing.

Bane lunged out with a simple overhand strike, but Fohargh responded with a quick parry to deflect the blow to the side. Instead of the crackle and hum of blades of pure energy crossing, there was a loud clang as the weapons clashed. Immediately the combatants spun away from each other and resumed their ready positions.

Bane rushed forward, his blade ascending diagonally from right to left in a long, swift arc. Fohargh managed to redirect the impact with his own weapon, but lost his balance and stumbled back. Bane tried to press his advantage, his training saber arcing up from left to right. His opponent spun out of harm's way, backpedaling quickly to create space. Bane broke off the half-completed sequence and settled back into the ready position.

Back on Apatros his latent abilities in the Force had allowed him to anticipate and react to the moves of his foe. Here, however, every opponent enjoyed the same advantage. As a result, victory required a combination of the Force and physical skill.

Bane had worked on acquiring that physical skill over the past months. As this ability grew, he was able to devote less and less of his mental energy to the physical actions of thrust, parry, and counterthrust. This allowed him to keep his mind focused so he could use the Force to anticipate his opponent's moves, while at the same time obscuring and confusing his enemy's own precognitive senses.

The last time he and Fohargh had fought, Bane had still been a novice. He had only learned a handful of sequences. Now he knew almost a hundred, and he was able to transition smoothly from the end of one sequence into the beginning of another, opening up a wider range of attack-and-defense combinations. And more options made it more difficult for a foe to use the Force to anticipate his actions.

Fohargh, despite his terrifying appearance, was smaller and lighter than his human opponent. Physically outmatched by the brute force of Bane's Form V, he was forced to rely on the defensive style of Form III to keep his larger opponent's overpowering attacks at bay.

Spinning his training saber in a quick flourish, Bane leapt high in the air and came crashing down from above. Fohargh parried the attack but was knocked to the ground. He rolled onto his back and barely managed to get his saber up in time to block Bane's next slashing attack. A chorus of metal on metal rang out as Bane's blows descended like rain. The Makurth kept him from landing a direct hit with a masterful defensive flurry, then swept Bane off his feet with a leg-whip, leaving them both supine.

They flipped to their feet simultaneously, mirror images, and their sabers met with another resounding crash before they disengaged once again. There were some whispers and mutters from the assembled crowd, but Bane did his best to tune them out. They had thought the battle was over . . . as had Bane himself. He was disappointed that he hadn't been able to finish off his fallen opponent, but he knew victory was near. Fohargh's survival had extracted a heavy toll: he was breathing in ragged gasps now, his shoulders slumping.

Bane rushed Fohargh again. This time, however, the Makurth didn't back away. He stepped forward with a quick thrust, switching from Form III to the more precise and aggressive Form II. Bane was caught off guard by the unexpected maneuver and was a microsecond slow in recognizing the change. His parry attempt knocked the tip of the blade away from his chest, only to have it slice across his right shoulder.

The crowd gasped, Fohargh howled in victory, and Bane screamed in pain as the saber slipped to the ground from his suddenly nerveless fingers. Mindlessly, Bane used his other hand to shove his opponent in the chest. Fohargh reeled backward, and Bane rolled away to safety.

Scrambling to his feet, Bane extended his left hand to the training saber lying on the ground three meters away. It sprang up and into his palm, and he once again assumed the ready position, his right arm dangling uselessly at his side. Some Sith learned to fight with either hand, but Bane hadn't yet reached that advanced stage. The weapon felt awkward and clumsy as he held it. Left-handed, he was no match for Fohargh. The fight was over.

His opponent sensed it, as well. "Defeat is bitter, human," he growled in Basic, his voice deep and menacing. "I have bested you; you have lost."

He wasn't asking Bane to yield; surrender was never an option. He was simply taunting him, publicly humiliating him in front of the other students.

"You trained for weeks to challenge me," Fohargh continued, drawing out his mockery. "You failed. Victory is mine again."

"Then come finish me!" Bane snapped back. There wasn't much else he could say. Everything his enemy said in his heavily accented Basic was true, and the words cut far deeper than the blunted training saber's edge possibly could.

"This ends when *I* choose," the Makurth replied, refusing to be baited.

The eyes of the other apprentices burned into Bane; he could feel them drinking in his suffering as they stared at him. They resented him, resented the extra attention he had been receiving from the Masters. Now they reveled in his failure.

"You are weak," Fohargh explained, casually twirling his own saber in a complex and intricate pattern. "You are predictable."

Stop it! Bane wanted to scream. *End this! Finish me!* But despite the emotion building up inside him, he refused to give his opponent the satisfaction of saying another word. Instead he let the all-but-useless saber fall once more to the ground. In the background he could see the Blademaster watching intently, curious to see how the confrontation would reach its inevitable end.

"The Masters cosset you. They give you extra time and attention. More than the others. More than me."

Bane barely even heard the words anymore. His heart was pounding so loud he could hear the blood coursing through his veins. Literally quaking with impotent rage, he lowered his head and dropped to one knee, exposing his bare neck.

"Despite this, you are still my inferior . . . *Bane* of the Sith."

Bane. Something in the way Fohargh said it caused Bane to glance up. It was the same way his father used to say the word.

"That name is mine," Bane whispered, his voice low and threatening. "Nobody uses it against me."

Fohargh either didn't hear him or didn't care. He took a leisurely step forward. "*Bane.* Worthless. An insignificant nothing. The Masters wasted their time on you. Time better spent on other students. You are well named, for you truly are this Academy's bane!"

"No!" Bane screamed, thrusting his good hand out palm-forward even as Fohargh leapt in to finish him off. Dark side energy erupted from his open palm to catch his opponent in midair, hurling him back to the edge of the crowd where he landed at Kas'im's feet.

The Master watched with an intrigued but wary expression. Bane slowly clenched his fist and rose to his feet. On the ground before him, Fohargh was writhing in agony, clutching at his throat and gasping for breath.

Unlike the Makurth, Bane had nothing to say to his helpless opponent. He squeezed his fist harder, feeling the Force rushing through him like a divine wind as he crushed the life out of his foe. Fohargh's heels pounded out a staccato rhythm on the temple's stone roof as his body convulsed. He began to gurgle, and pink froth welled up from between his lips.

"Enough, Bane," Kas'im said in a cold, even voice. Though he stood only centimeters away from the death throes of his student, his eyes were fixed on the one still standing.

A final surge of power roared up in the core of Bane's being and exploded out into the world. In response, Fohargh's body went stiff and his eyes rolled back in his head. Bane released his hold on the Force and his fallen enemy, and the Makurth's body went limp as the last vestiges of life ebbed away.

"Now it's enough," Bane said, turning his back on the corpse and walking toward the stairs that led back inside the temple. The circle of students quickly opened a path for him to pass. He didn't need to look back to know that Kas'im was watching him with great interest.

––––––––

Bane felt the presence of someone following him down the stairs from the temple roof long before he heard the footsteps. He didn't change his pace, but he did stop at the first landing and turn to face whoever it was. He half expected to see Lord Kas'im, but instead of the Blademaster he found himself staring into the orange eyes of Sirak, another apprentice at the Academy. Or rather, the top apprentice at the Academy.

Sirak was a Zabrak, one of three apprenticing here on Korriban. Zabrak tended to be ambitious, driven, and arrogant—perhaps it was these traits that made the Force-sensitives of the race so strong in the ways of the dark side—and Sirak was the perfect embodiment of those characteristics. He was far and away the strongest of the three. Wherever Sirak went, the other two usually followed, trailing at his heel like obedient servants. They made a colorful trio: red-skinned Llokay and Yevra, and pale yellow Sirak. But right now the other two were conspicuously absent.

There were rumors that Sirak had begun studying the ways of the dark side under Lord Qordis nearly twenty years ago, long before the Academy at Korriban had been resurrected. Bane didn't know if the rumors were true, and he hadn't thought it wise to ask about it. The Iridonian Zabrak was both powerful and dangerous. So far Bane had done his best to avoid drawing the attention of the Academy's most advanced student. Apparently, that strategy was no longer an option.

The rush of adrenaline he'd felt as he'd ended Fohargh's life was fading, along with the confidence and sense of invincibility that had led to his dramatic exit. Bane wasn't exactly afraid as the Zabrak approached him, but he was wary.

In the dim torchlight of the temple, Sirak's pale yellow skin had taken on a sickly, waxen hue. Unbidden, it brought back memories of Bane's first year working the mines on Apatros. A crew of five—three men and two women—had been trapped in a cave-in. They had survived the collapsing tunnel by escaping into a reinforced safety chamber dug out of the rock, but noxious fumes released in the collapse had seeped into their haven and killed them all before rescue teams could dig them out. The complexion of their bloated corpses was the exact same color as Sirak's: the color of a slow, agonizing death.

Bane shook his head, pushing the memory away. That life belonged to Des, and Des was gone. "What do you want?" he asked, trying to keep his voice calm.

"You know why I am here" was the icy response. "Fohargh."

"Was he a friend of yours?" Bane was genuinely confused. With the exception of his fellow Zabrak, Sirak rarely mingled with the other students. In fact, many of the accusations Fohargh had leveled at Bane—such as preferential treatment from the Masters—could easily be applied to Sirak, as well.

"The Makurth was neither friend nor enemy" was the haughty reply. "He was beneath my notice, as were you. Until now."

Bane's only reply was a steady, unblinking stare. The flickering torchlight reflecting off the Zabrak's pupils made it seem as if hungry flames licked away at the inside of his skull.

"You are an intriguing opponent," Sirak whispered, taking a step closer. "Formidable . . . at least compared with the other so-called apprentices here. I am watching you now. I am waiting."

He reached out slowly and pressed his finger into Bane's chest. Bane had to fight the urge to take a step back.

"I do not issue challenges," the Zabrak continued. "I have no need to test myself against a lesser opponent." Flashing a cruel smile, he lowered his finger and took a step back. "However, when you fool yourself into believing you are ready, you will inevitably challenge me. I shall be looking forward to it."

With that he brushed past Bane on the narrow landing, bumping him slightly with his shoulder as if unaware of him, then continuing on down the stairs to the level below.

The message of that slight bump was not lost on Bane. He knew Sirak was trying to intimidate him . . . and to goad him into a confrontation Bane wasn't ready for. He wasn't about to fall for the trap. Instead he stood motionless at the top of the landing, refusing to turn and watch Sirak depart. Only when he heard the sounds of the rest of the class descending from the roof did he move again, spinning on his heel and continuing down the stairs to the lower levels and the privacy of his own room.

11

The next morning Bane was not with the other students on the temple roof as they sparred. Lord Qordis wanted to speak with him. Privately.

He strode through the virtually empty halls of the Academy toward the meeting, his outward appearance calm and confident. Inside he was anything but.

All night, as he lay surrounded by the silence and darkness of his room, the duel had played itself over and over in his head. Free from the emotion of the battle, he knew he had gone too far. He had proven his dominance over Fohargh by pinning him with the Force; he had achieved dun möch. The Makurth would never dare to challenge him again. Yet for some reason Bane hadn't been able to stop there. He hadn't wanted to stop.

At the time he had felt no guilt over his actions. No remorse. Yet once his blood cooled, part of him couldn't help but feel he had done something wrong. Had Fohargh really deserved to die?

But another part of him refused to accept the guilt. He'd had no love for the Makurth. No feelings at all. Fohargh had been nothing but an obstacle to Bane's progress. An obstacle that had been removed.

He had given himself over to the dark side completely in that moment. It had been more than simple rage or bloodlust. It went deeper, to the very core of his being. He'd lost all reason and control . . . but it had felt *right.*

Bane had spent a long and sleepless night trying to reconcile the two emotions: triumph and remorse. But when the summons came that morning his inner conflict had been swept away by more immediate concerns.

Fohargh's death would have repercussions. Combat was supposed to test the apprentices, harden their mettle through struggle and pain. It wasn't meant to kill. Each and every disciple at the Academy, from Sirak down to the least and lowest of the students, had the ability to become a Master. Each possessed an extremely rare gift in the dark side—a gift that was meant to be used against the Jedi, not against one another.

In killing Fohargh, Bane had thinned the ranks of potential Sith Masters. He had dealt a serious blow to the war effort. Each apprentice at the Academy was valued more highly than an entire division of Sith troopers. He had destroyed an invaluable tool. For that, Bane suspected, he would be punished severely.

As he marched toward the meeting that could decide his fate he tried to push both fear and guilt from his mind. Nothing he did now could bring Fohargh back. The Makurth was gone, but Bane was still here. And he was a survivor. He had to be strong. He had to find some way to justify his actions to Lord Qordis.

He was already putting together his arguments. Fohargh had been weak. Bane hadn't just killed him: he'd exposed him. Qordis and the other Masters encouraged rivalry and dissension among their charges. They understood the value of challenge and competition. Those who showed promise—the individuals who elevated themselves above the others— were rewarded. They received one-on-one instruction with the Masters to reach their full potential. Those who could not keep up were left behind. That was the way of the dark side.

Fohargh's death was no more than a natural extension of the dark side philosophy. His death was the ultimate failure—his own failure. Why should Bane be blamed for another's weakness?

His pace quickened and he clenched his teeth in angry frustration. No wonder his emotions were so conflicted. The teachings of the Academy were self-contradictory. The dark side allowed for no mercy, no forgiveness. Yet the apprentices were expected to pull back once they had bested their opponents in the dueling ring. It was unnatural.

He had reached the threshold of Qordis's door. He hesitated, briefly wavering between fear of what his punishment would be and anger at the impossible situation he and all the other apprentices were put in every day.

Anger, he finally decided, would serve him best.

He knocked sharply at the door, then opened it when the command to enter came from within. Qordis was kneeling in the center of the chamber, deep in meditation. Bane had been in this room before, but he couldn't help but marvel at the extravagance. The walls were adorned with expensive tapestries and hangings. Golden braziers and censers burning heavy incense were scattered haphazardly about to provide a dim glow in the hazy air. In one corner was a large, luxuriant bed. In another was an intricately carved table of obsidian, a small chest atop it.

The lid of the chest was open, revealing the jewelry inside: necklaces and chains of precious metals, rings of gold and platinum encrusted with ostentatious gemstones. Qordis took great pains to surround himself with material goods and the trappings of wealth, and he took greater pains to make sure others noticed his opulence. On some level, Bane suspected, the Sith Lord derived pleasure—and power—from the covetous desire and greed his possessions inspired in others.

The trinkets held little interest for Bane, however. He was more impressed with the manuscripts and tomes that lined the bookshelves along the wall, each a magnificent volume clad in leather embossed with gold leaf. Many of the volumes were thousands of years old, and he knew they contained the secrets of the ancient Sith.

At last Lord Qordis rose to his feet, standing tall and straight so he could look down on his student with his gray, sunken eyes.

"Kas'im told me what happened yesterday morning," he said. "He tells me you are responsible for Fohargh's death." The tone of his voice gave Bane no clues as to his emotional state.

"I am not responsible for his death," Bane answered calmly. He was angry, but he wasn't stupid. He chose his next words very carefully; he wanted to convince Lord Qordis, not enrage him. "Fohargh was the one who let his guard down. He left himself vulnerable in the ring. It would have shown weakness not to take advantage of it."

His statement wasn't entirely factual, but it was close enough to the truth. One of the first lessons Kas'im taught students was how to build a protective shield around themselves in combat to prevent an enemy from using the Force against them. A Force-talented opponent could yank away your lightsaber, knock you off balance, or even extinguish your lightsaber's blade without the touch of a hand or weapon. A Force-shield was the most basic—and most necessary—protection there was.

It had become instinctive for all the appentices, almost second nature. As soon as the blade was drawn, the protective veil went up. Guarding against the Force powers of the enemy and obscuring your own intentions required as much concentration and energy as augmenting your physical prowess or anticipating the moves of your foe. It was that unseen part of combat, the invisible battle of wills, not the obvious interaction of bodies and blades, that more often than not decided the fate of a duel.

"Kas'im says Fohargh did not lower his guard," Qordis countered. "He says you simply ripped through it. His defenses could not stand before your power."

"Master, are you saying I should hold back if my opponent is weak?"

It was a loaded question, of course. One Qordis didn't even bother to answer.

"It is one thing to defeat an opponent in the ring. But even once he was down, you continued to attack him. He was beaten long before you killed him. What you did was no different from striking with the blade against a fallen and unconscious foe . . . something that is not permitted in the training ring."

The words struck too close to home, dredging up the guilt Bane had tried to bury even as he had made his way to this meeting. Qordis was silent, waiting for Bane's reaction. Bane had to make some type of reply. But the only answer he could come up with was a question he had wrestled with in the twilight hours before dawn. "Kas'im knew what was happening. He could see what I was doing. Why didn't he stop me?"

"Why not, indeed?" Qordis replied smoothly. "Lord Kas'im wanted to see what would happen. He wanted to see how you would act in that situation. He wanted to see if you would be merciful . . . or if you would be strong."

And suddenly Bane realized he hadn't been called into the Master's room to be punished. "I . . . I don't understand. I thought it was forbidden to murder another apprentice."

Qordis nodded. "We cannot have the students attacking each other in the halls; we want your hatred to be directed against the Jedi, not one another." The words echoed the argument Bane had been having with himself only minutes earlier. But what came next was something he hadn't anticipated.

"Despite this, Fohargh's death may turn out to be a minor loss if it helps you to achieve your full potential. Exceptions can be made for those who are strong in the dark side."

"Like Sirak?" Bane asked, the words out of his mouth before he even realized what he was saying.

Fortunately, the question seemed to amuse Lord Qordis rather than offend him. "Sirak understands the power of the dark side," he said with a smile. "Passion fuels the dark side."

"Peace is a lie, there is only passion." Bane muttered out of habit. "Through passion, I gain strength."

"Exactly." Qordis seemed pleased, though with himself or his student it was hard to tell. "Through strength, I gain power; through power, I gain victory."

"Through victory my chains are broken," Bane dutifully recited.

"Understand this—*truly understand it*—and your potential is limitless!"

Qordis gave a dismissive wave of his hand, then settled back onto his meditation mat as Bane turned to go. At the door of the room, though, the young man paused and turned back.

"What is the Sith'ari?" he blurted out.

Qordis tilted his head to the side. "Where did you hear that word?" His voice was grave.

"I . . . I've heard some of the other students use it. About Sirak. They say he could be the Sith'ari."

"Some of the old texts speak of the Sith'ari," Qordis answered slowly, gesturing with a ring-laden claw at the books scattered about the room. "They say the Sith will one day be led by a perfect being, one who embodies the dark side and all we stand for."

"Sirak is this perfect being?"

Qordis shrugged. "Sirak is the strongest student at the Academy. For now. Perhaps in time he will surpass Kas'im and me and all the other Sith Lords. Perhaps not." He paused. "Many of the Masters do not believe in the legend of the Sith'ari," he continued after a moment. "Lord Kaan discounts it, for one. It goes against the philosophy underlying the Brotherhood of Darkness."

"What about you, Master? Do you believe in the legend?"

Bane waited while Qordis considered his reply. It felt like forever.

"These are dangerous questions to ask," the Dark Lord finally said. "But if the Sith'ari is more than a legend, he will not simply be born as the exemplar of all our teachings. He—or she—must be forged in the crucibles of trial and battle to attain such perfection. Some might argue such training is the purpose of this Academy. But I would counter by insisting that we train our apprentices to join the ranks of the Sith Lords so they may stand alongside Kaan and the rest of the Brotherhood."

Realizing that was as good an answer as he was going to get, Bane nodded and left. He had been absolved of his crime, given a pardon because of his power and potential. He should have been exultant, triumphant. But for some reason all he could think about as he headed up to the roof to join the other students was the sticky gurgles of Fohargh's dying breaths.

———

That night, in the privacy of his room, Bane struggled to make sense of what had happened. He sought the deeper wisdom behind the Master's words. Qordis had said that his emotions—his anger—had let him summon up the strength to defeat Fohargh. He said passion fueled the dark side. Bane had felt this enough times to know it was true.

But he couldn't shake the feeling that there was more to it than that. He didn't consider himself a cruel person. He didn't believe he was ruthless or sadistic. Yet how else to explain what he had done to the helpless

Makurth? It had been murder, or execution . . . and Bane was having trouble accepting it.

He had a lot of blood on his hands: he'd killed hundreds, maybe even thousands, of Republic soldiers. But that had been war. And the ensign he'd killed on Apatros had been a case of self-defense. Those were all cases of *kill or be killed,* and he had no regrets about what he'd done. Unlike yesterday.

No matter how he tried, he couldn't find a way to justify what had happened in the ring. Fohargh had taunted him, feeding his rage and lethal fury. Yet he couldn't even use the excuse that he'd been swept up in the heat of the moment. Not if he was being honest with himself. He'd felt his emotions raging through him as he'd drawn on the dark side, but the act itself had been cold and deliberate. Calculating, even.

Lying in his bed, Bane couldn't help but wonder if the relationship between passion and the dark side was more complex than Qordis had made it seem. He closed his eyes, thinking back on what had happened. He took slow, deep breaths, trying to stay calm and detached so he could analyze what had gone wrong.

He had been humiliated and embarrassed, and he'd responded with anger. His anger had let him summon the dark side to lash out at his enemy. He could remember a feeling of elation, of triumph, when Fohargh went sprawling through the air. But there was something else, too. Even in victory, his hatred had kept growing, rising up like the flames of a fire that could be quenched only with blood.

Passion fueled the dark side, but what if the dark side also fueled passion? Emotion brought power, but that power increased the intensity of those emotions . . . which in turn led to an increase in the power. In the right circumstances, it would create a cycle that would end only when a person reached the limits of his or her ability to command the Force—or when the target of his or her anger and hatred was destroyed.

Despite the heat in his room, a cold shiver ran down Bane's spine. How was it possible to contain or control a power that fed on itself? The more he, as an apprentice, learned to draw on the Force, the more his emotions would control him. The stronger a person became, the less rational he would be. It was inevitable.

No, Bane thought. He was missing something. He had to be. If this were true, the Masters would be teaching the students techniques to avoid this situation. They would be learning to distance themselves from their own emotions, even as they used them to draw upon the dark side. But there was nothing of this in their training, so Bane's analysis had to be wrong. It had to be!

Somewhat reassured, Bane let his thoughts drift into the comfort of sleep.

"You make me sick," his father spat. "Look how much you eat! You're worse than a kriffing zucca pig!"

Des tried to ignore him. He hunkered down in his seat at the dinner table and concentrated on the food on his plate, shoveling slow forkfuls into his mouth.

"Did you hear me, boy?" his father snapped. "You think that food in front of you is free? I gotta pay for that food, you know! I worked every day this week and I still owe more now than I did at the beginning of the blasted month!"

Hurst was drunk, as usual. His eyes were glassy, and he still reeked of the mines; he hadn't even bothered to shower before hitting the bottle he kept tucked away beneath the covers of his cot.

"You want me to start working double shifts to support you, boy?" he shouted.

Without looking up from his plate Des muttered, "I work just as many shifts as you do."

"What?" Hurst said, his voice dropping down to a menacing whisper. "What did you just say?"

Instead of biting his lip, Des looked up from his plate and right into his father's red, bleary eyes. "I said I work as many shifts as you do. And I'm only eighteen."

Hurst pushed his chair away from the table and rose. "Eighteen, and still too dumb to know when to keep your mouth shut." He shook his head from side to side in exaggerated disappointment. "Bloody bane of my existence is what you are."

Throwing his fork down on his plate, Des pushed his own chair back from the table and stood up to his full height. He was taller than his father now, and his frame was beginning to fill out with muscles earned in the tunnels.

"Are you going to beat me now?" he snarled at his father. "Going to teach me a lesson?"

Hurst's jaw dropped open. "What the brix is wrong with you, boy?"

"I'm sick of this," Des snapped. "You blame all your problems on me, but you're the one who's drinking away all our credits. Maybe if you sobered up we could get off this stinking world!"

"You smart-mouthed, mudcrutch whelp!" Hurst roared, flipping the table so it crashed against the wall. He leapt across the now empty space between them and grabbed Des by his wrists in a grip as unbreakable as a pair of durasteel binders. The young man tried to wrench free, but his father outweighed him by twenty-some kilos, almost half of which was muscle.

Knowing it was hopeless, Des stopped struggling after a few seconds. But he wasn't going to cower and cry. Not this time. "If you're going to beat me tonight," he said, "remember that it might be the last time, old man. You better make it a good one."

Hurst did. He lit into his son with the savage fury of a bitter, hopeless man. He broke his nose; he blackened both his eyes. He knocked out two of his teeth, split his lip, and cracked his ribs. But throughout it all Des never said a word, and he didn't shed a single tear.

That night, as Des lay in his bed too bruised and swollen to sleep, a single thought kept running through his mind, drowning out the loud drunken snores of Hurst passed out in the corner.

I hope you die. I hope you die. I hope you die.

He'd never hated his father as much as he did at that moment. He envisioned a giant hand squeezing his father's cruel heart.

I hope you die. I hope you die. I hope you die.

The words rolled over and over, an endless mantra, as if he could make them come true through sheer force of will.

I hope you die. I hope you die. I hope you die.

The tears he'd held back during the brutal thrashing finally came, hot drops streaming down his purple, swollen face.

I hope you die. I hope you die. I hope you—

Bane woke with a start, his heart pounding and his body bathed in terror sweat as he thrashed against the covers tangled around his legs. For a brief second he thought he was back on Apatros in the cramped room filled with Hurst and the overwhelming stench of booze. Then he realized where he was, and the nightmare began to fade. A horrible realization swept in to take its place.

Hurst *had* died that night. The authorities had ruled it a natural death. A heart attack, brought on by a combination of too much alcohol, a life working the mines, and the overexertion of nearly beating his own son to death with his bare hands. They never suspected the real cause. Neither had Bane. Not until now.

Trembling slightly, he rolled over, exhausted but knowing sleep wouldn't come again this night.

Fohargh wasn't the first person he had murdered with the Force. He probably wouldn't be the last. Bane was smart enough to understand that.

He shook his head to clear away the memory of Hurst's death. The man had deserved neither pity nor mercy. The weak would always be crushed by the strong. If Bane wanted to survive, he had to become one of the strong. That was why he was here at the Academy. That was his mission. That was the way of the dark side.

But the realization did nothing to quell the queasy feeling in his stomach, and when he closed his eyes he could still see father's face.

12

"**N**o!" Kas'im barked, disdainfully slapping Bane's training saber aside with his own weapon. "Wrong! You're too slow on the first transition. You're leaving your left side wide open for a quick counter."

The Blademaster was teaching him a new sequence; he'd been teaching it to him for more than a week. But for some reason Bane couldn't seem to grasp the intricacies of the movements. His blade felt clumsy and awkward in his hand.

He stepped back and resumed the ready position. Kas'im studied him briefly, then dropped into a defensive stance in front of him. Bane took a deep breath to focus his mind before letting his body trigger the sequence once again.

His muscles moved instinctively, exploding into action. There was a hiss as the downstroke of his blade carved through the air in the first move, a blur of motion . . . but far too slow. Kas'im responded by slipping to the side and bringing his own double-bladed weapon around in a long, swift arc that struck Bane hard in the ribs.

The breath whooshed out of him and he felt the searing pain of the pelko barbs, followed by the all-too-familiar numbness spreading up through the left side of his torso. He staggered back, helpless, as Kas'im watched silently. Bane struggled to stay upright and failed, collapsing awkwardly to the floor. The Blademaster shook his head in disappointment.

Bane dragged himself to his feet, trying not to let his frustration show. It had been nearly three weeks since he had beaten Fohargh in the ring, and since that time he had been training with Kas'im in individual sessions to improve his lightsaber combat. But for some reason he wasn't making any progress.

"I'm sorry, Master. I will go practice the drills again," he said through gritted teeth.

"Drills?" the Twi'lek repeated, his voice cruel and mocking. "What good will that do?"

"I . . . I must learn the sequence better. To become faster."

Kas'im spat on the ground. "If you truly believe that, then you're a fool."

Bane didn't know how to respond, so he kept silent.

The Blademaster stepped forward and gave him a sharp cuff on his ear. It was meant not to hurt, but to humiliate. "Fohargh was better trained than you," he snapped. "He knew more sequences, he knew more forms. But they couldn't save him.

"The sequences are just tools. They help you free your mind so you can draw upon the Force. That is where you will find the key to victory. Not in the muscles of your arms or the quickness of your blade. You must call upon the dark side to destroy your enemies!"

Clenching his jaw from the burning pain now spreading through the entire left side of his body, Bane could only nod.

"You're holding back," the Master went on. "You aren't using the Force. Without it, your moves are slow and predictable."

"I . . . I'll try harder, Master."

"Try?" Kas'im turned away in disgust. "You've lost your will to fight. This lesson is over."

Realizing he had been dismissed, Bane slowly made his way to the stairs leading down from the temple roof. As he reached them, Kas'im called out one last piece of advice.

"Return when you are ready to embrace the dark side instead of pulling away from it."

Bane didn't turn to look back: the pain and numbness of his left side made that impossible. But as he hobbled down the stairs, Lord Kas'im's words echoed in his ears with the ring of truth.

This wasn't the first training session he had failed in. And his failures weren't limited to Kas'im and the lightsaber. Bane had gained in both reputation and prestige when he defeated Fohargh; several of the Masters had shown a sudden willingness to give him individual, one-on-one training. Yet despite the extra attention, Bane's skills hadn't progressed at all. If anything, he'd actually taken several steps back.

He made his way through the halls to his room, then lay down gingerly on his bed. There wasn't anything he could do while he was temporarily crippled by the pelko venom except rest and meditate.

It was obvious something was wrong, but he couldn't say exactly what. He no longer felt sharp. He no longer felt *alive.* When he had first become conscious of the Force flowing through him, his senses had become hyper-aware: the world had seemed more vibrant and more real. Now everything was muted and distant. He walked through the halls of the Academy as if he was in some kind of trance.

He wasn't sleeping well; he kept having nightmares. Sometimes he dreamed of his father and the night he died. Other times he dreamed of his fight with Fohargh. Sometimes the dreams blended together, merging into one terrible vision: the Makurth beating him in the apartment on Apatros, his father lying dead in the dueling ring atop the temple on Korriban. And each time Bane would wake choking back a scream, shivering even though his body was bathed in sweat.

But it was more than just lack of sleep that left him in a dazed stupor. The passion that had driven him was gone. The raging fire inside him had vanished, replaced by a cold emptiness. And without his passion, he was unable to summon the power of the dark side. It was becoming harder and harder to command the Force.

The changes were subtle, barely noticeable at first. But over time small changes built up. Now moving even small objects left him exhausted. He was slow and clumsy with the training saber. He could no longer anticipate what his opponents would do; he could only react after the fact.

He couldn't deny it any longer: he was regressing. Apprentices he had surpassed long ago had caught up to him again. He could tell he was falling behind just by watching the other students during their studies . . . which meant they could probably tell, too.

He thought back on what the Twi'lek Master had told him. *You've lost your will to fight.*

Kas'im was right. Bane had felt it slipping away since his first dream of his father. Unfortunately, he had no idea how to reclaim the anger and competitive fire that had fueled his meteoric rise through the hierarchy of Sith apprentices.

Return when you are ready to embrace the dark side instead of pulling away from it.

Something was holding him back. Some part of him recoiled from what he had become. He would meditate for hours each day, concentrating his mind in search of the swirling, pulsing fury of the dark side locked away within him. Yet he searched in vain. A cold veil had fallen across the core of his being, and try as he might he couldn't tear it aside to seize the power that lay beneath.

And he was running out of time. So far nobody had dared to challenge him in the dueling ring—not since Fohargh's death. The Makurth's gruesome end still inspired enough fear in the other students for them to steer clear of him. But Bane knew they wouldn't keep their distance much longer. His confidence and abilities were waning, and his failures were becoming more public. Soon it would be as obvious to the other students as it was to him.

In those first days after Fohargh's death his only true rival had been Sirak. Now every apprentice on Korriban was a potential threat. The hopelessness of the situation tore away at his guts. It made him want to scream and claw at the stone walls in impotent rage. Yet for all his frustrations, he was unable to summon the passion that fed the dark side.

Soon a challenger would step forward in the dueling ring, eager to take him down. And there was nothing he could do to stop that moment from coming.

————

Lord Kaan paced restlessly on the bridge of *Nightfall* as it orbited the industrial world of Brentaal IV. The Sith fleet occupied the Bormea sector, the region of space where the Perlemian Trade Route and the Hydian Way intersected. The Brotherhood of Darkness now controlled two of the most important hyperspace lanes serving the Core Worlds; Republic re-sistance to the ever-advancing Sith fleet was crumbling.

And yet despite this most recent victory, Kaan felt something wasn't right. If anything, their conquest of the Bormea sector had been *too* easy. The worlds of Corulag, Chandrila, and Brentaal had all fallen in rapid succession, their defenders offering only token resistance before retreat-ing in the face of the invading horde.

In fact, he had sensed only a handful of Jedi among the Republic forces opposing them. This was not the first time the Jedi had been virtually ab-sent from key battles: during encounters at Bespin, Sullust, and Taanab, Kaan had expected to be confronted by a fleet led by Jedi Master Hoth, the only Republic commander who seemed capable of winning victories against the Sith. But General Hoth—despite the reputation he had earned in the early stages of the war—was never there.

At first Kaan suspected it was a trap, some elaborate scheme arranged by the wily Hoth to ensnare and destroy his sworn enemy. But if it was a trap, it had never been sprung. The Sith were pressing in from all sides; they were almost sitting on the doorstep of Coruscant itself. And the Jedi had all but vanished, seemingly having deserted the Republic in its time of greatest need.

He should have been ecstatic. Without the Jedi, the war was as good as over. The Republic would fall in a matter of months, and the Sith would rule. But where had the Jedi gone? Kaan didn't like it. The strange message Kopecz had sent just a few hours earlier had only added to his unease. The Twi'lek was coming to meet *Nightfall* with urgent news about Ruusan, news he wouldn't transmit across regular channels. News so important he felt he had to deliver it in person.

"An interceptor has just docked in *Nightfall*'s landing bay, Lord Kaan," one of the bridge crew reported.

Despite his anxiousness to hear Kopecz's news, Lord Kaan resisted the urge to go down to the landing bay to meet him. He felt something had gone very, very wrong, and it was important to maintain an appearance of calm assurance before his troops. Yet patience was not a virtue many of the Sith Lords possessed, and he couldn't keep himself from pacing as he waited for the Twi'lek to make his way to the bridge and deliver his ominous report.

After what seemed like hours but was no more than a few minutes, Kopecz finally arrived. His expression did nothing to alleviate Kaan's growing apprehension as he crossed the bridge and gave a perfunctory bow.

"I must speak with you in private, Lord Kaan."

"You may speak here," Kaan assured him. "What we say will not leave this ship." The bridge crew of *Nightfall* had been handpicked by Kaan himself. All had sworn an oath to serve with absolute loyalty; they knew the harsh consequences should they break that oath.

Kopecz glanced suspiciously around the bridge, but the crew were all focused on their stations. None of them seemed even to notice him. "We've lost Ruusan," he said, whispering despite Kaan's assurances. "The base set up on the surface, the orbiting fleet . . . all of it wiped out!"

For a moment Kaan didn't speak. When he did his voice had dropped to the same level as Kopecz's. "How did this happen? We have spies throughout the Republic military. All their fleets have fallen back to the Core. All of them! They couldn't possibly have mustered enough strength to take back Ruusan. Not without us knowing!"

"It wasn't the Republic," Kopecz replied. "It was the Jedi. Hundreds of them. Thousands. Jedi Masters, Jedi Knights, Jedi Padawans: an entire army of Jedi."

Kopecz cursed loudly. None of the crew so much as glanced in his direction, a testament to their training and their fear of their commander.

"Lord Hoth realized that the strength of the Jedi order was spread too thin trying to defend the Republic," Kopecz continued. "He's gathered them all into a single host with only one goal: destroy the users of the dark side. They don't care about our soldiers and fleets anymore. All they want to do is wipe us out: the apprentices, the acolytes, the Sith Masters . . . and especially the Dark Lords. Lord Hoth himself is leading them," the Twi'lek added, though Kaan had already guessed this for himself. "They call themselves the Army of Light."

Kopecz paused to let the news sink in. Kaan took several deep breaths, silently reciting the Code of the Sith to bring his whirling thoughts back into focus.

And then he laughed. "An Army of Light to oppose the Brotherhood of Darkness."

Kopecz stared at him with a bewildered expression.

"Hoth knows the Jedi aren't capable of defeating our vast armies," Kaan explained. "Not anymore. The Republic is doomed. So now he concentrates exclusively on us: the leaders of those armies. Cut off the head and the body will die."

"We should send our fleet to Ruusan," Kopecz suggested. "All of them. Crush the Jedi in one fell swoop and wipe them from the galaxy forever."

Kaan shook his head. "That's exactly what Hoth wants us to do. Divert our armies from the Republic, draw them away from Coruscant. Give up all the ground we have gained in a foolish and pointless attack on the Jedi."

"Pointless?"

"You say he has an army of Jedi: thousands of them. What chance does a fleet of mere soldiers have against such an enemy? Ships and weapons are no match for the power of the Force. Hoth knows this."

Finally Kopecz nodded in understanding. "You always said this war would not be decided by military might."

"Precisely. In the end the Republic is merely an afterthought. Only through the complete annihilation of the Jedi order can we achieve true victory. And Hoth has been kind enough to gather them all in one place for us."

"But the Brotherhood is no match for the massed strength of the entire Jedi order," Kopecz protested. "There are too many of them and not enough of us."

"Our numbers are greater than you think," Kaan said. "We have academies scattered throughout the galaxy. We can swell our numbers with Marauders from Honoghr and Gentes. We can gather all the assassins trained at Umbara. We will command the students at Dathomir, Iridonia, and all the rest of the academies to join the ranks of the Brotherhood of Darkness. We will assemble our own army of Sith—one capable of destroying Hoth and his Army of Light!"

"And what of the Academy on Korriban?" Kopecz asked.

"They will join the Brotherhood, but only after they have completed their training under Qordis."

"We could use them against the Jedi," Kopecz pressed. "Korriban is home to the strongest of our apprentices."

"That is precisely why it is too dangerous to bring them into this conflict," Kaan explained. "With strength come ambition and rivalry. In the heat of battle their emotions will take over their minds; they will turn against each other. They will divide our ranks with infighting while the Jedi remain united." He paused. "It has happened to the Sith too many times in the past; I will not allow it to happen again. They will stay with Qordis and complete their training. He will teach them discipline and loyalty to the Brotherhood. Only then will they join us on the field of battle."

"Is that what you believe," Kopecz asked, "or what Qordis has been telling you?"

"Don't let your mistrust of Qordis blind you to what we are trying to accomplish," Kaan chided. "His pupils are the future of the Brotherhood. The future of the Sith. I will not expose them to this war until they are ready." His tone clearly brooked no further argument. "The apprentices at Korriban will join the Brotherhood in due time. But that time is not now."

"Well, it better be soon," Kopecz muttered, only partially mollified. "I don't think we can beat Hoth without them."

Kaan reached out and grasped the Twi'lek's meaty shoulder in a firm grip. "Never fear, my friend," he said with a smile. "The Jedi will be no match for us. We will slaughter them at Ruusan and wipe them from the face of the galaxy. The apprentices may be the future of the Brotherhood, but the present belongs to us!"

Much to Kaan's relief, Kopecz returned his smile. The leader of the Brotherhood would have been less pleased if he had known that much of the Twi'lek's satisfaction came from the knowledge that Qordis would miss out on the glory of the coming victory.

———

Lord Kas'im entered the opulently decorated chamber and gave a nod in the direction of his fellow Master. "You wanted to see me?"

"News from the front," Qordis said, rising slowly from his meditation mat. "The Jedi have massed together under a single banner on Ruusan. General Hoth is leading them. Lord Kaan has gathered his own army. Even now they are headed there to engage the Jedi."

"Are we going to join them?" Kas'im asked, his voice eager, his lekku twitching at the thought of pitting his skills against the greatest warriors of the Jedi order.

Qordis shook his head. "Not us. None of the Masters. And none of the students, unless you feel one of the apprentices is ready."

"No," Kas'im replied after a moment's consideration. "Sirak, perhaps. He is strong enough. But his pride is too great, and he still has much to learn."

"What about Bane? He showed great promise in disposing of Fohargh."

Kas'im shrugged. "That was a month ago. Since then he has made almost no progress. Something is holding him back. Fear, I think."

"Fear? Of the other students? Of Sirak?"

"No. Nothing like that. He's finally seen what he is truly capable of; he's seen the full power of the dark side. I think he's afraid to face it."

"Then he is of no further use to us," Qordis stated flatly. "Focus on the other students. Don't waste your time on him."

The Blademaster was momentarily taken aback. He was surprised that Qordis would be so quick to give up on a student with such undeniable potential.

"I think he just needs more time," he suggested. "Most of our apprentices have been studying the ways of the Sith for many years. Ever since they were children. Bane didn't begin his training with us until he was a full-grown adult."

"I'm well aware of the circumstances surrounding his arrival at this Academy!" Qordis snapped, and Kas'im suddenly realized what was really going on. Bane had been brought to Korriban by Lord Kopecz, and there was precious little love lost between Kopecz and the leader of the Academy. Bane's failure would ultimately become a poor reflection on Qordis's most bitter rival.

"The next time Bane approaches you, turn him away," the Dark Lord told him, his tone leaving no doubt that his words were a command and not a request. "Make sure all the Masters understand that he is no longer worthy of our teachings."

Kas'im nodded his understanding. He would do as ordered. It wasn't fair to Bane, of course. But nobody ever claimed the Sith were fair.

13

Bane knew he had to do something. His situation was becoming desperate. He was still floundering, unable to call upon the power he had used to destroy Fohargh. But now his weakness had become public.

Yesterday during the evening training session he had approached Kas'im to arrange a time for more one-on-one practice, hoping to break free of the lethargy that gripped him. But the Blademaster had refused him, shaking his head and turning his attention to one of the other students. The message was clear to everyone: Bane was vulnerable.

As the students gathered in a circle on the top of the temple after the morning drills, Bane knew what had to be done. His reputation had protected him from the challenges of the other students. Now that reputation was gone. But he couldn't sit back passively, waiting for one of the other students to challenge him and take him down. He had to seize the initiative; he had to go on the attack. Today he had to be the first one to step into the ring.

Of course, if he challenged one of the lesser students, everyone would see it as confirmation of the weakness he was trying to hide. There was only one way he could redeem himself in the eyes of the school and the Masters; there was only one opponent he could call out.

Several of the apprentices were still milling about, trying to find a place where they would be able to clearly observe the morning's action. It was customary to wait until everyone was in place before issuing a challenge, but Bane knew that the longer he waited, the harder his task would be. He stepped boldly into the center of the circle, drawing curious stares from the other students. Kas'im fixed him with a disapproving gaze, but he tried to put it out of his mind.

"I have a challenge," he proclaimed. "I call out Sirak."

There was an excited buzz among the students, but Bane could barely hear it above the pounding of his own heart. Sirak rarely fought in actual combat; Bane had never even seen him in action. But he'd heard other students talk of Sirak's prowess in the dueling ring, telling wild tales of his unbeatable skills. Ever since the Zabrak had approached him on the stairs, Bane had watched his opponent during training sessions in preparation for this confrontation. And from what he'd seen, the seemingly exaggerated accounts of his prowess were all too accurate.

Unlike most of the students, Sirak preferred the double-bladed training saber to the more traditional single blade. Apart from Kas'im himself, Sirak was the only one Bane had ever seen wield the exotic weapon with any signs of skill. His technique seemed almost perfect to Bane's inexpert eye. He always seemed in complete control; he was always on the attack. Even in simple drills his superiority over his opponents was obvious. Where most students took two to three weeks to learn a new sequence, Sirak was able to master one in a matter of days. And now Bane was about to face him in the dueling ring.

The Zabrak stepped out from the crowd, moving slowly but gracefully as he responded to the challenge. Even walking to the center of the ring he exuded an air of menace. He casually flourished his weapon as he approached, the twin durasteel blades carving long, languid arcs through the air.

Bane watched him come, feeling his heart and breathing quicken as his body released adrenaline into his system, instinctively readying itself for the coming battle. In contrast with his physical body, however, Bane felt no significant change in his emotional state. He had expected to feel a surge of fear and anger as Sirak approached, emotions he could feed off to rip through the lifeless veil and unleash the dark side. But the lethargic stupor still enveloped him like a dull, gray shroud.

"I wish you had challenged me earlier," Sirak whispered, his voice just loud enough for Bane to hear. "In the first week after Fohargh's death many thought you were my equal. I would have gained great prestige in defeating you. That is no longer the case."

Sirak had stopped his advance and was standing several meters away. His double-bladed training saber still danced slowly through the air. It moved as if it were alive, a creature anticipating the hunt, too excited to remain motionless.

"There will be little glory in defeating you now," he repeated. "But I will take great pleasure in your suffering."

Behind Sirak, Bane saw Llokay and Yevra, the other Zabrak apprentices, push their way to the front of the crowd to get a better view of their champion. The brother wore a cruel grin; the sister, an expression of hungry anticipation. Bane did his best to tune out the eagerness on their red faces, letting them blend into the unimportant background scenery of the spectators.

All his concentration was focused on the fluid movements of the unfamiliar weapon in Sirak's hands. He had tried to memorize the sequences Sirak worked on during the drills. Now he was looking for clues that would tip his opponent's hand—that might reveal which sequence he planned to use to begin the battle. If Bane guessed right, he could counterattack and possibly end the battle in the first pass. It was his best chance at victory, but without being able to draw on the Force, his odds of correctly guessing which sequence his foe would choose were very, very slim.

Sirak raised the double-bladed saber up above his head, spinning it so fast it was nothing but a blur, then lunged forward. One end came down in a savage overhead strike that Bane easily parried. But the move was only a feint, setting up a slashing attack at the waist from the opposite blade. Recognizing the maneuver at the last second, Bane could do nothing more than throw himself into a backward roll, narrowly escaping injury.

His foe was on him even before he got to his feet, the twin blades slicing down in an alternating rhythm of attacks: left–right–left–right. Bane blocked, rolled, twisted, and blocked again, turning back the flurry. He tried a leg-sweep, but Sirak anticipated the move and nimbly leapt clear, giving Bane just enough time to scramble to his feet.

The next round of attacks kept Bane in full retreat, but he was able to prevent Sirak from gaining an advantage by giving ground and reverting to basic defensive sequences. He was still desperately trying to gain some advantage by watching his opponent's moves. At one moment Sirak seemed to be using the jabs and thrusts of Vaapad, the most aggressive and direct of the seven traditional forms. But in the middle of a sequence he would suddenly shift to the power attacks of Djem So, generating such force that even a blocked strike caused Bane to stagger back. A quick turn or rotation of the weapon and one of the twin blades was suddenly swinging in again at an awkward angle, causing Bane to reel off balance as he knocked it aside.

There was a brief lull in the action as the two combatants paused to reevaluate their strategies, each breathing heavily. Sirak twirled his weapon in a quick, complex sequence that brought the saber under his right arm, around behind his back, over his left shoulder, and around to the front. Then he smiled and did it in reverse.

Bane watched the extravagant flourish with a sinking feeling. Sirak had been toying with him in the first few passes, dragging the fight out so his victory would seem more impressive. Now he was showing his true skill, using sequences that blended several forms at once, switching rapidly among different styles in complex patterns Bane had never seen before.

It was just one more sign of the Zabrak's superiority. If Bane tried to combine different styles into a single sequence, he'd probably gouge out an eye or smack himself in the back of the head. It was clear he was overmatched; his only hope was that his enemy would get careless and make a mistake.

Sirak moved in again, his training saber moving so quickly that Bane could hear the sizzle as it split the air. Bane leapt forward to meet the challenge, trying to call up the power of the dark side to anticipate and block the dual blades moving too fast for his eyes to see. He felt the Force flowing through him, but it seemed distant and hollow: the veil was still there. He was able to keep the paralyzing edges of Sirak's saber at bay, but it required him to concentrate all his attention on controlling his own blade . . . leaving him vulnerable to the real purpose of the attack being unleashed against him.

Bane's skull exploded as Sirak's forehead slammed into his face. Pain turned his vision into a field of silver stars. The cartilage of his nose gave way with a sickening crunch, a geyser of blood gushing forth. Blind and dazed, he was able to parry the next strike only by instinct guided by the faintest whisper of the Force. But Sirak spun as his saber was turned away and delivered a back roundhouse kick that shattered Bane's kneecap.

Screaming, Bane collapsed, his free hand slamming into the ground as he braced his fall. Sirak crushed the fingers under his boot, grinding them into the unyielding stone of the temple roof. A knee came up, fracturing his cheek and jawbone with a thunderous crack.

With a last, desperate burst Bane tried to hurl his opponent backward with the dark side. Sirak brushed the impact aside, easily deflecting it with the Force-shield he had wrapped himself in at the start of the duel. Then he moved in close to finish the job with his blades. The first blow hit with the impact of a landspeeder slamming into an irax, breaking Bane's right wrist. The training saber dropped from his suddenly nerveless grasp. The next strike took him higher up on the same arm, dislocating his elbow.

A simple kick to the face sent jagged bits of tooth shooting out of his mouth and bolts of pain shooting through his broken jaw. He slumped forward, barely conscious, as Sirak stepped back and lowered his saber, reaching out with a free hand to grab Bane around the throat with the crushing grip of the Force. He raised his arm, lifting the muscular Bane as if he were a child, then hurled him across the ring.

Bane felt another bone snap as he crashed to the ground, but his body had passed into a state of shock and there was no longer any pain. He lay motionless in a crumpled, twisted heap. Blood from his nose and mouth clogged his throat. A coughing fit racked his body, and he heard rather than felt the grinding of his broken ribs.

Everything began to go dim. He caught a glimpse of a pair of blood-flecked boots striding toward him, and then Bane surrendered himself to the merciful darkness.

———

Kopecz shook his head as he studied the battle plan Kaan had laid out on a makeshift table in the middle of his tent. The holomap of Ruusan's ter-

rain showed the positions of the Sith forces as glowing red triangles floating above the map. The Jedi positions were represented by green squares.
Despite this high-tech advancement, the rest of the map was a simple
two-dimensional representation of the surrounding area's topography. It
did nothing to convey the grim devastation that had left Ruusan a virtual
wasteland, ravaged by war.

Three great fleet battles had taken place high above the world in the
past year, scattering debris from the losing side across the sparsely populated world each time. Scorched and twisted hulls that had once been
ships had crashed into the lush forests, igniting wildfires that had reduced
much of the small world's surface to ash and barren soil.

Ruusan, despite its meager size, had become a world of major importance to both the Republic and the Sith. Strategically located on the edges
of the Inner Rim, it also stood at what most considered the border between the Republic's dangerous frontier and its safe and secure Core.
Ruusan was a symbol. Conquering it represented the inevitable advance
of the Sith and their conquest of the Republic; liberating it would be em-
blematic of the Jedi's ability to drive the invaders away and protect the Republic's citizens. The result was an endless cycle of battles, with neither
side willing to admit defeat.

The First Battle of Ruusan had seen the invading Sith fleet rout the Republic forces using the elements of surprise and the strength of Kaan's
battle meditation. The second battle saw the Republic try to reclaim control of Ruusan and fail, driven back by the enemy's superior numbers and
firepower.

The third battle in the skies above Ruusan marked the emergence of
the Army of Light. Instead of Republic cruisers and fighters, the Sith
found themselves facing a fleet made up primarily of one- and two-crew
fighters piloted exclusively by Jedi. The common soldiers who had joined
Kaan's army were no match for the Force, and Ruusan was saved . . . for a
time.

The Sith had responded to the Army of Light by amassing the full
numbers of the Brotherhood of Darkness into a single army, then unleashing it on Ruusan. The war that had ravaged the world from on high
moved down to the surface, with far more devastating consequences.

Compared with space fleet battles, ground combat was brutal, bloody, and visceral.

Kopecz slammed his fist down on the table. "It's hopeless, Kaan."

The other Dark Lords gathered in the tent murmured in agreement.

"The Jedi positions are too well defended; they have all the advantages," Kopecz went on angrily. "High ground, entrenched fortifications, superior numbers. We can't win this battle!"

"Look again," Kaan replied. "The Jedi have spread themselves too thin."

The big Twi'lek studied the map in more detail and realized Kaan was right. The Jedi perimeter extended too far out from their base camp. It took him barely a moment to realize why.

The clash between armies of Jedi and Sith, led by Jedi Masters and Dark Lords, had shaken the foundations of the world. The power of the Force raged unchecked across the battlefields like the thunder of an exploding star. Towns, villages, and individual homes caught up in the storm had been wiped out, leaving only death and destruction behind. Civilians caught up in the wake of war had been forced to flee, becoming refugees of an epic battle between the champions of light and dark.

Seeing their suffering, the Jedi had sought to console, comfort, and protect the innocent citizens of Ruusan. They planned their strategies around defending civilian settlements and homesteads, even at the expense of resources and tactical advantage. The Sith, of course, made no such concessions.

"The Jedi's compassion is a weakness," Kaan continued. "One we can exploit. If we concentrate our full numbers on a single point, we can breach their lines. Then the advantage will be ours."

The assembled generals and strategists of the Brotherhood of Darkness nodded in agreement. Several raised their voices in roars of triumph and congratulations. Only Kopecz refused to join in the celebrations.

"The Army of Light still outnumbers us two to one," the heavyset Twi'lek reminded them. "Their lines may be overextended in some places, but we don't know where they are vulnerable. They know our scouts are watching; they hide their numbers just as we hide ours. If we attack a location where their numbers are strong, we'll be slaughtered!"

The rest of the generals stilled their voices, no longer swept up in their leader's enthusiasm now that the glaring flaw in his plan had been exposed. Again, there were rumbles of disagreement and displeasure. Kopecz ignored the reaction of the other Dark Lords. For all their power, for all their ambition, they were like so many banthas, blindly following the rest of the herd. In theory everyone in the Brotherhood of Darkness was equal, but in practice Kaan ruled the others.

Kopecz understood this, and he was willing to follow him. The Sith needed a strong and charismatic leader, a man of vision, to quell the infighting that had plagued their ranks. Kaan was just such a leader, and he was normally a brilliant military tactician. But this plan was madness. Suicide. Unlike the rest of the rabble, Kopecz wasn't about to follow their leader into certain death.

"You underestimate me, Kopcez," Kaan reassured him, his voice calm and confident, as if he had anticipated this question all along and had an answer prepared. Perhaps he did. "We won't strike until we know exactly where they are most vulnerable," the Dark Lord explained. "By the time we attack, we'll know the precise number and composition of every unit and patrol along their perimeter."

"How?" Kopecz demanded. "Even our Umbaran shadow spies can't provide us with that kind of detail. Not quickly enough to use it in planning our attack. We have no way of getting the information we'd need."

Kaan laughed. "Of course we do. One of the Jedi will give it to us."

The flaps covering the entrance of the long tent serving as the Sith war room parted as if on cue, and a young human woman clad in the robes of the Jedi order stepped through. She was of average height, but that was the only thing about her that could ever be called average. She had thick, raven hair that tumbled down past her shoulders. Her face and figure were perfect examples of the human female form; her tricopper-hued skin was set off by green eyes smoldering with a heat that was both a warning and an invitation. She moved with the lithe grace of a Twi'lek dancer as she walked the length of the assembled Dark Lords, a coy smile on her lips as she pretended not to hear their whispers of surprise.

Kopecz had seen many striking females in his time. Several of the female Dark Lords gathered in the tent were gorgeous, renowned as much for their incredible beauty as their devastating power. But as the young

Jedi drew closer, he found he was unable to take his eyes off her. There was something magnetic about her, something that transcended mere physical attractiveness.

She carried her head high, her proud features issuing an unspoken challenge as she approached. And Kopecz saw something else: naked ambition, raw and hungry.

At his side Kaan whispered, "Remarkable, isn't she?"

She reached the front of the tent and dipped smoothly to one knee, bowing her head ever so slightly in deference to Lord Kaan.

"Welcome, Githany," he said, motioning for her to rise. "We've been waiting for you."

"It's my pleasure, Lord Kaan," she purred. Kopecz felt his knees go momentarily weak at her sensual voice, then snapped to rigid attention. He was too old and too wise to let himself be blinded by this woman's charms. He cared only about what she could offer them against the Jedi.

"You have information for us?" he asked abruptly.

She tilted her head to one side and gave him a curious glance, trying to find the reason for his cold reception. After a moment's pause she answered, "I can tell you exactly where to strike at their lines, and when. Lord Hoth put a Jedi named Kiel Charny in charge of coordinating their defenses. I got the information directly from him."

"Why would this Charny share that kind of information with you?" Kopecz asked suspiciously.

She gave him a sly grin. "Kiel and I were . . . close. We shared many things. He had no idea I would come to you with the information."

Kopecz narrowed his eyes. "I thought the Jedi disapproved of that sort of thing."

Her smile became a sneer. "The Jedi disapprove of a lot of things. That's why I've come to you."

Kaan stepped forward before he could ask any more questions, placing a familiar hand on her hip and turning her away from Kopecz.

"We don't have time for this, Githany," he said. "You must give us your report and return to the Jedi camp before anyone notices you're missing."

She flashed a dazzling smile at Kaan and nodded. "Of course. We have to hurry."

He gently ushered her over to the holomap, and a knot of strategists closed in, shielding her from view as she gave them the details of the Jedi guard. A few seconds later Kaan emerged from the crowd and walked back over to stand beside Kopecz.

"Ambition, betrayal—the dark side is strong in her," the Twi'lek whispered. "I'm surprised the Jedi ever took her in."

"They probably believed they could turn her to the light," Kaan replied, speaking just as softly. "But Githany was born to the dark side. Like me. Like you. It was inevitable she would join the Sith someday."

"The timing is fortunate," Kopecz noted. "Maybe a little too fortunate. It may be a trap. Are you sure we can trust her? I think she's dangerous."

Kaan dismissed the warning with a soft laugh. "So are you, Lord Kopecz. That's what makes you so useful to the Brotherhood."

Bane was floating, weightless, surrounded by darkness and silence. It seemed he was adrift in the black void of death itself.

Then consciousness began to return. His body, jerked from blissful unawareness, thrashed in the dark green fluid of the bacta tank, creating a stream of bubbles that rose silently to the surface. His heart began to pound; he could hear the blood rushing through his veins.

His eyes popped open in time to see a med droid come over to adjust some of the settings on his tank. Within seconds his heart rate slowed and the involuntary thrashing of his bruised and broken limbs settled. But though his body was calmed by the tranquilizer, Bane's mind was now fully alert and aware.

Memories of motion and pain flickered across his mind. The sights, sounds, and smells of combat. He remembered the approach of blood-stained boots: his blood. Kas'im must have stepped in after he'd blacked out and kept Sirak from killing him. They must have brought him here to heal.

At first he was surprised that they would bother to help him recover. Then he realized that he, like all the students at the Academy, was too valuable to the Brotherhood to simply throw away. So he would survive . . . but his life was essentially over.

Since coming to the Academy he had worked toward one clear goal. All his studying, all his training had been for one single purpose: to understand and command the power of the dark side of the Force. The dark side would bring him power. Glory. Strength. Freedom.

Now he would be a pariah at the Academy. He would be allowed to listen in on the group lessons, to practice his skills in Kas'im's training sessions, but that would be all. Any hope he might have had of getting one-on-one training with any of the Masters had been crushed in his humiliating defeat. And without that specializing guidance, his potential would wither and die.

In theory all in the Brotherhood were equal, but Bane was smart enough to see the real truth. In practice the Sith needed leaders, Masters like Kaan, or Lord Qordis here at the Academy. The strong always stepped forward; the weak had no choice but to follow.

Now Bane was doomed to be one of the followers. A life of subservience and obedience.

Through victory my chains are broken. But Bane had not found victory, and he understood all too well the chains of servitude that would bind him forevermore. He was destroyed.

Part of him wished Sirak had just finished the job.

14

There was an air of unusual celebration in the halls of the Sith Academy. The Brotherhood of Darkness had scored a resounding victory over the Jedi on Ruusan, and the jubilation of the feast Qordis had thrown to mark the victory lingered in the air. During training sessions, drills, and lessons, students could be heard whispering excitedly as details of the battle were shared. The Jedi on Ruusan had been completely wiped out, some said. Others insisted Lord Hoth himself had fallen. There were rumors that the Jedi Temple on Coruscant was defenseless, and it was only a matter of days before it was ransacked by the Dark Lords of the Sith.

The Masters knew that much of what was being said was exaggerated or inaccurate. The Jedi on Ruusan had been routed, but a great many had managed to escape the battle. Lord Hoth was not dead; most likely he was rallying the Jedi for the inevitable counterattack. And the Jedi Temple on Coruscant was still well beyond the reach of Kaan and the Brotherhood of Darkness. On the orders of Qordis, however, the instructors allowed the enthusiasm of their apprentices to go unchecked for the sake of improving morale.

The exultant mood at the Academy had little effect on Bane, however. It had taken three weeks of regular sessions in the bacta tank before he'd fully recovered from the horrific beating Sirak had given him. Most of the time a loss in the dueling ring required only a day or two in the tanks before the student was ready to resume training. Of course, most of the students didn't lose as badly as Bane had.

Hurst had been free with his fists, and Bane had suffered more than a few severe thrashings growing up. The punishments of his youth had taught him how to deal with physical pain, but the trauma inflicted by Sirak was far worse than anything he'd endured at his father's hands.

Bane shuffled slowly down the halls of the Academy, though his measured pace was one of choice rather than necessity. The lingering discomfort he felt was insignificant. Thanks to the bacta tanks his broken bones had mended and his bruises had vanished completely. The emotional damage, however, was more difficult to reverse.

A pair of laughing apprentices approached, regaling each other with supposedly factual accounts of the Sith victory on Ruusan. Their conversation stopped as they neared the solitary figure. Bane ducked his head to avoid meeting their eyes as they passed. One whispered something unintelligible, but the contempt in her tone was unmistakable.

Bane didn't react. He was dealing with the emotional pain in the only way he knew how. The same way he'd dealt with it as a child. He withdrew into himself, tried to make himself invisible to avoid the scorn and derision of others.

His defeat—so public and so complete—had destroyed his already suspect reputation with both the students and the Masters. Even before the duel many had sensed that his power had left him. Now their suspicions had been confirmed. Bane had become an outcast at the Academy, shunned by the other students and disregarded by the Masters.

Even Sirak ignored him. He had beaten his rival into submission; Bane was no longer worthy of his notice. The Zabrak's attention, like the attention of nearly all the apprentices, had turned to the young human female who had come to join them shortly after the battle on Ruusan.

Her name was Githany. Bane had heard that she had once been a Jedi Padawan but had rejected the light in favor of the dark side . . . a common enough story at the Academy. Githany, however, was anything but common. She had played an integral role in the Sith victory on Ruusan, and had arrived at Korriban with the fanfare of a conquering hero.

Bane hadn't been strong enough to attend the victory feast where

Qordis had introduced the new arrival to the rest of the students, but he had seen her several times at the Academy since then. She was stunningly beautiful; it was obvious that many of the male students lusted after her. It was just as obvious that several of the female students were jealous of her, though they kept their resentment well hidden for their own sake.

Githany was as arrogant and cruel as she was physically becoming, and the Force was exceptionally strong in her. In only a few weeks she'd already developed a reputation for crushing those who got in her way. It was no surprise she had quickly became a favorite of Qordis and the other Dark Lords.

None of this really mattered to Bane, however. He trudged on through the halls, head down, making his way to the library located in the depths of the Academy. Studying the archives had seemed the best way to supplement the teachings of the Masters in the early stages of his development. Now the cold, quiet room far beneath the Temple's main floors offered him his only place of refuge.

Not surprisingly, the massive room was empty save for the rows of shelves stacked with manuscripts haphazardly arranged and then forgotten. Few students bothered to come here. Why waste time contemplating the wisdom of the ancients when you could study at the feet of an actual Dark Lord? Even Bane came here only as a last resort; the Masters wouldn't waste their time on him anymore.

But as he perused the ancient texts, a part of him he'd thought dead began to reawaken. The inner fire—the burning rage that had always been his secret reserve—was gone. Still, even if only faintly, the dark side called to him, and Bane realized that he wasn't ready to give up on himself. And so he gave himself up to studying.

It wasn't permissible for students to remove records from the archive room, so Bane did all his reading there. Yesterday he had finally completed a rather long and detailed treatise by an ancient Sith Lord named Naga Sadow on the uses of alchemy and poisons. Even in that he had found small kernels of deeper wisdom he had claimed for his own. Bit by bit his knowledge was growing.

He walked slowly up and down the rows, glancing at titles and authors, hoping to find something useful. He was so intent on his search that he failed to notice the dark, hooded figure that entered the archives and stood silently in the doorway, watching him.

———

Githany didn't say a word as the tall, broad-shouldered man wandered through the archives. He was physically imposing; even under his loose-fitting robes his muscles were obvious. Concentrating as she had been taught by the Jedi Masters before she'd betrayed them, she was able to feel the power of the dark side in him; he was remarkably strong in the Force. Yet he didn't carry himself like a man who was strong or powerful. Even here, away from the eyes of anyone else, he walked stooped over, his shoulders hunched.

This was what Sirak could do to a rival, she realized. This was what he could do to her if she went up against him and lost. Githany had every intention of challenging the Academy's acknowledged top student . . . but only once she was certain she could beat him in the dueling ring.

She had sought out Bane hoping to learn from his mistakes. Seeing him now, weak and broken, she realized she might be able to get more from him than just information. Normally she would be wary of allying herself with another student, particularly one as strong as Bane. Githany preferred to work alone; she knew all too well how devastating the consequences of unexpected betrayal could be.

But the man she saw was vulnerable, exposed. He was alone and desperate; he was in no position to betray anyone. She could control him, using him as necessary and disposing of him when she was done.

He took a book down from one of the shelves and walked slowly over to the tables. She waited until he had settled himself in and begun his reading. She took a deep breath and cast back her hood, letting her long tresses cascade down her shoulders. Then she put on her most seductive smile and moved in.

———

Bane carefully opened the pages of the ancient volume he had taken down from the archive shelves. It was titled *The Rakata and the Unknown*

World, and according to the date was nearly three thousand standard years old. But it wasn't the title or subject matter that had grabbed him. It was the author: Darth Revan. Revan's story was well known to Sith and Jedi alike. What intrigued Bane was the use of the *Darth* title.

None of the modern Sith used the *Darth* name, preferring the designation *Dark Lord.* Bane had always found this puzzling, but he had never asked the Masters about it. Perhaps in this volume by one of the last great Sith to use the designation he could find out why the tradition had fallen into disuse.

He had barely begun to read the first page when he heard someone approaching. He glanced up to see the Academy's newest apprentice— Githany—striding toward him. She was smiling, making her already remarkable features even more attractive. In the past Bane had only seen her from a distance; up close she literally took his breath away. As she swept into the seat beside him, the faintest whiff of perfume tickled his nose, causing his already racing heart to quicken its beat.

"Bane," she whispered, speaking softly even though there was no one else in the archives to be disturbed by their conversation. "I've been looking for you."

Her statement caught him by surprise. "Looking for me? Why?"

She placed a hand on his forearm. "I need you. I need your help against Sirak."

Her closeness, the brief contact with his arm, and her alluring fragrance sent his head spinning. It took him several moments to figure out what she meant, but once he did her sudden interest in him became obvious. News of his humiliation at the Zabrak's hands had reached her ears. She had come to see him in person, hoping she might learn something that would keep her from falling victim to a similar failure.

"I can't help you with Sirak," he said, turning away from her and burying his face in his book.

The hand on his forearm gently squeezed, and he looked up again. She had leaned in closer, and he found himself staring right into her emerald eyes.

"Please, Bane. Just listen to what I have to say."

He nodded, not sure if he'd even be able to speak while she was pressed so close against him. He closed the book and turned slightly in his chair to better face her. Githany gave a grateful sigh and leaned back slightly. He felt a small flicker of disappointment as her hand slipped from his arm.

"I know what happened to you in the dueling ring," she began. "I know everyone believes Sirak destroyed you; that somehow the defeat robbed you of your power. I can see you believe it, too."

Her face had taken on an expression of sorrow. Not pity, thankfully. Bane didn't want that from anyone—especially not her. But she showed genuine regret as she spoke.

When he didn't reply she took a deep breath and continued. "They're wrong, Bane. You can't just lose your ability to command the Force. None of us can. The Force is part of us; it's part of our being.

"I heard accounts of what you did to that Makurth. That showed what you were capable of. It revealed your true potential; it proved you were blessed with a mighty gift." She paused. Her gaze was intense. "You may believe you've squandered that gift, or lost it. But I know better. I can sense the power inside you. I can feel it. It's still there."

Bane shook his head. "The power may be there, but my ability to control it is gone. I'm not what I used to be."

"That's not possible," she said, her voice gentle. "How can you believe that?"

Though he knew the answer, he hesitated before replying. It was a question he had asked himself countless times while floating in the weightless fluid of the bacta tank. After his defeat he'd had plenty of opportunity to struggle with his failure, and he'd eventually come to realize what had gone wrong . . . though not how to fix it.

He wasn't sure he wanted to share his personal revelation with a virtual stranger. But who else was he going to tell? Not the other students; certainly not the Masters. And even though he hardly knew Githany, she had reached out to him. She was the only one to do so.

Exposing personal weakness was something only a fool or an idiot would risk here at the Academy. Yet the hard truth was that Bane had nothing left to lose.

"All my life I've been driven by my anger," he explained. He spoke slowly, staring down at the surface of the table, unable to look her in the eye. "My anger made me strong. It was my connection to the Force and the dark side. When Fohargh died—when I killed him—I realized I was responsible for my father's death. I killed him through the power of the dark side."

"And you felt guilty?" she asked, once again placing a soft hand on his arm.

"No. Maybe. I don't know." Her hand was warm; he could feel the heat radiating through the fabric of his sleeve to his skin underneath. "All I know is that the realization changed me. The anger that drove me was gone. All that was left behind was . . . well . . . nothing."

"Give me your hand." Her voice was stern, and Bane hesitated only an instant before reaching out. She clasped his palm with both her hands. "Close your eyes," she ordered, even as she shut her own.

In the darkness he became acutely aware of how tightly she had clenched his hand: squeezing the flesh so hard he could feel the beating of her heart through her palms. It was quick and urgent, and his already racing heart accelerated in response.

He felt a tingling in his fingers, something beyond mere physical contact. She was reaching out with the Force.

"Come with me, Bane," she whispered.

Suddenly he felt as if he were falling. No, not falling: diving. Swooping down into a great abyss, the black emptiness inside his very being. The chill darkness numbed his body; he lost all sensation in his extremities. He could no longer feel Githany's hands wrapped about his own. He didn't even know if she was still sitting beside him. He was alone in the freezing void.

"The dark side is emotion, Bane." Her words came to him from a long way off, faint but unmistakable. "Anger, hate, love, lust. These are what make us strong. Peace is a lie. There is only passion." Her words were louder now, loud enough to drown out the drumming of his heart. "Your passion is still there, Bane. Seek it out. Reclaim it."

As if in response to her words his emotions began to well up inside him. He felt anger. Fury. Pure, pulsing hatred: hatred of the other students for ostracizing him, hatred of the Masters for abandoning him. Most of all he hated Sirak. And with the hate came the hunger for revenge.

Then he felt something else. A spark; a flicker of light and heat in the cold darkness. His mind lunged out and grasped the flame, and for one brief instant he felt the glorious power of the Force burning through him once more. Then Githany let go of his hand and it was gone—snuffed out as if he had merely imagined it. But he hadn't. It was real. He'd actually felt it.

He opened his eyes warily, like a man waking from a dream he was afraid to forget. From the expression on Githany's face, he knew she must have felt something, too.

"How did you do that?" he asked, trying and failing to keep the desperation out of his voice.

"Master Handa taught me when I was studying under him in the Jedi order," she admitted. "I lost touch with the Force once, just as you have. I was still a young girl when it happened. My mind simply couldn't cope with something so vast and infinite. It created a wall to protect itself."

Bane nodded, remaining fervently silent so she could continue.

"Your anger is still there. As is the Force. Now you must break through the walls you've built around it. You have to go back to the beginning and learn how to connect with the Force once more."

"How do I do that?"

"Training," Githany answered, as if it was obvious. "How else does one learn to use the Force?"

The faint hope her revelation had kindled inside him died.

"The Masters won't train me anymore," he mumbled. "Qordis has forbidden it."

"I will train you," Githany said coyly. "I can share with you everything I learned from the Jedi about the Force. And whatever I learn about the dark side from the Masters I can teach to you, as well."

Bane hesitated. Githany was no Master, yet she had trained as a Jedi for many years. She probably knew much about the Force that would be new to him. At the very least he'd learn more with her help than without it. And yet something bothered him about her offer.

"Why are you doing this?" he asked.

She gave him a sly smile. "Still don't trust me? Good. You shouldn't. I'm only in this for myself. I can't defeat Sirak on my own. He's too strong."

"They say he's the Sith'ari," Bane muttered.

"I don't believe in prophecies," she countered. "But he has powerful allies. And the other Zabrak apprentices here are completely loyal to him. If I'm ever going to challenge him, I need somebody on my side. Somebody strong in the Force. Somebody like you."

Her reasons made sense, but there was still something bothering him. "Lord Qordis and the other Masters wouldn't approve of this," he warned her. "You're taking an awful risk."

"Risks are the only way to claim the rewards," she replied. "Besides, I don't care what the Masters think. In the end those who survive are the ones who look after themselves."

It took Bane a second to realize why her words sounded so familiar. Then he remembered the last thing Groshik had said to him before he left Apatros. *In the end each of us is in this alone. The survivors are those who know how to look out for themselves.*

"You help me regain the Force, and I'll help you against Sirak," he said, extending his arm. She clasped it in her own, then stood up to leave. Bane held his grip, forcing her to sit back down. There was a dangerous glint in her eye, but he didn't let go.

"Why did you leave the Jedi?" he asked.

Her expression softened, and she shook her head. She extended her free hand and placed it gently on his cheek. "I don't think I'm quite ready to share that with you."

He nodded. He didn't need to push her now, and he knew he hadn't earned the right yet.

The hand on his cheek fell away, and he let go of her arm. She gave him one last appraising glance, then rose and walked away with brisk, purposeful strides. She never glanced back, but Bane was content to follow her swaying hips until she was out of sight.

————

Githany knew he was watching her make her exit. Men always watched her; she was used to it.

All in all she felt the meeting had gone well. For a split second at the end—when he'd refused to let go of her arm—she had wondered if she'd underestimated him. His defiance had caught her off guard; she'd expected someone weak and subservient. But once she'd looked into his eyes she'd realized he was clinging to her out of desperation and fear. One single meeting and he already couldn't bear to let her go.

Even though she'd been with the Sith only a short time, the ways of the dark side came naturally to her. She felt no pity or sorrow for him; his vulnerability only made him easier to control. And unlike the Jedi, the Brotherhood of Darkness rewarded ambition. Each rival she brought low proved her worth and elevated her status within the Sith.

Bane would make the perfect tool to bring her rivals down, she thought. He was incredibly strong in the Force. Even stronger than she'd first realized. She'd been amazed at the power she'd felt inside him. And now he was completely wrapped around her finger. She just had to make sure he stayed that way.

She'd bring him along slowly, always keeping him just behind her own abilities. It was a dangerous game, but one she knew she could play well. Knowledge was power, and she alone controlled what knowledge he would gain. She'd teach him. String him along, twist him to her will, then use him to crush Sirak. And then, if she felt Bane was growing too powerful, she'd destroy him, too.

––––––––

Night had fallen over Korriban; sputtering torches cast eerie shadows in the halls of the Academy. Bane made his way through those halls wrapped in a black cloak, little more than a shadow himself.

It was forbidden for apprentices to leave their rooms after curfew—one of the steps Qordis had taken to reduce the "unexplained" deaths that seemed to be all too common in academies populated by rival students of the dark side. Bane knew that if he was caught, the punishment would be severe. But this was the only time he could act without fear of being seen by the other students.

He wound his way through the dormitory floor that housed the students until he reached the stairway leading to the upper levels and the Masters' quarters. He glanced quickly from side to side, peering into the flickering shadows cast on the stone walls. He paused, listening for the sound of anyone who might catch him in the halls. He had memorized the routes of the night sentries who patrolled the corridors after dark; he knew it would be almost an hour before they returned to this floor of the temple. But there were many other underlings—kitchen staff, cleaning staff, groundskeepers—who served the needs of the Academy and might be wandering about.

Hearing only silence, he proceeded up the stairs. He made his way quickly past the personal quarters of Qordis, somewhat relieved to see that even the Sith Master felt the need to close and lock his door at night. He continued on past another half a dozen doors, pausing only when he reached the entrance to the Blademaster's room.

He knocked once softly, careful not to wake the others. Before he could knock a second time, the door swung open to reveal the Twi'lek. For a split second Bane thought he must have been standing on the other side waiting for him. But that was impossible, of course. More likely the Blademaster's highly tuned reflexes had reacted to the first knock so quickly that he had already crossed the room and opened the door by the time the second rap came.

He was clad in a pair of pants, but his torso was bare, showing his scarred and tattooed chest. His confused expression confirmed Bane's assumption that the Blademaster hadn't known he was coming, and the speed with which he reached out to grab Bane and haul him inside the room confirmed his suspicions about his extraordinary reflexes.

Before Bane even realized what was happening, the door was closed and locked behind him, sealing the two of them together in the small, dark room. His host lit a small glow rod on a stand by the bed and turned to glare at his uninvited guest.

"What are you doing here?" he hissed, keeping his voice low.

Bane hesitated, uncertain how much to tell him. He had been thinking about Githany's offer, and what she had said to him. He had decided she was right: he had to look out for himself if he was to survive. That meant he had to be the one to bring Sirak down, not her.

"I want you to train me again," Bane whispered. "I want you to teach me all you know about the art of lightsaber combat."

Kas'im shook his head in response, but Bane thought he sensed a brief hesitation before he did so.

"Qordis will never allow it. He has made it very clear that none of the Masters is to waste any more time on you."

"I didn't think you answered to Qordis," Bane countered. "Aren't all the Masters equal in the Brotherhood of Darkness?"

It was a blatant appeal to the Blademaster's pride, and the Twi'lek easily recognized it for what it was. He smiled, amused at Bane's boldness. "True enough," he admitted. "But here on Korriban the other Lords defer to Qordis. It avoids . . . complications."

"Qordis doesn't have to know," Bane pointed out, taking heart in the fact that Kas'im hadn't flat-out refused him yet. "Train me in secret. We can meet at night on the temple roof."

"Why should I do this?" the Twi'lek asked, crossing his muscular arms. "You ask for the teachings of a Sith Lord, but what are you offering me in return?"

"You know my potential," Bane pressed. "Qordis has cast me aside. If I succeed now, he cannot take the credit. If I become an expert warrior for the Brotherhood, Lord Kaan will know you were the one who trained me. And if I fail, no one will ever suspect your part in this. You have nothing to lose."

"Nothing but my time," the other replied, scratching his chin. "You've lost your will to fight. You proved that against Sirak." His lekku were quivering ever so slightly, and Bane took it as a sign that, despite his words, he was seriously considering the offer.

Again, Bane hesitated. How much did he dare to reveal? He still planned to let Githany teach him about the Force and the ways of the dark side. But he had realized that if she was his only teacher, he would forever be beneath her in power. If he wanted to be the one to take out Sirak, he'd need Kas'im to help him . . . and he'd need to keep her from finding out.

"My will to fight is back," he finally said, deciding not to reveal Githany's involvement in his sudden resurrection. "I'm ready to embrace the power of the dark side."

Kas'im nodded. "Why are you doing this?"

Bane knew this was the final test. Kas'im was a Dark Lord of the Sith. His talent and skill were reserved for those who would one day rise up and join the Masters in the Brotherhood of Darkness. He wanted more than proof that Bane was truly ready for this. He wanted proof that Bane was worthy.

"I want revenge," Bane replied after careful consideration. "I want to destroy Sirak. I want to crush him like an insect beneath the heel of my boot."

The Blademaster smiled in grim satisfaction at his answer. "We will begin tomorrow."

15

Bane made his way down the hall with careful, measured steps. But though his pace was somber and subdued, his mood was one of elated triumph. In the weeks since his fateful meeting with Githany his situation had turned around completely.

As promised, she was teaching him. The first few sessions had gone slowly as she'd helped him work through his mind's fear of its own potential. Bit by bit the black veil had been torn away. Piece by piece she was helping him reclaim what he had lost, until once again he felt the power of the dark side coursing through his veins.

Since then the training had gone much more quickly. His hunger for revenge drove his studies. It fueled his ability to use the Force. It enabled him to understand the lessons that the Masters had taught Githany and she had then passed on to him. Despite being ignored by the instructors, he was once again learning everything the other apprentices were being taught—and learning it rapidly.

As another student passed Bane bowed his head, keeping up the pretense of subservience. It was important that none of the others suspected anything had changed. He kept his training with Githany hidden from everyone, even Kas'im . . . just as the Blademaster's training was kept secret from her.

Kas'im knew he was growing more formidable with the blade, but didn't know he was making similar strides in other areas. Githany could see his progress in unleashing his true potential with the Force, but wasn't aware he was also mastering the intricacies of lightsaber combat. As a result, they were both likely to underestimate the full scope of his abilities. Bane liked the subtle edge that gave him.

His days were now filled with study and training. In the darkest hours before morning's first light he would meet Kas'im to practice drills and techniques. He would meet with Githany in the archives in the midday, where she could share instruction with him without fear of interruption or discovery. And whenever he wasn't training with Kas'im or studying with Githany, he read the ancient texts.

Another apprentice approached and Bane moved to the side, projecting an image of weakness and fear to hide his remarkable metamorphosis. He waited until the other apprentice's footsteps faded away before heading down the stairs toward the tomes in the temple's lowest levels.

Qordis or one of the other Masters might have been able to pierce the false front he projected and sense his true power, were they not blinded by their own arrogance. They had dismissed him as a failure; now he was beneath their notice. Fortunately, this anonymity suited Bane just fine.

He hardly slept at all anymore. It seemed his body no longer needed sleep; it fed on his growing command of the dark side. An hour or two of meditation each day was enough to keep his body energized and his mind invigorated. He consumed knowledge with the appetite of a starving rancor, devouring everything he got from his secret mentors and always hungering for more. The Blademaster was amazed at his progress, and even Githany—despite her years of study with the Jedi—was hard-pressed to keep ahead of him. Everything he learned from them he supplemented with the wisdom of the ancients. On his first arrival he had sensed the value of the archives, only to turn his back on them as he had been drawn into the daily routine and intense lessons of the Academy. Now he understood that his initial instincts had been right after all: the knowledge contained in the yellowed parchments and leather-bound manuscripts was timeless. The Force was eternal, and though the Masters at the Academy now walked a different path than their Sith forebears had, they all sought answers in the dark side.

He smiled at the irony of this life. He was the outcast, the student Qordis had wanted left behind. Yet with Githany, Kas'im, and his own study of the archives, he was receiving far more education than any other apprentice on Korriban.

The truth would be revealed soon enough. When the time was right, Sirak would discover that he had underestimated Bane. They all would.

———

"Excellent!" Kas'im said as Bane blocked the Dark Lord's flurry and countered with one of his own. He didn't actually score a direct hit, but he did force the Blademaster to take a full step back under the fury of his assault.

Suddenly the Twi'lek leapt high in the air, spinning and twisting so he could lash down at Bane as he flipped over the top of him. Bane was ready, switching from offense to defense so smoothly it all seemed to be a single action. He parried both blades of Kas'im's weapon even as he ducked out of the way and rolled clear to safety.

He spun to face his foe, only to see that Kas'im had lowered his weapon, signifying the end of the lesson.

"Very good, Bane," the Twi'lek said, giving him a slight bow. "I thought you might be caught off guard by that move, but you were able to anticipate and defend it with near-perfect form."

Bane basked in his Master's praise, but he was sorry to know the session was over. He was breathing hard, his muscles glistening with sweat and twitching with adrenaline, yet he felt as if he could have continued fighting for hours. Sparring and drills had become much more than mere physical exertion for him now. Each movement, every strike and thrust, had become an extension of the Force acting through the corporeal shell of his flesh-and-bone body.

He longed to engage another opponent in the dueling ring. He hungered for the challenge of testing himself against the other apprentices. But it wasn't time. Not yet. He still wasn't good enough to defeat Sirak, and until he could take the Zabrak down he had to keep his rapidly developing talent hidden.

Kas'im tossed him a towel. Bane was pleased to see that the Twi'lek was sweating, too—though nowhere near as profusely as he was.

"Do you have anything you want me to work on for tomorrow?" Bane asked eagerly. "A new sequence? A new form? Anything?"

"You've moved far beyond sequences and forms," the Master told him. "In that last pass you broke off your attack in the middle of one sequence and came at me from a completely different and unexpected angle."

"I did?" Bane was surprised. "I . . . I didn't really mean to."

"That's what made it such a potentially devastating move," Kas'im explained. "You're letting the Force guide your blade now. You act without thought or reason. You're driven by passion: fury, anger . . . even hate. Your saber has become an extension of the dark side."

Bane couldn't help smiling, but then his brow furrowed in consternation. "I still couldn't get past your defenses," he said, trying to re-create the battle in his mind. No matter what he had tried to do, it seemed one side of the Twi'lek's twin-bladed weapon was always there to parry his attack. A seed of doubt crept into his mind as he recalled that Sirak used a similar style of weapon. "Does the double-bladed lightsaber give you an advantage?" he asked.

"It does, but not in the way you believe," Kas'im replied.

Bane was silent, waiting patiently for further explanation. After a few seconds his Master obliged him.

"As you already know, the Force is the real key to victory in any confrontation. However, the equation is not so simple. Someone well trained in lightsaber combat can defeat an opponent who is stronger in the Force. The Force allows you to anticipate your opponent's moves and counter them with your own. But the more options your foe has available, the more difficult it is to predict which will be chosen."

Bane thought he understood. "So the double-bladed weapon gives you more options?"

"No," Kas'im replied. "But you think it does, so the effect is the same."

For several seconds Bane thought about the Blademaster's strange words, trying to decipher them. In the end he had to admit defeat. "I still don't understand, Master."

"You know the single-bladed lightsaber well; you use it yourself and you've seen most of the other apprentices use it, as well. My double-bladed weapon seems strange to you. Unfamiliar. You don't fully understand what it can and cannot do." From the lack of impatience or exasperation in the Twi'lek's tone, Bane could tell this was something he hadn't been expected to grasp on his own.

"In combat, your mind tries to keep track of each blade separately, effectively doubling the number of possibilities. But the two blades are connected: by knowing the location of one, you are automatically aware of the location of the other. In actual practice, the double-bladed lightsaber is more limited than the traditional lightsaber. It can do more damage, but it is less precise. It requires longer, sweeping movements that don't transition well into a quick stab or thrust. Because the weapon is difficult to master, however, few among the Jedi—or even the Sith—understand it. They don't know how to attack or defend effectively against it. That gives those of us who use it an advantage over most of our opponents."

"Like Githany's whip!" Bane exclaimed. Githany eschewed traditional weaponry in favor of the very rare energy whip: just one of the many traits that made her stand out from the other apprentices. It operated on the same basic principles as a lightsaber, but instead of a steady beam, the energy of the crystals was projected in a flexible ribbon that would twist, turn, and snap in response to both Githany's physical motions and her use of the Force.

"Exactly. The energy whip is far less efficient than any of the lightsaber blades. However, nobody ever practices against the whip. Githany knows that her enemies' confusion at being confronted with the whip gives her an edge."

"By telling me this secret, you've given up your advantage," Bane noted, smiling as he pointed to Kas'im's double saber.

"Only to a very small degree," the Twi'lek said. "You now understand why an exotic weapon or unfamiliar style will be more difficult to defend against, but until you become an expert in a particular style, in the heat of combat your mind will still struggle to grasp its limitations."

Bane kept pressing, eager to turn this new insight into something practical he could use. "So by studying different styles, I could negate that advantage?"

"In theory. But time spent studying other styles is time away from mastering your own form. Your best progress will come from focusing more on yourself and less on your opponent."

"Then why even bother telling me all this?" Bane blurted out, frustrated.

"Knowledge is power, Bane. My purpose is to give you that knowledge. It is up to you to figure out how best to use it."

With those words the Blademaster left him, heading down the temple stairs to steal a few hours of sleep before the morning sun rose. Bane remained behind, wrestling with the lesson until it was time to meet Githany in the archives.

————

The smell of burning ozone wafted through the archives, filling Githany's nostrils as she watched Bane practicing his latest exercise. The room crackled and hissed as he channeled the energy of the Force and flung it about the room in great arcing bolts of blue-violet lightning.

Githany stood with Bane at the center of a maelstrom. A fierce wind swirled around them, tearing at her hair and the folds of her robe. It rocked and shook the bookshelves, knocking manuscripts to the floor and rifling their pages. The air itself was charged with electricity, causing her skin to itch.

In the midst of it all, Bane laughed, then raised his arms in triumph and launched another blast to ricochet off the far wall. Each time the lightning flared, the intensity of the flash burned Githany's retinas, causing her to shield her eyes. She noticed that Bane didn't look away: his eyes were wide and wild with the rush of power.

The thunder was almost deafening, and the storm was still building. If Bane wasn't careful, the echoes would reach the levels above the archives, revealing their secret training ground to the rest of the Academy.

Moving carefully, Githany reached out and touched his arm. He snapped his head around to face her, and the madness in his eyes almost made her recoil. Instead she smiled.

"Very good, Bane!" she shouted, trying to make her voice heard above the din. "That's enough for today!"

She held her breath in anticipation until he nodded and lowered his arms. Instantly she felt the power of the storm abating. Within a few seconds it was gone; only the mess it had made remained.

"I've—I've never felt anything like that before," Bane gasped, his face still showing his exhilaration.

Githany nodded. "It's a remarkable sensation," she agreed. "But you must be careful not to lose yourself in it." She was parroting the words of Master Qordis, who had taught her how to summon Force lightning only a few days earlier. However, she had never conjured anything even approaching the majesty of what Bane had just unleashed.

"You must maintain control, or you could find yourself swept up in the storm along with your enemies," she told him, trying to mimic the calm, slightly condescending tone the Masters used with their apprentices. She couldn't let him know that he had already surpassed her in this new talent. She couldn't let him know that she had felt the cold grip of fear clutching at her during his performance.

He looked around at the toppled shelves, taking in the books and scrolls strewn about the room. "We'd better clean this up before somebody sees it and wonders what happened in here."

She nodded again, and the two of them set to restoring the archives to their previous state. As they worked, Githany couldn't help but wonder if she had made a mistake in allying herself with Bane.

Only the top apprentices had been present when Qordis had taught them to use the dark side to corrupt the Force into a deadly storm. None of them—not even Sirak—had been able to create much more than a few jolts of energy that first day. Yet only an hour after being taught the technique by Githany, Bane had summoned enough energy to rip apart an entire room.

This wasn't the first time Bane had taken a lesson she had taught him and exceeded her achievements on his first attempt. He was far stronger in the Force than she had realized, and he seemed to be growing more so each day. She worried that she might lose her control over him.

She was careful, of course. She wasn't foolish enough to tell him everything she learned from the Sith Masters. Yet that didn't seem to be giving her an advantage over her pupil anymore. Sometimes she wondered if all his study of the ancient texts was actually giving him an advantage over *her.* Learning at the feet of a true Master should be more beneficial than reading theoretical works written thousands of years earlier . . . unless the current-day Sith were somehow flawed.

Unfortunately, she didn't know how she could test her theory. If she suddenly started spending hours each day in the archives, Bane would wonder what she was up to. He might decide that her teachings weren't as valuable as what he could learn on his own. He might decide she was expendable. And if it came down to a confrontation, she was no longer sure she could defeat him.

But Githany prided herself on her adaptability. Her initial plan of keeping him as a subservient apprentice was no longer viable. She still wanted Bane on her side, though; he could prove to be a powerful ally— beginning with his killing Sirak.

They worked in silence for the next hour, gathering up the books and straightening the shelves. By the time the room was restored to some semblance of order, Githany's back ached from the constant bending, lifting, and reaching. She collapsed into one of the chairs, giving Bane a tired smile.

"I'm exhausted," she said with an exaggerated sigh.

He made his way over and stepped behind her, placing his large hands on her shoulders, just at the base of her long neck. He began to massage the muscles, his caress surprisingly gentle for a man so large.

"Mmm . . . that feels nice," she admitted. "Where did you learn to do this?"

"Working the cortosis mines teaches you a lot about aches and pains," he replied, working his thumbs deep into her shoulder blades. She gasped and arched her back, then went slowly limp as her muscles melted beneath his touch.

He rarely spoke of his past life, though over their time together she had pieced most of it together. In contrast, she had always been much more guarded with what she revealed about herself.

"You asked me once why I left the Jedi," she mumbled, feeling herself drifting away on the rhythmic pressure of his fingers on her neck. "I never told you, did I?"

"We all have things in our past we would rather not revisit," he replied without stopping. "I knew you would tell me when you were ready."

She closed her eyes and let her head fall back as he continued to knead her shoulders.

"My Master was a Cathar," she said softly. "Master Handa. I studied under him for almost as long as I can remember; my parents gave me over to the order when I was just a toddler."

"I've heard the Jedi care little for the bonds that hold families together."

"They only care about the Force," she admitted after a moment's consideration. "Worldly attachments—friends, family, lovers—cloud the mind with emotion and passion."

Bane chuckled, a deep, low sound she felt thrumming through the tips of his fingers. "Passion leads to the dark side. Or so I've heard."

"It wasn't a joke to the Jedi. Especially not to Master Handa. The Cathar are known as a hot-blooded species. He was always warning me and Kiel about the dangers of giving in to our emotions."

"Kiel?"

"Kiel Charny. Another of Handa's Padawans. We often trained together; he was only a year older than me."

"Another Cathar?" Bane asked.

"No, Kiel was human. Over the years we became close. Very close."

The slight increase in the pressure of his touch told her that Bane had taken in the full meaning of her words. She pretended not to notice. "Kiel and I were lovers," she continued. "The Jedi are forbidden from forming such attachments. The Masters fear it will cloud the mind with dangerous emotions."

"Were you really attracted to him, or just to the idea of disobeying your Master?"

She thought about it for a long time. "A bit of both, perhaps," she said finally. "He was handsome enough. Strong in the Force. There was an undeniable attraction."

Bane only grunted in response. His hands had stopped massaging, and were now resting on her neck.

"Once we became lovers it didn't take long for Master Handa to find out. Despite all his preaching about controlling emotion, I could tell he was furious. He commanded us to set our feelings aside and forbade us from continuing our relationship."

Bane snorted his contempt. "Did he really think it would be that simple?"

"The Jedi see emotion as part of our bestial nature. They believe we must transcend our baser instincts. But I know passion is what makes us strong. The Jedi only fear it because it makes their Padawans unpredictable and difficult to control.

"Master Handa's reaction made me realize the truth. Everything the Jedi believed about the Force was a perversion of reality, a lie. I finally understood I would never reach my full potential under Master Handa. That was the moment I turned my back on the order and began planning my defection to the Sith."

"What about Kiel Charny?" He was rubbing her shoulders once again, but his hands were a little rougher now.

"I asked him to come with me," she confessed. "I told him we had a choice to make: the Jedi, or each other. He chose the Jedi."

The tension in Bane's hands eased ever so slightly. "Is he dead?"

She laughed. "Did I kill him, do you mean? No, he was still alive the last I heard. He may have died battling the Sith on Ruusan since then, but I didn't feel the urge to kill him myself."

"Then I guess your feelings for him weren't as strong as you thought."

Githany stiffened. It might have been a joke, but she knew there was truth in Bane's words. Kiel had been convenient. Though there was a physical attraction, he had become more than a friend mostly because of her situation: studying day and night with him under Master Handa; the pressure of living up to the unrealistic ideals of a Jedi; the stress of being trapped in the seemingly endless war on Ruusan.

Bane ringed her neck with his hands, his touch firm but not tight. He leaned down and whispered in her ear, causing her to shiver at the warmth and closeness of his breath. "When you finally betray me, I hope you care enough to try to kill me yourself."

She jumped up from the chair, slapping his hands away and spinning to face him. For a split second she saw a self-satisfied expression on his face. Then it was gone, replaced by a look of apologetic concern.

"I'm sorry, Githany. It was just a joke. I didn't mean to upset you."

"I opened up a painful part of my past, Bane," she said warily. "It's not something I want to make light of."

"You're right," he said. "I . . . I'll go."

She studied him as he turned and made his way out of the archives. He seemed genuinely sorry for what he'd said, as if he regretted hurting her. The perfect situation to give her the emotional leverage she had been looking for . . . if only she hadn't seen that flicker of something else.

Once he was gone she shook her head, trying to make sense of the situation. Bane looked like a great, hulking brute of a man, but there was wisdom and cunning beneath his heavy brow and bald skull.

She thought back on the last twenty minutes, trying to determine when she had lost control of the situation. There had been sparks between them, just as she had intended. Bane had done nothing to hide his desire for her; she'd sensed the heat as he caressed her neck. Still, something had gone wrong with her carefully planned seduction.

Was it possible she actually felt something for him?

Githany unconsciously bit her lower lip. Bane was powerful, intelligent, and bold. She needed him if she was going to eliminate Sirak. But he had a knack for surprising her. He kept challenging and defying her expectations.

She had to admit she found him intriguing in spite of this. Or perhaps because of it. Bane was everything Kiel hadn't been: ambitious, impulsive, unpredictable. Despite her best intentions, some small part of her was drawn to him. And that, more than anything else, made him a very dangerous ally.

16

High atop the temple of Korriban, beneath the light of a blood-red moon, two figures stood poised in silhouette: one human, one Twi'lek. A chill wind swept across the roof, but though both combatants had stripped off their robes to fight bare-chested, neither shivered from the cold. They might have been statues, still and hard as stone, were it not for the smoldering heat in their eyes.

Without warning the figures lunged, moving so swiftly it would have been impossible for an observer to say which one acted and which reacted. They met with a thunderous crash of their savage blades.

Even as he desperately fought to hold his ground, Bane was studying Kas'im carefully. He was acutely aware of every feint and strike, analyzing and memorizing each block, parry, and counterstrike. The Blademaster had said his time would be better spent focusing on improving his own technique, but Bane was determined to negate Sirak's advantage by absorbing all he could from the Twi'lek's double-bladed fighting style.

The exchange lasted well over a minute, with no break or lull in the action, until Bane spun away to regroup. He had sensed his attacks slipping into an unconscious pattern, and predictability was death against an opponent as skilled as Kas'im. He had fallen into that trap once the previous week. He wasn't about to make the mistake twice.

The two combatants faced each other once again, motionless save for their eyes, which flicked and darted in search of any sign they could use to gain some slight advantage.

Over the past month their training sessions had become less frequent but far more intense. Part of Bane believed Kas'im actually found value in sparring against him: the Blademaster had to grow bored crossing blades with apprentices and students so far beneath his own level.

Of course, Bane had yet to land a telling blow against his Master. But each time they sparred he felt as if he was getting closer and closer to a victory. Kas'im's form and technique were flawless, but Bane was aware that the slightest miscue was all the opening he needed.

Both fighters were breathing hard; the session had gone far longer than any before it. Their battles typically ended when the Twi'lek landed a scoring blow, disabling one of his student's limbs with the burning pelko venom. On this night, however, Kas'im had yet to land such a blow.

Kas'im charged forward, and the clang and clash of their weapons rang out over the rooftop in a sharp staccato rhythm. They stood toe-to-toe, hammering away at each other, neither giving ground or quarter. Ultimately Bane was forced to disengage, breaking off the melee before the Blademaster's superior skill broke down his defenses.

This time it was Bane who initiated the charge. Once again their training sabers rained down, and once again they broke apart with both combatants unscathed. This time, however, the outcome of the battle was no longer in doubt.

Bane hung his head and lowered his blade in an admission of defeat. The last pass he had held Kas'im off, but with each swing of his saber he had grown a microsecond slower. Fatigue was setting in. Even the Force couldn't keep his muscles fresh forever, and the seemingly endless duel had finally taken too great a toll. The Blademaster, on the other hand, had lost almost none of his speed and sharpness.

Bane doubted he would get through the next pass, and even if he did, the one after that would bring certain defeat. It was inevitable, so there was no point in pressing to the point that he actually suffered the pain of getting hit.

Kas'im seemed momentarily surprised at the concession, then nodded in acceptance of the victory. "You were smart to recognize that the battle was over, but I expected you to fight on until the end. There is little honor in surrender."

"Honor is a fool's prize," Bane replied, reciting a passage from one of the volumes he had recently read in the archives. "Glory is of no use to the dead."

After pondering his words for a moment, the Blademaster nodded. "Well said, my young apprentice."

Bane wasn't surprised that Kas'im didn't recognize the quote. The words had been written by Darth Revan nearly three millennia earlier. The Masters were as lax as the students when it came to studying the ancient writings. It seemed the Academy had turned its back on the past champions of the dark side.

True, Revan had eventually gone back over to the Jedi and the light after being betrayed by Darth Malak. Still, Revan and Malak had come within a hairsbreadth of wiping out the Republic. It was foolish to discount all they accomplished, and even more foolish to ignore the lessons that could be learned from them. Yet Qordis and the other Masters stubbornly refused to spend any time studying the history of the Sith order. Fortunately for Bane, it was a trait they passed along to their students.

It had given him an undeniable advantage over the other apprentices. If nothing else, it had shown him the true potential of the dark side. The archives were filled with accounts of incredible feats of power: cities laid waste, worlds brought low, entire star systems swallowed up when a Dark Lord caused the sun to go nova. Some of these tales were likely exaggerations, myths that had grown with each retelling before being set down on parchment. Yet they had their roots in truth, and that truth had inspired Bane to push himself farther and faster than he otherwise would have dared.

Thinking of Revan and the Sith Lords of the past brought to mind another question that had been troubling him for some time. "Master, why don't the Sith use the *Darth* title anymore?"

"It was Lord Kaan's decision," the Twi'lek told him as he toweled off. "The *Darth* tradition is a relic of the past. It represents what the Sith once were, not what we are now."

Bane shook his head, dissatisfied with the answer. "There has to be more to it than that," he said, stooping to retrieve the robe he had cast off at the start of their duel. "Lord Kaan wouldn't throw out the ancient traditions without justification."

"I see you won't be satisfied with the easy answer," Kas'im said with a sigh, pulling on his own robe. "Very well. To understand why the title is no longer used, you must understand what it truly represents. The *Darth* title was more than just a symbol of power; it was a claim of supremacy. It was used by those Dark Lords who have sought to enforce their will on the other Masters. It was a challenge—a warning to bow down or be destroyed."

Bane already knew this from his studies, but he didn't think it was wise to interrupt. Instead he crossed his legs and lowered himself into a sitting position, looking up at his Master and just listening.

"Of course, few of the Dark Lords would ever submit to another's will for long," Kas'im continued. "Wherever one of our order took up the *Darth* title, deception and betrayal were always close at hand to snatch it away. There can be no peace for a Master who dares to use the *Darth* name."

"Peace is a lie," Bane replied. "There is only passion."

Kas'im raised an eyebrow in exasperation. "*Peace* was a poor choice of words. What I meant was *stability*. Those Masters who chose the *Darth* title spent as much time guarding against their supposed allies as they did battling the Jedi. Kaan wanted to put an end to such wastefulness."

From where he sat, it seemed to Bane as if the Blademaster was trying to convince himself as much as his student.

"Kaan wants us to focus all our resources on our true enemy instead of one another," Kas'im asserted. "That is why we are all equals in the Brotherhood of Darkness."

"Equality is a myth to protect the weak," Bane argued. "Some of us are strong in the Force, others are not. Only a fool believes otherwise."

"There are other reasons the *Darth* title was abandoned," Kas'im insisted with just a hint of frustration. "It attracted the attention of the Jedi, for one. It revealed our leaders to the enemy; it gave them easy targets to eliminate."

Bane still wasn't convinced. The Jedi knew who the real leaders of the

Sith were; whether they called themselves *Darth* or *Lord* or *Master* made no difference. But he could tell the Twi'lek was uncomfortable with the discussion, and he knew enough to let the matter drop.

"Forgive me, Lord Kas'im," he said, bowing his head. "I meant no offense. I only sought to draw upon your wisdom to explain that which I could not understand myself."

Kas'im looked down at him with the same expression he had used when Bane had abruptly ended their duel a few moments earlier. Eventually, he asked, "So now you see the wisdom behind Lord Kaan's decision to end the tradition?"

"Of course," Bane lied. "He is acting for the good of us all." As he rose to his feet he thought, *Kaan's acting like one of the Jedi. Worrying about the greater good. Seeking to bring harmony and cooperation to our order. The dark side withers and dies under those conditions!*

Kas'im stared at Bane as if he wanted to say more. In the end, however, he let it drop. "That's enough for today," he said. In the distance the sky had turned the faint gray of first light; dawn was only an hour away. "The other students will be arriving for their training soon."

Bane bowed once more before taking his leave. As he made his way down the temple steps he realized that Kas'im, for all his skill with the lightsaber, couldn't teach him what he really needed to know. The Twi'lek had turned his back on the past; he had abandoned the individualistic roots of the Sith in favor of Kaan's Brotherhood.

The mysteries of the dark side's true potential were beyond his reach—and likely beyond the reach of every Master at the Academy.

———

Githany could sense that something was troubling Bane. He was barely paying attention as she shared what she had learned from the Sith Masters in her most recent lessons.

She didn't know what was bothering him. In truth, she didn't care. Unless it interfered with her own plans.

"Something's on your mind, Bane," she whispered.

Lost in his thoughts, he took a moment to react. "I'm . . . I'm sorry, Githany."

"What's wrong?" she pressed, trying to sound genuinely concerned. "What are you thinking about?"

He didn't answer at first; he seemed to be weighing his words carefully before speaking. "Do you believe in the power of the dark side?" he asked.

"Of course."

"And is it what you envisioned? Does the Academy live up to your expectations?"

"Few things ever do," she replied with a hint of a smile. "But I've learned a lot from Qordis and the others since I've come here. Things the Jedi could never have taught me."

Bane gave a derisive snort. "Most of what I've learned has come from these books." He waved a hand at the shelves.

She wasn't sure what to say next, so she said nothing.

"You once told me the Masters didn't know everything," Bane continued. "You meant the Jedi Masters at the time, but I'm starting to believe it applies to the Sith, as well."

"They were wrong to turn their backs on you," she said, seeing the opportunity she had long been waiting for. "But you have to place your blame where it belongs. We both know who is responsible for doing this to you."

"Sirak," he said, spitting out the name as if it were poison.

"He must pay for what he did to you, Bane. We've waited long enough. It's time."

"Time for what?"

Githany allowed the hint of a tremor into her voice. "Tomorrow morning I'm going to challenge him in the dueling ring."

"*What?*" Bane shook his head. "Don't be stupid, Githany! He'll destroy you!"

Perfect, she thought. "I have no choice, Bane," she said gravely. "I've already told you I don't believe in the legend of the Sith'ari. Sirak may be the top student in the school, but he's not invincible."

"He may not be the Sith'ari, but he's still too strong for you. You can't face him in the dueling ring, Githany. I've studied him; I know how good he is. You can't beat him."

She let his words hang in the air for a long time before dropping her head in defeat. "What other choice is there? We have to destroy him, and the only way is by facing him in the dueling ring."

Bane didn't reply right away; she knew he was mulling over another solution. They both knew there was only one possible course of action, one answer he would inevitably come to. They'd have to kill Sirak outside the ring. Assassinate him. It was a blatant violation of the Academy's rules, and the consequences would be severe if they were caught.

That's why it had to be Bane who came up with the idea. Once it was out there, Githany was confident she could maneuver him into performing the actual deed by himself. It was the perfect plan: get rid of Sirak and have Bane assume all the risk.

Later she could "accidentally" tip off the Masters about Bane's involvement . . . if she needed to. She wasn't so sure about that part of her plan anymore, though. She wasn't convinced she wanted to betray Bane. But she didn't mind manipulating him.

He drew in a long breath, gathering himself to speak. She prepared herself to give a very convincing—and very contrived—exclamation of surprise.

"You can't face Sirak in the ring, but I can," he said.

"What?" Githany's surprise was completely genuine. "He nearly beat you to death last time! He'll kill you for sure this time!"

"This time I intend to win."

The way he spoke made Githany realize she was missing something. "What's going on, Bane?" she demanded.

He hesitated a moment before admitting, "I've been training with Lord Kas'im in secret."

That made sense, she saw. In fact, she should have figured it out on her own. *Maybe you would have if, if you hadn't let Bane get to you,* she chided herself. *You knew you were starting to have feelings for him; you let them cloud your judgment.*

Out loud she said, "I don't like being played for a fool, Bane."

"Neither do I," he said. "I'm not stupid, Githany. I know what you wanted from me. I know what you expected me to say. I will get my revenge on Sirak. But I'm taking my own path."

Without even realizing it she had begun chewing on her lower lip. "When?"

"Tomorrow morning. Just as you said you were going to."

"But you know I wasn't serious."

"And you know I am."

Unbidden, Githany's finger began to twine itself in a lock of her hair. She pulled her arm down sharply as soon as she realized what she was doing.

Bane reached out a hand and let it rest gently on her shoulder. "You don't have to worry," he reassured her. "Nobody will know you were involved."

"That's not what I'm worried about," she whispered.

He tilted his head to one side, studying her closely to see if she was being honest with him. Much to her own surprise, she actually was.

Bane must have sensed her sincerity, because he leaned in close and kissed her softly on the lips. He drew back slowly, letting his hand slip from her shoulder. Without another word, he rose to his feet and made his way toward the door leading out of the archives.

She watched him go in silence, then at the last second called out, "Good luck, Bane. Be careful."

He stopped as if he'd taken a blaster bolt in the throat, his body rigid. "I will," he replied without looking back. And then he was gone.

Moments later Githany felt her face burning. She absently brushed away a tear coiling down her cheek, then brought her hand up slowly, staring in disbelief at the moisture smeared across her palm.

Disgusted at her own weakness, she wiped the tear away on the folds of her cloak. She stood up from the chair and threw her shoulders back, bracing her spine and holding her head high and proud.

So what if things hadn't quite gone according to plan? If Bane killed Sirak in the ring, her rival would still be dead. And if Bane failed, she could always find someone else to assassinate the Zabrak. It would all work out the same in the end.

But as she marched smartly from the room, part of her knew that wasn't true. No matter how this played out, things were going to be very different from anything she had imagined.

———

The morning sky was dark with storm clouds. Far in the distance thunder could be heard rumbling across the empty plains that separated the temple from the Valley of the Dark Lords.

Bane hadn't slept that night. After his confrontation with Githany, he had returned to his room to meditate. Even that had proved difficult; his mind was churning with too many thoughts to properly focus.

Memories of the gruesome beating he had suffered kept forcing themselves to the fore, dragging doubt and the fear of failure behind them. So far he'd managed to resist the whispers that threatened his resolve, and he'd stayed firm in his original plan.

The apprentices were gathering, some casting sour glances at the clouds overhead. The temple roof was completely exposed to the elements, but no matter how wet, cold, and miserable the students got, they knew the drills and challenges would not be canceled. A little rain was nothing to a Sith, Kas'im was fond of saying.

Bane found his place amid the throng in preparation for the group drills. The apprentices around him studiously ignored his presence. It had been this way ever since his loss to Sirak: he was shunned; he had become anathema to the other students. Though he trained with them in all the group sessions, it was as if he didn't really exist. He was a silent shadow lurking on the fringes, excluded in spirit if not in actual physical presence.

He scanned the crowd for Githany, but when he caught her eye she quickly looked away. Still, he found her presence reassuring. He believed she wanted him to succeed, or at least part of her did. He believed that some of what they felt for each other was more than just part of the game they had both been playing.

As the drills began he made a point not to look over at Sirak. He had studied the Zabrak in excruciating detail over the past months; anything he happened to notice now would only cause him to second-guess himself. Instead he focused on his own technique.

In the past he had purposefully worked errors and mistakes into his routines during the drills in order to keep his growing talent hidden from any student who might happen to cast a glance in his direction. Now, however, the time for secrecy was gone. After the challenges today everyone would know what he was capable of—or he would be dead and forgotten forever.

The rain began to come down. Slowly at first; fat, heavy drops spaced enough apart that he could make out the sound as each one landed. But then the clouds opened up and the rain came in a steady, pounding rhythm. Bane barely even noticed. He'd escaped inside himself, digging down deep to confront his fear. As his body went through the motions of basic attack and defense stances along with the rest of the class, he slowly transformed the fear into anger.

It was impossible for Bane to say how long the training session lasted: it seemed to go on forever, but in actual fact Kas'im probably kept it brief in light of the steady downpour soaking his charges. By the time it ended and the apprentices had gathered into the familiar circle around the dueling ring, the young man had turned his seething anger into white-hot hate.

As he had done the last time he challenged Sirak, he entered the ring before anyone else had a chance to act, pushing his way through the crowd from his position on the outermost edge. There was a murmur of surprise when the others recognized who had stepped forward.

He could feel the dark side churning inside him, a storm far fiercer than the one pelting down on him from the sky. It was time for his hate to set him free.

"Sirak!" he shouted, his voice carrying over the rising wind. "I challenge you!"

17

Bane's challenge hung in the air, as if the relentless sheets of rain had somehow trapped his words. Through the darkness of the storm he saw the crowd part and Sirak step slowly forward.

The Zabrak moved with a quiet confidence. Bane had hoped the unexpected challenge might unsettle his enemy. If he could rattle Sirak, catch him off guard or confuse him, he would have an advantage before the fight even began. But if his opponent felt anything at all, he kept it carefully masked beneath a cold, calm veneer.

Sirak handed his long, double-bladed training saber to Yevra, one of the Zabrak siblings who always seemed to follow in his wake, then stripped off his heavy, rain-soaked cloak. Beneath his robes he wore a simple pair of breeches and a sleeveless vest. Without a word he held out his balled-up cloak and Llokay, the other Zabrak, scampered out from the crowd and took it from him. Then Yevra scurried in to return his weapon to his open and waiting hand.

Bane peeled off his own cloak and let it drop to the ground, trying to ignore the cold sting of the rain on his naked torso. He hadn't really expected Sirak to be flustered by his challenge, but at the very least he'd hoped the Zabrak would be overconfident. There was, however, a ruthless efficiency in Sirak's preparation—an economy and precision of movement—that told Bane he was taking this duel very seriously.

Sirak was arrogant, but he was no fool. He was smart enough to understand that Bane wouldn't challenge him again unless he thought he had some plan for victory. Until he understood what that plan was, he wasn't going to take his opponent for granted.

Bane knew he could probably beat Sirak now. Like Githany, he didn't believe in the legend of a chosen one who would rise up from the Sith ranks: he was convinced Sirak was not, in fact, the Sith'ari. He didn't want just to beat him, however. He wanted to destroy him, just as Sirak had destroyed him in their last meeting.

But Sirak was too good; he'd never leave himself exposed the way Bane had. Not at first. Not unless Bane somehow lured him into it.

Across the ring Sirak assumed the ready position. His rain-slicked skin seemed to glow in the darkness: a yellow demon emerging from the shadows of a nightmare into reality's harsh light.

Bane leapt forward, opening the melee with a series of complex, aggressive attacks. He moved quickly . . . but not too quickly. There were gasps of astonishment from the crowd at his obvious and unexpected skill, though Sirak turned aside his assault easily enough.

In response to the inevitable counterattack, Bane let himself stagger back into a stumbling retreat. For a brief instant he saw his opponent overextend, leaving his right arm vulnerable to a strike that would have ended the contest right then and there. Fighting his own finely honed instincts, Bane held back. He'd worked too long and too hard to claim victory with a simple blow to the arm.

The battle continued in the familiar rhythm of combat, the ebb and flow of attack and defense. Bane made sure his attacks were effective yet crude, trying to convince his enemy that he was a dangerous but ultimately inferior opponent. Each time he warded off one of Sirak's charges he embellished his defensive maneuvers, transforming quick parries into long, clumsy swipes that seemed to keep the double-bladed saber at bay as much through blind luck as intention.

With the surge and swell of each exchange Bane gently prodded with the Force, testing and searching for a weakness he could exploit. It took only a few minutes until he recognized it. Despite his training, the Zabrak had no real experience in long, drawn-out battles—none of his opponents had ever lasted long enough to truly push him. Imperceptibly, the strikes of his foe became less crisp, the counters less precise, and the transitions less elegant as Sirak gradually wore down. The fog of exhaustion was slowly clouding his mind, and Bane knew it was only a matter of time until he made a crucial—and fatal—miscalculation.

Yet even though he was battling the Zabrak, Bane's real struggle was with himself. Time and again he had to pull back to keep from lunging through an opening presented by his enemy's increasingly desperate assault. He understood that the crushing victory he sought would only come through patience—a virtue not normally encouraged in followers of the dark side.

In the end his patience was rewarded. Sirak became more and more frustrated as he continually tried and failed to bring his bumbling, stumbling opponent down. As the prolonged physical exertion began to take its toll, his swings became wild and reckless, until he abandoned all pretense of defense in an effort to end the duel he sensed was slipping away from him.

When the Zabrak's desperation turned to hopelessness, every impulse in Bane screamed with the desire to take the initiative and end the fight. Instead he let the tantalizing closeness of Sirak's defeat feed his appetite for vengeance. The hunger grew with each passing second until it became a physical pain tearing away at his insides: the dark side filled him and he felt it on the verge of ripping him apart, splitting his skin and gushing out like a fountain of black blood.

He waited until the last possible second before unleashing the energy bottled up inside him in a tremendous rush of power. He channeled it through his muscles and limbs, moving so fast it seemed as if time had stopped for the rest of the world. In the blink of an eye he knocked the saber from Sirak's hand, sliced down to shatter his forearm, then spun through and brought his saber crashing into his opponent's lower leg. It splintered under the impact and Sirak screamed as a shard of gleaming white bone sliced through muscle, sinew, and finally skin.

For an instant none of the spectators was even aware of what had happened; it took their minds a moment to catch up and register the blur of action that had occurred so much quicker than their eyes could see.

Sirak lay crumpled on the ground, writhing in agony and clutching with his one good hand at the chunk of bone protruding from his shin. Bane hesitated a split second before moving in to finish him off, savoring the moment . . . and giving Kas'im the opportunity to intervene.

"Enough!" the Blademaster shouted, and the apprentice obeyed, freezing his saber even in the act of chopping it down on his helpless foe. "It's over, Bane."

Slowly, Bane lowered his saber and stepped away. The fury and focus that had turned him into a conduit of the dark side's unstoppable power was gone, replaced by a hyperconscious awareness of his physical surroundings. He was standing atop the temple roof in the middle of a raging storm, drenched in cold rain, his body half frozen.

He began to shiver as he cast about the ground for his discarded cloak. He picked it up but, finding it soaked completely through, didn't bother to put it on.

Kas'im stepped from the crowd, smoothly placing himself between Bane and the helpless Zabrak.

"You have witnessed an amazing victory today," he told the assembled throng, shouting to be heard above the pounding rain. "Bane's triumph was as much a result of his brilliant strategy as his superior skill."

Bane was barely listening to the words. He merely stood in the center of the ring, silent save for the chattering of his teeth.

"He was patient and careful. He didn't just want to defeat his opponent . . . he wanted to destroy him! He achieved dun möch—not because he was better than Sirak, but because he was smarter."

The Blademaster reached out a hand and placed it on Bane's bare shoulder.

"Let this be a lesson to you all," he concluded. "Secrecy can be your greatest weapon. Keep your true strength hidden until you are ready to unleash the killing blow."

He let go of Bane's shoulder and whispered, "You should go inside before you catch a chill." Then he turned to address the stunned Zabrak siblings standing at the edge of the circled students. "Take Sirak down to the medcenter."

As they moved forward to carry their moaning and barely conscious champion away, Bane turned toward the stairs. Kas'im was right: he had to get out of the rain.

Feeling strangely surreal, he walked stiffly toward the stairs that led into the warmth and shelter of the rooms below. The crowd parted quickly to let him through. Most of the other apprentices were staring at him with expressions of fear and open wonder, yet he barely noticed. He descended the steps to the temple's main floor, walking in a stupor that was broken only when he heard Githany call his name.

"Bane!" she shouted, and he turned to see her hurrying down the stairs after him. Her drenched hair was plastered haphazardly to her face and forehead. Her soaked clothes clung tightly to her body, accentuating every curve of her shapely form. She was breathing hard, though whether from excitement or the exertion of catching up to him he couldn't say.

He waited at the base of the stairs as she approached. She ran down the steps toward him, and for a moment he thought she would continue on into his arms. At the last second she stopped, however, and stood mere centimeters from him.

Githany took a second to catch her breath before she spoke. When she did, her words were harsh, though her voice was low. "What happened up there? Why didn't you kill him?"

Part of him had been expecting this reaction, though another part of him was hoping she had come to congratulate him on his victory. He couldn't help but feel disappointed.

"He sent me to the bacta tank in our first duel. Now I've done the same to him," he replied. "That's vengeance."

"That's foolish!" she shot back. "You think Sirak's going to just forget about this? He'll come after you again, Bane. Just like you came after him. That's the way this works. You missed your chance to put a permanent end to this feud, and I want to know why."

"My blade was raised for the killing blow," Bane reminded her. "Lord Kas'im stepped in before I could finish Sirak off. The Masters don't want one of their top students to end up dead."

"No," she said, shaking her head. "Your blade was raised, but Kas'im didn't stop you. You hesitated. Something held you back."

Bane knew she was right. He had hesitated. He just wasn't sure why. He tried to explain it . . . to Githany and himself. "I've already killed one foe in the ring. Qordis chastised me for Fohargh's death. He warned me not to let it happen again. I guess . . . I guess I was worried about what the Masters would do to me if I killed another apprentice."

Githany's eyes narrowed in anger. "I thought we'd finally stopped lying to each other, Bane."

It wasn't a lie. Not exactly. But it wasn't entirely accurate, either. He shifted uncomfortably, feeling guilty beneath her furious glare.

"You couldn't do it," she said, reaching out and jabbing him hard in the chest with her finger. "You felt the dark side swallowing you up, and you pulled back."

Now it was Bane's turn to get angry. "You're wrong," he snapped, swiping her accusing hand away. "I retreated from the dark side after I killed Fohargh. I know how that felt. This is different."

His words carried the righteous weight of truth. Last time he'd felt hollow inside, as if something had been taken from him. This time he could still feel the Force flowing through him in all its savage glory, filling him with its heat and power. This time the dark side remained his to command.

Githany wasn't convinced. "You still aren't willing to give yourself fully to the dark side," she said. "Sirak showed weakness, and you showed him mercy. That's not the way of the Sith."

"What do you know of the ways of the Sith?" he shouted. "I'm the one who's read the ancient texts, not you! You're stuck learning from Masters who've forgotten their past."

"Where in the ancient texts does it say to show compassion to a fallen enemy?" she asked, her voice dripping with scorn.

Stung by the words, Bane shoved her sharply backward and turned away. She took a quick step to balance herself, but kept her distance.

"You're just angry because your plan fell apart," he muttered, suddenly unwilling to face her. He wanted to say more, but he knew the rest of the students would be down soon. He didn't want anyone to see them talking together, so he simply walked away and left her standing there alone.

Githany followed him with cold, calculating eyes. She'd been impressed watching him toy with Sirak in the ring; he'd seemed invincible.

But when he'd failed to kill the helpless Zabrak, she was quick to recognize and identify what had happened. It was a flaw in Bane's character, a weakness he refused to recognize. Yet it was there nonetheless.

Once the passion of the moment had faded—once he was no longer driven by the dark side—his seething bloodlust had cooled. He hadn't even been able to kill his most hated enemy without provocation. Which meant he probably wouldn't be able to kill Githany if it ever came down to it.

Knowing this changed the nature of their relationship once again. Recently she'd begun to fear Bane, afraid that if he ever turned on her, she wouldn't be strong enough to stand against him. Now she knew that this would never happen. He simply wasn't capable of killing an ally without justification.

Fortunately, she didn't have the same limitations.

————

Bane was still thinking about what Githany had said later that night as he lay in bed, unable to sleep. Why hadn't he been able to kill Sirak? Was she right? Had he pulled back out of some misguided sense of compassion? He wanted to believe he had embraced the dark side, but if he had, he would have cut Sirak down without a second thought—no matter what the consequences.

However, it was more than this that was bothering him. He was frustrated by how he'd left things with Githany. He was undeniably drawn to her; she was hypnotic and compelling. Each time she brushed up against him he felt chills down his spine. Even when they were apart he often thought of her, memories lingering like the scent of her intoxicating perfume. At night her long black hair and dangerous eyes haunted his dreams.

And he honestly believed she felt something for him, too . . . though he doubted she would ever admit it. Yet as close as they'd become during their secret lessons together they'd never consummated their yearning. It just seemed wrong while Sirak was still the top apprentice at the academy. Defeating him had been the underlying goal for each of them; neither one had wanted any distractions from that goal. He was a common foe that united them to a single cause, but in many ways he had also been a wall keeping them apart.

Taking Sirak down should have leveled that wall into rubble. But Bane had seen the disappointment in Githany's face after the battle. He'd promised to kill their enemy, and she'd believed in him. Yet in the end his actions had proved he wasn't up to her expectations, and the wall between them had suddenly grown much, much stronger.

Someone knocked softly at the door of his chamber. It was well after curfew; none of the apprentices had any reason to be in the halls. He could think of only one person who might be wandering the halls at this hour.

Leaping from his bed he crossed the floor in one quick stride and yanked open the door. He quickly masked his disappointment at seeing Lord Kas'im standing beyond the threshold.

The Blademaster stepped through the open door without waiting for an invitation; he gave Bane a nod that told him to close it once he was inside. Bane did as he was bidden, wondering at the purpose of the unannounced late-night visit.

"I have something for you," the Twi'lek said, brushing away the folds of his cloak and reaching for his lightsaber on his belt. No, Bane realized. Not *his* lightsaber. The handle of Kas'im's weapon was noticeably longer than most, allowing it to house two crystals, one to power each blade. This hilt was smaller, and it was fashioned with a strange curve, giving it a hooked appearance.

The Blademaster ignited the lightsaber: its single blade burned a dark red. "This was the weapon of my Master," he told Bane. "As a young child I would watch for hours as my Master performed his drills. My earliest memories are of dancing ruby lights moving through the sequences of battle."

"You don't remember your parents?" Bane asked, surprised.

Kas'im shook his head. "My parents were sold in the slave markets of Nal Hutta. That's where Master Na'daz found me. He noticed my family on the auction blocks; perhaps he was drawn to them because we were Twi'leks like himself. Even though I was barely old enough to stand, Master Na'daz could sense the Force in me. He purchased me and took me back to Ryloth, to raise me as his apprentice among our own people."

"What happened to your parents?"

"I don't know," Kas'im replied with an indifferent shrug. "They had no special connection to the Force, so my Master saw no reason to purchase them. They were weak, and so they were left behind."

He spoke casually, as if the knowledge that his parents had lived and probably died as slaves in the service of the Hutts had no effect on him whatsoever. In a way his apathy was understandable. He'd never known his parents, so he had no emotional ties to them, good or bad. Bane briefly wondered how his own life might have been different if he had been raised by someone else. If Hurst had been killed in the cortosis mines when he was just an infant, would he still have ended up here at the Academy on Korriban?

"My Master was a great Sith Lord," Kas'im continued. "He was particularly adept in the arts of lightsaber combat—a skill he passed on to me. He taught me how to use the double-bladed lightsaber, though as you can see he preferred a more traditional design for himself. Except for the handle, of course."

The blade flickered out of existence as he shut off the weapon and tossed it to Bane, who caught it easily, wrapping his hand around the hooked handle.

"It feels strange," he muttered.

"It requires a minor variation in your grip," Kas'im explained. "Hold it more in the palm, farther away from the fingertips."

Bane did as instructed, letting his body grow accustomed to the odd heft and balance. Already his mind was beginning to run through the implications of the new grip. It would give the wielder more power on his overhand strikes, and it would change the angle of the attacks by the merest fraction of a degree. Just enough to confuse and disorient an unsuspecting opponent.

"Some moves are more difficult with this particular weapon," Kas'im warned. "But many others are far more effective. In the end I think you'll find this lightsaber will suit your personal style quite well."

"You're giving this to me?" Bane asked incredulously.

"Today you proved you were worthy of it." There was just a hint of pride in the Blademaster's voice.

Bane ignited it, listening to the sweet hum of the power pack and the crackling hiss of the energy blade. He performed a few simple flourishes, then abruptly shut it off.

"Does Qordis approve?"

"The decision is mine, not his," Kas'im stated. He almost sounded offended. "I haven't held on to this blade for ten years just so Qordis can decide who I give it to."

Bane answered with a respectful bow, fully aware of the great honor that Kas'im had just bestowed upon him. To fill the uncomfortable silence that followed he asked, "Your Master gave you this when he died?"

"I took it when I killed him."

Bane was so stunned that he couldn't cover his reaction. The Blademaster saw it and smiled slightly.

"I had learned everything I could from Master Na'daz. As strong as he was in the dark side, I was stronger. As skilled as he was with the lightsaber, I became better."

"But why kill him?" Bane asked.

"A test. To see if I was as strong as I believed. This was before Lord Kaan rose to power; we were still trapped in the old ways. Sith versus Sith, Master versus apprentice. Foolishly pitting ourselves against one another to prove our dominance. Fortunately, the Brotherhood of Darkness put an end to all that."

"Not completely," Bane muttered, thinking of Fohargh and Sirak. "The weak still fall to the strong. It is inevitable."

Kas'im tilted his head to the side, trying to gauge the meaning behind his words. "Don't allow yourself to be blinded by this honor," he warned. "You are not ready to challenge me, young apprentice. I have taught you everything you know, but I haven't taught you everything *I* know."

Bane couldn't help but smile. The notion of facing Kas'im in a real fight was preposterous. He knew he was no match for the Blademaster. Not yet. "I will keep that in mind, Master."

Satisfied, Kas'im turned to go. Just before Bane closed the door behind him he added, "Lord Qordis wants to see you first thing in the morning. Go to his chambers before the morning drills."

Even the sobering prospect of meeting with the Academy's grim overseer couldn't dampen Bane's elated spirit. As soon as he was alone in his room he reignited the lightsaber and began practicing his sequences. It was many hours before he finally put the weapon away and crawled wearily into bed, all thoughts of Githany long banished from his mind.

––––––––

The morning's first light found Bane at the door leading into the private quarters of Lord Qordis. It had been many months since he had last been here. At that time he had been chastised for killing Fohargh. This time he had severely injured one of the top students of the Academy—one of Qordis's personal favorites. He wondered what was in store for him.

Summoning his courage, he knocked once.

"Enter," came the voice from within.

Trying to ignore a feeling of trepidation, Bane did as he was told. Lord Qordis was in the center of the room kneeling on his meditation mat. It was almost as if he hadn't moved: his position was exactly the same as it had been at their last meeting.

"Master," Bane said, making a low bow.

Qordis didn't bother to rise. "I see you have a lightsaber on your belt."

"Lord Kas'im gave it to me. He felt I earned it with my latest victory in the ring." Bane suddenly felt very defensive, as if he was under attack.

"I have no wish to contradict the Blademaster," Qordis replied, though his tone suggested the opposite. "However, though you now carry a lightsaber, do not forget that you are still an apprentice. You still owe your obedience and allegiance to the Masters here at the Academy."

"Of course, Lord Qordis."

"The way in which you defeated Sirak has left quite an impression on the other students," Qordis continued. "They will look to emulate you now. You must set an example for them."

"I will do my best, Master."

"That means your private sessions with Githany must end."

A chill washed over Bane. "You knew?"

"I am a Sith Lord, and Master of this Academy. I am not a fool, and I am not blind to what is happening within the walls of the temple. I tolerated such behavior when you were an outcast because it did no harm to the other apprentices. Now, however, many of the students will be watching you closely. I do not want them following your path and trying to train one another in a misguided attempt to duplicate your success."

"What will happen to Githany? Will she be punished?"

"I will speak with her just as I am speaking with you. It must be clear to the rest of the apprentices that the two of you are not training together in private. That means you cannot see her anymore. You must avoid all contact except in the group lessons. If you both obey me in this, there will be no further consequences."

Bane understood Lord Qordis's concerns, but he felt the solution went too far. There was no need to cut him off from Githany so completely. He wondered if the Masters knew of his attraction to her. Did they fear she would be a distraction?

No, he realized, that wasn't it. This was simply about control. Bane had defied Lord Qordis; he had succeeded despite being shunned by the rest of the Academy. Now Qordis wanted to claim ownership of Bane's accomplishments.

"That is not all," Qordis continued, interrupting Bane's thoughts. "You must also put an end to your study of the archives."

"Why?" Bane burst out, surprised and angry. "The manuscripts contain the wisdom of the ancient Sith. I have learned much about the ways of the dark side from them."

"The archives are relics of the past," Qordis countered sharply. "They are from a time that has long since vanished. The order has changed. We have evolved beyond what you learned in those musty scrolls and tomes. You would understand this if you had been studying with the Masters instead of rushing off on your own path."

You're the one who forced me down that path, Bane thought. "The Sith may have changed, but we can still build on the knowledge of those who came before us. Surely you understand that, Master. Why else would you have rebuilt the Academy on Korriban?"

There was a flash of anger in the Dark Lord's eyes. He obviously didn't like being challenged by one of his students. When he spoke, his voice was cold and menacing. "The dark side is strong on this world. That is the only reason we chose to come here."

Bane knew he should let the matter drop, but he wasn't ready to back down. This was too important. "But what about the Valley of the Dark Lords? What about the tombs of all the dark Masters buried on Korriban, and the secrets hidden inside them?"

"Is that what you seek?" Qordis sneered. "The secrets of the dead? The Jedi pillaged the tombs when Korriban fell to them three thousand years ago. Nothing of value remains."

"The Jedi are servants of the light," Bane protested. "The dark side has secrets they will never understand. There may be something they missed."

Qordis laughed, a harsh and scornful bark. "Are you really so naïve?"

"The spirits of powerful Sith Masters are said to linger in their tombs," Bane insisted, stubbornly refusing to be cowed. "They appear only to those who are worthy. They would not have revealed themselves to the Jedi."

"Do you really believe ghosts and spirits still linger in their graves, waiting to pass on the great mysteries of the dark side to those who seek them out?"

Bane's thoughts turned back to his studies. There were too many such accounts documented in the archives to be mere legend. There had to be some truth to it.

"Yes," he answered, though he knew it would infuriate Qordis even more. "I believe I can learn more from the ghosts in the Valley of the Dark Lords than the living Masters here at the Academy."

Qordis leapt to his feet and slapped Bane hard across the face, his talon-like fingernails drawing blood. Bane held his ground; he didn't even flinch.

"You are an impudent fool!" his Master shouted. "You worship those who are dead and gone. You think they hold some great power, but they are nothing but dust and bone!"

"You're wrong," Bane said. He could feel the blood welling up in the scratches on his face, but he didn't reach up to wipe it away. He simply stood still as stone in front of his seething Master.

Even though Bane didn't move, Qordis took half a step back. When he spoke, his voice was more composed, though it still dripped with anger. "Get out," he said, extending a long, bony finger toward the door. "If you value the wisdom of the dead so much, then go. Leave the temple. Go to the Valley of the Dark Lords. Find your answers in their tombs."

Bane hesitated. He knew this was a test. If he apologized now—if he groveled and begged the forgiveness of his Master—Qordis would probably let him stay. But he knew Qordis was wrong. The ancient Sith were dead, but their legacy remained. This was his chance to claim it as his own.

He turned his back on Lord Qordis and marched from the room without a word. There was no point in continuing the argument. The only way he could win was by finding proof. And he wasn't going to find it standing here.

18

Bane had missed the morning practice session. It wasn't hard for Kas'im to figure out who was responsible for his absence.

He didn't bother to knock on Lord Qordis's door; he simply used the Force to burst apart the lock, then kicked it open. Unfortunately, the element of surprise he'd been hoping for had been lost.

Qordis had his back to the door, examining one of the magnificent tapestries that hung beside his oversized bed. He didn't turn when the Blademaster burst in; he didn't react at all. Which meant he'd been expecting the intrusion.

Kas'im gestured violently with his hand, and the door slammed shut. What he was about to say wasn't for the ears of the students. "What in blazes did you do, Qordis?"

"I assume you are referring to apprentice Bane" came the too-casual reply.

"Of course I kriffing mean Bane! No more games, Qordis. What did you do to him?"

"*To* him? Nothing. Not in the way you're thinking. I merely tried to reason with him. Tried to make him understand the necessity of working within the structure of this institution."

"You manipulated him," Kas'im said with a sigh of resignation. He knew Qordis had no fondness for Bane. Not with Lord Kopecz—his longtime rival—being the one who'd brought him here. The Blademaster realized he should have warned the young apprentice to be on his guard.

"You twisted his mind somehow," he continued, trying to draw out a reaction. "You forced him down a path you wanted him to take. A path of ruin."

There was no immediate reply. Tired of staring at Qordis's back, he stepped forward and reached up to grab the taller man by the shoulder, whirling him around to face him. "Why, Qordis?"

In the first brief second that the overseer of the Academy was spun around, Kas'im caught a glimpse of uncertainty and confusion in the gaunt, drawn features. Then those features twisted into a mask of rage, dark eyes burning in sunken sockets. Qordis slapped Kas'im's hand away.

"Bane brought this on himself! He was willful! Obsessed with the past! He is of no use to us until he accepts the teachings of this Academy!"

Kas'im was taken aback: not by the sudden outburst, but by the unexpected glimpse of uncertainty that had preceded it. Suddenly he wondered if maybe the meeting hadn't gone exactly as planned. Perhaps Qordis had tried to manipulate Bane and failed. It wouldn't be the first time they'd underestimated their unusual apprentice.

Now Kas'im felt more curious than angry. "Tell me what happened, Qordis. Where is Bane now?"

Qordis sighed, almost regretful. "He's gone into the wastelands. He's heading for the Valley of the Dark Lords."

"What? Why would he do that?"

"I told you: he's obsessed with the past. He believes there are secrets out there that will be revealed to him. Secrets of the dark side."

"Did you warn him of the dangers? The pelko swarms? The tuk'ata?"

"He never gave me a chance. He wouldn't have listened anyway."

That much, at least, Kas'im believed. Yet he wasn't sure if he trusted the rest of Qordis's story. The Master of the Academy was subtle, crafty. It would be just like him to trick someone into venturing through the deadly Valley of the Dark Lords. If he wanted to eliminate Bane without being held accountable, this would be one of the ways to do it—except for one small thing.

"He's going to survive," Kas'im stated. "He's stronger than you know."

"If he survives," Qordis replied, turning back to the tapestry, "he will learn the truth. There are no secrets in the valley. Not anymore. Everything of value has been taken: stripped away first by Sith seeking to preserve our order, and later by Jedi seeking to wipe it out. There is nothing left in the tombs but hollow chambers and mounds of dust. Once he sees this for himself, he will give up his foolish idealization of the ancient Sith. Only then will he be ready to join the Brotherhood of Darkness."

The conversation was over; that much was clear. Qordis's words made sense, if this was all part of a larger lesson to make Bane finally abandon the old ways and accept the new Sith order and Kaan's Brotherhood.

Yet as he turned and left the room, Kas'im couldn't shake the feeling that Qordis was rationalizing events after the fact. Qordis wanted others to believe he had been in control the whole time, but the haunted look the Blademaster had glimpsed gave evidence to the real truth: Qordis had been scared by something Bane had done or said.

That thought brought a smile to the Twi'lek's lips. He had every confidence Bane would survive his journey into the Valley of the Dark Lords. And he was very interested to see what would happen when the young man returned.

————

Sirak was moving gingerly. He'd spent the past thirty-six hours in a bacta tank, and though his injuries were completely healed, his body still instinctively reacted to the memories of the wounds inflicted by Bane's saber. Slowly, he gathered up his personal effects, anxious to return to the familiar surroundings of his own room and leave the solitude of the med-center behind.

One of the med droids floated in, bringing him a pair of pants, a shirt, and a dark apprentice's robe. The clothes smelled of disinfectant; it was common practice to sterilize everything before bringing it into the med-center. The garments fit, but he knew as soon as he put them on that they had never been worn before.

He hadn't seen a single being other than the med droids since being carried unconscious from the dueling ring. Nobody had come to check up on him while he'd floated in the healing fluid: not Qordis, not Kas'im, not even Llokay or Yevra. He didn't blame them.

The Sith despised weakness and failure. Whenever apprentices lost in the dueling ring, they were left alone with the shame of their defeat until strong enough to resume their studies. It happened to everyone sooner or later . . . except it had never before happened to Sirak.

He had been invincible, untouchable—the top apprentice in every discipline. He'd heard the rumors and the whispers. They called him the Sith'ari, the perfect being. Only they wouldn't be calling him the Sith'ari now. Not after what Bane had done to him.

He turned to the door and found Githany standing there, watching him.

"What do you want?" he asked warily.

He knew who she was, though he'd never actually spoken to her. On the day of her arrival he'd identified her as a potential threat. He'd watched her, and he'd seen her watching him, each measuring and gauging the other, trying to determine who had the upper hand. Sirak was wary of all potential challengers, or so he had thought—until the one student he'd feared the least had brought him down.

"I came to speak to you," she answered. "About Bane."

He twitched involuntarily at the name, then cursed himself for his re-action. If Githany had noticed, she gave no indication.

"What about him?" he asked curtly.

"I'm curious as to what your plans are now. How are you going to han-dle this situation?"

It was a struggle to summon up his old arrogance, yet somehow he managed a satisfactory sneer. "My plans are my own."

"Are you going to seek revenge?" she pressed.

"In time, perhaps," he finally admitted.

"I can help you."

She took a step farther into the room. Even in that single step Sirak could see that she moved with the sensual grace of a Zeltron veil dancer.

He narrowed his eyes suspiciously. "Why?"

"I helped Bane defeat you," she said. "I recognized his potential from the moment I first saw him. When Qordis and the other Masters turned their backs on him, I secretly taught him their lessons in the Force. I knew the dark side was strong in him. Stronger than in me. Stronger than in you. Maybe even stronger than in the Masters themselves."

Sirak couldn't see the point of her story. "You still haven't answered my question. You got what you wanted out of Bane. Why help me now?"

She shook her head sadly. "I was wrong about Bane. I thought if I helped him grow stronger, he would embrace the dark side. Then I could learn from him and gain power of my own. But he is incapable of embracing the dark side. Everyone else believes his triumph over you was a great victory. Only I recognized it as a failure."

She was toying with him. Mocking him. And he didn't like it. "No one ever beat me in the dueling ring before Bane!" he snapped. "How can you call him a failure?"

"You're still alive," she said simply. "When the moment came to strike you down and end your life, he hesitated. He couldn't bring himself to do it. He was weak."

Intrigued, Sirak didn't respond right away. Instead he waited for her to elaborate.

"He plotted and planned for months to take his revenge on you," she continued. "His hate gave him the strength to surpass you . . . and at the last instant he showed mercy and let you live."

"*I* left *him* alive at the end of our first duel," Sirak reminded her.

"That was no act of mercy—it was an act of contempt. You thought you had utterly destroyed him. If you knew he would rise up to one day challenge you again, you would have taken his life regardless of the rules of the Academy.

"You underestimated him. A mistake I know you won't make again. But Bane does not underestimate you. He knows you are powerful enough to represent a true threat. Yet still he left you alive, knowing you would one day seek revenge against him. He is either a weakling or a fool," she concluded, "and I want no part of either."

There was some truth in what she said, but Sirak still wasn't convinced. "You change allegiances too quickly, Githany. Even for a Sith."

She was silent for a long time, trying to figure out how to answer him.

Then suddenly she looked down at the floor, and when she looked up her eyes were filled with shame and humiliation.

"It was Bane who ended this alliance, not me," she admitted, nearly choking on the words. "He abandoned me," she continued, making no attempt to hide her bitterness. "He left the Academy. He never told me why. He never even said good-bye."

Suddenly everything fell into place. Sirak understood her sudden desire to join with him in a partnership against her former ally. Githany was used to being in control. She was used to being in charge. She was used to being the one who ended things. And she didn't like being on the other side.

It was like the old Corellian expression: *Fear the wrath of a female scorned.*

"Where did he go?" he asked.

"The students are saying Qordis sent him out into the Valley of the Dark Lords."

Sirak nearly blurted out, *Then he's dead already!* but at the last second he remembered her admonishment not to underestimate Bane again. Instead he said, "You expect he will return."

"I'm certain of it."

"Then we will be ready," Sirak promised. "When he comes back, we will destroy him."

————

As Bane marched across the scorched sand of Korriban's wastelands, he noticed the sun sinking quickly below the horizon. He'd been walking for hours beneath its heat; the small city of Dreshdae and the temple that towered over it were far behind him. They had been reduced to mere specks on the horizon; if he was to look back, he would have just been able to make them out in the fading light.

He didn't look back. He marched doggedly onward. The blazing heat hadn't slowed him; neither would temperatures that were about to drop to near freezing with the setting of the sun. Physical discomfort—cold, heat, thirst, hunger, fatigue—had no significant effect on him, sustained as he was by the power of the Force.

Still, he was troubled. He remembered the first time he'd set foot on Korriban. He'd sensed the power of the world: Korriban was alive with the dark side. Yet the feeling had been faint and distant. During his time at the Academy he'd grown so accustomed to the almost subconscious hum that he barely even noticed it anymore.

When he'd left the temple and the starport behind, he'd expected that feeling to grow stronger. With each step drawing him closer to the Valley of the Dark Lords he thought he'd feel the dark side growing in its intensity.

Instead he'd felt nothing. No noticeable change at all. He was only a few kilometers away from the valley's entrance; he could see the shaded outlines of the nearest tombs carved from the stone walls. And still the dark side was no stronger than a hollow echo, no more than the lingering memory of distant words spoken in the distant past.

Pushing his doubts and reservations aside, he redoubled his pace. He wanted to reach the valley before complete darkness. He had grabbed a handful of glow rods before leaving the Academy; he could use them to find his way if necessary. Unfortunately, their light would act like a beacon in the darkness, signaling his location to anyone—or any*thing*. With his new lightsaber at his side he was confident he could survive almost any encounter, but there were things that lurked near the tombs whose attention he would rather not attract.

The last few rays of light still hung in the air when he finally reached his destination. The Valley of the Dark Lords lay sprawled out before him, hidden beneath the cover of twilight's gloom. He briefly considered stopping for the night and making camp until dawn, then rejected the idea. Day or night would make no difference once he was inside the tombs: he'd have to use the glow rods no matter what time it was. And now that he was finally here he was too eager to see what he could find to put it off any longer.

He chose the nearest temple, the only one he could actually make out in the dim light. Like all the tombs, this one had been dug out from the high stone cliffs that boxed in the valley on either side. The grand archway at the entrance had been built out from the cliff face, but the chambers that housed the remains of the Dark Lord interred within wound their way deep into the rock.

As he got closer, he could make out intricate designs carved into the archway. Something was written across the top in letters he didn't recognize. He guessed that the craftsmanship would have been awe inspiring at one time, but eons of desert winds had worn away most of the detail.

He paused on the threshold, taking in the air of forbidden mystery that surrounded the entrance to the tomb. He still sensed no change in the Force, however. Stepping up to the entrance, he was shocked to see that the great stone slab of a door had been split asunder. He ran his fingers along the edges of the fissure. Smooth. Worn. Whoever had broken the door had done it long ago.

Bane stood up straight and marched boldly through the shattered portal. He made his way down the long entrance tunnel, moving slowly through the gloom. Half a dozen meters in, the darkness became absolute, so he pulled out a glow rod and activated it.

An eerie blue light filled the tunnel, sending a small swarm of deadly pelko bugs scurrying for refuge beyond the dim circle of illumination. They had been stalking him, closing in from all sides. He could still sense them there, lurking in the shadows all around him, but he wasn't afraid. After all, it wasn't the light keeping them at bay.

Pelko bugs, like many of the creatures indigenous to Korriban, were attuned to the Force. They would have sensed Bane's arrival even before he entered the tomb; his power would inevitably draw them in. Yet it also kept them and their paralyzing spines at a safe distance. Instinctively, the pelko bugs could sense the sheer scope of his power; they were wary of him. They wouldn't come close enough to actually attack him, making them nothing more than a nuisance. Larger predators, like the tu'kata, might pose a real threat. But he'd deal with them if and when the time came.

Right now he was more concerned with the potential dangers the builders of the tomb might have left behind. Sith mausoleums were notorious for their fiendishly lethal traps. Bane reached out with the Force, carefully probing the walls, ground, and ceiling in front of him for anything out of the ordinary. He was relieved—and slightly disappointed—to discover nothing. Part of him had hoped he would stumble across an undiscovered chamber, something the Jedi had missed.

He continued down the tunnel, winding his way past various chambers where the wealth and treasures would have been buried with the deceased Dark Lord—along with his still-living lesser servants. The rooms held no interest for him; he wasn't a grave robber. Instead he continued deeper and deeper until he reached the burial chamber itself.

The pelko bugs matched his progress, endlessly circling just beyond the blue illumination cast by his glow rod. He could hear the high-pitched clicking—*skreek skreek skreek*—of the frustrated swarm: powerless to assail their prey, yet irresistibly caught up in the wake of his passing.

The burial chamber was easily identifiable by the enormous stone sarcophagus in the center of the room, resting atop a small stone pedestal. It was little more than a blocky shadow on the fringes of the glow rod's light, but it filled him with a sense of both fear and awe.

Still using the Force to scan for traps, he cautiously approached the tomb, his trepidation growing as the blue light washed over it to reveal more and more details. The stone was carved with symbols similar to those on the crypt's entrance, but these hadn't suffered untold centuries of erosion. They stood out starkly, brutal and sharp. He couldn't read the unfamiliar language or identify the Dark Lord from the crest, yet he knew this was the resting place of an ancient and mighty being.

He reached the platform; it stood a little higher than his knee. He put one foot on it, then reached out to grip a protruding edge of one of the carved symbols on the side of the sarcophagus itself. He half expected to receive a sharp jolt or shock, but all he felt was cold stone beneath his palm.

Using his hold to maintain his balance, he hauled himself up so that he was standing with both feet on the platform, looking down at the top of the tomb. To his horror, he could now see that the stone slab sealing the sarcophagus had been virtually destroyed. Whatever had been inside was gone, replaced by rubble, dust, and a few bits of broken bone that might once have been the fingers or toes of the Dark Lord's skeletal remains.

He stepped down from the platform, frustrated but still not willing to give up. Slowly, he turned in a great circle, as if he expected to find the stolen remains lying in a corner of the burial chamber. There was nothing: the tomb had been robbed and defiled.

Bane hadn't been sure what he expected to find, but it wasn't this. The spirits of the ancient Dark Lords were beings of pure dark side energy; they were as eternal as the Force itself. The spirit would linger for centuries—millennia, even—until a worthy successor came along. Or so the texts in the archive had led him to believe.

Yet the harsh evidence before him was undeniable. The ancient manuscripts had failed him. He had gambled everything on the truth of their words—even defying Qordis himself—and he had lost.

In desperation he cast his head back and threw his arms to the uneven rock of the ceiling above. "I'm here, Master!" he cried. "I've come to learn your secrets!" He paused, listening for a response. Hearing nothing, he shouted, "Show yourself! By all the power of the dark side, show yourself!"

His words reverberated off the walls, sounding empty and hollow. He dropped to his knees, his arms falling to his sides and his head slumping forward. As the echo died away, the only sound was the shrill clicking of the pelko bugs.

———

Kopecz spit on the ground as he surveyed the camp. He was surrounded by an army, but it was an army of inferiors. Everywhere he looked he saw the minions of the Sith: battle ragers, assassins, and apprentices. But there were precious few Sith Masters. The seemingly endless war against the Jedi on the battlefields of Ruusan was taking a heavy toll on Kaan's Brotherhood of Darkness. Without reinforcements they would be forced to retreat—or be wiped out by General Hoth and his hated Army of Light.

The heavyset Twi'lek rose to his feet, spurred to action by the realization that something had to be done. He made his way through scattered pockets of soldiers, noticing how many were injured, exhausted, or simply defeated. By the time he reached the entrance to Lord Kaan's tent the contempt he felt for his so-called Brothers had reached a boiling point.

When Kopecz entered, Lord Kaan took one look at him and dismissed his other advisers with a sharp wave of his hand. They filed out, none of them daring to come too close.

"What is it, my old friend?" Kaan asked. His voice was charming as ever, but his eyes were wide and wild, like a hunted beast.

"Have you seen what passes for our army out there?" Kopecz snarled, poking a thumb over his shoulder as he walked slowly forward. "If this is all we have to stand against Lord Hoth, we may as was well burn our black robes and start practicing the Jedi Code."

"We have reinforcements coming," Lord Kaan assured him. "Two more full divisions of foot soldiers, another core of snipers. Half a platoon of repulsorcraft armed with heavy guns. There are many who are drawn to the glory of our cause. More and more each day. The Brotherhood of Darkness cannot fail."

Kopecz took little comfort in his promises. Lord Kaan had always been the strength of the Brotherhood of Darkness, a man who had rallied the Dark Lords to a single cause through the greatness of his personality and vision. Now, however, he looked like a man on the edge. The strain of constantly battling the Jedi had left him frazzled.

Kopecz shook his head in disgust. "I'm not one of your sycophantic advisers," he said, his voice rising. "I won't grovel and scrape before you, Lord Kaan. I won't heap praise on your fool head when I can see with my own eyes that you are leading us to our destruction!"

"Keep your voice down!" Kaan snapped. "You will destroy the morale of our troops!"

"They have no morale left to destroy," Kopecz shot back, though he did lower his volume. "We can't defeat Jedi with ordinary soldiers. There are too many of them and not enough of us."

"By *us* you mean those worthy of joining the ranks of the Dark Lords," Kaan replied. He sighed and stared down at the holomap spread out on the table before him.

"You know what you have to do," Kopecz told him, his voice losing some of the anger. He had chosen to follow Kaan; he wouldn't abandon him now. But he wasn't about to sit idly by and face certain defeat. "We face an army of Jedi Knights and Masters. We can't stand against them without our own Masters from the Academy. The students, too. All of them."

"They are mere apprentices," Kaan protested.

"They are the strongest of our order," Kopecz reminded him. "We both know even the lowliest students on Korriban are stronger than half the so-called Dark Lords here on Ruusan."

"Qordis's work is not yet complete. The students there still have so much to learn," Kaan insisted, though without much force. "So much untapped potential. The Academy represents the future of the Sith."

"If we cannot defeat the Jedi here on Ruusan, then we have no future!" Kopecz insisted.

Lord Kaan clutched his head with his hands, as if a great pain threatened to burst his skull in two. He began to tremble in the grip of some terrible palsy. Kopecz involuntarily stepped back.

It only took a few seconds for Kaan to regain his composure and lower his hands. The haunted look in his eyes was gone, replaced by the calm self-assurance that had drawn so many to the Brotherhood in the first place.

"You're right, old friend," he said. The words were smooth and easy; he spoke as if a great weight had been lifted from him. He radiated confidence and strength. He seemed to glow with a violet aura, as if he were the very embodiment of the dark side. And suddenly, inexplicably, Kopecz was reassured.

"I will send word to Qordis," Kaan continued, the Force emanating from him in palpable waves. "You are right. It is time for those at the Academy on Korriban to truly join the ranks of the Sith."

19

Bane had never been so hungry in his life. It twisted his stomach into knots, causing him to hunch over as he trudged slowly across Korriban's wastes toward Dreshdae. For thirteen days he had searched the tombs in the Valley of the Dark Lords, sustaining himself only with the Force and the hydration tablets he'd brought along for the desert journey. He never slept, but rested his mind from time to time through meditation. Yet for all its power, even the Force couldn't create something from nothing. It could ward off starvation for a time, but not forever.

Twice he'd been set on by packs of tuk'ata, the guardian hounds that prowled the crypts of their former Masters. The first time he'd driven them away with the Force, seizing the body of the alpha male and hurling it into the rest of the pack, injuring several of the beasts. They'd scurried away with high-pitched howls that had sent shivers down his spine. The second attack had been far bloodier. While exploring one of the most recent tombs he'd found himself surrounded by a dozen tuk'ata: a pack twice the size of the first. He'd unleashed his lightsaber on them, slicing through flesh and bone. When the pack finally broke and fled, only four of the twelve tuk'ata still lived.

After that the tuk'ata left him alone, which was a good thing, because he was no longer sure he'd be able to hold them off if they attacked again. To fuel his muscles for the ongoing search through tomb after tomb, he'd overtaxed his body's reserves, literally devouring himself from the inside out. Now he was paying the price.

He could have eased his suffering by slipping into a meditative trance, slowing his heartbeat and vital functions to preserve his energy. Yet in the end that would accomplish nothing. Nobody would come to find him, and eventually even a state of hibernation would end in a slow, if relatively painless, death.

Death was not an option he was ready to consider. Not yet. Despite his futile search, despite the crushing disappointment, he wasn't ready for that. Not if it meant that the truth he had discovered would die with him. So he endured the pain, and willed his rapidly failing flesh to take him back. Back to the Academy.

It had taken him only a day to walk to the valley at the beginning of his quest. He was now on the third day of his trip back. He had been strong and fresh when he'd first set out; now he was famished and weak. But there was more to his slowed pace than mere physical wanting.

Before he had been buoyed by expectation. Now he was weighed down by the burden of failure. Qordis had been right: the ancient Dark Lords of Korriban were gone. Nearly three thousand years had passed between the time the Sith had been driven from Korriban by Revan, and the day Kaan's Brotherhood of Darkness officially reclaimed this world for the order. In that time the legacy of the original Sith had been completely wiped away.

He'd gone into the desert seeking enlightenment, but found only disillusionment. Korriban was no longer the cradle of darkness; it was a husk, a withered, desiccated corpse that had been picked clean by scavengers. Qordis had been right . . . yet Bane now understood that he was also very, very wrong.

Bane hadn't found what he was looking for in the tombs. But in the long trek back across the desert his mind had finally become clear. Hunger, thirst, exhaustion: the physical suffering cleansed his thoughts. It stripped away all his illusions and exposed the lies of Qordis and the Academy. The spirits of the Sith were gone from Korriban forever. But it was Lord Kaan's Brotherhood of Darkness—not the Jedi—who were to blame.

They had twisted and perverted the ancient order of the Sith. The Academy's teachings flew in the face of everything Bane had learned in the archives about the ways of the dark side. Kaan had cast aside the true power of the individual and replaced it with the false glory of self-sacrifice in the name of a worthy cause. He sought to destroy the Jedi through might of arms, rather than cunning. Worst of all, he proclaimed that all were equal in the Brotherhood of the Sith. But Bane knew equality was a myth. The strong were meant to rule; the weak, to serve.

The Brotherhood of Darkness stood for everything that was wrong with the modern Sith. They had fallen from the true path. Their failure was the reason the spirits of the Dark Lords had vanished. None on Korriban— not Master, not apprentice—had been worthy of their wisdom; none worthy of their power. They had simply faded away, scattered like a handful of dust cast across the desert sand. Bane could see the truth so clearly now. Yet Qordis and the others were forever blind. They followed Kaan as if he had bound them up with some secret spell.

A faint gust of wind brought the sound of distant voices to his ears. Glancing up, he was surprised to see the temple of the Academy looming ahead of him, less than a kilometer away. Caught up in his philosophical ramblings, he hadn't realized how far he'd come. He was close enough to see small figures moving at the base of the building: servants, or possibly a handful of students from the Academy out wandering the surrounding grounds. One of them noticed him approaching and scurried back inside, probably to deliver news of his return to Qordis and the other Masters.

Bane wasn't sure what kind of reception they'd give him. In truth he didn't care, as long as they brought him food. Beyond that they were of no use to him anymore. He despised them all: Masters and apprentices alike. They were no better than the Jedi who had looted Korriban three millennia before. The Academy was an abomination, a testament to how far the Sith had fallen from the true ideals of the dark side.

Bane alone understood this. He alone saw the truth. And he alone could lead the Sith back to the way of the dark side.

He wouldn't be foolish enough to say so, of course. The Brotherhood would never follow him; neither would Qordis or any of the others at the Academy. Weak and ignorant as they were, they could still overwhelm him with their numbers. If he was to restore the Sith to their true glory, he would need an ally.

Not one of the Masters: they were all too close to Kaan. And the apprentices were nothing but groveling servants, blindly following their Masters. They had no real understanding of the dark side. They didn't sense that they were being led down a false path. Not a single one of them was worthy.

No, Bane corrected himself. There was one. Githany.

She wasn't intimidated by the Masters. She had defied them to train Bane. The fact that she'd done it for her own selfish reasons only offered further proof that she understood the true nature of the dark side.

He wished now that he had spoken to her before he'd left the Academy. He could have at least tried to explain why he had to go. She had been disappointed in him for letting Sirak survive. Rightfully so. But in the end he was the one who had turned away from her. He was the one who left her behind while he went in search of Korriban's hidden secrets. What could she possibly think of him now?

As he reached the edge of the temple grounds the scents of the midday meal being prepared in the kitchens wafted out to him, driving all other thoughts from his mind. Mouth watering and stomach rumbling, he hobbled up the steps toward the ever-nearing prospect of food.

———

The news that Bane had returned did not sit well with Qordis. The timing couldn't have been worse. Lord Kaan had sent an urgent message: everyone from the Academy was to come to Ruusan to join the battle against the Jedi. The apprentices were all to be presented with lightsabers and given seats in the Brotherhood of Darkness, elevating them to the ranks of the Dark Lords of the Sith.

It wouldn't do to show up with one of his most powerful students being as defiant as Bane had been at their last meeting. It would be even worse if Bane spurned the offer and went off on his own, disobeying the command to go to Ruusan. Lord Kaan had managed to keep the Brotherhood together, but it was an alliance that was always on the verge of disintegrating. In the face of their repeated failure to drive the Jedi from

Ruusan, the refusal of one prominent Sith to fall into line might be all it took to make everything unravel.

One defection could lead to others, and things would return to a state of chaos: Sith fighting Sith as the various Dark Lords sought to dominate and destroy their rivals. The Jedi would survive and rebuild their order, all the while laughing at the foolishness of their mortal enemies.

If only Bane had perished out in the wastes of Korriban! Unfortunately, he had returned, and Qordis couldn't do anything to eliminate him now. Not after Kaan's directive. They had need of every lightsaber and every Sith, especially one as strong as Bane. For the sake of the Brotherhood—for the sake of Lord Kaan's glorious vision—Qordis would have to find some way to make amends.

————

News that Bane had returned spread quickly through the Academy. Sirak wasn't surprised. If anything, he was relieved. When Master Qordis had informed the students they would soon be shipping out to Ruusan, he'd feared they would leave before Bane returned, denying him his vengeance.

Instead fortune had smiled on him. He'd have to act quickly, though. Once they left Korriban it would be too late. Lord Kaan would have all the apprentices swear vows of loyalty and fealty to each other when they joined the Brotherhood. Killing his enemy after that would be an act of betrayal punishable by death. He wanted revenge, but not at the cost of his own life.

He knew Yevra and Llokay would help him, but he'd need more than them to destroy an enemy as strong as Bane. He needed Githany.

Knocking on the door to her room, he waited for her to call "Enter" before going in.

She was lying on her bed, looking casual and relaxed. In contrast, Sirak felt taut as a wire stretched beyond its limit.

"He's back" was all he said.

"When?" She didn't need to ask who he was talking about.

"He staggered in an hour ago. Maybe less. He went straight to the kitchens."

"The kitchens?" She seemed surprised. Or offended. No doubt she'd expected him to come to her first.

"He's vulnerable," Sirak pointed out, his hand dropping to the hilt of his newly acquired lightsaber. "Half starved. Exhausted. We should go after him now."

"Don't be stupid," she snapped. "What would the Masters do to us if we chopped him down in the kitchens?"

She was right. "Do you have a plan?"

She nodded. "Tonight. Wait in the archives. I'll bring him to you there."

"I'll bring Yevra and Llokay."

A sour grimace puckered up her face. "I suppose we'll need them," she conceded, making no effort to hide her distaste.

Sirak's mouth twisted into a cruel grin. "I only ask one more thing. Let me be the one who deals the killing blow."

––––––––

Bane collapsed into his bed, his belly full to bursting. He'd gorged himself in the kitchen, tearing into the food with the manners of a Gamorrean soldier at the barracks trough. He'd stuffed himself with everything in sight until his ravenous hunger was sated. It was only then that he remembered he hadn't actually slept in nearly two weeks.

Hunger had given way to exhaustion, and he'd wandered from the kitchen to his room in a daze. Within seconds he had dropped into a deep, dreamless sleep.

He woke several hours later to a knocking at his door. Still groggy, he forced himself to his feet, lit a glow rod, and opened the door.

Qordis was standing in the hall. He barged in without waiting for an invitation, closing the door behind him. Bane was too busy trying to shake off the last vestiges of sleep to protest.

"Welcome back, Bane," the Master said. "I trust your journey was . . . educational."

Puzzled at Qordis's cordial tone, Bane only nodded.

"I hope you understand now why I let you go," Qordis said.

Because you were too much of a coward to try and stop me, Bane thought, but didn't say anything aloud.

"This was the final phase of your training," the Master continued. "You had to understand why we have abandoned the old ways. This is a new age, and you could understand that only once you recognized the old age was truly gone."

Bane maintained his stoic silence, not agreeing with Qordis but unwilling to argue the point.

"Now that you have learned your final lesson, the Academy has nothing left to teach you." On that point, at least, they were in complete agreement. "You are no longer an apprentice, Bane. You are now fit to join the ranks of the Masters. You are now a Dark Lord of the Sith."

He paused, as if expecting some kind of reaction. Bane stood still as the stone statues he'd seen guarding the tombs of the ancient Sith in some of the older crypts.

Qordis cleared his throat, breaking the uncomfortable silence. "I know Lord Kas'im has already given you a lightsaber. I, too, have a gift for you." He held out his hand, a lightsaber crystal in his palm.

When Bane hesitated, Qordis spoke again. "Take it, Lord Bane." He put a special emphasis on the new title. It sounded sour in Bane's ears: an empty honor bestowed by a fool who believed himself a Master. But he said nothing as the other continued speaking.

"This synthetic crystal is stronger than the one powering your lightsaber now," Qordis assured him. "And it is much, much stronger than the natural crystals the Jedi use in their own weapons."

Moving slowly, Bane reached out and took it in his hand. It was cold to the touch at first, but as he gripped it the six-sided stone quickly grew warm.

"The timing of your return from the wastes couldn't have been better," Qordis continued. "We are making preparations to leave Korriban. Lord Kaan has need of us on Ruusan. All the Sith must be united in the Brotherhood of Darkness if we are to defeat the Jedi."

"The Brotherhood will fail," Bane stated, boldly declaring what he knew to be true only because he knew the other wouldn't believe. "Kaan does not understand the dark side. He is leading you down the path of ruin."

Qordis drew in a sharp breath, then spat it out in an angry hiss. "Some might consider that talk to be treason, Lord Bane. You would do well to keep such ideas to yourself in the future." He wheeled away and strode angrily to the door, wrenching it open. His reaction was exactly as Bane had expected.

The tall Master spun back to face Bane one more time. "You may be a Dark Lord now, Bane. But there is still much about the dark side you do not understand. Join the Brotherhood and we can teach you what we know. Reject us, and you will never find what you seek."

The Master stalked out; Bane watched silently as the door swung shut behind him. Qordis was wrong about the Brotherhood, but he was right about one thing: there was still much about the dark side Bane needed to understand.

And there was only one place in the galaxy he could go to learn it.

20

Bane crawled back into bed after Qordis left. He thought about going to see Githany, but he was still exhausted. *Tomorrow,* he thought as he drifted off to sleep.

Several hours later he was again disturbed by a knock on his door. This time he felt more refreshed when he woke. He sat up quickly and lit a glow rod, casting the room in soft light. There were no windows in his chamber, but he guessed it must be close to midnight: well past curfew.

He rose to his feet and went to greet his second uninvited visitor. This time he was not disappointed when he opened the door.

"Can I come in?" Githany whispered.

Bane stepped aside, catching the scent of her perfume as she brushed past him. As he silently closed the door behind her, she walked over to the bed and sat down on the edge. She patted the space beside her, and Bane dutifully sat down, turning slightly so he could look her in the eye.

"Why are you here?" he asked.

"Why did you leave?" she responded.

"It's . . . it's hard to explain. You were right about what happened with Sirak. I should have finished him, but I didn't. I was foolish and weak. I didn't want to admit that to you."

"You left the Academy so you wouldn't have to face me?" The words sounded compassionate, as if she were seeking to understand him. But Bane could sense the contempt beneath them.

"No," he explained. "I didn't leave because of you. I left because you were the only one who recognized my failing. Everyone else congratulated me for my great victory: Kas'im, Qordis . . . everyone. They were blind to the true nature of the dark side. As blind as I had been until you opened my eyes.

"I left because the Academy had nothing more to offer me. I went to the Valley of the Dark Lords hoping to find the answers I couldn't find here."

"And you never thought to come tell me all this?" Her voice had changed; the veil of false compassion was gone. Now she just sounded angry. Angry and hurt. Bane was relieved that she still felt strongly enough about him to reveal some genuine emotion.

"I should have come to you," he admitted. "I acted rashly. I let my anger at Qordis drive me away."

She nodded: passion and reckless actions were something he knew Githany could relate to.

"I've answered your question," he said. "Now you answer mine. Why are you here?"

She hesitated, her teeth biting down softly on her lower lip. Bane recognized the unconscious gesture; it meant she was lost in thought, trying to sort something out.

"Not here," she said at last, rising stiffly from the bed. "I have something to show you. In the archives."

Without looking back to see if he was following, she made her way from his room and into the dim hall beyond, moving quickly. Bane scrambled to his feet and trotted after her, breaking into a jog to keep up.

She stared straight ahead, her boots making crisp snaps as they struck the stone floor with each brisk stride. The sharp sound echoed in the empty halls, but Githany appeared not to care. Bane could tell that something was bothering her, but he had no idea what it could be.

They found the door to the archives open. Githany didn't seem surprised; she passed right through without slowing down. Bane paused for only an instant before following her.

At the far side of the room, beyond the rows of shelves, she stopped and turned to face him. There was an expression he couldn't quite decipher on her haughty but beautiful features.

He crossed to the middle of the room then stopped short when she held up her hand, palm extended. "Githany," he said, perplexed, "what's going—"

His words were cut off by the hollow boom of the archive door slamming shut behind him. He whirled around to see Sirak, flanked by Yevra and Llokay. The Zabrak's pale yellow lips were pulled back in a cruel smile so wide it gave him the appearance of a grinning skull. Bane couldn't help but notice the lightsaber handles dangling from the belts of all three.

When Githany spoke from behind him he had to resist the urge to turn and face her. It wouldn't be wise to expose his back to the Zabrak trio.

"Why did you follow me, Bane?" she asked, her voice a mixture of anger, disgust, and regret. "How could you be so stupid? Didn't you realize you were walking into a trap?"

Githany had betrayed him. The conversation in his room had been a test—one that he'd failed. He knew her well enough to expect something like this. He should have been wary of a trap. Instead he'd been a blind and obedient fool.

He knew he'd brought this on himself. Now he had to discern a way out.

"Is this what you want, Githany?" he asked, trying to stall for time.

"She wants what all Sith want," Sirak answered for her. "Power. Victory. She knows to side with the strong."

"I'm stronger than he is," Bane told Githany. "I proved that in the dueling ring."

"There's more to strength than physical prowess," Sirak replied, igniting his lightsaber. It was the double-bladed variety. Bane's eyes were focused squarely on the bright red blades, but he heard the hiss as the other two Zabrak followed suit. Githany, however, still hadn't fired up her whip.

"Strength means more than just the ability to use the Force," Sirak continued, starting to advance. "It means intelligence. Cunning. Ruthlessness."

"You know how easily I defeated you in the ring," Bane said, finally speaking directly to Sirak, though his words were still meant for Githany. "Are you so certain you can defeat me now?"

"Four against one, Bane. And you left your lightsaber back in your chambers. I like those odds."

Bane laughed and turned his back on Sirak. The Zabrak was close enough to lunge in and kill him with one blow, but Bane was gambling he would hold back, wary of being lured into a trap. It was a dangerous gamble, but he wanted to be looking directly into Githany's eyes when he spoke what might be his last words.

"This fool actually believes you brought me here for his sake," he said to her. Behind him he could sense Sirak's confusion and uncertainty. No attack came yet.

Githany met his stare with a cold, unflinching gaze and didn't answer. But her teeth worried her lower lip.

"We both know why you brought me here, Githany," he said, speaking quickly. Sirak wouldn't wait for long. "You don't want to side with Sirak. You've been plotting ways to get me to kill him ever since you first arrived."

"Enough!" Sirak shouted. Bane threw himself forward, rolling out of the way at the last second as the double-bladed lightsaber sliced a deep furrow into the spot where he had been standing. As he rolled to his feet, he saw Githany move; when she tossed his lightsaber to him, he was already extending his hand and using the Force to guide the hilt into his grasp.

The weapon flared to life and he turned just in time to block Sirak's charge. Yevra and Llokay were a few meters behind, rushing forward to join the fray.

Bane counterattacked, slashing down at Sirak's legs. The Zabrak parried the blow, and their blades collided with a burning hum. On the edge of his awareness Bane heard the sound of Githany's whip igniting.

A quick flurry caused Sirak to retreat. Bane feinted as if he was going to press forward, then took a step back, opening a full meter of space between them. It gave him just enough time to cast out his arm in the direction of the unsuspecting Yevra. Catching her up with the Force, he hurled her against one of the nearby shelves hard enough to splinter the wood.

She crumpled to the floor, dazed. Before she had a chance to rise, Githany lashed out with her whip and ended the Zabrak female's life.

Bane barely had time to register her death before Llokay was on him. The red-skinned Zabrak was overmatched, but his grief and rage empowered him, and he drove his much larger opponent back with a brutal series of desperate slashes and strikes.

Staggering back, Bane was almost too distracted to see Sirak unleashing a bolt of crackling blue lightning at him. At the last second he twisted and caught the potentially lethal blast with the blade of his lightsaber, absorbing its energy. The move had been one of instinct and last resort, and it had left him vulnerable to a single quick thrust from Llokay. But Githany's whip was snapping and cracking at Llokay's eyes and face, and his blade was busy frantically warding off the blows.

Bane turned his attention back to Sirak, who hesitated. At that moment there was a scream from Llokay: he had misjudged the erratic path of Githany's energy whip and lost an eye. A second scream would have followed, but she gashed open his throat, the burning tip of her weapon searing his vocal cords so he died in agonized silence.

Outnumbered, Sirak extinguished his lightsaber, dropped it to the ground, and fell to his knees.

"Please, Bane," he begged, his voice cracking. "I yield. You are a true Sith Lord. I know that now."

Githany whispered, "End it now, Bane."

Bane advanced until he towered over his groveling foe. Suddenly it wasn't just Sirak he saw before him. It was everyone he'd ever struck down. Every life he'd ever taken. Fohargh, the Makurth. The nameless Republic soldier he'd killed on Apatros. His father.

He was responsible for their deaths. Even now, they weighed on him. Guilt over Fohargh's death had left him numb to the dark side for months. It had shackled him like iron. He didn't want to suffer through that again.

"Listen to me," Sirak pleaded. "I'll serve you. I'll do anything you command. You can use me. I can help you. Please, Bane—have mercy!"

Bane steeled himself. "Those who ask for mercy," he answered coldly, "are too weak to deserve it."

His blade decapitated his helpless foe. The torso remained upright for a full second, the charred edges of the cauterized stump where the head had once been attached still smoking. Then it toppled forward.

Staring down at it, Bane felt only one thing: freedom. The guilt, the shame, the weight of responsibility had all vanished in that single, decisive act. He had opened himself to the dark side completely. It surged through him, filling him with confidence and power.

Through power, I gain victory. Through victory my chains are broken.

He turned to see Githany smiling, her eyes filled with hunger.

"I of all people should have known better than to underestimate you," she said. "You saw me take your lightsaber! That's why you followed me."

"No," Bane replied, still heady from the rush of killing his enemy. "I didn't see anything. I was just guessing."

For a brief moment her expression darkened; then she burst out with a laugh. "You never cease to amaze me, Lord Bane."

"Don't call me that," he said.

"Why not?" she asked. "Qordis has given all the students the rank of Dark Lord of the Sith."

Seeing him wince, she stepped forward and wrapped her arms around his neck, looking up into his face. "Bane," she breathed, "we're going to fight the Jedi! We're going to join Lord Kaan's Brotherhood of Darkness!"

He reached up and grasped her delicate hands in his own massive ones, then gently unwound her arms from around his neck. Puzzled, she offered no resistance as he brought his hands together at his chest, her own clasped between them.

How could he make her understand? He was of the dark side now; Sirak's execution had been the final step. He had crossed the threshold; there was no going back. He would never hesitate again. Never doubt again. The transformation he had begun when he'd first come to the Academy was complete: he was Sith.

Now, more than ever, he understood the failings of the Brotherhood.

"Kaan is a fool, Githany," he said, staring intently into her eyes to read her expression.

She recoiled slightly and tried to pull her hands away. He held them tight.

"You've never even met Lord Kaan," she said defensively. "I have. He's a great man, Bane. A man of vision."

"He's blind as an Orkellian cave slug," Bane insisted. "The Brotherhood of Darkness, this Academy, everything the Sith have become is a monument to his ignorance!" He clasped her hands even more tightly. "Come with me. There is nothing left for us on Korriban, and only death on Ruusan. But I know somewhere else we can go. A place where the dark side is still strong."

She squirmed her hands free and pulled away from him. "Lord Kaan has united the Sith in a single glorious cause. We can join them on Ruusan."

"Then go!" Bane spat. "Join the others on Ruusan. Be united with them in their defeat."

He turned and stormed angrily away as she called out "Wait, Bane. Wait!"

If she had made any move to follow him, he might have.

———

Bane kicked open the door to Qordis's chamber; it slammed against the wall with a crash that reverberated down the hall. The Academy's Master had been awake and already dressed, meditating on the mat in the center of his room. Now he leapt to his feet, anger darkening his face.

"What is the meaning of this?"

"Did you send Sirak to kill me?" Bane blurted out. The time for subtlety was gone.

"What? I . . . did something happen to Sirak?"

"I killed him. Yevra and Llokay, too. Their bodies are in the archives."

The shock and horror of his reaction made it clear that Qordis had known nothing about the attack. "You did this on the eve of our departure for Ruusan?" he asked, his voice rising shrilly.

A few of the other Masters had gathered in the corridor outside, drawn by Bane's loud arrival. A handful of the students, as well. Bane didn't care.

"You can go to Ruusan," Bane snapped. "I will have nothing to do with the Brotherhood of Darkness."

"You are a student of this Academy," Qordis reminded him. "You will do as you are told!"

"I am a Dark Lord of the Sith," Bane countered. "I serve no one but myself."

Glancing over Bane's shoulder at the gathering crowd of curious on-lookers, Qordis dropped his voice to a threatening whisper. "We leave for Ruusan tomorrow, Lord Bane. You will be coming with us. This is not a matter for discussion."

"I am leaving tonight," Bane replied, lowering his voice to match and mock the tone of Qordis's own. "And none of you here is strong enough to stop me."

He turned his back on the head of the Academy and walked slowly from the room. For a brief second he felt the spurned Master gathering the Force, and Bane braced himself for a confrontation. But a second later he felt the power fading away.

At the threshold he halted. When he spoke, he was addressing the assembled gawkers as much as Qordis.

"Someone here once told me the *Darth* title was no longer used because it promoted rivalry among the Sith. It gave the Jedi an easy target. It was easier just to abandon the custom. To have all the Sith Masters use the same title of *Dark Lord*."

He raised his voice slightly, speaking loud enough for all to hear. "But I know the truth, Qordis. I know why none of you claims that name for yourself. Fear. You're cowards."

He half turned and looked back at Qordis. "None of the Brotherhood is worthy of the *Darth* title. Least of all you."

There was a gasp from the assemblage. Some of the students stepped back, expecting some type of reaction. Of course there was none.

Shaking his head in disgust, Bane left them there. As he passed the other Masters, Kas'im stepped in front of him, placing a hand on his chest.

"Don't go," the Blademaster said. "Let's talk about this. If you just meet with Kaan you'll understand. That's all I ask, Bane."

"It's *Darth* Bane," he said, slapping the Twi'lek's hand away and pushing past him.

Nobody else tried to stop him as he made his way through the temple's halls. Nobody tried to follow him or even called out as he mounted the stairs to the small landing pad on the roof.

There was only a single ship at the starport: the *Valcyn*, a T-class long-range personal cruiser. The blade-shaped vessel was one of the finest in the Sith fleet, equipped with the latest and most advanced technology. It had arrived just the day before: a gift from Kaan to Qordis, in recognition of his work with the apprentices at the Academy.

Bane lowered the access hatch and climbed inside. During his stint in the military he'd been given rudimentary training in the basics of piloting a standard hyperdrive vessel. Fortunately, the *Valcyn*'s controls matched all intergalactic standards of operation and were designed for ease of use. He sat himself down in the pilot's chair and fired up the thrusters, punching in the hyperspace coordinates of his destination even as he began the liftoff sequence. A moment later the *Valcyn* rose up from the landing pad's surface then shot off into the atmosphere, leaving Korriban and the Academy behind.

PART THREE

21

Lord Hoth, Jedi Master and acting general of the Republic forces on Ruusan, sat huddled on a stump outside his tent and stared up at the dark clouds hovering above the camp. He scowled at the brooding sky as if he could banish the coming storm with the fierceness of his expression.

"Is something troubling you, Lord Hoth?"

The voice of Master Pernicar, his longtime friend and right hand during this never-ending campaign, snapped his attention back to where it belonged.

"What isn't troubling me, Pernicar?" he asked with a heavy sigh. "We're low on food and medpacs. Our injured outnumber our hale. The scouts report that reinforcements are on their way to assist Kaan and his Sith." He slapped his hand down on one knee. "All we have coming to *our* aid are youths and children."

"Children who are strong in the Force," Pernicar reminded him. "If we don't recruit them to our side, the Sith will claim them for theirs."

"Blast it, Pernicar, they're just children! I need Jedi. Fully trained. All we can spare. But there are still members of our own order who refuse to help us."

"Perhaps it's how you ask them," a new voice said from behind him.

Hoth rubbed his temples but didn't turn to face the speaker. Lord Valenthyne Farfalla had been one of the first Jedi Masters to join the Army of Light on Ruusan. He had fought in nearly every confrontation, and the Sith had come to know him well: Farfalla was hard to miss even in the chaos of battle.

He had long, flowing curls of golden hair that hung down past his shoulders. The breastplate of his armor was also gold, buffed and polished until it gleamed before every battle. It was trimmed with bright red sleeves and adorned with rubies that matched the color of his eyes and contrasted with his pale skin.

Lord Hoth found him insufferable. Farfalla was a loyal servant of the light, but he was also a vain and prancing fool who spent more time selecting his wardrobe before each battle than he did planning strategy. Farfalla was the last person he wanted to deal with now.

"If you showed more tact, Lord Hoth," Farfalla continued, gliding into view, "you might have rallied more Jedi to your cause."

"I shouldn't have to persuade them!" Hoth roared, leaping to his feet and waving his arms in exasperation. Farfalla hopped nimbly out of the way. "We're fighting the Sith! The dark side must be destroyed! We could do it if more Jedi were here!"

"There are some who don't see it that way," Pernicar said calmly. He had become used to Hoth's outbursts during their time on Ruusan, and had learned to ignore them, for the most part.

"There are other Republic worlds besides this one that are under attack," Farfalla chimed in. "Many Jedi are aiding the Republic troops in other sectors, helping them against the Sith fleets."

Hoth spat on the ground and was pleased to see Farfalla's look of horrified disgust. "Those fleets might fly the banner of the Sith, but they're made up of ordinary beings. The Republic has the numbers to beat them back. They don't need the help of the Jedi to do it. All the real Sith—the Dark Lords—are here now. If we defeat the Brotherhood of Darkness, the Sith rebellion will collapse. Don't they understand that?"

There was a long silence as the other two exchanged uneasy looks. It was Pernicar who finally found the courage to answer.

"Some of the Jedi believe we shouldn't be here. They feel the only thing keeping the Brotherhood together is their hatred of the Army of

Light. They claim if we disband and surrender Ruusan, then the Sith will quickly turn against each other, and the Brotherhood will tear itself apart."

Hoth shook his head in disbelief. "Don't they see what a great opportunity we have here? We can wipe out the followers of the dark side once and for all!"

"Some might argue that is not the purpose of our order," Farfalla suggested gently. "The Jedi are defenders of the Republic. They feel the Army of Light is prolonging the rebellion by strengthening the Sith resolve. They say you are actually causing harm to the Republic you were sworn to defend."

"Is that what *you* think?" Hoth snarled.

"Lord Farfalla has been with us since the beginning," Pernicar reminded him. "He is only telling you what others are saying—those Jedi who have not come to Ruusan."

"The Sith are getting reinforcements from Korriban," Hoth grumbled. "We barely have enough numbers to hold them off as it is. I'll just have to make them understand!"

"We would probably have more success if someone else approached them," Farfalla said. "There are some who believe this has become a personal vendetta for you. They do not see Ruusan as the ultimate struggle between the light and the dark, but rather as a feud between you and Lord Kaan."

Hoth sat back down wearily. "Then we are doomed. Without reinforcements we will be overwhelmed."

Farfalla crouched down beside him, laying a perfectly manicured, heavily perfumed hand on Hoth's brawny shoulder. It took every ounce of the general's Jedi discipline not to shrug him off.

"Send me, my lord," Farfalla said earnestly. "I have been here since the beginning; I believe in this cause as strongly as you."

"Why should they listen to you any more than me?"

Farfalla gave a high, twittering laugh that set Hoth's teeth on edge. "My lord, for all your skill in battle and all your strength in the Force, you are somewhat lacking in the delicate art of diplomacy. You are a brilliant general, and your taciturn nature serves you well when giving orders to your troops. Unfortunately, it can set those who are not under your command on edge."

"You are too blunt, my lord," Pernicar clarified.

"That's what I just said," Farfalla insisted with just a hint of annoyance. Then he continued, "On the other hand, people find me witty and charming. I can be quite persuasive when necessary. Give me leave to recruit others to our cause, and I will return with a hundred—no, three hundred!—Jedi ready to join the Army of Light."

Hoth dropped his head into his hands again. His temples were throbbing: Farfalla always seemed to have that effect on him.

"Go," he muttered without looking up. "If you're so certain you can bring me reinforcements, then bring them."

Farfalla gave an extravagant bow, then turned with a flourish and left, his golden locks streaming out behind him in the rising wind of the coming storm.

As soon as he was out of earshot, Pernicar spoke again. "Is that wise, my lord? Our numbers are already thin. How long do you think we can survive without him?"

The rain began to fall in great, heavy drops, and an idea sprang into Hoth's mind. "The Sith can't defeat us if we don't stand and fight," he said. "We won't give them a chance. The wet season is here; the rains will make it impossible for their trackers to find us. We'll hide in the forest, harrying them with quick attacks and ambushes before we vanish back into the trees."

"That strategy won't work once the dry season comes," Pernicar warned.

"If Farfalla hasn't brought me my reinforcements by then, it won't matter," Hoth replied.

———

The five Interlopers—small, midrange multitroop transport ships used by the Sith—swept in low over Ruusan's horizon. Each vessel carried a crew of ten, comprised entirely of former students and Masters from Korriban's Academy.

In the lead ship Githany worked the controls with the calm precision of a highly trained pilot. She'd actually learned to fly on a Republic vessel, but the basics were the same.

The Interlopers were lighter and quicker than the Bivouac transports preferred by the Republic. The Interlopers had less armor plating, sacrificing the safety of the occupants inside in exchange for greater range and maneuverability. As if to prove the point, she banked her vessel down and hard to port, bringing it so close to the planet's surface that the leaves on the trees of Ruusan's great forest trembled in the wake of the ion drive.

The other vessels followed her lead, never breaking formation. Linked to Githany through the Force, the other pilots reacted in perfect unison to her every move. If she made a mistake, the entire convoy would go down. But Githany didn't make mistakes.

"It might be safer to climb higher above the tree line," Lord Qordis observed from his seat at Githany's side in the cockpit.

"I don't want the Jedi picking anything up on their scanners," she explained, her attention focused on keeping the ship from smashing into the ocean of wood mere meters below the hull. "The Brotherhood hasn't secured this region. If a squad of seekers locks on to us, these transports aren't equipped with enough firepower to hold them off."

Far in the distance half a dozen small fighters came into view, their trajectory bringing them on a direct line to intercept the Interlopers' path. Qordis swore, and Githany braced herself to begin evasive maneuvers.

A second later she recognized the distinctive outline of the Sith Buzzards and breathed a sigh of relief. "Our escort's here," she said.

They'd be at the Sith base camp in a few minutes, and with the Buzzards there to pick off any incoming Jedi fighters there was no need to fly so dangerously close to the treetops anymore. She could have eased back on the stick to bring the ship up to a safer altitude.

Instead she held her course. She enjoyed the thrill of being one tiny miscue from an instantaneous and fiery end. From his rigid posture in the copilot's chair, it was clear Qordis didn't share her opinion.

Once they cleared the forest she throttled back their speed, then brought the ship down gracefully in the landing field at the edge of Lord Kaan's encampment.

A small collection of Sith Masters, Kaan standing at their head, waited to greet the reinforcements as they disembarked. They might have been only fifty in number, but each one of them was a Sith Lord: more powerful than an entire division of soldiers.

As she made her way down the ship's exit ramp, Githany was quick to understand why their presence had been so urgently requested. Beyond the assemblage of Dark Lords the rest of the camp spread out to the limits of her vision, and all she could see was a picture of grim despair. Ragged, ramshackle tents arranged in tight rings of five housed the bulk of the army: cloth domiciles stained and torn by wind and rain. Scattered among them were repulsorcraft, heavy turrets, and other instruments of war. The equipment was caked with dried mud and spots of rust, as if efforts to keep it properly maintained had been abandoned.

The troops were spread out in small pockets, huddled around cook fires built in the circles of tents. Their uniforms were covered in dust and grime; many wore dirty bandages over wounds they had given up all hope of keeping clean or sterile. Their faces were all scarred by the bitter taste of far too many defeats at the hands of their enemy, and it was the hopelessness of their expressions that made the greatest impression.

Lord Qordis seemed similarly taken aback at the dismal scene, and he grimaced as Lord Kaan approached.

Kaan appeared thin, his face drawn and etched with lines of worry. His hair was bedraggled and unkempt. A day's worth of stubble shadowed his chin, making him look old and weary. He seemed physically smaller than Githany remembered him. Diminished. Less commanding. The spark she had found so compelling when she'd first met him was no longer there. His eyes had once burned with the fire of a man absolutely confident of his imminent success. Now they burned with something else. Desperation. Madness, perhaps. She couldn't help but wonder if Bane had been right.

"Welcome, Lord Qordis," Kaan said, grasping the newcomer's arm in greeting. He released his grip and turned to address the rest of them. "Welcome, all of you, to Ruusan."

"I didn't expect to see your army in such sorry shape," Qordis mumbled.

A look that might have been anger flickered across Kaan's features. Then it was gone, replaced by the beaming confidence Githany remembered. He threw his shoulders back and stood a little straighter.

"You can't judge the victor of a war without seeing the condition of both sides," he said crisply. "The Jedi are in far worse shape. My intelligence reports that their casualties are far greater than ours. Their supplies are running low; their numbers are dwindling. We have medpacs, food, and greater numbers. And they do not have fresh reinforcements."

He lifted his voice so that it carried throughout the camp, his words booming across the tented landscape. "Now that you are here, the Brotherhood of Darkness is at last whole!"

The troops in camp paused and looked up at him. A few rose expectantly to their feet. There was fire in that single bold statement; it rekindled hope from the damp ashes of their fatigue and despair.

"The full power of the Sith Lords is now united here on Ruusan," he continued, projecting his words to even the most distant of his followers. Reaching out to them with the undeniable power of the Force, he fed them, rejuvenated them, and filled their hollow spirits. "We are strong. Stronger than the Jedi. We are the champions of the dark side, and we will crush Lord Hoth and his servants of light!"

A great shout roared up from his troops. Those who were seated leapt to their feet. Those who were standing thrust their fists up in the air. The echo of their cheers shook the camp like a groundquake.

Githany felt it as surely as the rest of the troops. It was more than just the words. It was the way he said them. All her doubts and fears simply vanished, crushed by the weight of that single brief speech. It was as if she had been compelled to obey by a power greater than herself.

They made their way through the camp, reveling in the newfound optimism of the troops as Lord Kaan led them to the great tent where he convened his war sessions. A thickset Twi'lek fell into step beside Lord Qordis just ahead of Githany. Swept up in the moment, it took her several seconds to remember him: Lord Kopecz.

"Where's Bane?" he asked Qordis, his voice so low that only Qordis and Githany likely heard him.

"Bane is gone," Qordis replied.

Kopecz grunted. "What happened? Did you kill him?" He made little attempt to hide his contempt.

"He still lives. But he has turned his back on the Brotherhood of Darkness."

"We need him," Kopecz insisted. "He's too strong for you to just let him go."

"It was his choice, not mine!" Qordis snapped.

They continued in without speaking. Kopecz at last broke the silence, sighing as he asked, "Do you at least know where he went?"

"No," Qordis said. "Nobody knows."

———————

Bane dropped the *Valcyn* out of hyperspace on the farthest edge of the remote system, then kicked in the ion drives and continued slowly toward the only habitable planet: a small world locked in orbit around a pale yellow star.

The planet's official name was Lehon—the same as the solar system—but it was more commonly referred to as the Unknown World. Nearly three thousand years before, in this insignificant system located beyond the farthest edges of explored space, Darth Revan and Darth Malak had discovered the Rakata: an ancient species of Force-users that had ruled the galaxy long before the birth of the Republic.

They had also discovered the Star Forge, an incredible orbiting space station and factory . . . and a monument to the power of the dark side. A great battle had been fought here between the Republic, led by the redeemed Jedi Master Revan, and Darth Malak's Sith. Malak had fallen, the Sith were routed, and the Star Forge had been destroyed, though at great cost to the Republic.

Even now the remnants of that titanic battle remained. Ships from both fleets had been engulfed in the cataclysmic explosion that had destroyed the Star Forge. Anything caught up in the shock waves of the detonation, including the massive factory itself, had been warped and shredded by the concussive force, then fused together by the heat of the blast into unrecognizable chunks of molten metal.

Much of the wreckage had coalesced into a wide band that encircled the small planet of Lehon like the rings common to many of the gas giants across the galaxy. The rest of the debris was scattered throughout the system, orbiting the sun like a vast asteroid field that made navigation difficult, if not impossible.

Bane switched the controls to manual and took over. Using the Force, he maneuvered his ship carefully through the treacherous obstacle course. It took nearly an hour to reach his destination, and by the time he finally passed beyond the ring and into the relative safety of the Unknown World's atmosphere, he was sweating from the intense concentration.

There was no other ship traffic to contend with, of course. Nobody hailed him as he dropped from the sky toward the planet's surface, looking for a place to land.

The Rakata had been a dying species on the verge of extinction when Revan and Malak discovered them. Virtually all evidence of their existence beyond their tiny homeworld had been wiped out; they had been purged from galactic memory. Nothing had significantly changed after the Battle of the Star Forge to alter that fact.

Republic officials had been aware of them, of course, but their existence had never been officially recognized beyond the classified reports of the conflict. It was believed that the general population wouldn't have reacted well to the sudden reemergence of an ancient species that had once enslaved most of the known galaxy. The few surviving Rakata had declined to leave their ancestral home, and their numbers had been insufficient to maintain a viable gene pool. Within a few more generations the long, slow extinction of their species was finally complete.

Keeping secret the existence of the Rakata had proven to be a surprisingly simple task. The system had never attracted much attention after the battle. Although there was a vast amount of starship material left over from the destruction of the Star Forge, no attempts were made to salvage any of it. Rather than desecrating the floating graves of its soldiers, the Republic chose to honor the memory of its dead by designating Lehon a protected historical site. That made it technically illegal for any ship to enter the system without official authorization.

Nobody ever bothered to seek such permission. The system had no inherent value or resources, other than the protected starship debris. It was located well beyond any of the established hyperspace lanes and trade routes—so far out that not even smugglers bothered with it. A small notation of its location was added to the official Republic records, and it began to show up as an insignificant speck on the fringes of some of the more detailed star charts. Beyond that, it might as well have not even existed.

Bane understood that it wasn't quite as simple as that. The Unknown World was a place strong in the Force. It may even have been the birthplace of the first servants of the dark side: the Rakata leaders who drove their people to conquer and enslave hundreds of worlds ten thousand years before the rest of the galaxy even discovered hyperdrive technology. That power had been concentrated and focused in the Star Forge, and would have been released with its destruction.

The Jedi understood this, and they feared what evil might breed in such a place. The Republic officials had acted on their instruction, isolating the entire system, effectively quarantining it from the rest of the galaxy. In the ensuing centuries the Jedi had worked to keep its secrets hidden. The story of Revan and Malak lived on, as did rumors and speculation regarding the Rakata, but the true nature of the Unkown World was buried beneath a shroud of secrets and lies of omission.

In the Academy archives Bane had come across bits and pieces that hinted at the truth. At first he hadn't even realized the implications of what he was seeing. A small mention of the world here. An allusion to it there. Understanding had come slowly as he'd unraveled the mysteries of the dark side. As his knowledge grew, he had come closer and closer to assembling the entire puzzle. He'd thought to complete it in the Valley of the Dark Lords but had failed. Now he had come here to claim the final piece.

Below him the world was a patchwork of small tropical islands separated by bright blue ocean. He used the *Valcyn*'s sensors to identify the largest landmass, then swooped in looking for a place to touch down. The island was almost completely covered by thick, lush jungle, and there were no clearings large enough for his ship. Finally, he pulled the throttle back and began a slow descent, landing the *Valcyn* on the crystal sand beach on the island's edge.

As soon as Bane's feet touched the Unknown World's surface he felt it: a deep thrumming, similar to what he'd first felt on Korriban but much, much stronger. Even the air felt different: heavy with ancient history and secrets long forgotten.

Standing with his back to the ocean, staring into the virtually impenetrable wall of forest that covered the island's interior, he sensed something else, as well: a presence; a life-force of immense size and strength. It was moving toward him. Quickly.

A few seconds later he could hear it crashing through the undergrowth. It must have been drawn by the ship's landing on the beach, an enormous hunter looking for fresh prey.

The rancor burst forth from the trees and began loping across the sand, bellowing its terrible cry. Bane held his ground, watching it come, marveling at the speed with which the massive beast moved. When it had closed the distance between them to less than fifty meters, he calmly held up a hand and reached out with the Force to touch the mind of the charging monster.

At his unspoken command it stumbled to a halt and stood in place, panting. Careful to keep the creature's predatory instincts firmly in check, Bane approached the rancor. It remained still, as docile as a tauntaun being inspected by its rider.

From its size Bane could see it was a full-grown male, though the bright coloration of its hide and the small number of scars suggested that it must have only recently come to adulthood. He laid his palm on one of its massive legs, feeling the trembling muscles beneath the skin as he probed deeper into its animal brain.

He found no awareness, concept, or understanding of the Masters who had once tamed such beasts for use as guardians and mounts. He wasn't surprised: the Rakata had vanished many centuries before this rancor had been born. But Bane was looking for something else.

A collage of images and sensations assailed him. Countless hunts through the forest, most ending in successful slaughter. The rending of sinew and bone. Feasting on the quarry's still-warm flesh. The search for a mate. Battling with another rancor for dominance. And then, finally, he found what he was searching for.

Buried deep in the creature's memories was the image of a great four-sided stone pyramid hidden deep within the jungle's heart. The rancor had seen it only once, back when it was still a youngling in the care of the herd mothers. Yet the structure had left an indelible mark on the brutish mind.

The rancor was an animal, the top of the Unknown World's food chain. It knew no fear, yet it let out a low moan as Bane dredged up the memory of that Temple. The beast shuddered, knowing what was expected of it, but it was powerless to flee; the Force compelled it to obey.

It crouched low to the ground, and Bane leapt up onto its back. It rose carefully to its feet, its rider perched on its great, hunched shoulders. At Bane's command the rancor lumbered off, leaving the beach behind and heading back into the forest, carrying him toward the ancient Rakatan Temple.

22

It took nearly an hour before Bane reached his destination. The vegetation around him was teeming with life, but as he was carried along through the jungle he saw nothing larger than insects or small birds. Most creatures scattered before the rancor's advance, vanishing long before Bane ever came close enough to catch even a glimpse of them. Yet though they scampered away, the rancor's keen sense of smell often picked up their trail, and more than once Bane had to rein in the beast's hunting instincts to keep it on course.

As difficult as it was to keep the beast from racing off in pursuit of its next meal, it became even more difficult to drive it forward as they neared the temple. Every few steps it would try to veer to the side or suddenly shy away from its course. Once it even tried to rear up and dislodge him from its shoulders.

Bane couldn't see more than a few meters ahead through the thick vegetation, but he knew they were close now. He could sense the power of the Temple, calling to him from behind the impenetrable curtain of tangled vines and twisted branches. Clamping down with the dark side, he crushed the last of the mighty rancor's will to resist and urged it forward.

Suddenly they broke through into a clearing, a circle nearly one hundred meters across. In the very center stood the Rakatan Temple. The structure rose nearly twenty meters to the sky, a monument of carved rock and stone. The only entrance was a broad archway at the peak of an enormous staircase carved into an outside wall of the Temple itself. Its surface was pristine: stark and pure, unsullied by clinging moss or climbing ivy. The grounds surrounding it were barren but for a carpet of short, soft grass. It was as if the jungle feared to creep forward and reclaim the tainted stone.

Bane leapt down from his mount, all his attention focused on the structure towering before him. Freed from his power, the rancor turned and fled back into the undergrowth. The terrible crashing cacophony of its escape was overlaid with its tortured howls, but Bane noticed neither sound. He had no more use for the rancor; he had found what he was searching for.

He took a trembling step forward before stopping short. He shook his head to clear it. The dark side was strong here, so strong it made him feel light-headed. That meant this was a place of danger; he couldn't afford to be wandering around in a stupor.

According to the accounts he'd read in the archives, the Temple had once been protected by a powerful energy shield, one that required an entire Rakatan tribe—of which each individual had been a powerful Force-user—to bring it down. He didn't sense any such barrier, but only a fool would proceed without caution.

As he had done in the tombs on Korriban, he began to probe the area around him with the Force. He felt the echoes of the safeguards that had once protected the Temple, but they were so weak as to be almost non-existent. He wasn't surprised. The shields around the Temple had been fueled by the power of the orbiting Star Forge. With its destruction, the shields had failed—along with all the other defenses that had made the Unknown World a graveyard of ships.

Wondering what else had been lost in the Star Forge's violent end, he crossed the surrounding courtyard and mounted the Temple steps. The staircase was steep but wide, and the stone was neither worn nor cracked despite its age. It ended at a small landing leading to the stone archway of the entrance, three-quarters of the way up. He paused at the threshold, then passed through. He had a brief sensation of what it must have felt like for those who came before him: the anticipation, the thrill of discovery. Once inside, however, it only took a few minutes of exploration for his excitement to fade.

Like Korriban, the Temple had been stripped of anything of value. He searched for hours, beginning with the top floor where he had first come in and proceeding deeper and deeper until he reached the bottom level, combing every centimeter of the empty halls and deserted rooms. Yet even though his search was proving futile, he didn't despair. The crypts in the Valley of the Dark Lords had felt drained—used up and sucked dry. The Unkown World felt different. There was still power here.

There had to be something here for him to find. He was certain of it. He refused to accept another failure.

It was in the lowest level of the Temple, far below the planet's surface, that his obsessive quest finally ended. When he first stumbled into the room his attention was immediately drawn by the remains of a massive computer, but it was clearly beyond any hope of repair. And then he noticed something on the stone wall behind the computer.

The surface was etched with a number of arcane symbols: the language of the Rakata, perhaps. They meant nothing to him, and he would have dismissed them without a second glance. Except that one of them was glowing.

He almost hadn't noticed it at first. It was subtle: a faint violet hue tracing the edges of one of the unusual shapes. It was almost perfectly level with his eye.

As he stared at it, the glow grew stronger. He stepped forward and reached out tentatively with his hand. The light winked out, startling him into taking a step back. He reached out again, but this time, instead of using his hand, he reached out with the Force.

The stone character flared to life.

Struggling to contain his eagerness, he again extended his hand and pressed hard against the glowing symbol. There was the sound of turning gears, and the grinding of stone on stone. The seams of a small square— less than half a meter on each side—took shape in the wall as a section of stone pushed out.

Bane stepped back as the chunk toppled down from the wall and shattered on the ground at his feet, revealing a small cubbyhole behind it. With no hesitation, he thrust his arm into the darkness to seize whatever was inside.

His fingers wrapped around something cold and heavy. He drew it out and stared in wonder at the artifact in his hand. Slightly larger than his fist, it had the shape of a four-sided pyramid—a tiny replica of the Temple in which he stood. Bane instantly recognized his prize for what it was: a Sith Holocron, a repository of forbidden knowledge just waiting to be unlocked.

The art of constructing Holocrons had been lost for countless millennia, but from his studies Bane knew something of the basic theory behind their design. The information they contained was stored within an interwoven, self-encrypted digital matrix. A Holocron's protection systems couldn't be circumvented or broken; the information couldn't be sliced or copied. There was only one way to access the knowledge captured within.

Each Holocron was imprinted with the personality of one or more Masters to serve as guardians. When accessed by one capable of understanding its secrets, the Holocron would project tiny, crude hologrammic images of the various guardians. Through interaction with the student, the programmed simulacra would teach and instruct in much the same way as would a flesh-and-blood mentor.

However, all accounts of Sith Holocrons had made mention of the ancient symbols adorning the four-sided pyramid. The Holocron he held in his hand was almost completely blank. Could this possibly predate even the Holocrons of the ancient Sith? Was this a relic of the Rakata themselves? Would the guardians of the Holocron be the imprinted personalities of alien Masters from a time even before the birth of the Republic? And if so, would they be willing to teach him their secrets? Would they even respond to him?

Moving carefully, he set the Holocron gently on the floor, then sat down before it. He crossed his legs and began the deep, slow breathing of a meditative trance. Gathering and focusing his energy, Bane projected a wave of dark Force power out to engulf the small relic on the floor. The Holocron began to sparkle and shimmer in response.

He held his breath in anticipation, unsure what would come next. A small beam of light projected out from the top, the particles scattered and diffused. They began to shift and spin, coalescing into a cloaked figure, its features completely hidden by the hood of its heavy robe.

Then a voice spoke, crisp and clear. "I am Darth Revan, Dark Lord of the Sith."

The empty halls of the Temple above trembled with the reverberations of Bane's triumphant, booming laughter.

———

To Bane it seemed the teachings contained within the single Holocron surpassed those of the Academy's entire archives. Revan had discovered many of the rituals of the ancient Sith, and as the Holocron's avatar explained their nature and purpose, Bane could barely wrap his mind around their awesome potential. Some of the rituals were so terrible—so dangerous to attempt, even for a true Sith Master—that he doubted he would ever dare to use them. Yet he dutifully copied them down on sheaves of flimsi, preserving them so he could study them in greater depth later.

And there was far more than just the ancient practices of dark side sorcerers stored inside the Holocron. In only a few short weeks he'd learned more about the true nature of the dark side than he had in all his time on Korriban. Revan had been a true Sith Lord, unlike the simpering Masters who bowed to Kaan and his Brotherhood. And soon all his knowledge—his understanding of the dark side—would belong to Bane.

———

Githany woke with a start, kicking the covers off her cot and onto the dirt floor of the tent. She was sweating and flushed, but it wasn't from the heat. Ruusan had entered its rainy season, and though the days were warm and humid, at night the temperature dropped enough that the sentries on duty could see the misty clouds of their own breath.

She'd been dreaming of Bane. No, not dreaming. The details were too sharp and clear to call it a dream; the experience too vivid and real. It was a vision. There was a link between the two of them, a bond established through their time together studying the Force. A connection between mentor and student was not unheard of, although Githany was no longer sure who had really been the Master and who the apprentice in their relationship.

Her vision had been one of stark clarity: Bane was going to come to

Ruusan. But he wasn't coming to join the Brotherhood. He was coming to destroy it.

She shivered, the perspiration cooling her skin in the chill night air. She rolled out of bed and pulled her heavy cloak on over her thin bedclothes. She had to speak to Kaan about this. It couldn't wait until morning.

The night was dark: the moon and stars were blocked out by the brooding storm clouds that had filled the sky ever since she and the others from Korriban had arrived. A light mist fell from the sky, a slight improvement from the steady drizzle that had been falling when she'd crawled wearily into bed.

A handful of other Sith were wandering the camp. A few mumbled unintelligible greetings as they passed, but most kept their heads down and their feet plodding steadily through the mud. The ardor Kaan had inspired when the reinforcements had arrived had been dulled by the seemingly endless stream of gray, wet days. It would be several more weeks before the rains abated and gave way to the sweltering heat of Ruusan's long summer. Until then Kaan's followers would continue to suffer from the damp and cold.

Githany paid no attention. Focused on her mission, she slowed only when she reached the entrance to the great tent that Kaan had made his personal quarters. There was a light burning inside; Lord Kaan was awake.

She entered tentatively. What she had to say was for his ears only. Fortunately, she found him alone. But she stopped in the entry, staring in morbid fascination at the apparition before her. In the dim glow of the lantern that served as the tent's only source of illumination, Kaan looked like a man gone mad.

He was pacing quickly up and down the length of the tent, his steps uneven and erratic. He was hunched over nearly double, muttering to himself and shaking his head. His left hand constantly strayed up to tug on a strand of his hair, then quickly jerked down as if it had been caught in some forbidden act.

She could hardly believe that this crazed being was the man she had chosen to follow. Was it possible Bane had been right all along? She was on the verge of slipping back out into the sodden night when Kaan turned and finally noticed her.

For a brief moment his eyes showed wild panic: they burned with the fear and desperation of a caged animal. Then suddenly he snapped to his full height, standing straight and tall. The look of terror left his eyes, replaced by one of cold anger.

"Githany," he said, his welcome as cold as his icy expression. "I was not expecting visitors."

Now it was she who felt fear. Lord Kaan radiated power: he could crush her as easily as she crushed the small beetles that sometimes scuttled across the floor of her tent. The memory of the craven, broken man was gone, blasted from her mind by the overwhelming aura of Kaan's authority.

"Forgive me, Lord Kaan," she said with a slight bow of her head. "I need to speak with you."

His anger seemed to soften, though he still maintained his undeniably commanding presence. "Of course, Githany. I always have time for you."

The words were more than cordial formality; there was something deeper beneath them. Githany was an attractive woman; she was used to being the object of innuendo and men's barely hidden desire. Usually it evoked little more than revulsion, but in Kaan's case it brought a warm flush to her cheeks. He was the founder of the Brotherhood of Darkness, a man of vision and destiny. How could she not be flattered by his attentions?

"I've had a premonition," she explained. "I saw . . . I saw Darth Bane. He was coming to Ruusan to destroy us."

"Qordis has made me well aware of Bane's views," he said, nodding. "This is not unexpected."

"He doesn't see the glory of our cause," Githany said, apologizing for Bane. "He's never met you in person. His only understanding of the Brotherhood comes through Qordis and the other Masters—the ones who turned their backs on him."

Kaan gave her a puzzled stare. "You came to warn me that Bane is planning to destroy us. Now it seems you are trying to justify his actions."

"The Force shows us what *may* be, not necessarily what *will* be," she reminded him. "If we can convince Bane to join us, he could be a valuable ally against the Jedi."

"I see," Kaan said. "You feel that if we bring him into the fold of the Brotherhood, then your premonition will not come true." There was a long pause, and then he asked, "Are you certain your personal feelings for him are not clouding your judgment in this matter?"

Embarrassed, Githany couldn't meet his eyes. "I'm not the only one who feels this way," she mumbled, staring down at the ground. "Many of the others from Korriban are troubled by his absence, as well. They've felt his strength. They wonder why one so strong in the dark side would reject the Brotherhood."

She raised her head when Kaan placed a comforting hand on her shoulder. "You might be right, Githany. But I cannot act on your suggestion. Nobody even knows where Bane is."

"I do. There is a . . . a bond between us. I can tell you where Bane has gone."

Kaan reached out to take her chin in his cupped palm. He tilted her head back ever so slightly. "Then I will send someone to him," he promised. "You did the right thing by coming to me, Githany," he added, gently releasing her and giving her a reassuring smile.

Githany, beaming with pride, smiled back.

————

She left a few minutes later, after explaining where Bane had gone and why. Kaan watched her go, her words troubling him though he was careful not to let it show. He had allayed her fears and he was confident she would remain loyal to the Brotherhood despite her obvious attraction to Bane. Githany imagined herself the object of every man's desire, but Kaan could see a similar desire burning brightly within her: she hungered for power and glory. And he was all too willing to feed her pride and ambition with his flirting, praise, and promises.

Still, he wasn't sure what to make of her vision. Though he was strong in the Force, his talents lay elsewhere. He could change the course of a war with his battle meditation. He could inspire loyalty in the other Lords through subtle manipulations of their emotions. But he had never experienced a premonition like the one that had brought her to his tent in the middle of the dark night.

His first inclination was to dismiss it as baseless worry brought on by low morale. The reinforcements from Korriban had brought expectations of a quick end to Ruusan's long war. But General Hoth was too clever to let his Army of Light be crushed by the superior Sith might. He had switched tactics, conducting a war of hit-and-run skirmishes, stalling for time as he tried to marshal more support for his own forces.

Now the Sith were growing impatient and restless. The glorious victory Kaan had promised them weeks earlier had not materialized. Instead they trudged through mud and never-ending rain, trying to defeat an enemy that wouldn't even stand and fight. Githany's visit hadn't surprised him. The only real surprise was that more of the Dark Lords hadn't come to voice their dissatisfaction.

But that only made Githany's warnings more dangerous. Bane had rejected the Brotherhood in a very public spectacle; all the recruits from Korriban claimed to have seen it in person. The story had spread through the camp like a plague. At first they had scoffed at his arrogance and stubbornness; he had chosen to walk alone, and he would not share in the triumph of the Brotherhood. In the absence of that triumph, however, some of the recruits had begun to wonder if Bane was right.

Lord Kaan had his spies among the Dark Lords. The whispers had reached his ears. The Lords were not ready to act on their doubts, but their resolve was weakening—along with their allegiance. He had forged a coalition of enemies and bitter rivals. Though the Brotherhood of Darkness appeared strong as durasteel, one firm voice of dissent could fracture it into a thousand fragile pieces.

He grabbed the lantern from his tent and headed out into the night's drizzle, his long stride propelling him quickly through the camp. He would deal with Bane, just as he had promised Githany. If the recalcitrant young man could not be convinced to join them, he would have to be eliminated.

Within a few minutes Kaan had reached his destination. He paused at the door, remembering his anger at Githany's unexpected entrance into his own tent. Not wishing to antagonize the man he had come to see, he called out, "Kas'im?"

"Come in," a voice answered a second later, and he heard the unmistakable *shuush* of a lightsaber powering down.

He entered to find the Twi'lek Blademaster clad only in breeches, sweating and breathing hard.

"I see you're up," he noted.

"It's not easy to sleep on the eve of battle. Even a battle that never seems to come."

Kas'im was a warrior; Kaan knew he chafed at their inactivity. Drills and exercises could not quench his desire for actual combat. At the Academy on Korriban the Blademaster had performed his duty without complaint. But here on Ruusan the promise of battle was too near, too insistent. The scent of blood was always in the air, mingling with the sweat of fear and anticipation. Here Kas'im could be satisfied only once he stood face-to-face with an enemy. Soon his frustration would boil over into rebellion, and Kaan could ill afford to lose the loyalty of the greatest swordsman of his camp. Fortunately, he had a way to deal with both his problems—Bane and Kas'im—in one fell swoop.

"I have a mission for you. A mission of great importance."

"I live to serve, Lord Kaan." Kas'im's answer was calm, but his head-tails twitched with anticipation.

"I must send you far from Ruusan. To the ends of the galaxy. You have to go to Lehon."

"The Unknown World?" the Blademaster asked, puzzled. "There is nothing there but the graveyard of our order's greatest defeat."

"Bane is there," Kaan explained. "You must go to him as my envoy. Explain that he must join the rest of the Sith here on Ruusan. Tell him that those who do not stand with the Brotherhood stand against it."

Kas'im shook his head. "I doubt it will make a difference. Once his mind is set he can be . . . stubborn."

"The dark side cannot be united in the Brotherhood if he stands alone," Kaan explained. As he spoke, he reached out with the Force, pushing ever so gently at the Twi'lek's wounded sense of pride. "I know he rejected you and the other Masters on Korriban. But you must make this offer once more."

"And when he refuses?" Kas'im's words were quick and sharp. Inwardly, Kaan smiled at the Blademaster's growing anger even as he pushed just a little more.

"Then you must kill him."

23

"Those who use the dark side are also bound to serve it. To understand this is to understand the underlying philosophy of the Sith."

Bane sat motionless, eyes riveted on the avatar of a Dark Lord three thousand years dead and gone. Revan's projected image winked out of existence, then slowly flickered back into view. The Holocron was failing. Dying. The material used to construct it—the crystal that channeled the energy of the Force to give the artifact life—was flawed. The more Bane used it, the less stable it became. Yet he couldn't set it aside, even for a single day. He had become obsessed with tapping all the knowledge trapped within, and he spent hours on end drinking in Revan's words with the same single-minded determination he had used when mining cortosis back on Apatros.

"The dark side offers power for power's sake. You must crave it. Covet it. You must seek power above all else, with no reservation or hesitation."

These words rang especially true for Bane, as if the preprogrammed personality of his virtual Master sensed it was nearing its end and had tailored its last lessons especially for him.

"The Force will change you. It will transform you. Some fear this change. The teachings of the Jedi are focused on fighting and controlling this transformation. That is why those who serve the light are limited in what they can accomplish.

"True power can come only to those who embrace the transformation. There can be no compromise. Mercy, compassion, loyalty: all these things will prevent you from claiming what is rightfully yours. Those who follow the dark side must cast aside these conceits. Those who do not—those who try to walk the path of moderation—will fail, dragged down by their own weakness."

The words almost perfectly described Bane as he had been during his time at the Academy. Despite this, he felt no shame or regret. That Bane no longer existed. Just as he had cast aside the miner from Apatros when he had taken his Sith name, so had he cast aside the stumbling, uncertain apprentice when he had claimed the *Darth* title for himself. When he'd rejected Qordis and the Brotherhood, he had begun the transformation Revan spoke of, and with the Holocron's help he was at last on the verge of completing it.

"Those who accept the power of the dark side must also accept the challenge of holding on to it," Revan continued. "By its very nature, the dark side invites rivalry and strife. This is the greatest strength of the Sith: it culls the weak from our order. Yet this rivalry can also be our greatest weakness. The strong must be careful lest they be overwhelmed by the ambitions of those beneath them working in concert. Any Master who instructs more than one apprentice in the ways of the dark side is a fool. In time the apprentices will unite their strength and overthrow the Master. It is inevitable. Axiomatic. That is why each Master must have only one student."

Bane didn't respond, but his lip instinctively curled up in disgust as he remembered his instruction at the Academy. Qordis and the others had passed the apprentices around from class to class, as if they were children in school instead of heirs to the legacy of the Sith. Was it any wonder he had struggled to reach his full potential in such a flawed system?

"This is also the reason there can be only one Dark Lord. The Sith must be ruled by a single leader: the very embodiment of the strength and power of the dark side. If the leader grows weak, another must rise to seize the mantle. The strong rule; the weak are meant to serve. This is the way it must be."

The image flickered and jumped, and then the tiny replica of Darth Revan bowed its head, drawing its hood up to hide its features once more. "My time here is ended. Take what I have taught you and use it well."

And then Revan was gone. The glow emanating from the Holocron faded away to nothing. Bane retrieved the small crystal pyramid from the floor, but it was cold and lifeless in his hands. He felt no trace of the Force inside it.

The artifact was of no more use to him. As Revan had taught him, it must therefore be discarded. He let it drop to the floor. Then, very slowly and deliberately, he crushed it with the power of the Force until only dust remained.

────────

The Sith Buzzard broke into Lehon's atmosphere and plummeted down through the clear blue sky. At the controls Kas'im made slight alterations to keep his vessel on its course, a direct line for the homing beacon of the *Valcyn*.

He'd half expected Bane to have disabled the beacon, or at least changed its frequency. But despite being aware of it—the beacon was standard on virtually all craft—he had left it alone. Almost as if he wasn't afraid of anyone coming after him. As if he welcomed it.

Within a few minutes Kas'im got a visual on his target. The ship that had once—briefly—belonged to Qordis before Bane had taken it for his own was resting on a beach of white sand, the azure waters of the Unknown World's vast oceans on one side and the impenetrable jungle on the other. Scans showed no signs of life in the immediate vicinity, but Kas'im was wary as he brought his own craft in to touch down beside it.

He powered down the Buzzard and climbed out of the hatch. He felt the energy of the world, and the unmistakable presence of Darth Bane, seemingly emanating from the jungle's dark heart. Leaping to the ground, he landed with a dull thud on the soft-packed sand, his feet sinking in ever so slightly. A cursory examination of the *Valcyn* confirmed what he'd already suspected: his prey wasn't here.

Any tracks Bane might have left in the sand had been washed away by the tides or carried away on the breeze. Yet he knew where he was going. Before him, the jungle loomed lush and vibrant, thick and forbidding: an almost impenetrable wall of vegetation, except for a wide swath carved through it.

Someone or something of massive size and strength had torn that path through the trees and undergrowth. Already the jungle was trying to reclaim it. Moss grew thick across the ground, and a vast network of creeping vines wound their way over the surface. But it was clear enough for the Twi'lek to follow.

Hidden eyes were watching him from the jungle: even without the Force he would have felt their gaze studying him, evaluating him, following his every move in an effort to determine if this newcomer to the ecosystem was hunter or prey. To help clarify his role, he drew out his great double lightsaber and ignited the twin blades, then began to jog slowly down the path.

As he ran, he probed the surrounding foliage with the Force. Most of the creatures he sensed posed little threat. Still, he was wary. Something had blazed the trail he was following. Something big.

Almost ten kilometers in—he'd been jogging for nearly an hour—the Blademaster finally encountered his first rancor. The trail took a sharp turn to the east, and as he wound around the corner the creature burst from the surrounding trees, snarling and howling.

Kas'im wasn't surprised in the least by the ambush. He'd sensed the rancor's presence from several hundred meters away, just as it had surely caught his scent and stalked him from some great distance. He met the creature's charge with calm, ruthless efficiency.

Ducking under the first swiping claw, he carved a deep gash along the beast's left foreleg. When it reared back to bellow in pain, he sliced another deep groove in its soft underbelly. The rancor didn't fall right away; it was far too massive to be felled by a pair of wounds from a lightsaber. Instead the pain drove it into a berserk rage. It flailed about with its teeth and talons, spinning, snapping, and slashing at everything around it.

Kas'im twisted and dodged, leaping over one attack, then dropping to the ground to roll beneath another. He moved so fast he would have been nothing but a blur had the rancor not been blinded by rage. And with each evasion he struck another blow, whittling away at the mountain of sinew and flesh like a master sculptor working a lump of lommite.

The rancor floundered, lumbering and stumbling as if it were performing some drunken spacer's dance. In contrast, Kas'im was quick and precise. With each passing second his opponent slowed, its strength ebbing away. At last, with a forlorn groan, the beast toppled forward and lay motionless.

Leaving the beast where it had collapsed, Kas'im pressed on with a newfound urgency to his pace. The battle, short and simple as it had proved, was the first time he'd been tested in a true life-or-death struggle since he'd agreed to help Qordis train the students at the Academy. He was pleased to see that his skills had not been diminished by the long layoff.

Kas'im had a feeling he was going to need those skills again before the day was through.

———

Bane was sitting cross-legged on the stone floor of the central chamber on the Rakatan Temple's uppermost floor. He was meditating on Revan's words as he had often done between the Holocron's lessons. Now that the artifact was gone, it was even more important to contemplate what he had learned about the nature of the dark side . . . and the path it would lead him down.

By its very nature, the dark side invites rivalry and strife. This is the greatest strength of the Sith: it culls the weak from our order.

The constant battling of the Sith since the beginning of recorded history served a necessary purpose: it kept the power of the dark side concentrated in a few powerful individuals. The Brotherhood had changed all that. There were now a hundred or more Dark Lords following Kaan, but most were weak and inferior. The Sith numbers were greater than they had ever been, yet they were still losing the war against the Jedi.

The power of the dark side cannot be dispersed among the masses. It must be concentrated in the few who are worthy of the honor.

The strength of numbers was a trap . . . one that had snared all the great Sith Lords who had come before. Naga Sadow, Exar Kun, Darth Revan: each had been powerful. Each had drawn disciples in, teaching them the ways of the dark side. Each had assembled an army of followers and unleashed them against the Jedi. Yet in each and every case the servants of light had prevailed.

The Jedi would always remain united in their cause. The Sith would always be brought low by infighting and betrayals. The very traits that drove them to individual greatness and glory—the unrelenting ambition, the insatiable hunger for power—would ultimately doom them as a whole. This was the inescapable paradox of the Sith.

Kaan had tried to solve the problem by making everyone equal in the Brotherhood. But his solution was flawed. It showed no understanding of the real problem. No understanding of the true nature of the dark side. *The Sith must be ruled by a single leader: the very embodiment of the strength and power of the dark side.*

If all are equal, then none is strong. Yet whoever rose from the swollen and bloated ranks of the Sith to claim the mantle of Dark Lord would never be able to hold it. *In time the apprentices will unite their strength and overthrow the Master. It is inevitable.* Together the weak would overwhelm the strong in a gross perversion of the natural order.

But there was another solution. A way to break the endless cycle dragging the Sith down. Bane understood that now. At first he had thought the answer might be to replace the order of the Sith with a single, all-powerful Dark Lord. No other Masters. No apprentices. Just one vessel to contain all the knowledge and power of the dark side. But he had quickly dismissed the idea.

Eventually even a Dark Lord would wither and die; all the knowledge of the Sith would be lost. *If the leader grows weak, another must rise to seize the mantle.* One alone would never work. But if the Sith numbered exactly two . . .

Minions and servants could be drawn in to the service of the dark side by the temptation of power. They could be given small tastes of what it offered, as an owner might share morsels from the table with his faithful curs. In the end, however, there could be only one true Sith Master. And to serve this Master, there could be only one true apprentice.

Two there should be; no more, no less. One to embody the power, the other to crave it. The Rule of Two.

This was the knowledge that would lead the dark side into a new age. A revelation that would bring an end to the infighting that had defined the order for a thousand generations. The Sith would be reborn, the new ways would be swept away—and Bane would be the one to do it.

But first he would have to destroy the Brotherhood. Kaan, Qordis—all who had studied with him on Korriban, all the Masters on Ruusan—had to be purged until he alone remained.

Darth Bane, Lord of the Sith. The title was his by right; there was no other strong enough in the dark side to challenge him. The only question that remained was who was worthy of being his apprentice. And how he would eliminate the others.

"Bane!" Kas'im's voice cut off his thoughts midstream. "I come with an invitation from Lord Kaan."

Bane leapt to his feet, whipping out his lightsaber, enraged at being disturbed on the cusp of enlightenment. He glared at Kas'im, as angry at himself for being too engrossed in his own thoughts to sense the Twi'lek's presence as he was at the interruption.

"How did you find me?" he asked, casting out with his mind to see who else might have invaded the Rakatan Temple and its inner sanctum. He felt a mixture of relief and disappointment when he realized Kas'im was alone. He had been hoping for one more . . . but she must have chosen not to come.

"Lord Kaan told me you had come to this world. Once I entered the atmosphere, I simply followed the *Valcyn*'s beacon," the Blademaster replied. "How Lord Kaan knew you would be here I couldn't say."

Bane suspected Githany must have told him, but he didn't bother telling that to the Twi'lek. Instead he asked, "Did Kaan send you to kill me?"

Kas'im gave a slight nod. "If you will not join the Brotherhood, I will leave your corpse on this barren and forgotten world."

"Barren?" Bane echoed, incredulous. "How can you say that? The dark side is strong here. Far stronger than it ever was on Korriban. This is where we will find the power to destroy the Jedi—not in Kaan's Brotherhood!"

"Korriban was once a place of great power, too," his former instructor countered. "Over the centuries thousands of Sith have explored its secrets, and none of them discovered any great strategy to defeat our enemy." The

Twi'lek ignited his double-bladed lightsaber before continuing. "It is time to end this foolish quest, Bane. The old ways have failed. The Jedi defeated those who followed them: Exar Kun, Darth Revan . . . they all lost! We have to find a new philosophy if we want to defeat them."

For a brief moment Bane felt the faint flicker of excitement. Kas'im's words echoed his own thoughts. Was it possible the Blademaster was the apprentice he sought?

Kas'im's next words brought Bane's hopes crashing down. "Kaan understands this. That is why he created the Brotherhood. The Brotherhood is the future of the dark side."

Bane shook his head. The Blademaster was as blind as all the others. For that he had to die. "Kaan is wrong. I will never follow him. I will never join the Brotherhood."

Kas'im sighed. "Then your life ends here." And he leapt in, his weapon moving with far more speed than he had ever shown during their practice sessions.

Parrying the first sequence Bane realized his former Master had always been holding something in reserve . . . just as Bane himself had done in the early stages of his battle against Sirak. Only now was he seeing Kas'im's true ability, and he was barely able to defend himself. Barely, but still able.

His opponent grunted in surprise when Bane warded him off, then stepped back to regroup. He'd come in hard and fast, expecting to end their battle quickly. Now he had to reevaluate his strategy.

"You're better than you were when we last fought," he said, clearly impressed and making no attempt to hide it.

"So are you," Bane responded.

Kas'im lunged in again, and the room was filled with the hiss and hum of lightsabers striking each other half a dozen times in the space of two heartbeats. Bane would have been carved to ribbons had he tried to react to each move individually. Instead he simply called upon the Force, letting it flow through him and guide his hand. He gave himself over to the dark side completely, without reservation. His weapon became an extension of the Force, and he responded to the Twi'lek's unstoppable attack with an impenetrable defense.

Then *he* went on the attack. In the past he had always been afraid to surrender his will to the raw emotions that fueled the dark side. Now he had no such limitations; for the first time he was calling on his full potential.

He drove Kas'im back with furious slashes, forcing his old mentor into a backpedaling retreat across the floor of the chamber. Kas'im flipped back and out through the door into the hall beyond, but Bane was relentless in his pursuit, leaping forward and coming within a centimeter of landing a crippling blow to the Twi'lek's leg.

His strike was turned aside at the last second, but he quickly followed it up with another series of powerful thrusts and stabs. The Blademaster continued to give ground, pushed inexorably back by the raging storm of Bane's onslaught. Each time he tried to change tactics or switch forms, Bane anticipated, reacted, and seized the advantage.

The outcome was inevitable. Bane was simply too strong in the Force. Only some unexpected maneuver could save Kas'im, but they had fought too many times in the past for him to surprise Bane now. Over the course of his training Bane had seen every possible sequence, series, move, and trick with the double-bladed lightsaber, and he knew how to counter and nullify them all.

The Blademaster became desperate. Leaping, spinning, ducking, rolling: he was wild and reckless in his retreat, seeking now only to escape with his life. But he didn't know the Temple like Bane did. Bane kept the routes to the outside cut off, slowly herding his opponent into a dead-end hallway.

Recognizing what was happening, Kas'im blew open the heavy door of a side room with the Force and dived inside. Bane knew there was no other exit, and he paused at the threshold of the room to savor his victory.

The Twi'lek stood in the center of the empty chamber, panting heavily, stooped ever so slightly, his head bowed. He looked up when Bane stepped through the doorway. But when his gaze met Bane's, there was no hint of defeat in his eyes.

"You should have finished me when you had the chance," he said. There was less than five meters between them, but it was just enough space for Kas'im to give the hilt of his lightsaber a quick twist. The long handle separated in the middle, and suddenly he was armed not with one double-bladed lightsaber, but with a pair of single blades, one in each hand.

Bane hesitated. Few of the students at the Academy had even attempted to use two sabers at once. The Blademaster had always discouraged them from this variation of the fourth form, saying it was inherently flawed. Now, as he saw the cruel and cunning expression on his enemy's face, Bane understood the real truth.

The battle was rejoined, but now it was Bane who was in full retreat. Without proper training, even his enormous command of the Force was unable to anticipate the unfamiliar sequences of the two-handed fighting style. His mind was flooded with a million options of what his opponent might attempt, and he had no experience to draw on to eliminate any of them. Overwhelmed, he staggered back, floundering with the desperation of a drowning man.

Within the first few passes Bane knew he couldn't win. Kas'im had trained his entire life for this moment. After years of study, he'd mastered all seven forms of the lightsaber. Then he'd honed his skill for decades, perfecting every move and sequence until he had become the perfect weapon and the greatest living swordsman in the galaxy. Maybe the greatest swordsman ever. Bane was no match for him.

The Blademaster was unrelenting in his pressure. He seemed to wield six blades rather than two: he attacked with a peculiar rhythm designed to keep his foe off balance, coming in with one blade high and the other low at the same time, striking from opposite sides at odd and opposing angles. Bane had no option but to fall back . . . and back . . . and back. He was fighting now with a single purpose: somehow escaping with his life. One hope gave him the strength to persevere in the face of overwhelming odds; one advantage the Blademaster had lacked during his own retreat. He knew the layout of the Temple, and he was able to work himself slowly toward the exit.

Battling through the halls and corridors, the combatants rounded a corner to bring them in sight of the Rakatan Temple's only entrance: the wide archway and the small landing beyond, with the wide staircase leading back down to the ground nearly twenty meters below. In the instant it took Kas'im to recognize where they were and realize that his opponent might still escape, Bane thrust out with the Force. He knocked the Twi'lek off balance for a brief second, then backflipped out through the archway and onto the landing. He dropped into a crouch, still facing his opponent. But in his haste Bane had leapt too far; he was balanced precariously on the precipice of the uppermost stair, the steps falling sharply away behind him.

Kas'im responded by using the Force to knock Bane backward, sending him tumbling down the great stone staircase, away from the Blademaster. The fall would have broken his neck—or at least fractured an arm or a leg—if Bane hadn't cocooned himself in the Force. Even so he reached the bottom bruised, battered, and momentarily stunned.

On the landing high above Kas'im stood beneath the massive arch of the Temple entrance, staring down at him.

"I will follow you wherever you run," he said. "Wherever you go I will eventually find you and kill you. Don't live your life in fear, Bane. Better to end it now."

"I agree," Bane replied, hurling out the wave of Force energy he had been gathering during the Blademaster's speech.

There was nothing subtle about Bane's attack: the massive shock wave shook the very foundations of the great Rakatan Temple. The concussive blast had enough power to shatter every bone in Kas'im's body and pulverize his flesh into a mass of pulpy liquid. But at the last possible instant he threw up a shield to protect himself from the attack.

Unfortunately, he couldn't shield the Temple around him. The walls exploded into great chunks of rubble. The archway collapsed in a shower of stone, burying Kas'im beneath tons of rock and mortar. A second later the rest of the roof caved in, drowning out the Twi'lek's dying screams with a deafening rumble.

Bane watched the spectacle of the Temple's implosion from the safety of the ground at the foot of the stairs. Billowing clouds of dust rolled out from the wreckage and down the stairs toward him. Exhausted by the long lightsaber battle and drained by the sudden unleashing of the Force, he simply lay there until he was covered in a layer of fine white powder.

Eventually he struggled wearily to his feet. Reaching out with the Force, he sought some sign that Kas'im might still be alive beneath the mountain of stone. He felt nothing. Kas'im—his mentor, the only instructor at the Academy who had ever actually helped him—was dead.

Darth Bane, Dark Lord of the Sith, turned his back and walked away.

24

There was neither time nor reason to mourn Kas'im's death. For all his use in the past, he had become simply an obstacle in Bane's path. An obstacle that was now gone. Yet his arrival on Lehon had prompted Bane to action. For too long he had separated himself from the events of the galaxy, seeking wisdom, understanding, and power. With the Temple's destruction there was no reason for him to remain on the Unknown World. And so he began the long trek through the jungle on foot, following the same path Kas'im had taken only hours before.

He could have used the Force to summon another rancor to speed him along, but he wanted time to think about what had happened . . . and how he would deal with the Brotherhood.

Kaan had perverted the entire Sith order, transforming it into a sickly assemblage of mewling sycophants. He had tricked them all into believing they could achieve victory over the Jedi through martial might, but Bane knew better. The Jedi were many, and they gained strength when united against a common foe: that was the nature of the light side. The key to defeating them wasn't fleets or armies. Secrecy and deception were the weapons to bring them down. Victory could only come through subtlety and cunning.

Subtlety was something Kaan lacked. If he had been smart, he would have sent Kas'im to Lehon in the guise of a disgruntled follower. The Blademaster could have arrived with a tale of how he had turned his back on the Brotherhood. Bane would have accepted him as an ally. He would have been suspicious, of course, but over time his vigilance would have waned. Sooner or later he would have let his guard down, and Kas'im could have killed him. Assassination was quick, clean, and effective.

Instead, Kas'im had come and issued an open challenge, following the rules of some foolish code of honor. There was no honor in his end; there was no such thing as a noble death. Honor was a lie, a chain that wrapped itself around those foolish enough to accept it and dragged them down to defeat. *Through victory my chains are broken.*

Bane followed the rancor's trail through the trees without incident; the denizens of the jungle steered well clear of him. He caught a brief glimpse of a pack of six-legged felines scavenging the corpse of a rancor along the path, but they scattered at his approach. They waited a long time after he was gone before slinking back to continue their meal.

By the time he arrived at the beach he had devised his plan. Kas'im's ship was sitting on the sand beside his own, and he quickly stripped it of supplies, including the message drones. He lugged them over to his own vessel, then made a quick inspection of the *Valcyn*. Finding all systems in working order, he boarded. Before liftoff, he programmed a course into the message drone using coordinates he had downloaded from Kas'im's ship. A few minutes later, the *Valcyn* launched from the Unknown World's surface, climbing higher and higher until it broke through the atmosphere into the black void of space. Bane punched in the hyperspace coordinates of his destination, then discharged the message drone.

The drone would reach Ruusan within a few days, offering Kaan a truce and delivering a gift—a gift he suspected Kaan would be too foolish and vain to recognize for what it really was.

The Brotherhood would never defeat the Jedi. And as long as they existed, the Sith would be tainted, befouled like a well poisoned at the source. Bane had to destroy them. All of them. To do that, he'd have to use the weapons Kaan had been too proud or too blind to use against him: deception and betrayal. The weapons of the dark side.

"I don't like splitting our squads like this," Pernicar whispered, following closely at Lord Hoth's heel. The general looked back along the ragtag line of soldiers trudging through the forest. Less than a score in total, half starved, most wounded and ill equipped, they looked more like refugees than warriors in the Army of Light. They were carrying supplies from the drop point back to the camp, as were two other caravans taking different routes.

"It's too dangerous to travel in one large group," Hoth insisted. "We need these supplies. Splitting us into three caravans gives us a better chance that at least some of them will make it back to camp."

Hoth glanced back along the path they had come, wary of signs of pursuit. The rains had stopped nearly a week earlier, but the ground was still soft. The passing of his troops left deep impressions in the loamy ground.

"Even a blind Gamorrean could track us now," he grumbled. Silently he wished for a return of the concealing rains he had so often cursed these past few months while sitting huddled and shivering beneath inadequate shelters fashioned from leaves and fallen branches.

Yet he knew it wasn't trackers they had to worry about. He cast out with the Force, trying to sense hidden enemies lying in wait in the trees ahead. Nothing. Of course if there were any Sith, they would be projecting false images to conceal themselves for their—

"Ambush!" one of the points screamed, and then the Sith were upon them. They came from everywhere: warriors wielding lightsabers, soldiers armed with blasters and vibroblades. The clash of durasteel and the hiss of crossing energy blades mingled with the screams of the living and the dying: screams of rage and triumph; of agony and despair.

A volley of blasterfire ripped through his lines, taking down those Padawans too inexperienced to deflect the shots. A second volley tore through the melee. The bolts ricocheted wildly as Sith and Jedi alike batted them aside, doing little real harm but adding to the chaos. Lord Hoth stood in the thickest of the fighting, hewing down foes foolish enough to come in range of his fierce weapon. His nostrils were filled with the greasy-sweet stench of charred flesh, and a wall of bodies was mounting around him. And still they kept coming, swarming over him like carrion beetles on a fresh kill, seeking to drag him down by sheer numbers.

Pernicar vanished beneath the sea of enemies, and Hoth redoubled his efforts to reach his fallen friend. He was unstoppable in his fury, like the devastating storms of the Maw itself. When he reached him, Pernicar was already dead. Just as the rest of them soon would be.

An explosion on the edge of the battle briefly drew his attention skyward. One eager minion of the Sith lunged forward, seeking glory beyond her wildest expectations by trying to kill the mighty general while he was distracted. Hoth never even turned his gaze, but merely cast out with the Force, imprisoning her in a stasis field. She stood helpless, frozen in place until struck down by the careless follow-through from a vibroblade wielded by one of her own side.

Her death barely even registered in Hoth's conscious thoughts. He was focused on the four swoopbikes barreling down on the battle, their heavy guns pounding into the enemy lines. The Sith ambush scattered, unable or unwilling to stand against heavy air support. It took all of Hoth's Jedi training not to chase after them and hack them down from behind as they fled into the safety of the trees.

A moment later the swoops landed to cheers from the dozen or so Jedi still standing. Lord Valenthyne Farfalla, looking as fastidiously proper as ever, dismounted and bowed low before his general.

"I heard you were bringing supplies, my lord," he said, rising with all the affected elegance of a Coruscant Senator. "We thought we'd come give you an escort."

"There are two other caravans," Hoth snapped. "Instead of standing here gloating, you should be heading out to help them."

Farfalla pursed his lips in displeasure, a peevish, pouty expression. "We have other swoops escorting them already." He hesitated, as if considering whether to say anything more. Hoth shot him an angry look that all but screamed at him to remain silent.

Despite this—or maybe because of it—he added, "I thought you'd be more welcoming to my reinforcements."

"You've been gone for months!" Hoth snarled. "While you've been out playing diplomat, we've been stuck here in a war."

"I did as I promised," Farfalla responded coldly. "I've brought three hundred Jedi reinforcements. They'll be in your camp as soon as we have enough fighters to break our transports through the Sith planetary blockade."

"Little comfort to those who gave their lives waiting for you to arrive," Hoth shot back.

Farfalla glanced at the corpses scattered on the ground. Seeing Pernicar among them, his expression fell. He crouched down beside the body and whispered a few short words, then touched the fallen soldier once in the center of his brow before standing up once more.

"Pernicar was my friend, too," he said, his tone softer now. "His death pains me as much as it does you, General."

"I doubt that," Hoth muttered angrily. "You weren't even here to see it."

"Do not let your grief consume you," Farfalla warned, the ice back in his voice. "That path leads to the dark side."

"Don't you dare speak to me of the dark side!" Hoth shouted, jabbing an angry finger in Farfalla's face. "I'm the one who's been here battling Kaan's Brotherhood! I know its ways better than anyone! I've seen the pain and suffering it brings. And I know what it will take to defeat it. I need soldiers. Supplies. I need Jedi willing to fight the enemy with the same hatred they feel for us." He let his finger drop and turned away. "What I don't need is some prancing dandy lecturing me on the dangers of the dark side."

"Pernicar's death is not your fault," Farfalla said, coming forward to place a comforting hand on Hoth's shoulder. "Let go of your guilt. *There is no emotion. There is peace.*"

Hoth wheeled around and slapped his hand away. "Get away from me! Take your blasted reinforcements and run back to Coruscant like the mincing cowards you are! We don't need your kind here!"

Now it was Farfalla who turned away, stomping angrily back to his swoopbike while the rest of the group watched in silent shock and horror. He threw one long leg over the seat and fired up the engines.

"Maybe the other Jedi were right about you!" he said, shouting to be heard over the roar of his swoop. "This war has consumed you. Driven you to madness. Madness that will lead you to the dark side!"

Hoth didn't bother to watch as Farfalla and the other swoops sped off into the distance. Instead he crouched down beside the body of his oldest friend and wept at his brutal, senseless end.

––––––––––

When Githany finally arrived, Kaan had to keep himself from snapping at her. She had already seen him with his guard down: uncertain, unsure. He had to be careful when dealing with her now, lest he lose her allegiance. And he needed her more than ever.

Instead he spoke in a casual tone that held only a hint of icy disapproval beneath its surface. "I sent for you nearly three hours ago."

She flashed him a fierce, savage smile. "There was a sortie going out against one of the Jedi supply caravans. I decided to go with them."

"I haven't heard the reports yet. What was the result?"

"It was glorious, Lord Kaan!" She laughed. "Three more Masters, six Jedi Knights, a handful of Padawans . . . all dead!"

Kaan nodded his approval. The tide of battle was ever changing on Ruusan, and with the end of the rainy season the pendulum had swung back in favor of the Sith. Of course he knew it was more than a change of weather that had restored the morale of his troops and brought them a string of resounding victories.

The Army of Light was fractured. Their numbers on Ruusan were dwindling. Valenthyne Farfalla was orbiting the world with reinforcements, but Kaan's spies reported a rift between Hoth and Lord Farfalla that kept the newcomers from joining the fray. Without Master Pernicar to blunt their sharp animosity, the two Jedi Masters' mutual antipathy was crippling the Jedi war effort.

The irony of the situation was not lost on Kaan. For a change it was the Jedi who were split by infighting and rivalries, while the Brotherhood of Darkness remained united and strong. Part of him found the strange reversal troubling. In the long nights when he couldn't sleep, he'd often walk the floor of his tent wrestling with the seeming paradox.

Had the armies on Ruusan crossed a line where light and darkness meet? Had the endless conflict between the Army of Light and the Brotherhood of Darkness drawn them both into a void where the ideologies became hopelessly intertwined? Were they all now Force-users of the Twilight, caught between the two sides and belonging to neither?

However, the arrival of the morning sun would inevitably banish such thoughts with news of yet another Sith victory in the field. And only a fool questioned his methods when he was winning. Which was why he wasn't sure what to make of the message he had recently received from Darth Bane.

"Kas'im is dead," he told Githany, getting directly to the matter at hand.

"Dead?" Her shocked reaction affirmed Kaan's decision not to share this news with the rest of the Brotherhood. He had been careful to keep the purpose of the Blademaster's departure secret until he knew the outcome of the confrontation. "Was it the Jedi?" she asked.

"No," he admitted, choosing his words carefully. "I sent him to parlay with Lord Bane. Kas'im thought he could convince him to join us. Instead, Bane killed him."

Githany's eyes narrowed. "I warned you about him."

Kaan nodded. "You know him better than any of us. You understand him. That is why I need you now. Bane sent me a message."

He reached over and flicked on the message drone sitting on the table. A tiny hologram of the heavily muscled Dark Lord materialized before them. Even though the details of his expression were difficult to make out at that size, it was clear he was troubled.

"Kas'im is dead. I . . . I killed him. But I've been thinking about what he said before . . . before he died."

Githany gave Kaan a curious look. He shrugged and tilted his head toward the hologram as it continued to speak.

"I came here searching for something. I'm . . . I'm not even sure what it was. But I didn't find it. Just like I didn't find it in the Valley of the Dark Lords on Korriban. And now Kas'im is dead and I . . . I don't know what to do . . ."

The projection bowed its head: lost, confused, and alone. Kaan could clearly see the scorn in Githany's expression as she watched the spectacle before her. At last the figure seemed to compose itself, and it looked up once more.

"I don't want Kas'im's death to be in vain," Bane said emphatically. "I should have listened to him in the first place. I . . . I want to join the Brotherhood."

Kaan reached out and flicked the drone off again. "Well?" he asked Githany. "Is he serious? Or is this just a trap?"

She chewed at her lower lip. "I think he's sincere," she finally said. "For all his power, Bane is still weak. He can't surrender himself fully to the dark side. He still feels guilt when he uses the Force to kill."

"Qordis mentioned something similar," Kaan said. "He told me Bane had a chance to kill a bitter rival in the dueling ring at the Academy, but he pulled back at the last moment."

Githany nodded. "Sirak. He just couldn't bring himself to do it. And Kas'im was his mentor. If Bane was forced to kill him, it would have been even harder for him to deal with it."

"So I should send an emissary to meet with him?"

She shook her head. "Bane is more trouble than he's worth. He's vulnerable now, but as his confidence returns he'll become as headstrong as ever. He'll bring dissension to the ranks. Besides," she added, "we don't need him anymore. We're winning."

"So how do you propose we deal with him? Assassins?"

She laughed. "If he could handle Kas'im, then I doubt anyone else will stand a chance against him. Anyone but me."

"You?"

Githany smiled. "Bane likes me. I wouldn't say he trusts me, exactly . . . but he *wants* to trust me. Let me go to him."

"And what will you do when you find him?"

"Tell him I miss him. Explain that we've considered his offer, and we want him to join the Brotherhood. Then, when his guard is down, I'll kill him."

Kaan raised his eyebrows. "You make it sound so simple."

"Unlike Kas'im, I know how to handle him," she assured him. "Betrayal is a far more effective weapon than the lightsaber."

She left the tent a few moments later, taking the message drone and the coordinates Bane had sent along for the meeting. Kaan had every confidence she'd get the job done. And he saw no reason to share with her the small package that had arrived in the message drone's storage compartment.

Bane had sent it to Lord Kaan as a peace offering; a way to atone for Kas'im's death. It wasn't much to look at: text written on several sheets of flimsi, the writing cramped and hurried as if it had been recorded while listening to someone else speak. Yet within its pages it contained a detailed description of one of the most fearsome creations of the ancient Sith: the thought bomb.

An ancient ritual that required the combined will of many powerful Sith Lords, the thought bomb unleashed the pure destructive energy of the dark side. There were risks involved, of course. That much power was highly volatile, making it difficult to control even for those who had the strength to summon it. It was possible the blast could annihilate the entire Brotherhood along with Hoth's Army of Light. The vacuum at the center of the blast could suck in the disembodied spirits of Sith and Jedi alike, trapping them side by side for all eternity in an unbreakable state of equilibrium at the heart of a frozen sphere of pure energy.

Kaan doubted he'd actually have need of such a weapon to finish off the Jedi here on Ruusan. After all, he was winning the war. Still, as he began his pacing for another long and sleepless night, he couldn't help studying the ritual of the thought bomb over and over again.

25

From a distance, Ambria looked beautiful. An orange world with striking violet rings, it was easily the largest habitable planet in the Stenness system. Yet anyone landing on the world would quickly realize that the beauty faded soon after entering the atmosphere.

Many centuries earlier, the failed rituals of a powerful Sith sorceress had inadvertently unleashed a cataclysmic wave of dark side energy across the surface of the world. The sorceress had been destroyed, along with almost all other life on Ambria. What survived was little more than barren rock, and even now plots of fertile ground were few and far between. There were no real cities on Ambria; only a few hardy settlers dwelled on its surface, scattered so far apart they might as well have been living on the planet alone.

The Jedi had once tried to cleanse Ambria of its foul taint, but the power of the dark side had permanently scarred the world. Unable to purify it, they succeeded only in concentrating and confining the dark side in a single source: Lake Natth. The homesteaders brave enough to endure Ambria's desolate environs gave the lake and its poisoned waters a wide, wide berth. Of course Bane had made his camp right on its shores.

Ambria was located on the fringes of the Expansion Region, only a quick hyperspace jump away from Ruusan itself. The evidence of several small battles that had been fought here between Republic and Sith troops during the most recent campaign was everywhere. Fallen weapons and armor littered the stark landscape; burned-out vehicles and damaged swoops were visible from kilometers away on the hard, cold plains. Apart from a few of the local settlers scavenging for parts, nobody had bothered to clean up the remains.

The ringed planet was an insignificant world: too few resources and too few people for the Republic fleets that now controlled the sector to worry about. Bane had heard that a healer of some skill—a man named Caleb—had come to the world once the fighting had ended. An idealistic fool determined to mend the wounds of war; a man not even worthy of Bane's contempt. By now, even that man might have forsaken this world once he'd seen how little salvageable remained here. For all intents and purposes, the world was forgotten.

It was the perfect place to meet Kaan's envoy. A Sith fleet would be quickly detected by the Republic vessels patrolling the region, but a small ship and a skillful pilot could sneak in without any trouble. Bane had no intention of setting up a meeting someplace where Kaan could send an armada to wipe him out.

He waited patiently in his camp for Kaan's emissary to arrive. Occasionally he glanced up at the sky or looked out across the horizon, but he wasn't worried about anyone sneaking up on him. He'd see a ship coming in to land from several kilometers away. And if they came to him in a ground vehicle—like the land crawler sitting on the edge of his camp—he'd hear the grinding of its engines or feel the unmistakable vibrations of its heavy treads as they churned their way over the uneven terrain.

Instead all he heard was the gentle lapping of Lake Natth's dark waters against the shore not five meters from where he sat. And all the while, his mind wrestled with the only question he still had no answer for.

Two there should be; no more, no less. One to embody the power, the other to crave it. Once he had rid the galaxy of the Brotherhood of Darkness, where would he find a worthy apprentice?

The whine of a Buzzard's engines pulled him away from his thoughts. He rose to his feet as the ship dropped from the sky and circled his camp once before touching down a short distance away. When the landing ramp lowered and he saw who came down, he couldn't help but smile.

"Githany," he said, rising to greet her once she had crossed the distance between them. "I was hoping Lord Kaan would send you."

"He didn't send me," she replied. "I asked to come."

Bane's heart began to beat a little quicker. He was glad to see her; her presence awakened a hunger inside him he had almost forgotten existed. Yet he was troubled, too. If anyone could see through his ruse, it was her.

"Did you see the message?" he asked, studying her carefully to gauge her reaction.

"I thought you were over this, Bane. Self-pity and regret are for the weak."

Relieved, he bowed his head to continue his charade. "You're right," he mumbled.

She stepped in closer to him. "You can't fool me, Bane," she whispered, and his muscles tensed in anticipation of what she would do next. "I think you're here for something else."

He held his ground as she leaned in slowly, poised to react at the first hint of threat or danger. He let his guard down only when she brushed her lips softly against his.

Instinctively his hands came up and seized her shoulders, pulling her in closer, pressing her lips and body hard up against his own as he drank her in. She wrapped her arms around his broad shoulders and neck, returning his insistence with her own urgency.

Her heat enveloped them. The kiss seemed to last for all eternity; her scent wrapped around their entwined flesh until he felt he was drowning in it. When she at last broke away he could see the fierce eagerness in her eyes and still taste the sweet fire of her lips. He could taste something else, too.

Poison!

Bedazzled by her kiss, it took him a second to realize what had happened. Whether Githany believed him or not hadn't mattered. She'd asked Kaan to let her come here so she could kill him. For a brief second he was worried . . . until he recognized the faint tricopper taste of rock worrt venom.

He laughed, gasping slightly for air. "Magnificent," he breathed. Secrecy. Guile. Betrayal. Githany may have been corrupted by the Brotherhood's influence, but she still understood what made the dark side strong. Was it possible she could be his one true apprentice, despite her allegiance to the Brotherhood?

She smiled coyly at his compliment. "Through passion we gain strength."

Bane could feel the poison working its way through his system. The effects were subtle. Had his growing strength in the dark side not made his senses hyperaware, he probably wouldn't even have noticed its presence for several hours. Yet once again, Githany had underestimated him.

Rock worrt venom was powerful enough to kill a bantha, but there were far more rare—and lethal—toxins she could have chosen. The dark side flowed through him, thick as the blood in his veins. He was Darth Bane now, a true Dark Lord. He had nothing to fear from her poison.

The fact that she had thought he wouldn't detect it on her lips—the fact that she thought it would even harm him—meant that she must have believed his performance. She suspected he had fallen away from the dark side again; she thought he was weak. He was glad: it made her decision to side with Kaan more forgivable. Maybe there was still hope for her after all. But he had to be sure.

"I'm sorry for abandoning you," he said softly. "I was blinded by dreams of past glory. Naga Sadow, Exar Kun, Darth Revan—I lusted after the power of the great Dark Lords of the past."

"We all crave power," she replied. "That is the nature of the dark side. But there is power in the Brotherhood. Kaan is on the verge of succeeding where all those before him have failed. We are winning on Ruusan, Bane."

Bane shook his head, disappointed. How could she still be so blind? "Kaan may be winning on Ruusan, but his followers are losing everywhere else. His great Sith army has crumbled without its leaders. The Republic has driven them back and reclaimed most of the worlds we conquered. In a few more months the rebellion will be crushed."

"None of that matters if we can wipe out the Jedi," she explained eagerly, her eyes blazing. "The war has taken a heavy toll on the Republic. Once the Jedi are gone, we can easily rally our troops and turn the tide of war. All we have to do is wipe them out, and the ultimate victory will be ours! All we have to do is win on Ruusan!"

"There are other Jedi besides those on Ruusan," he replied.

"A few, but they are scattered in ones and twos across the galaxy. If the Army of Light is destroyed, we can hunt them down at our leisure."

"Do you really believe Kaan will win? He has claimed imminent victory before, then failed to deliver on his promise."

"For one who claims to want to join the Brotherhood," she noted with some suspicion, "you don't seem particularly devoted to the cause."

Bane's arm shot out and grabbed her by the waist, pulling her in close for another savage kiss. She gasped in surprise, then closed her eyes and gave in to the physical pleasure of the moment. This time it was she who finally pulled back with a faint sigh.

"You were right when you said I came back for something else," he said, still holding her close. The treacherous poison on her lips tasted just as sweet the second time.

"The Brotherhood cannot fail," she promised. "The Jedi are on the run, cowering and hiding in the forests."

He let her go and stepped away, turning his back to her. He desperately wanted to believe she was capable of becoming his apprentice once he'd destroyed Kaan and the Brotherhood. But he still wasn't sure. If she truly believed in what the Brotherhood stood for, then there was no hope.

"I just can't accept what Lord Kaan preaches," he confessed. "He says we are all equals, but if all are equal, then none can be strong."

She stepped up behind him and placed her hands on his shoulders, applying gentle pressure until he turned to face her once again. Her expression was one of amusement.

"Do not believe everything Kaan says," she warned, and he could hear the naked ambition in her voice. *One to embody the power, the other to crave it.* "Once the Jedi are destroyed, many of his followers will discover that some of us are more equal than others."

He swept Githany up in his mighty arms with a joyful roar, spinning her around and around as he gave her another long, hard kiss. This was what he wanted to hear!

When he finally set her down she stumbled back half a step, unsteady after his unexpected outburst. She regained her balance and gave a startled laugh. "I guess you accept," she said with a sly smile on her poison-slicked lips. "You pack up your camp. I'll go ahead to let Kaan know you're coming."

"I can't wait to see the look on his face when you tell him about this meeting," he replied, still pretending he was unaware of the poison raging unchecked through his blood.

"Neither can I," she replied, her voice giving nothing away. "Neither can I."

———

As the surface of Ambria fell away beneath her and the glorious rings came into view, Githany couldn't help but feel a twinge of regret. The passion she'd awakened in Bane had given him a sudden, surprising strength; she'd felt it in each of his kisses. But it was clear Bane was interested in *her*, not in joining the Brotherhood of Darkness.

She punched in the coordinates for the jump back to Ruusan and leaned back in her seat. Her head was spinning from the poison that had coated her lips. Not the rock worrt venom; that was only there to lull Bane into a false sense of security. But the synox she had mixed in with it—the colorless, odorless, tasteless toxin favored by the infamous assassins of the GenoHaradan—was having an effect despite the antidote she had taken. She had no doubt Bane would soon be feeling much, much worse than she did. A single kiss would have been enough to kill him, and he had received a triple dose.

She was going to miss Bane, she realized. But he was a threat to everything Lord Kaan was working for. She had to side with one or the other, so naturally she had chosen the one with an entire army of Sith at his command.

It was, after all, the nature of the dark side.

———

Bane watched the Buzzard until it disappeared in the sky before turning his attention to gathering up his camp. He would have to act carefully now. Githany would tell Kaan she'd tried to poison him. When he showed up at the camp still alive things could become . . . difficult.

He could simply stay away and let events run their course. The Jedi on

Ruusan would rally, turning the tide of the battle once again. It was a given; Bane was counting on it. Desperate, Kaan would then turn to the gift Bane had sent him. He would unleash the thought bomb, unaware of its true nature. And then every Force-user on Ruusan—Sith and Jedi alike—would be destroyed.

This was the most likely scenario. But Bane had come too far to leave the end of the Brotherhood of Darkness to chance. When Kaan's army faltered this time, there were those in his camp—like Githany—who might turn against him. They could flee Ruusan, scattering before the Jedi. And then Bane would have to deal with each of his rivals separately before he could become the unchallenged leader of the Sith.

Better to be on hand, guiding the events to the outcome he desired. That, however, meant he'd have to come up with a plausible story to explain his desire to join the Brotherhood even after a failed assassination.

He thought about it for nearly an hour, considering and discarding a number of ideas. In the end there was only one reason any of them would believe that he had come back. He had to make them all think he wanted to overthrow Kaan and become the new leader of the Brotherhood.

Bane smiled at the subtle beauty of the plan. Kaan would be suspicious, of course. But all his effort and attention would be focused on holding on to his position. He wouldn't realize his rival's true purpose: to exterminate the Brotherhood completely; to destroy every last Sith on Ruusan.

Plus, there was the added advantage of having another opportunity to convince Githany to join him. Once she understood what he had truly become—and how he had manipulated Kaan and the other so-called Dark Lords—she might actually accept his offer to become his apprentice. At the very least he would get a chance to see her face once she realized her poison had failed to—

"Ungh!" Bane let out a grunt and doubled over as a vicious pain ripped through his stomach. He tried to straighten up, but his body was suddenly racked with a prolonged coughing fit. He raised his hand to cover his mouth, and when he let it fall it was covered in frothy red flecks of blood.

Impossible, he thought, even as another stabbing pain through his guts dropped him to his knees. Revan had shown him how to use the Force to ward off poison and disease. No simple toxin should be able to affect anyone strong enough in the dark side to be a Lord of the Sith.

Another coughing fit paralyzed him until it passed. He reached up to wipe the sweat rolling down his face and felt something warm and sticky on his cheek. A thin trickle of crimson tears was leaking from the corner of his eye.

He rose shakily to his feet, turning his focus inward. The poison was still there. It had spread throughout his entire body, polluting and corrupting his system and damaging his vital organs. He was hemorrhaging internally, bleeding from his eyes and nose.

Githany! He would have laughed if he hadn't been in such unbearable agony. He had been so confident, so arrogant. So convinced she was underestimating him. Instead he had underestimated her. A mistake he vowed never to make again . . . if he survived.

He had read enough about synox to recognize the symptoms. If he had detected it immediately, he would have been able to cleanse it from his system, just as he had done with the rock worrt venom that had concealed its presence. But synox was the subtlest of poisons; the insidious toxin had sapped his strength as it had spread unnoticed throughout his body.

Summoning all his resources, he tried to purge the poison from his body, burning it away with the cold fire of the dark side. The poison was too strong . . . or rather, he was too weak. The damage was already done. The synox had crippled him, leaving his power a mere shadow of what it had been only hours earlier.

He could dull its effects, slow its progress, and temporarily hold the most lethal symptoms at bay. But he couldn't cure himself. Not now, weakened as he was.

There was power in Lake Natth, but it was power he couldn't draw on. The ancient Jedi had been careful to lock the dark side safely away within its depths. The black, stagnant waters were the only evidence of the power that lay forever trapped beneath its surface.

Desperate to find some other way to survive, he staggered over to the land crawler on the edge of his camp. Ignoring the protests of his sud-

denly weary limbs, he clambered in behind the wheel and began to drive. He needed a healer. If the one called Caleb was still on this world, Bane had to find him. It was his only chance.

He headed for the nearest battleground, a barren plain several kilometers away where the remains of those who had fought and died still lay strewn about the ground. The rough rumble of the land crawler's treads jarred him with each turn, and he gritted his teeth against the agonizing pain. As he drove, his world became a waking nightmare of darkness and shadow, all tinged with red. He was barely even conscious of where he was going, letting the Force guide him even as he tried to use it to keep his body from succumbing to the effects of Githany's poison.

The fear of death wrapped itself around him, smothering his thoughts. His will began to falter; it would be so easy to just surrender now and let it all end. Just let it all slip away and be at peace . . .

Snarling, he shook his head, dragging his thoughts back from the brink by repeating the first line of the Sith mantra over and over: *Peace is a lie.* He reached back into his training as a soldier, taking his fear and transforming it into anger to give him strength.

I am Darth Bane, Dark Lord of the Sith. I will survive. At any cost.

Far ahead—at the very limits of his rapidly fading vision—he saw another vehicle moving slowly across the other side of the battlefield. Settlers. Scavengers, picking through the remains.

He pointed the nose of his land crawler at them, groaning with the effort required to simply turn the wheel. Reaching out with the Force, he tried to touch the spirits of those who had fallen at this site. Only a few months earlier, scores of beings had died here. He tried to drink in what remained of their tortured ends, hoping the agony of their final moments would bolster his own flagging power. But it wasn't enough; their suffering was too distant, the echo of their screams too faint.

Glancing up, he noticed that his vehicle had begun to veer off course, listing hard to one side as his grip on the wheel weakened. His arms were numb and tingling; they had become almost completely unresponsive. He could feel his heart laboring with every beat.

The front tread struck a large rock and the land crawler suddenly

turned over, dumping Bane out onto hard dirt and jagged stone. He tried to look up again to locate the people he had seen in the distance, but the effort to raise his head was too much. Exhausted, his world went black.

The heavy *whump-whump-whump* of a land crawler's treads stirred him back to consciousness. The other vehicle was here. He doubted they would even see him: his body had fallen behind his tipped-over crawler and they had approached from the other side. Even if they did, there was nothing they could do to save him now. Yet there was something he could do to save himself.

The engines cut out and he heard the sound of voices: children's voices. Three young boys scampered down from the back of the land crawler and began to hunt eagerly through the wreckage.

"Mikki!" came the voice of their father, calling after one of his sons. "Don't go too far."

"Look!" one of the boys shouted. "Look what I found!"

The weak must serve the strong. That is the way of the dark side.

"Wow! Is it real? Can I touch it?"

"Let me see, Mikki! Let me see!"

"Settle down, boys," the father said wearily. "Let's take a look."

Bane listened to the crunching of his boots across the small stones as he approached. *I am strong. They are weak. They are nothing.*

"It's a lightsaber, Father. But there's something weird about the handle. See? It's got a strange hook in it."

He felt the sudden fear that gripped the father's chest like a vise.

Survive. At any cost.

"Throw it away, Mikki! Now!"

Too late.

The lightsaber sprang to life in the boy's hand, spinning in the air and striking him dead on the spot. The father screamed; his brothers tried to run. The blade leapt after the eldest, cutting him down from behind.

Bane, drawing strength from the horror of their deaths, rose to his feet, coming into view like an apparition disgorged from the bowels of the planet.

"*Nooo!*" the father howled, desperately clutching his youngest son to

his chest. "Spare this one, my lord!" he begged, tears streaming down his face. "He's the youngest. The last one I have."

Those weak enough to beg for mercy do not deserve it.

Still too weak to even raise his arms Bane reached out once more with the Force, bringing the lightsaber up to hover over his helpless victims. He waited, letting their horror mount, then plunged the burning blade into the young boy's heart.

The father clutched the corpse to his breast, his tortured laments echoing across the empty battlefield. "Why? Why did you have to kill them?"

Bane feasted on his anguish, gorging himself, feeling the dark side growing stronger in him. The symptoms of the poison receded enough so that he could raise his arm without the muscles trembling. The lightsaber sprang to his hand.

The father cowered before him. "Why did you make me watch? Why did you—"

One quick swipe of the lightsaber cut him off, sending the father to the same tragic fate as his sons.

26

Lord Hoth tossed and turned, unable to sleep. The creaking of his cot joined the whining buzz of the bloodsucking insect swarms that followed his army wherever they made camp. The noise was compounded by the whirring hum of small-winged night birds swooping in to feast on the insects that feasted on his soldiers. The result was a shrill, maddening cacophony that hovered on the edges of hearing.

But it wasn't the noises that were keeping him awake, or the unrelenting heat that left him with a constant sheen of sweat on his brow, even at night. It wasn't the military strategies and battle plans constantly running through his mind. It wasn't any one of these things, but rather the sum of all of them together—and the fact that there seemed to be no end in sight to this blasted, cursed war. Minor annoyances that had been tolerable during the first months on Ruusan had been magnified by frustration and futility into unbearable torments.

With an angry growl he cast aside the thin blanket he slept under, tossing it into the far corner of his tent. He swung his legs over the side and sat up on the edge of the cot, leaning forward with his elbows on his knees and his head clasped between his hands.

For two standard years he had waged his campaign against the Brotherhood of Darkness here on Ruusan. In the beginning many Jedi had rallied to his side. And many Jedi had died—too many. Under Lord Hoth's command they had sacrificed themselves, offering up their own lives for the sake of a greater cause. Yet now, after six major battles—not to mention countless skirmishes, raids, minor clashes, and indecisive engagements— nothing had been decided. The blood of thousands stained his hands, yet he was no closer to his goal.

Frustration was beginning to give way to despair. Morale was the lowest it had ever been. Many of the soldiers grumbled that Farfalla was right: the general had let Ruusan become his mad obsession and was leading them to their doom.

Hoth no longer even had the strength to argue with them. Sometimes he felt as if he had forgotten the reasons he had come here in the first place. Once there may have been virtue in this war, but such nobility had long since been stripped away. Now he fought for revenge in the name of those Jedi who had fallen. He fought out of hatred of the dark side and what it stood for. He fought out of pride and a refusal to admit defeat. But most of all, he fought simply because he no longer knew anything else.

Yet if he gave up now, would it make any difference? If he ordered his troops to retreat, to evacuate the planet in Farfalla's ships, would anything change? If he stepped aside and left the burden of battling the Sith—here on Ruusan or elsewhere in the galaxy—to another, would he finally find peace? Or would he simply be betraying all those who had believed in him?

To disband the Army of Light now, while the Brotherhood of Darkness still existed, dishonored the memory of all those who had perished in the conflict. To press on meant many more would surely die—and he himself might be lost to the light forever.

He lay back down and closed his eyes again. But sleep would not come.

"When all the options are wrong," he muttered to himself in the darkness, "what does it matter which one I choose?"

"When the way before you is not clear," an ethereal voice answered, "let your actions be guided by the wisdom of the Force."

Hoth snapped his head up to peer through the darkness of the tent. A figure was just barely visible in the shadows, standing on the other side.

"Pernicar!" he exclaimed, then suddenly asked, "Is this real? Or am I actually sound asleep in my cot, and all this nothing but a dream?"

"A dream is only another kind of reality," Pernicar said with an amused shake of his head. He crossed the tent slowly, moving closer. As he approached, Hoth realized he could actually see through him.

The apparition settled itself on the cot. The springs didn't creak; it was as if he had no weight or substance at all.

This had to be a dream, Hoth realized. But he didn't want to wake. Instead he clung desperately to the chance to see his old friend again, even if it was just an illusion conjured up by his own mind. "I've missed you," he said. "Your counsel, your wisdom. I need them now more than ever."

"You were not so eager to listen to me when I was alive," the Pernicar of his dream replied, striking at the most secret guilt and regrets buried deep in Hoth's subconscious. "There was much you could have learned from me."

A funny thought struck the general. "Was I your Padawan all this time, Master Pernicar? So young and foolish that I didn't even know you were trying to instruct me in the ways of the Force?"

Pernicar laughed lightly. "No, General. Neither one of us is young—though we both have had more than our share of foolish moments."

Hoth nodded somberly. For a moment he said nothing, just enjoying Pernicar's presence once again, even if he was only here in spirit. Then, knowing there must be some purpose to this elaborate charade his subconscious had created for him, he asked, "Why have you come?"

"The Army of Light is an instrument of good and justice," Pernicar told him. "You fear you may have lost your way, but look to the Force and you will know what you must do to find it again."

"You make it sound so simple," Hoth said with a slight shake of his head. "Have I really fallen so far that I cannot even remember the most basic teachings of our order?"

"There is no shame in falling," Pernicar said, standing up. "There is only shame if you refuse to rise once again."

Hoth sighed heavily. "I know what I must do, but I lack the tools to do it. My troops are on the verge of collapse: exhausted and outnumbered. And the other Jedi no longer believe in our cause."

"Farfalla still does," Pernicar noted. "Though you had your differences, he was always loyal."

"I think I've driven Farfalla away for good," Hoth admitted. "He wants nothing more to do with the Army of Light."

"Then why are his ships still in orbit?" Pernicar countered. "You drove him away with your anger, and he fears you may have fallen to the dark side. Show him this is not so and he will follow you again."

Pernicar took a step back. Hoth could sense himself beginning the slow climb to consciousness again. He could have fought against it. He could have struggled to stay in the dream world. But there was work to be done.

"Good-bye, old friend," he whispered. Slowly, his eyes opened, revealing the waking world and the empty darkness of his tent. "Good-bye."

Sleep did not return to him that night. Instead he thought long and hard about what Pernicar had said to him in his dream. Pernicar had always been the one he'd turned to in times of confusion and trouble. It made sense that his mind would conjure up the image of his dearest friend to set him on the proper path again.

He knew what he had to do. He would swallow his pride and ask Farfalla's forgiveness. They had to set aside their personal differences for the sake of the Jedi.

First thing in the morning he emerged from his tent, determined to send an envoy to Farfalla. But to his surprise he found that one of Farfalla's people had come to speak with him.

"I wondered if I had made this trip in vain," the messenger admitted once Lord Hoth had welcomed her into his tent. "I was afraid you would refuse to even see me."

"Had you come a day earlier you probably would have been right," he confessed. "Last night I had a . . . revelation that changed things."

"I guess we're lucky I came today, then," she replied with a cordial tilt of her head.

"Yes, lucky," he muttered, though part of him believed the timing of the dream had nothing to do with luck at all. Truly, the Force was a powerful and mysterious ally.

————

Bane could still feel the poison in his system as he drove the land crawler across Ambria's vast and empty plains. The rumble of the engine couldn't quite drown out the rattle and clank of the junk piled in the back. The clatter kept him from pushing the memories of the vehicle's previous owners completely from his mind, but he felt no remorse over their deaths.

He'd left their bodies lying where they'd fallen—in the midst of the battlefield where they'd gathered their prizes. Their deaths had given him the strength to press on, but already the surge of power he had felt was fading. He had the strength to keep the synox at bay for a few more hours, but he needed to find a permanent cure.

He needed to find Caleb. If he could reach the healer, there was still hope. But the man's dwelling was still many kilometers away.

It was only a matter of time until his body succumbed to the paralysis and his mind was swallowed by the fevered madness brought on by the toxin. For now, though, his anger allowed him to keep his thoughts clear.

He wasn't angry at Githany. She had only acted as a servant of the dark side should. His rage was directed inward—toward his own weakness and misplaced arrogance. He should have anticipated the true depth of her cunning.

Instead he had let her poison him. And if he died now, his great revelation—the Rule of Two, the salvation of the Sith—would end with him.

———

Caleb felt the land crawler's approach long before he saw or heard it. It was like a storm on the wind, a black sky rushing in to cover the sun. When the vehicle rolled to a stop before his hut he was already sitting outside waiting for it.

The man who climbed out was large and muscular, a sharp contrast with Caleb's own thin and wiry frame. He wore dark clothing, and a hook-handled lightsaber dangled from his belt. His skin was gray as ash, and his features were twisted into an expression of cruelty and contempt. Even were he not sensitive to the ways of the Force, it wouldn't have been hard for Caleb to recognize him as a servant of the dark side. What he might not have sensed was how powerful this grim visitor truly was.

But Caleb had dealt with powerful men and women before. Jedi and

Sith alike had come to him in the past, and he had turned them all away. He was a servant of the common people, those who could not help themselves. He wanted no part of the war between light and darkness.

The man began walking toward him, moving stiffly. The foul stench of poison wafted out from the dying Sith's pores, smothering the scent of the boiling soup hanging over Caleb's fire. Jabbing a stick into the coals to stir up more heat, Caleb now understood his visitor's unnatural complexion. The effects of synox were unmistakable. He figured the doomed man had at most a day before he died.

He didn't speak until the man stood directly above him, looming like the specter of death itself.

"There is venom in your body," Caleb said placidly. "You have come for the cure," he continued. "I will not give it to you."

The man didn't speak. Not surprising, given his state. The poison would have left his tongue cracked and swollen, his mouth parched and blistered. But he didn't need words to convey his message as his hand dropped to the hilt of his lightsaber.

"I am not afraid to die," Caleb said, with no change in his voice. "You may torture me if you want," he added. "Pain means nothing to me."

To prove his point, he plunged his hand into the bubbling cauldron. The scent of seared flesh mingled with the smells of soup and poison. His expression never changed, even as he withdrew his hand and held it up to show the scalded flesh.

He saw doubt and confusion in the newcomer's eyes, a look he had witnessed many times before. In the past his stoicism had served him well, usually thwarting the plans of those Sith or Jedi who had sought him out for one reason or another. They couldn't understand him, and that was how he wanted it.

He cared nothing for their war or what either side valued. In fact, there was only one thing he cared about in all the galaxy. And this performance was his only hope of protecting it from the monster standing above him.

———

The implacable man before him puzzled Bane. His only hope for survival had just been denied him, and he wasn't sure what he could do about it.

He could sense the power in this man, but it wasn't the power of either the dark side or the light. It wasn't even the power of the Force in any normal sense of the word. He drew his strength from ground and stone; mountain and forest; the land and the sky. Despite this difference, Bane could sense that the man's power was formidable in its own way. Bane found its strangeness disturbing, unsettling. Was it possible he was actually going to lose this battle of wills? Was it possible this simple man—a man with only the faintest flicker of the Force inside him—was actually able to defy a Dark Lord of the Sith?

Had the healer's mind been weak Bane could have simply compelled him to do his bidding, but his will was as unyielding as the black iron of the pot he had plunged his hand into. He had demonstrated that pain and threat of death would be ineffective tools in convincing him to change his mind, as well. Even now Bane could sense his mind building up walls to block out the pain; burying it so deep it almost seemed to disappear. And there was something else he was burying as well. Something he was desperately trying to keep Bane from uncovering.

Bane's eyes narrowed as he recognized what it was. He was trying to hide the presence of another, shielding whoever it was from the Dark Lord's hazy, fevered perceptions. He turned his attention to the healer's small, ramshackle hut. The man made no move to stop him. In fact, he had no reaction at all.

The door was blocked by nothing but a long curtain that flowed gently in the breeze. Bane stepped forward and flipped it aside to reveal a small, ramshackle room. A young girl, her eyes wide with terror, huddled silently against the far wall.

A grim smile of relief touched the corners of Bane's lips as he realized the truth. Caleb had a weakness after all; he cared about something. All his strength of will was useless because of this one failing. And Bane was not above exploiting it to get what he needed.

With a single mental command he swept the terrified girl up into the air, carrying her out to suspend her upside down above the healer's boiling pot.

Caleb leapt to his feet, showing real emotion for the first time. He reached out to her, then pulled his hand back, his eyes flicking between his daughter and the man who literally held her life in his grasp.

"Daddy," she whimpered, "help me."

The man's head dropped in defeat. "All right," he said. "You win. You will have your cure."

The healing ritual lasted all through the night and into the next day. Caleb drew on all manner of herbs and roots: some cooked in the boiling waters of his pot; others ground up into paste; still others placed directly on Bane's swollen tongue. Throughout the entire process Bane was wary, ready to unleash his vengeance against the healer's child should the man try to betray him.

But as the hours went by he slowly felt the synox leaching from his body, drawn out by the medicines. By evening of the next day all traces of the poison were gone.

Bane returned to his camp and packed up. A few hours later he was ready to lift off and leave Ambria behind.

After the completion of the healing ritual he had briefly considered slaying both father and daughter for the crime of seeing him in his moment of weakness. But those were the thoughts of a man blinded by his own arrogance. His recent encounter with Githany had shown him the dangers of that path.

Neither Caleb nor his daughter presented any threat to him or his goals. And Caleb had a skill he might one day need again. For all its power, the dark side was weak in the healing arts.

So he had let them live. There was no purpose or advantage in their deaths. Killing without reason or gain was a petty pleasure of sadistic fools.

And Bane was determined—as he punched the coordinates for Ruusan into the nav computer—to cleanse the dark side of fools.

27

When the *Valcyn* arrived at Ruusan, Bane was surprised to find both Sith and Jedi fleets in the system. The Sith had formed a blockade around the planet, obviously trying to prevent the Jedi from bringing reinforcements to their fellows on the surface.

Yet to Bane's eye it appeared that the Jedi were making no effort to run the blockade. Their ships seemed content to wait, lurking just beyond the range of enemy fire. And the Sith couldn't attack without breaking formation and exposing their lines. The result was a tense stalemate, with neither side willing to make the first move.

Despite the blockade, Bane was able to land his ship on Ruusan without drawing the attention of either fleet. The Jedi weren't concerned with ships going to the planet, and the Sith were patrolling in patterns designed to guard against large-scale incursions. The blockade was meant to stop troop transports, supply ships, and their escorts; it was all but useless against a single scout vessel or fighter.

His sensors picked up the Sith encampment soon after he breached the atmosphere, and he brought the *Valcyn* in on the far side of the world. The blockade patrols hadn't spotted him, and he'd disabled the ship's beacon before leaving Lehon. Nobody knew he was here. He planned to keep it that way for a while longer.

He set the ship down in the cover of a small range of foothills several kilometers from the encampment. He would draw less attention approaching on foot, and he wanted to keep the *Valcyn*'s location secret in case he needed it to make a quick escape. He disembarked and began the long hike to meet up with Kaan and his fellow Sith.

The feel of this planet was far different from any of the others he had been on. This was a tired world, weary and spent with the endless wars being waged across its surface. There was a malaise in the air, like some infectious disease of mind and spirit. The Force was strong on Ruusan— inevitable given the vast numbers of Sith and Jedi there. Yet he sensed it was in turmoil, a maelstrom of confusion and conflict. Neither the dark nor light held sway. Instead they collided and fused, becoming an obscene, indecisive gray.

Far to the east he could see the edges of Ruusan's great forests. He could sense the Jedi hiding deep within them, though they used the light side to mask their exact location. The Sith encampment was to the west, several kilometers away from the forest's borders. Between them stretched a vast panorama of gently rolling hills and plains: the site of all the major battles that had been fought on Ruusan so far. The constant fighting had been punctuated by six full-scale engagements, battles where each side had brought its full strength to bear in an effort to wipe out the enemy— or at least drive them from the world. Three times Hoth and the Army of Light had seized the upper hand; the other three had gone to Kaan and his Brotherhood. Yet none of the victories had been decisive enough to bring an end to the war.

From the pungent smell of death Bane suspected some smaller confrontation had been recently fought over this territory, as well. His suspicions were confirmed when he crested a rise and came across a scene of slaughter. It was hard to tell who had won: bodies clad in the garb of each side were everywhere, intermingled as if the combatants had remained locked together in hatred long after they had all been slain. Most of the dead were likely to be followers of the Jedi or minions of the Sith, rather than actual Jedi Knights or members of the Brotherhood, though he noticed dark Sith robes on a handful of the bodies.

Hovering above the killing field were the bouncers, a unique species native to Ruusan. There were at least half a dozen, spherical in shape and of various sizes, with most being between one and two meters across. Their round bodies were covered with thick green fur, as were the finlike appendages protruding from their sides and the long ribbonlike tails that streamed out behind them. They had no visible facial features other than dark, lidless eyes.

Reports indicated they were sentient, yet to Bane they looked like animals scavenging the remains of the battle. As he approached he realized they were communicating, though they possessed no mouths. Somehow they were projecting mental images of succor and comfort, as if they sought to heal the wounds of the scarred land beneath them.

They scattered at Bane's approach, whisking themselves away like a bizarre school of fish capable of swimming through the skies. As he drew nearer, he realized they had been congregating over one of the fallen. The human man was not quite dead, though the gaping wound in his gut gave stark evidence that he wouldn't live to see the night.

He wore the robes of the Sith, and the shattered remains of a lightsaber's hilt lay near his outstretched hand. Bane recognized him as one of the lesser students from the Academy on Korriban: so weak in the dark side, it wasn't even worth the bother of learning his name. Yet he knew Bane.

With a groan the man rolled onto his back and hauled himself up to a sitting position, leaning his head and shoulders against a nearby stone. His eyes—glazed and dilated—cleared momentarily and came into focus. "Lord Bane . . . ," he gasped. "Kaan told us . . . you were dead."

There was no point in replying, so Bane said nothing.

"You missed the fight . . . ," the man mumbled, the words hard to hear through the choking bubbles of blood welling up in his throat. A coughing fit cut off what he was going to say next. He was too weak to even bring up his hand to cover his mouth as he spewed red spots over Bane's dark boots.

"The battle was glorious," he finally croaked out. "It's an honor to . . . fall in such a splendid battle."

Bane laughed loudly, the only appropriate response to such ridiculous stupidity. "Glory means nothing for the dead," he said, though it wasn't clear if the man could even hear him in his fevered state.

He turned to go, then paused when he felt a feeble tug on his heel. "Help me, Lord Bane."

Lifting his boot free of the clutching hand, Bane answered, "My name is *Darth* Bane." There was a sickening crunch as his boot slammed down, grinding the man's skull into the rocks propping him up. His body convulsed once then lay still.

The purging of the Sith had begun.

———

Lord Kaan lay on his back on the small cot in his tent, eyes closed, gently massaging his temples. The strain of keeping his followers united in a common cause was taking a heavy toll, and his head constantly pulsed with a dull and relentless ache.

Despite their success in recent battles with the Jedi on Ruusan, the mood in the Sith camp was tense. They had been on Ruusan too long—far too long—and reports kept filtering in of Republic victories in distant systems. Even with his ability to manipulate and influence the minds of the other Dark Lords, it was becoming more and more difficult to keep the Brotherhood focused on their battle against the Army of Light.

He knew there was one sure way to end the war, and end it quickly. The thought bomb. He had spent many nights wondering if he dared to use it. If they lured the Jedi in and unleashed the thought bomb, its blast would completely obliterate their enemies. But would the combined will of the Brotherhood be strong enough to survive such power? Or would they get swept up in the backlash of the explosion?

Time and again he had dismissed it as too dangerous, a weapon so terrible that even he—a Dark Lord of the Sith—was afraid to use it. Yet each time he considered it for a few moments longer before backing away from the abyss.

A sound outside the tent caused him to open his eyes and sit up sharply. A second later Githany, now seen by many as his right hand, poked her head in. "They're ready for you, Lord Kaan."

He nodded and rose to his feet, taking a second to calm and compose himself. If he showed any weakness, the others might turn against him. He couldn't let that happen. Not now, when they were so close to ultimate victory. That was why he had summoned the other Dark Lords: one final gathering to strengthen their resolve and assure their continued loyalty.

Githany led the way through the camp, and he followed her to the large tent where the other Sith Lords were waiting for him. He entered with conviction and purpose, projecting an aura of confidence and authority.

As was customary whenever he entered a room, those in the assemblage rose to their feet as a sign of respect. There was one, however, who remained seated, arms folded across his thick chest.

"Are you too heavy to rise, Lord Kopecz?" Githany asked pointedly.

"I thought we were all equals in the Brotherhood," the Twi'lek snarled back, speaking more to Kaan than to her.

Kaan knew he had to tread carefully. This was not the first time Kopecz had been the voice of dissent, and many of the others took their cues from him. Unfortunately, he was also one of the most difficult to influence and control.

"Equals. Quite right, Lord Kopecz," he said with a weary smile. "Remain seated. All of you. We have no need of these pointless formalities."

The rest of the group did as he bade and found their seats once more, though it was clear everyone still felt the tension between the two of them. He let a wave of soothing reassurance ripple out across the room as he crossed over to the strategy table.

"The war against the Jedi is almost won," he declared. "They are on the verge of collapse. They have retreated into the forests, but they are running out of places to hide."

Kopecz snorted derisively. "We've heard that refrain one too many times."

It took tremendous effort to maintain his composure, but somehow Lord Kaan managed to reply in a calm, even voice. "Anyone who has doubts about our strategy here on Ruusan is free to speak," he offered. "As has already been pointed out in this meeting, we are all equals in the Brotherhood of Darkness."

"It's not just Ruusan I'm worried about," Kopecz replied, accepting the bait and rising to his feet. "We've lost ground everywhere else in the galaxy. We had the Republic reeling. But instead of finishing them off, we let them regroup!"

"Most of our early victories came before the Jedi joined their cause," Kaan reminded him. "The point of attacking the Republic in the first place was to draw the Jedi out. We wanted to force them into a battle of our choosing: this battle, here on Ruusan.

"Now we are on the verge of wiping them out. And with the Jedi gone, we can easily reclaim the worlds that have slipped back under the Republic's control—and many more besides."

Though Kopecz was silent, there were murmurs of agreement from the other Sith Lords. Kaan pressed his point even farther.

"Once we wipe out the enemy here on Ruusan our armies will sweep across the galaxy virtually unopposed. Conquering territory in every sector, we will encircle Coruscant and the other Core Worlds like a noose, drawing ever tighter until we choke the very life out of the Republic!"

There was a roar of approval from the crowd. When Kopecz spoke again, even he seemed to have lost some of his hostility.

"But victory here is not assured. We may have Hoth's army surrounded and pinned down, but there's a Jedi fleet with hundreds of reinforcements lurking on the edges of this system."

"Their reinforcements are on the edge of the system," Kaan admitted with a nod, not bothering to deny what every single one of them knew to be fact. "Just as they have been for the past week. And that's exactly where they will stay: far away from the surface where they are needed.

"The bulk of our fleet is in orbit around Ruusan itself, and the Jedi lack the numbers or the firepower to break through our blockade. If they can't unite their numbers with those here on the surface, Hoth and his followers will fall. And once we have finished them off we can mop up the tattered remnants of the Order at our leisure."

Kopecz, mollified, sat down with one final comment. "Then let's finish Hoth off quickly and get off this blasted rock."

"That's exactly the point of this strategy conference," Kaan said with a smile, knowing he had once again averted a potential schism in the Brotherhood. "We may have lost a few skirmishes here and there, but we are about to win the war!"

Githany stepped up and handed him a holomap with the latest data from their reconnaissance drones. He gave her a nod of thanks and unfurled it on the table, then bent down for a closer look.

"Our spies indicate Hoth's main camp is located here," he said, jabbing a finger at a heavily wooded section of the map. "If we can flush them out of the forest we might be able to—"

He stopped short as a dark shadow fell across the map. "What now?" he demanded, pounding his fist on the table and snapping his head up to find the cause of this latest interruption.

An enormous mountain of a man stood in the doorway, blocking the light streaming in from outside. He was tall and completely bald, with a heavy brow and hard, unforgiving features. He wore the black armor and robes of the Sith, and a hook-handled lightsaber hung at his side. Though he had never met the man before, Lord Kaan had heard enough about him to know exactly who he was.

"Darth Bane!" he exclaimed. He cast a quick glance in Githany's direction, wondering if she had betrayed him. From the expression on her face, it was obvious she was just as surprised as he was to see their visitor alive and well.

"We . . . we thought you were dead," he began uncertainly. "How did—"

"I'm tired," Bane interrupted. "Do you mind if I sit?"

"Of course," Kaan quickly agreed. "Anything for a Brother."

The big man sneered as he settled into one of the nearby chairs. "Thank you, *Brother.*"

There was something in his tone that put Kaan's guard up. What was he doing here? Did he know that Githany had tried to poison him? Did he know Kaan had sent her?

"Please continue with your strategy," Bane urged with a casual wave of his hand.

Kaan's hackles rose. It was as if he was being given permission to continue; as if Bane was the one in charge. Gritting his teeth, he looked down at the map again and resumed where he had left off. "As I was saying, the Jedi are hiding in the forests. We can flush them out if we split our numbers. If we deploy our fliers, we can flank their southern lines—"

"Bah!" Bane spat out, slapping his open palm down hard on the table. "Deploying fliers and flanking armies," he mocked, rising to his feet and thrusting an accusing finger at Kaan. "You're thinking like a dirt general, not a Sith Lord!"

A heavy silence had fallen across the room; even Kaan was left speechless. He could feel all eyes on him, watching intently to see what would happen next. Bane stepped in close, his face just centimeters from Kaan's own.

"How did you ever find the guts to poison me?" he asked in a low, menacing whisper.

"I . . . that wasn't me!" Kaan stammered as Bane turned his back on him.

"Don't apologize for using cunning and trickery," the big man admonished, moving over to the strategy table. "I admire you for it. We are Sith: the servants of the dark side," he continued, bending down to study the troop positions and tactical layouts spread out before him. "Now look at this map and think like a Sith. Don't just fight in the forest . . . *destroy the forest!*"

It was Githany who finally broke the ensuing silence, asking the question on everyone's mind. "And just how do you propose we do that?"

Bane turned back to them with an evil grin. "I can show you."

————

Night had fallen, but in the lights of the blazing campfires Bane could see the others scurrying to and fro, making the preparations as he had instructed. When he sensed Githany approaching from behind him, he turned. She was holding a bowl of steaming soup and wore a cautious, uncertain expression.

"It will be another hour before they are ready to begin this ritual of yours," she said by way of greeting. When he didn't reply she added, "You look tired. I brought you something to restore your strength."

He took the bowl from her but didn't raise it to his lips. He had discovered the ritual she spoke of while studying Revan's Holocron: a way to unite the minds and spirits of the Sith through a single vessel so their strength could be unleashed upon the physical world. In many ways the process was similar to the one used to fashion a thought bomb from the Force, though this was less powerful than the ritual he had sent as a peace offering to Kaan—and far less dangerous.

He realized Githany was still studying him closely, so he tilted his head toward the soup. "Come to poison me again?" he asked. There was just a hint of playful teasing in his voice.

"You knew all along, didn't you?" she said.

He shook his head. "Not until I tasted the poison on your lips."

She raised a single eyebrow and gave him a coy smile. "But you came back for a second helping. And a third."

"Poison should not harm a Dark Lord," he told her. Then he admitted, "Yet it almost killed me." He paused, but she didn't say anything. "There are too many Sith Lords in the Brotherhood," he went on. "Too many who are weak in the dark side. Kaan doesn't understand this."

"Kaan's afraid you've come back to take over the Brotherhood." After a moment she added, "I think he's right."

Not take over, he thought, *but obliterate.* He didn't bother to correct her, though; it wasn't the time yet. He still needed further proof that she was the right one to become his apprentice. *Two there should be; no more, no less. One to embody the power, the other to crave it.* It was a choice he wasn't about to rush into.

"I can show you the true power of the dark side, Githany. Power beyond what any of these others can even imagine," he said.

"Teach me," she breathed. "I want to learn. You can show me everything . . . after you've taken Kaan's place as leader of the Brotherhood!"

He couldn't help but wonder if she was still trying to manipulate him. Did she want to play him and Kaan against each other? Or was she looking for him to usurp Kaan as proof of his newfound strength?

No, he admitted. *She still doesn't understand that the entire Sith order must be torn apart and rebuilt from scratch. Maybe she won't ever understand.*

"Tell me something," he said. "Was it your idea to poison me? Or Kaan's?"

With a slight laugh, she ducked beneath his arm holding the bowl of soup and came up close against his chest, looking right up into his eyes. "It was my idea," she confessed, "but I was careful to make sure Kaan thought it was his."

There might be hope for her yet, Bane thought.

"I know I made a mistake before," she continued, moving away from him. "I should have gone with you when you left Korriban. I didn't realize what you were after; I didn't understand the secrets you were seeking. But I understand them now. You are the true leader of the Sith, Bane. I'll follow you from now on. And so will the rest of the Brotherhood, after we use your ritual to destroy the Jedi."

"Yes," he agreed, keeping his voice carefully neutral and taking a sip of the steaming soup. "After we've destroyed the Jedi."

Bane knew they couldn't really destroy the Jedi. Not here on Ruusan. Not like this. Somehow the Jedi would survive. No ordinary war could completely eliminate the servants of the light. Only the tools of the dark side—cunning, secrecy, treachery, betrayal—could do that.

The same tools he would use to wipe out the entire Brotherhood of Darkness . . . beginning with the ritual tonight.

28

Kaan, Githany, and the rest of the Dark Lords had gathered atop a barren plateau overlooking the vast forests where Hoth and his army were hiding. They had come on their fliers: short-range, single-person, airborne vehicles front-mounted with heavy blaster guns. The fliers were parked at the edge of the plateau, fifty meters away from where the Sith sat in a loose circle. The ritual had begun.

They were communing with the Force, all of them slipping into a meditative trance as one. Their minds drifted deeper and deeper into the well of power contained within each individual, drawing on their strength and combining it through a single conduit. Bane stood in the center of the circle, urging them on.

"Touch the dark side. The dark side is one. Indivisible."

The night sky filled with dark clouds and a fierce wind swirled across the plateau, tearing at the cloaks and capes of the Sith. The air shook with the thunder and crackle of a mounting electrical storm. Bolts of blue-white lightning arced through the air, and the temperature suddenly dropped.

"Give yourself over to the dark side. Let it surround you. Engulf you. Devour you."

The Brotherhood slipped deeper into the collective trance, barely even aware of the storm now raging about their physical selves. Bane stood at the eye of the storm, drawing the bolts of lightning into himself, feeding on them. He felt his strength surge as he channeled and focused the dark side from the others.

This is how it should be! All the power of the Brotherhood in one body! The only way to unleash the full potential of the dark side!

"Do you feel invincible? Invulnerable? Immortal?"

He had to shout to be heard above the howling wind and thunder. A web of lightning spiraled out from his body, connecting him to each of the other Sith. He shivered then suddenly went stiff, arms spread out at his sides. Slowly, his rigid body began to rise into the air.

"Can you feel it?" he screamed, feeling as if the raw power of the Force roaring through him might rip his very flesh asunder. "Are you ready to kill a world?"

———

There was very little in the galaxy that could scare a man like General Hoth. Yet as he sat looking over the latest situational reports from his scouts he felt the first glimmers of real fear gnawing away at the base of his skull.

The rift between himself and Farfalla had been mended, but now there was no way to get the reinforcements down to Ruusan's surface. Small messenger ships with a crew of one or two had been able to slip past the Sith blockade undetected, though on occasion even these vessels had been spotted and destroyed. Anything larger would never make it.

But his fear was more than the result of his frustration at having help so near yet so impossibly far away. There was something sinister in the air. Something evil.

Suddenly an image leapt unbidden to his mind: a premonition of death and destruction. He sprang to his feet and ran from his tent. Even though it was the middle of the night, he was only mildly surprised to see that most of the rest of the camp was up and about. They had felt it, too. Something coming for them. Coming fast.

They were looking to him for leadership, waiting for him to take command. He did so with a single, shouted order.

"Run!"

The storm rolled down from the plateau and rumbled across the forest. Hundreds of forks of searing lightning shot down from the sky—and the forest erupted. Trees burst into flames, the blaze racing through the branches and spreading out in all directions. The underbrush smoldered, smoked, and ignited; and a wall of fire swept across the planet's surface.

The inferno consumed everything in its path.

Heat and fire. There was nothing else in Bane's world. It was as if he had become the storm itself: he could see the world before him, swallowed up in red and orange and reduced in seconds to ash and embers by the unchained fury of the dark side.

It was glorious. And then suddenly it was gone.

There was a jarring thump as his body dropped from where it had been hovering five meters above the ground. For several seconds he was completely disoriented, unable to figure out what happened. Then he understood: the connection had been broken.

He rose to his feet slowly, uncertain of his balance. All around him were the forms of the Sith, no longer kneeling in meditation but collapsed or rolling on the ground, their minds reeling from the sudden end to the joining ritual. One by one they also regained their composure and stood, most looking as confused as Bane had been only seconds before.

Then he noticed Lord Kaan standing off to the side, over by the fliers.

"What happened?" Bane demanded angrily. "Why did you stop?"

"Your plan worked," Kaan replied curtly. "The forest is destroyed, the Jedi have fled to open ground. They are exposed, vulnerable. Now we go to finish them off."

Kaan had broken the connection, and somehow he had managed to drag the others out along with him, as if he had some hold over their minds. *Perhaps he does,* Bane thought. Further proof that they all had to be destroyed if the Sith were to be cleansed.

As the others regained their senses, Kaan was shouting out orders and battle plans. "The fire flushed the Jedi out into the open. We can mow them down from the sky. Hurry!"

They jumped at his command, rushing to their waiting vehicles and taking to the sky with battle cries and shouts of triumph.

"Come on, Bane," Githany said, rushing past him. "Let's join them!"

He grabbed her arm, pulling her up short. "Kaan is still trying to win this war through blasters and armies," he said. "That is not the way of the dark side."

"It's more fun this way," she said, the excitement obvious in her voice. She shook free of his grasp.

As he watched her run to join the others he realized that she had been corrupted by the teachings of Qordis and the Academy on Korriban. Despite her promise to follow Bane, she couldn't see beyond the Brotherhood and its limitations. She was tainted—unfit to be his apprentice. She would have to die with all the others.

There was the faintest hint of regret as he made the decision, but the regret was hollow: the echo of a feeling, the last vestiges of an emotion. He snuffed it out quickly, knowing it could only make him weak.

"You frighten us, Bane," a voice said from behind. He turned to see Kopecz studying him carefully.

"When we were focusing the Force through you, it felt as if you had your teeth on our throats," the Twi'lek continued. "As if you were trying to suck us dry."

"The power of the dark side is strongest if it is concentrated in one vessel," Bane replied. "Not spread out among many. I did it for the sake of the dark side."

Kopecz shook his head and climbed onto his flier. "Well, we know you weren't doing it for us."

Bane watched him soar off. Then he climbed onto his own flier, but instead of following Kaan to the battle he set a course back to the Sith camp. The first phase of his plan to destroy the Brotherhood was complete.

———

When he arrived back at the camp twenty minutes later, he wasn't surprised to find it completely deserted. All the Dark Lords had been on the plateau for the ritual, and they had all flown off in Kaan's wake to face the suddenly vulnerable Jedi. The soldiers, servants, and followers who made up the bulk of the Sith army had originally been left behind at the camp, but they had since received commed orders from Kaan and the others to join them at the battlefield.

Bane brought his flier in for a landing in the heart of the camp, right beside Lord Kaan's tent. He killed the engine and was surprised to hear the distant whine of another flier approaching. He looked up, curious. When it swooped in low, he recognized the rider.

The vehicle was bearing down on him in a direct line. Bane let his hand drop to his lightsaber, ready to unclip it at a moment's notice. The Force welled up within him, prepared to throw up a protective shield if the flier's front-mounted blasters should open fire.

But the flier didn't attack. Instead it swooped a few meters over his head, banked sharply, then came in for a landing beside his own.

"You have no need of your weapon," Qordis said as he dismounted. "I've come with an offer."

Realizing there was no immediate threat, Bane let his hand drop back to his side. "An offer? What could you possibly have to offer me?"

"My allegiance," Qordis said, dropping to one knee.

Bane stared down at him, his expression a mixture of horror, amusement, and contempt. "Why would you give your allegiance to me?" he asked. "And why should I even want it?"

Qordis rose slowly to his feet, a cunning smile on his lips. "I am not blind, Lord Bane. I see you speaking with Githany. I see how you are undermining Kaan. I know the real reason you have come to Ruusan."

Perplexed, Bane wondered if it was possible that Qordis—the founder of the Academy on Korriban, the most ardent proponent of all that was wrong with the Sith—had finally seen the truth.

"What exactly are you proposing?" he asked through clenched teeth.

"I know what happened to Kas'im. He sided with Kaan against you. He paid for that decision with his life. I am not so foolish. I know you're here to take over the Brotherhood," he declared. "I believe you will succeed. And I want to help you."

"You want to help me take over the Brotherhood?" Bane laughed; Qordis was as blind and misguided as the rest of them. "Replace one leader with another, and you and the rest of the Brotherhood continue on as before? That's your brilliant plan?"

"I can prove quite useful to you, Lord Bane," Qordis insisted. "Many of the Brotherhood are former students of my Academy. They still look to me for wisdom and guidance."

"And therein lies the problem." Bane lashed out with the dark side, seizing Qordis in an immobilizing, crushing grip. His opponent tried to protect himself, throwing up a field to deflect the incoming assault, but Bane's attack tore through the pitiful defense, wiping it away as if it hadn't even been there.

There was a strangled cry of pain from Qordis as the Force tightened around him and lifted him up from the ground.

"Your *wisdom* has destroyed our order," Bane explained casually, watching as Qordis struggled helplessly above him. "You have polluted the minds of your followers; you and Kaan have led them down the path of ruin."

"I—I don't understand," Qordis gasped, barely able to speak as the breath was squeezed inexorably from his lungs.

"That has always been the problem," Bane replied. "The Brotherhood must be purged. The Sith must be destroyed and rebuilt. You, Kaan, and all the others must be wiped from the face of the galaxy. That is why I have returned."

Dawning horror spread across Qordis's long, drawn features. "Please," he groaned, "not . . . like this. Release me. Let me . . . draw my lightsaber. Let us fight . . . like Sith."

Bane tilted his head to the side. "Surely you know I could kill you just as easily with my lightsaber as I could with the Force."

"I . . . know." Qordis's skin was turning red, and his body was trembling as the pressure mounted. Each word he spoke took tremendous effort, yet somehow the dying man found the strength to make his final plea. "More . . . honor . . . in . . . death . . . by . . . combat."

Bane gave an indifferent shrug. "Honor is for the living. Dead is dead."

A final push with his mind tightened the invisible vise. Qordis let out a final scream, but with no air in his lungs it came out only as a rattling gasp that was lost beneath the snapping and crackling of his bones.

Had Bane still been capable of such emotions he might actually have pitied the man. As it was, he simply let the corpse fall to the ground then wandered into Kaan's tent and the communications equipment inside. It was time to enact the second phase of his plan.

————

On the deck of *Nightfall*, great flagship of the Sith fleet, acting commander Admiral Adrianna Nyras responded to the hailing frequency coming from the private comlink on her wrist.

"This is Admiral Nyras," she said into it. "I await your orders, Lord Kaan."

"Lord Kaan is not here," an unfamiliar voice replied. "This is Lord Bane."

She hesitated for only a second before answering. Kaan rarely let anyone else use his personal transceiver, but on occasion it did happen. And with the security encryption on the equipment, it was virtually impossible for anyone else to tap into the frequency. The message had to be coming from the Sith camp, which meant she really was speaking to one of the Dark Lords.

"Forgive me, Lord Bane," she apologized. "What are your orders?"

"Status report."

"Unchanged," she replied, her voice sharp with military precision and efficiency. "The blockade is intact. The Jedi fleet still hovers just beyond our range."

"Engage."

"Pardon?" she asked, so surprised that she momentarily forgot whom she was speaking to.

"You heard me, Admiral," the voice on the other end snapped. "Engage the Jedi fleet."

The order made no sense. The last time Kaan had spoken to her, he had ordered her to hold their position at all costs. As long as they maintained location in orbit, their blockade was virtually impenetrable. If they broke formation and attacked the Jedi fleet, however, they wouldn't be able to stop drop ships from landing reinforcements on the surface.

Still, she had been given strange orders before during her service with the Sith. There were rumors that Kaan had some mystic power, some way to influence the outcome of a battle through the power of the Force that could make traditional strategies fall by the wayside. And if a Dark Lord was giving her a direct order, using the personal communications equipment in Lord Kaan's tent, she wasn't about to run the risk of refusing to obey.

"As you command, Lord Bane," she answered. "We will engage the Jedi."

———

The fire drove General Hoth and his army from the sheltering confines of the forest. Leaving most of their supplies and equipment behind, his troops ran through the trees, a mad scramble to escape the searing heat and flames. Those who stumbled or fell were instantly swallowed up by the conflagration. Somehow most managed to stay ahead of the deadly fires, eventually bursting out of the woods and into the rocky plains where so many battles had already been fought.

The Sith were there waiting for them.

The first wave of Hoth's followers to emerge from the forest were mowed down by blasterfire. Those just behind were able to draw their lightsabers and deflect many of the deadly bolts as they raced out onto the plains, only to be swallowed up by the throngs of Sith soldiers rushing forward to engage them.

Though outnumbered, the Jedi more than held their own. They drove the Sith ranks back, breaking their lines and throwing them into chaos and disarray. But Hoth knew that the real trap had yet to be sprung.

Hewing down any foe foolish enough to come in range of his lightsaber, the general could sense these were not the true Sith. The Dark Lords were not among them: these were the faceless hordes, nothing more than a distraction.

Where are they? What is Kaan up to?

The answer came an instant later when a battalion of fliers swooped in over the horizon, unleashing a deadly barrage across the battlefield. Guided by the power of the dark side, the heavy guns were deadly in their accuracy, decimating Hoth's troops and turning the tide of the battle back in favor of the Sith.

Hoth had faced impossible odds before and triumphed. Yet he knew this battle was fated to be his last.

But I will make a last stand worthy of story and song, he thought defiantly, *even though there won't be anybody left to sing it.*

The world dissolved into the numbing fog of war. Screams and the sounds of battle became a dull, indistinguishable roar. The spray of dirt and stone from the blaster bolts exploding into the ground showered down on him from above, mingling with the sweat and blood of both friend and foe. He swung each blow as if it might be his last, knowing that sooner or later one of the fliers would lock in on him and swoop down to finish him off.

———

Lord Kaan's flier carved a path back and forth above the milling soldiers on the battlefield below, soaring over the chaos like a grim bird of prey. From his vantage point it was clear the battle was theirs. Yet even though they were ill equipped, outnumbered, and badly outgunned, the Jedi fought bravely to the bitter end. There was no hint of retreat, no breaking of their ranks. He couldn't help but admire such courage and such devotion to a cause even in the face of certain death. If his own troops had been so steadfast in their loyalty and purpose, he would have won this war long ago. It wasn't that they lacked discipline: the Sith armies were just as well trained as those of the Jedi or the Republic. They simply lacked conviction.

Too often their morale had been held together only by the sheer force of Kaan's will, his battle meditation strengthening their resolve whenever the situation seemed grim or desperate. But his battle meditation could only do so much. Against an entire army of Jedi on guard against the Force powers of the Sith, it could do little more than instill a vague sense of unease. A small advantage, but one easily overcome. Here on the surface of this wretched world, the Brotherhood of Darkness and its minions had been forced to fight on their own merits, without his intervention. And far too many times they had come up short.

There had been occasions when he'd questioned the ability of his followers to succeed on their own. There were instances when he wondered if the Sith troops had become so reliant on the enormous advantage of his battle meditation that they had forgotten how to fight effectively without it. But now, at last, the ultimate victory had been achieved. The Jedi were making a last, desperate stand—one glorious to behold—yet the outcome was inevitable. There was just one thing left for Lord Kaan to do before the fighting ended.

He continued to weave back and forth, firing sporadically at the enemy below as he searched for his real prey. Then at last he saw him: General Hoth, standing in the very center of the fray, surrounded by a bulwark of valiant allies and a relentless sea of Sith foes that broke against them again and again and again.

Locking his flier's guns on his target he swooped in, intent on taking his rival's life in a spectacular strafing run. But a mere second before he fired, a massive explosion rocked his flier, causing it to veer to the left. His shots carved a deep furrow in the ground several meters to the left of the general, leaving him miraculously unharmed.

Hoth continued fighting as if he hadn't even noticed, but Kaan banked his vehicle around sharply to see what had happened. Before he completed the turn, another explosion shook the sky beside him, and he saw one of the other fliers careen out of control and crash into the ground.

He looked up, realizing they were under attack from above. A pair of massive gunships were descending on the battle, their batteries blasting the Sith fliers from the sky one by one. On the underside of each ship, the colors of Jedi Master Valenthyne Farfalla were clearly visible.

Impossible! Kaan cursed silently. *There is no way they could have broken through the blockade! Not with ships like this!* Yet somehow they had.

Another series of blasts took out three more of the small fliers, and Kaan realized it was his army that was now suddenly overmatched. The fliers were quicker and more maneuverable than the Jedi gunships, but their blasters wouldn't even make a dent in the larger vessels' heavily armored hulls.

For a brief second he thought he might be able to rally the other Dark Lords. If they concentrated their attacks, they might be able to bring the gunships down—though their own losses would be heavy. But he dismissed that idea as quickly as it had come.

He wasn't the only one who had noticed the arrival of the Jedi reinforcements. Faced with overwhelming odds, the Dark Lords under his command had reacted in the only manner they understood: self-preservation through flight. Already most of the other fliers had broken off their strafing runs and were executing evasive maneuvers, intent only on escaping the battlefield alive. And with their Lords and Masters fleeing the engagement, the hordes of Sith soldiers on the ground would be quick to follow. Imminent victory was about to become disasterous defeat.

Swearing vile oaths against both the Jedi and his own people, Lord Kaan knew there was only one option left. Weaving and darting to avoid a pair of bolts intended to blow him from the sky, he joined the retreat.

29

General Hoth couldn't help but offer the ragged hint of a smile despite the dead and wounded that lay scattered across the battlefield. The Sith had sprung their trap, and somehow the Army of Light had survived.

He recognized Farfalla's colors on the gunships that were now circling the field, keeping the Sith stragglers pinned down under whatever cover they could find until the troops on the ground could surround them and demand their surrender. Most were quick to comply. Everyone knew the Jedi preferred taking prisoners over killing their enemies, just as everyone knew the Jedi treated their prisoners humanely. The same could not be said for the Sith, of course.

A small convoy of personal fliers was emerging from the gunships, flying down to join the survivors on the ground. The general recognized Farfalla aboard the lead flier, even as Farfalla caught sight of him and came in to land.

The younger Jedi stepped off his flier, not speaking but extending his hand by way of cautious greeting. He was dressed in clothes as bright and outlandish as ever, but for some reason it didn't bother Hoth as it once had. Hoth stepped over to him and clasped him in a firm embrace, causing Farfalla to laugh in surprise. Hoth only released him from the fierce hug when Farfalla began to cough and sputter.

"Greetings, Lord Hoth," Farfalla said once he was released, making a deep bow and a flourish. Standing up, he gazed out across the battlefield, and his expression became more serious. "My only regret is we couldn't get here sooner."

"It's a miracle you're here at all, Farfalla," Hoth replied. "I'm afraid to even ask how you managed to run the blockade, in case this all turns out to be nothing more than the fevered dream of a doomed and dying man."

"Rest assured, General, I am quite real. As to how we arrived, that is easy enough to explain: the Sith broke the ranks of their blockade to engage our fleet. With our capital ships drawing the focus of their cruisers and Dreadnaughts, we were able to send several gunships down to your aid."

"What about the rest of our fleet?" Hoth asked in concern. "The Sith had nearly double the numbers of your ships."

"They held their own long enough for us to get through the blockade, then disengaged and retreated with surprisingly few casualties."

"Good." The general nodded. Then he frowned. "But I still don't understand why they would engage your fleet at all. It makes no sense!"

"I can only assume that they received orders to do so from someone here on the surface."

"Kaan was on the verge of wiping us out," Hoth insisted. "The last thing he would do is give the order to engage."

Both Jedi were silent for a moment, pondering the implications of what had happened. Finally Farfalla asked, "Is it possible we have an unknown ally among the Brotherhood of Darkness?"

Hoth shook his head. "I doubt it. More likely the Sith are finally beginning to turn on each other. It was inevitable."

Master Farfalla nodded his agreement. "It is the way of the dark side, after all."

Kaan was fuming as his flier touched down back at the Sith camp. How could everything have gone so terribly wrong in such a short time? They had been on the cusp of victory, and now suddenly they were on the knife's edge of defeat.

He stormed across the camp toward his tent, ignoring the questioning looks of Githany and the others. They wanted an explanation, but he didn't have one to give. Not yet. Not until he got a status report from Admiral Nyras. *How did Farfalla break through the kriffing blockade?*

His anger was so great that he didn't notice Qordis's flier parked near his tent, or the droplets of blood scattered on the ground nearby. If he had, he might have searched the area and found the body stashed in the nearby undergrowth. But all of Kaan's focus was concentrated on reaching his tent and the communications equipment inside.

He found Bane there waiting for him, standing still as stone.

"Back so soon, Kaan?" he asked. "What happened to your glorious battle?"

"Reinforcements," Kaan snarled. "Somehow Farfalla found a way to break through our blockade."

"I told your fleet to engage the Jedi," Bane said, his words as casual as if he had been discussing the weather.

Kaan's jaw dropped. He had suspected treachery, but he wasn't prepared for the traitor to openly admit it! "But . . . why?"

"I wanted all the Jedi here on Ruusan at the same time," Bane replied.

"You blasted fool!" Kaan shouted, waving his arms madly as if they were gripped by uncontrollable spasms. "Victory was ours! We had Hoth beaten!"

"That is your goal, not mine. I'm after a prize far greater than the death of General Hoth. He is but one man."

Kaan barked out a harsh laugh. "We all know what prize you seek, *Darth* Bane. You're here to take over the Brotherhood."

Bane shrugged indifferently, as if it didn't matter one way or the other to him.

He seemed so calm, so certain of what he was doing. It was all Kaan could do to keep himself from leaping at the larger man's throat. Didn't he understand what he had done? Couldn't he see that he had doomed them all?

Kaan slumped wearily into a chair. "If you lead them against the Jedi, you lead them to their slaughter."

Now it was Bane who laughed—a low, sinister chuckle. "How quickly you've fallen into despair, Kaan. It seemed only hours ago you were certain of victory."

"That was before Farfalla and his reinforcements arrived," Kaan shot back. "Back when we had the advantages of numbers and air superiority. All that is gone, thanks to you. We can't possibly defeat them now."

"I can," Bane vowed.

Kaan sat up straighter in his chair. Again, there was that unwavering confidence. Bane knew something he didn't. Some trick. "Another ritual like the last one?" he guessed.

"I know many rituals. Many secrets. And I have the strength to use them."

Dread gripped Kaan. "The thought bomb," he breathed.

"Your leadership has failed," Bane declared. "Now I will take the Brotherhood down the path to victory."

"And what of me?" Kaan asked, already knowing the answer.

"You can swear your loyalty to me with all the others," Bane told him, "or you can die here in this tent."

Lord Kaan knew he was no match for Bane, either physically or through the power of the Force. Yet he wasn't about to surrender so easily. Not while he still had cunning, guile, and his unique talents of persuasion on his side.

"Do you really believe the others will follow you?" he asked, pushing out with the Force to plant the first seeds of doubt in his rival's mind. "They are still wary of you after your last ritual."

A flicker of uncertainty passed across Bane's hard features. Kaan increased the pressure of his invisible compulsions and continued to speak. "The Brotherhood is about equality, not servitude. Asking the others to bow down before you will only drive them away—or turn them against you."

He rose from his chair as Bane nervously stroked his chin, weighing the arguments. "How do you think the others will react when I tell them how you orchestrated the arrival of the Jedi reinforcements?"

Bane's dark eyes flashed angrily, and his hand dropped to the hilt of his lightsaber.

"Killing me won't keep your secret," Kaan warned him. "The others know you weren't at the battle when Farfalla's ships arrived. More than a few of them probably already suspect you of betraying them."

Kaan pushed even harder with the Force, trying to twist and warp Bane's very thoughts. "You may be the strongest among us, but you can't defeat us all. Not by yourself, Bane."

The big man staggered and clutched at his head. He stumbled over to the chair and collapsed in it, the wood groaning under his massive frame. He hunched forward, hands pressing hard on his temples.

"You're right," he said through tightly clenched teeth. "You're right."

"There's still hope, though," Kaan said, stepping over and placing a reassuring hand on Bane's broad shoulder. "Follow me and I will keep the others from turning against you. Join us in the Brotherhood!"

Bane nodded slowly, then turned his head to stare up at Kaan with a desperate, hopeless expression in his eyes. "What about the Jedi? What about their gunships?"

Kaan stood, slowly releasing his mental hold over the other man. "We can nullify their air superiority by retreating into the caves," he said. "I know General Hoth; he will follow us. And there we will unleash the thought bomb against them."

Bane leapt to his feet eagerly. Kaan was pleased to see that his powers of Force persuasion were as strong as ever. Even Bane was not immune to his manipulations. "I will do as you say, Lord Kaan!" he exclaimed. "Together we will destroy the Jedi!"

"Peace, Bane," Kaan urged, extending tendrils of soothing calm. He had nullified the threat to his position that Bane represented, but he knew the effect was only temporary. In time Bane's hostility would return, as would his dreams of usurping the mantle of leadership. Kaan needed to find a more permanent solution.

"Unfortunately," he said, "there are still . . . complications."

"Complications?"

"I can convince the rest of the Brotherhood to forgive your treasonous acts, but only after the Jedi are destroyed. Until then, you will have to remain hidden from the others."

The confused and hurt expression on Bane's face was pitiful, but Kaan was used to eliciting such naked emotion in those he manipulated.

"I will lead the Brotherhood to the caves," he explained. "I am strong enough to join their minds and unleash the power of the thought bomb without your help. You stay here in the tent until nightfall, then sneak out of the camp. Stay safely out of view until the deed is done."

"And once the Jedi are destroyed you will return for me?"

"Yes," Kaan promised, his voice solemn. "Once the Jedi are gone, I will return for you with the full strength of the Brotherhood." That much, at least, was truth. He would leave nothing to chance; he wouldn't underestimate his opponent anymore. Bane had already survived one assassination attempt. This time he would unleash the full numbers of his followers against his foe.

"I will do as you command, Lord Kaan," Bane replied, dropping to one knee and bowing his head. Kaan turned and marched out into the camp, heading for his own tent where the pages containing the ritual of the thought bomb were hidden away.

Bane stayed in the position of supplication until the Dark Lord was well out of sight, then stood up and brushed the dirt from his knees with a grim scowl. He had felt Kaan's efforts to dominate his mind, but they had had no more effect than a rusted knife scraping against the hide plates of a Halurian ice-boar. Yet he had seized on the opportunity and delivered a performance worthy of the greatest dramatist on Alderaan.

Kaan was convinced the thought bomb was the key to Sith victory, and he was about to ensnare the rest of the Brotherhood in his web of madness. The second phase of Bane's plan was set in motion. By nightfall the next day it would all be over.

———

On the perimeters of the Jedi camp, patrols circled endlessly throughout the night, ever vigilant and watchful. It wasn't just attacks from the Sith they stood guard against, but also the invasions of the floating, fur-covered bouncers.

The previously peaceful and docile native creatures of Ruusan had been driven mad by the cataclysm that had swept through the forest. Before, they had been a familiar and welcome sight: gathering in groups over the sick and wounded to project images of comfort and healing. Now they emerged from the night's gloom in terrible packs, inflicting twisted nightmares that brought suffering, terror, and panic to all in the vicinity.

There was nothing the patrols could do but shoot the tormented creatures on sight, before they spread their madness among the Jedi. A grim task, but necessary—as so many other things here on Ruusan had been.

Fortunately, the patrols had managed to keep the bouncers at bay, and the mood within the confines of the Jedi camp itself was one of cautious optimism. After the hopeless despair of the past months their subdued enthusiasm almost felt like jubilant revelry to General Hoth.

They were no longer the hunted, cowering in the depths of the forest, surviving only as long as they remained hidden. The Jedi had gained the upper hand: their new camp had been set up on the open plains along the edges of the very battlefield where the war had turned. And now it was the Sith who had gone into hiding.

The general, though still exhausted by the desperate escape from the flames and the fighting that followed, refused to sleep. There were too many details to see to, too many things that needed his attention.

In addition to organizing the patrols to protect against the bouncers, he also had to oversee the distribution of fresh supplies. Farfalla's ships had delivered desperately needed food, medpacs, and fresh power cells for blasters and personal shields. With most of their other stores lost to the unnatural wildfire that had devastated the forests, the general wanted to make sure all his troops were properly reequipped and tended to before he granted himself the luxury of rest.

He wove his way through dozens of dying campfires and scores of snoring bodies. They were still short on tents for the troops, but those without were more than content to spend the warm nights splayed out on the ground sleeping beneath the open sky.

"General," a voice called out, surprisingly loud in the otherwise still night. Hoth turned to see Farfalla running toward him, sure-footed despite the darkness as he leapt nimbly over the slumbering soldiers in his way.

Pausing to let him catch up, Hoth returned his now customary—yet still extravagant—bow with a courteous nod. "Do you have news, Master Farfalla?"

The younger man nodded excitedly. "Our scouts have spotted the Sith on the move. Kaan is leading them east, toward the foothills."

"Probably heading into the caves and tunnel systems," Hoth guessed. "Trying to take away our advantage in the air."

Farfalla smiled. "Fortunately, we've already done some reconnaissance on the area. We know most of the major access points to and from the surface. Once they go into the tunnels we can surround the exits. They'll be trapped!"

"Hmmm . . ." Hoth stroked his heavy beard. "It isn't like Kaan to make such an obvious tactical mistake," he muttered. "He's up to something."

"I could instruct some of the scouts to follow them into the tunnels and keep an eye on them," Farfalla suggested.

"No," Hoth said firmly after only a moment's consideration. "Kaan will be watching for spies. I won't deliver any of our people into his hands for interrogation."

"Maybe we could starve them out," Farfalla offered. "Force them to surrender without any more bloodshed."

"That would be the best solution," the general admitted. "Unfortunately, I don't think we can afford that kind of time." He gave a deep sigh and a weary shake of his head. "I don't know why Kaan's heading into the caves . . . I just know we have to do something to stop him." Resolve hardened his face. "Sound the reveille and assemble the troops. We'll go in after him."

"Not to question your orders, General," Farfalla began, as tactfully as he could, "but is it possible Kaan is luring you into a trap?"

"I'm almost certain of it," Hoth conceded. "But it's a trap he's going to spring sooner or later anyway. I'd rather not give him time to prepare. If we're lucky we can catch him before he's ready."

"As you command, General," Farfalla said with another of his grandiose bows. Then he added, "You, however, should get some sleep. You look as pale and drawn as one of the Sith yourself."

"I can't sleep now, my friend," Hoth answered, placing a heavy hand on Farfalla's delicate shoulder. "I was here at the start of this war. I was the one who led the Army of Light here to Ruusan to face Kaan's Brotherhood of Darkness. I must see this out to the end."

"But how much longer can you go without sleep, General?"

"Long enough. I get the feeling this will all be over by tomorrow's end—one way or another."

30

The caves were cool and damp, but they were far from dark. The rock walls and ceiling were laced with crystals that caught the dim light from the glow rods, reflecting and refracting their illumination throughout the cavern. Small pools shimmered on the floor, and enormous stalagmites jutted up toward the roof. An inverted forest of stalactites hung down, water dripping steadily from their tips to splash and ripple the pools far below. In some places the protrusions on the floor and ceiling had actually fused, joined by centuries of sediment deposits from the endless trickles of moisture. The enormous columns were magnificent: massive, yet at the same time delicate and fragile.

Kaan had no time to marvel at the natural beauty of their surroundings. He knew the Jedi scouts had marked their exodus to this underground refuge. And he knew General Hoth wouldn't wait long before coming after him.

The cavern, though large, was crowded with the rest of the Brotherhood. Every surviving Sith Lord—with the notable exception of Darth Bane—was gathered with him here to make their final stand. The rest of his army was guarding the main entrances to the subterranean tunnels, with orders to hold off the inevitable Jedi attack for as long as possible.

Eventually those outside would be overwhelmed, but Kaan was confident their numbers would delay Hoth long enough for the ritual of the thought bomb to be completed.

"Gather 'round," he called out to the others. "It is time."

———

Githany knew there was something very wrong with Lord Kaan. She had suspected something was amiss when they had fled the arriving Jedi reinforcements. When they landed back at camp, Kaan had disappeared into the communications tent, then reappeared moments later and gone into his own tent without speaking a word. But when he emerged from his tent, the irresistible force of his charisma was back in place. He came to them then not as a defeated leader seeking to make amends but as a conquering hero, defiant and unbowed. He stood proud, the picture of might and glory.

He spoke to them, his voice strong and his words bold, radiating authority. He spoke of leading them in a joining of their minds, a ritual that would far surpass the one Bane had led them in only hours earlier. He told them of a terrible weapon they would unleash against their foes. He rekindled their faith and hope by revealing the existence of the thought bomb.

He had promised them victory, as he had done so many times before. And, as they had always done in the past, the Brotherhood had followed him once again. Followed him here to this cave, though Githany wasn't sure if it was more accurate to say they had been led—or lured.

She had followed him along with everyone else, compelled by the passion of his words and the sheer magnitude of his personality and presence. All thoughts that he might be unstable or unfit to lead them had been forgotten in the heady pilgrimage through the night to the shelter of this cave. Once they reached their destination, though, the exhilarating rush had faded away, replaced by a stark and undeniable clarity. And she had finally seen the truth revealed in the illumination of the glow rods reflected in the crystals of the cavern walls.

Kaan's appearance and garb weren't unusual, apart from the dust, grime, and blood of the recent battle. But now Githany could see a crazed look in his eyes; they were wide and wild and shone with a fierce intensity, sparkling as brightly as the crystal shards all around them. Those eyes brought back memories of the night she had surprised Kaan in his tent. The night she had seen her vision of Bane's return.

He had looked disheveled and frantic, lost and confused. For a brief moment she had glimpsed him as he truly was: a false prophet, unable to see past his own delusions. And then the flickering vision had disappeared, forgotten until this instant.

Now, however, the memory came flooding back, and Githany knew she was following a madman. The arrival of the Jedi reinforcements and the shocking defeat had caused something inside him to snap. Kaan was leading them to their doom, and none of the others could sense it.

She didn't dare to speak out against him. Not here in this cave, surrounded by his once again fanatically loyal followers. She wanted to sneak away, slip quietly off into the darkness beyond the radiance of the glow rods, and escape this horrible fate. But she was caught up by the crush of bodies that surged forward at Kaan's command.

"Gather in. Closer. Form a circle; a ring of power."

She felt his hand grab her tightly by the wrist and pull her in so that her body pressed up against his. Even in the chill of the cave, his touch was freezing. "Stand beside me, Githany," he whispered. "We will share in this moment of exaltation."

Loudly he shouted, "Join your hands as we must join our minds."

The fingers of his right hand wrapped around her left, seizing it in a grip cold as ice and unyielding as durasteel. One of the other Sith Lords took her other hand, and she knew all hope of escape was gone.

Beside her, Kaan began to chant.

———

Githany was not the only one who sensed something wrong with Lord Kaan. Like all the others, Lord Kopecz had been swept up in the excitement of the thought bomb. He had cheered with all the rest when Kaan described how it would obliterate the Jedi and imprison their spirits. And he had eagerly joined in the throng that had followed him to the cave.

Now, however, his zeal had faded. He was thinking rationally again, and he realized the plan was utter insanity. They were at ground zero of the thought bomb's detonation. Any weapon powerful enough to destroy the Jedi would destroy them, too.

Kaan had promised them that the strength of their combined will would allow them to survive the blast, but now Kopecz had his doubts. The promise stank of wishful thinking birthed from a desperate mind that refused to admit defeat. If Kaan had had this thought bomb all along, why hadn't he used it before?

The only logical answer was that he was afraid of the consequences. And though Kaan, in his madness, may have let go of that fear, Kopecz was still sane enough to cling to his.

The rest of the Sith pressed forward in response to Kaan's command, but Kopecz fought against the momentum of the crowd and moved in the opposite direction. None of the others seemed to notice.

A wall of bodies surrounded Kaan, blocking much of the light from the glow rods. In the shadows the Twi'lek moved carefully toward the cavern's main exit, surprisingly silent for such a large being. He didn't turn or look back as he entered the tunnel to the surface, and picked up his pace only once he heard the Brotherhood begin a slow, rhythmic chant.

Escape was impossible, of course. By now the Jedi would already have the entire tunnel complex surrounded. Soon they would engage the Sith troops out on the surface, trying to break through their barricade to come after Kaan and end the last great battle of Ruusan. Kopecz didn't know if they would make it in time. Part of him actually hoped they would.

In the end, though, he wanted to make sure it didn't matter to him. He'd join the defenders on the surface in one last stand against the Jedi. Death was inevitable; he was willing to accept that fact. But he also knew he'd rather die from a lightsaber or a blaster shot than be caught by the thought bomb's detonation.

————

The chant was simple, and after repeating it only once Kaan was joined by the rest of the Brotherhood. They recited the unfamiliar catechism in a steady, constant rhythm. Their voices bounced off the cavern walls, the ancient words mixing and mingling in counterpoint as they echoed throughout the cave.

Githany could feel the power beginning to gather in the center of the ring, like a fierce whirlpool spinning faster and faster. She felt the pull on her conscious thoughts as they were dragged down, her awareness, her mind, and even her identity swallowed up in the vortex. The cool dampness of the cave faded, as did the reverberation of their voices. She could no longer smell the mildew and fungus growing in the hidden corners, or feel the pressure of the hands that gripped her own. Finally, the shimmering of the reflective crystals and the pale light from the glow rods melted away.

We are one. The voice was Kaan's, yet it was hers, as well. *We are the dark side. The dark side is us.*

Though she could no longer hear the sound of their chanting she could sense it, even as her mind slipped deeper and deeper into the center. Realizing she would soon lose both the ability and the desire to free herself from Kaan's ritual, she tried to fight against what was happening to her.

It was like swimming against the relentless undertow of an ocean's heart. She felt the words of their recurring mantra taking physical shape. They wrapped around their collective will, trapping it, shaping it, and binding it into a rapidly coalescing form.

Feel the power of the dark side. Surrender to it. Surrender to the unified whole. Let us become one.

From deep within herself Githany summoned her last reserves of resistance. Somehow they were enough, and she was able to wrench her mind free from the unholy conclave.

She staggered back with a gasp, her sense crashing over her like floodwaters bursting through a retaining wall. Sight, sound, smell, and touch returned all at once, overwhelming her frantic mind. The light from the glow rods had grown faint and dim, as if it, too, was being swallowed by the ritual. The chant continued, so loud now it actually hurt her ears. The temperature had dropped so sharply that she was able to see her breath, and tiny crystals of frost had begun to form on the stalactites and along the edges of the tiny puddles and pools.

Suddenly she realized that neither Kaan nor anyone else had a grip on her hands. They were all standing in the ring, arms raised toward its center, oblivious to the world around them. At first it looked as if they were grasping at nothing, but as her eyes adjusted to the gloom she caught sight of a strange distortion in the air.

Githany couldn't bear to look at it for more than a moment. There was something terrible and unnatural about the wavering fabric of reality, and she turned away in horror.

Bane was right, she realized. *Kaan has brought us to ruin!*

There was a faint tug on her mind. A gentle pull that was quickly growing stronger, threatening to draw her in with the others. She stumbled away from the profane ceremony and its doomed celebrants, squinting to see her way along the uneven footing.

Bane tried to warn me, but I wouldn't listen. Her thoughts were a chaotic jumble of regret, desperation, and fear. Even as one part of her brain chastised her for her mistake, another was forcing her to back away from the abomination being birthed by the Brotherhood.

Her retreat brought her to one of the cavern walls and she followed along it, looking for a way out. The compulsion of the ritual was growing stronger. She could feel it calling to her, inviting her to join the others and share their fate.

She had no plan, no sense of where she was going. She simply had to escape, flee, get out. Get away from here before she was sucked in once again. A small space opened in the stone: a narrow tunnel entrance just wide enough for her to sneak through. She squeezed her body into the crevice, the jagged stone slicing through cloth and skin.

The pain was nothing to her. The physical world was slipping away again. Desperately, Githany managed to throw herself forward, crashing to the ground, then crawled frantically on her hands and knees down the tunnel.

Away. She had to get away. Away from the ritual. Away from Kaan. Away from the thought bomb before it was too late.

The Sith soldiers guarding the entrance to the subterranean tunnels were strong in number but weak in spirit. They offered only token resistance to Farfalla and the rest of the Jedi advance units who came against them. The last battle of Ruusan quickly transformed into a mass surrender, with the enemy throwing down their weapons and begging for their lives.

Farfalla walked among his troops, surveying the scene. General Hoth was close behind with the bulk of the army. He'd be surprised to find the war already over when he arrived.

"How goes it?" Farfalla asked one of the unit commanders.

"The Sith troops have us outnumbered three to one," the commander answered gruffly. "And they're all trying to surrender at the same time. This is going to take awhile."

Farfalla gave him a hearty laugh and slapped him on the shoulder. "Well said," he agreed. "Sometimes I think people only follow the Sith because they know we will take them alive if they lose."

"Don't you dare take me alive, Farfalla," a voice gurgled. Turning his head sharply, he saw a heavyset Twi'lek lying wounded on the ground.

The injured Twi'lek struggled to his feet, and Farfalla was surprised to see that he wore the robes of a Sith Lord. His face was so covered in blood and gore, most of it his own, that it took the Jedi a moment to recognize him.

"Kopecz," he said at last, remembering him from days long gone, back when Kopecz had been a Jedi. "You are hurt," Farfalla continued, extending his hand in an offer of friendship. "Lay down your weapons and we can help you."

The Twi'lek's meaty hand lashed out to slap him away. "I chose my side long ago," he spat. "Promise me death, Jedi, and I will give you a warning. I will tell you Kaan's plan."

One look at the Dark Lord's wounds told Farfalla his enemy didn't have long to live in any case. "What do you know?"

Kopecz coughed, choking on the blood welling up in his throat. "Promise me, first," he wheezed.

"I will grant you death, if that is what you truly seek. I swear it."

The Twi'lek laughed, pink froth bubbling up on his lips. "Good. Death is an old friend. What Kaan has planned is far worse." And he told Farfalla about the thought bomb, his words sending a chill down the Jedi Master's spine. When Kopecz had finished he bowed his head and took a deep breath to gather his strength, then activated his lightsaber.

"You promised me death," he said. "I wish to fall in combat. If you hold back at all, you will be the one who dies here today. Do you understand?"

Master Farfalla nodded grimly, igniting his own weapon.

Lord Kopecz fought valiantly despite his wounds, though he was no match for a fresh and uninjured Jedi Master. In the end, Farfalla fulfilled his promise.

31

The scene that greeted General Hoth as his army came upon the battlefield was as unexpected as it was welcome. He had braced himself for a vision of grim and bloody slaughter, fierce combat with neither side giving nor asking quarter. He had imagined the corpses of the dead would be strewn about, trampled beneath the feet of those still fighting desperately to hang on to their lives. He had come expecting to see a war.

Instead he was witness to something so unbelievable his initial reaction was one of suspicion. Was it a trick? A trap? His fears were quickly allayed when he recognized the familiar and smiling faces of other Jedi all around him.

As he surveyed the aftermath of the last battle of Ruusan, his own face broke into a smile. There were only a handful of dead, and from their dress it was clear that few of them had served in the Army of Light. Most of the enemy had been taken prisoner: they were sitting calmly on the ground in large groups, surrounded by armed Jedi. Yet even though the Jedi were keeping close watch on their captured foes, they were laughing and joking with one another.

He reached out with the Force, and he felt wave after wave of relief and joy washing out from Farfalla's troops. The soldiers under his command were quick to feel it, too. Seeing the obvious victory, they broke ranks and ran cheering and laughing down to join their fellows in celebration. Hoth resisted the urge to shout out a command to regroup and simply let them go.

The endless war was over!

But as he walked through the milling throngs, accepting the salutes and congratulations of his followers, he realized something was wrong. The battlefield was full of placid, unarmed Sith . . . but he saw not a single Dark Lord among their numbers.

The sight of Master Farfalla running at full speed toward him from the far side of the field did little to soothe his unease.

"General," Farfalla said, sliding to a stop and gasping for breath. He snapped off a quick salute. The lack of his typical over-the-top bow further fueled Hoth's mounting concern.

"I must have taken longer to assemble my forces than I thought," the general joked, hoping his disquiet was simply misplaced paranoia. "It seems you've already won the war."

Farfalla shook his head. "The war isn't over. Not yet. Kaan and the Brotherhood—the true Sith—have taken refuge in the caves. They're going to unleash some kind of Sith weapon. Something called a thought bomb."

A thought bomb? Hoth had heard mention of such a weapon long ago, studying at the feet of his Master back at the Jedi Temple on Coruscant. According to legendary accounts, the ancient Sith had the ability to forge the dark side into a concentrated sphere of power and then unleash its energy in a single, devastating blast. All those sensitive to the Force—Sith and Jedi alike—would be consumed by the explosion, their spirits trapped in the great vacuum created at the epicenter of the detonation.

"Is Kaan mad?" he said aloud, though the very question was answer enough.

"We have to evacuate, General," Farfalla insisted. "Get everyone away as fast as possible."

"No," Hoth answered. "That won't work. If we retreat, Kaan and the Brotherhood will escape. It won't take them long to rally support and begin this war all over again."

"But what about the thought bomb?" Valenthyne demanded.

"If Kaan has such a weapon," the general explained grimly, "then he will use it. If not here, then somewhere else. Maybe in the Core Worlds. Maybe on Coruscant itself. I can't allow that.

"Kaan wants to witness my death. I have to go into the cave to face him. I have to force him to detonate the bomb here on Ruusan. It's the only way to truly end this."

Farfalla dropped to one knee. "Then I will go by your side, General. As will all who follow me."

Reaching out with his strong, weathered hands, General Hoth took Farfalla by the shoulders and hauled him to his feet. "No, my friend," he said with a sigh, "you cannot walk this journey with me."

When the other started to protest he held up a hand for silence and continued. "When Kaan unleashes his weapon, all within that cave will die. The Sith will be wiped out, but I won't let that happen to our entire order. The galaxy will have need of Jedi to rebuild once this war is over. You and the other Masters must live so that you may guide them and defend the Republic as we have done since its foundation."

There was no real argument against the wisdom of his words, and after a moment's deliberation Master Farfalla dropped his head in mute acceptance. When he looked up again there were tears in his eyes.

"Surely you're not going in alone?" he protested.

"I wish I could," Hoth replied. "But if I do the Dark Lords will simply take me down with their lightsabers. That would solve nothing. Kaan has to see that his only choice is to surrender or . . ." He left the thought unspoken.

"You'll need enough Jedi to convince the Brotherhood that a physical battle would be hopeless. At least a hundred. Any less and he won't detonate the thought bomb."

Hoth nodded. "Nobody will be ordered to go in with me. Ask for volunteers. And make sure they understand none of us will ever be coming out."

————

Despite the danger, virtually every single member of the Army of Light volunteered for the mission. General Hoth realized that he shouldn't have been surprised. After all, these were Jedi, willing to sacrifice everything— even their lives—for the greater good. In the end he did what he knew he would have to do all along: he himself chose who would accompany him to certain death.

He selected exactly ninety-nine others to go with him. The decision was agonizingly difficult. If he took less, the Sith might be able to fight their way out of the cave and escape, only to detonate their thought bomb somewhere else. But the more he took, the more Jedi lives he might be needlessly throwing away.

Choosing who would go with him was even more difficult. Those Jedi who had served at his side the longest, the ones who had joined the Army of Light at the very beginning of the campaign, were those he knew best. He knew how much they had already given in this war, and these were the ones he least wanted to lead to their doom. Yet these were the ones with the most right to stand by his side when the end finally came, and when all was said and done that was how he made his selection. Those with the most seniority would go with him; the others would fall back with Lord Farfalla.

The hundred Jedi—the ninety-nine chosen plus Hoth himself—stood anxiously at the entrance of the tunnels. The sky above was growing dark as night fell and ominous storm clouds rolled in. Still, the general did not give the command to advance. He wanted to give Farfalla and the others enough time to get clear. If it had been possible, he would have ordered all those not going into the cave to leave Ruusan. But there wasn't time. They would simply have to get as far away as possible, then hope they were beyond the range of Kaan's thought bomb.

As the first drops of rain began to fall, he realized he could wait no longer, and he gave the command to advance. They marched in an orderly fashion into the tunnel, down into the caverns far beneath the planet's surface.

The first thing Hoth noticed as they descended was how cold the tunnel quickly became, as if all the heat had been sucked away. The next thing he felt was the tension in the air. It actually pulsed with vast, unimaginable power just barely held in check; the power of the dark side. He didn't allow himself to think about what would happen when that power was released.

They advanced slowly, wary of traps or an ambush. They found none.

In fact, they saw no sign of the Sith at all until they reached the large central cavern at the heart of the tunnel system.

General Hoth led the way, a glow rod in one hand and his drawn lightsaber in the other. As he stepped into the cavern, his glow rod suddenly flickered and went very dim. Even the illumination from his lightsaber seemed to die, becoming the thinnest sliver of incandescence.

As his eyes grew accustomed to the heavy shadows he was able to pick out the shapes of the Sith Lords, standing in a circle on the far side of the cave. They faced inward, their hands raised to its center. They stood without moving, their mouths hanging open, their features slack, their eyes blank. Cautiously, he approached the still forms, wondering if they were alive, dead, or trapped in some nightmare state in between.

Drawing closer he could make out a single figure standing in the center of the circle: Lord Kaan. He hadn't seen him at first; the middle of the ring was darker than the rest of the cave. There seemed to be a black cloud hovering above him, tendrils of inky darkness extending down to wrap and twist around him in a sinister embrace.

One look at the leader of the Brotherhood and any hope the general had of convincing Lord Kaan to listen to reason died. The Sith Lord's face was pale and taut; his features were stretched as if his skin had become too tight for his skull. A thin layer of ice coated his hair and lashes. His expression was one of cruel arrogance, and his left eye trembled and twitched uncontrollably. He stared straight ahead with a frozen intensity, unblinking and unmoving as Hoth and his Jedi slowly filled the cavern.

Only after all the Jedi were inside did he speak. "Welcome, Lord Hoth." His voice was tight and strained.

"Are you trying to scare me, Kaan?" Hoth asked, stepping forward. "I do not fear death," he continued. "I do not mind dying. I would not mind all the Jedi dying if it meant the end of the Sith."

Kaan turned his head quickly from one side to the other, his eyes darting back and forth across the cave as if he were counting the Jedi who stood before him. His lip curled into a sneer, and he raised his hands up.

The general made his move, lunging forward to try to end Kaan's life before he could unleash his ultimate weapon. He wasn't quick enough.

The Dark Lord clapped his hands together sharply—and the thought bomb exploded.

In an instant every living soul in the cave was snuffed out of existence. Clothing, flesh, and bone were vaporized. The stalactites, the stalagmites, even the massive stone columns were reduced to clouds of dust. The rumbling echo of the blast rolled down every tunnel, crevice, and fissure leading out of the cavern as the destructive wave of energy began to spread.

———

Githany was trapped in the labyrinth of subterranean passages. In fleeing Kaan's ritual she had lost her bearings, and now she wandered aimlessly down kilometer after kilometer of natural tunnels as she searched in vain for an exit to the surface.

In the dim light of her glow rod she saw a small opening on her left and followed it for many meters before it came to a dead end. Shouting out a curse, she turned and made her way back again.

She was furious. Furious at Kaan for bringing the Brotherhood to the brink of destruction. Furious at herself for following him there. And furious at Bane. There was no doubt in her mind that he had somehow orchestrated all this. He had manipulated Kaan and the rest of the Brotherhood, driving them toward their own destruction. Yet that betrayal wasn't what enraged her. Bane had abandoned her. He'd cast her aside with the others, leaving her to die while he went off to rebuild the Sith.

Ahead of her the tunnel branched in two directions. She paused, drawing on the Force to heighten her senses in the hope she might find some hint as to which path to take. At first there was nothing. Then she caught the faintest whisper of a breeze coming from the tunnel on the left. The air smelled fresh and clean: it led to the surface!

As she raced up the passage, her frustration and rage fell away. She was going to survive! The uneven ground began to slope sharply upward, and she could see a hint of natural light far in the distance. She redoubled her efforts, and her thoughts turned to how she would exact her revenge.

She would have to be subtle and cunning. She had underestimated

Bane too many times in the past. This time she would be patient, not striking until she was certain the moment was right.

The first step was to find him and offer to be his apprentice. There was no doubt in her mind he would accept. He needed someone to serve him; it was the way of the dark side. She would learn at his feet, subjugating herself to his will. It might take years, maybe decades, but in time he would teach her everything he knew. Only then, after all his secrets were hers, would she turn on him. She would become the Master and take an apprentice of her own.

Escape was less than fifty meters away when Githany felt the first effects of the thought bomb. It began with a trembling in the ground. Her initial instinct was fear of a groundquake or cave-in that would bury her beneath tons of dirt and stones within sight of the surface. But when she felt the power of the dark side rushing up the passage toward her, she realized she was about to suffer a far more horrible fate. Those at the epicenter of the blast had been vaporized. Caught on the fringes of the thought bomb's radius, Githany was not so lucky. The wave of pure dark side energy swept over her an instant later. It tore through her like some terrible wind, sucking the essence of life from her body and ripping her spirit from its corporeal shell. Her flesh withered and shrank, her beautiful features mummified before she even had time to scream. And then, as quickly as it had come, the wave had passed. For one frozen moment her lifeless husk stood in perfect balance, before it toppled and struck the ground, disintegrating into ash.

———

On the surface many kilometers away, Farfalla and the other Jedi felt the ground shake, and they knew their general was no more. A moment later their minds erupted with the tortured screams of the Jedi and Sith caught up in the blast, their life-force ripped away and sucked into the vacuum at the heart of the blast.

Many of the Jedi wept in anguish, understanding how great the sacrifice of their fallen comrades had been. The spirits of the dead were bound for all eternity, forever frozen in stasis.

Master Valenthyne Farfalla, now the leader of what remained of the

Army of Light, felt the sorrow as deeply as any of them. But this was not the time for grief. With General Hoth's passing, the burden of command was his to bear, and there were things that still needed to be done.

"Captain Haduran, assemble a team," he ordered. "We're going to search the area in and around the tunnels for survivors." He knew no living creature could have withstood the power of the thought bomb, but it was possible a few of the Sith might have fled before the detonation. After all that had been sacrificed, he had no intention of letting any of the Brotherhood escape.

The captain gave him a quick salute and turned to go. Just before he left Farfalla added, "And have your troops keep an eye out for the bouncers. The last Sith ritual drove them to madness. Who knows what this one did to them."

"And if we spot them, sir?"

"Shoot to kill."

———

Many kilometers in the opposite direction, Darth Bane also felt the reverberations of the blast. He sensed the wave of dark side energy pass over him, strong enough to leave him shivering even at this distance. Once it was gone he reached out with the Force to seek out any who might have escaped. As he expected, he felt nothing. They were all gone: Kaan, Kopecz, Githany . . . all of them.

The Brotherhood of Darkness had been purged. As far as the Jedi knew, the Sith were now extinct. Bane intended to keep it that way.

He was the only Dark Lord of the Sith, the last of his kind. The burden of rebuilding the order would fall to him. But this time he would do it right. Instead of many there would be only two: one Master and one apprentice. One to embody the power, and one to crave it.

To survive, the Sith had to vanish, becoming creatures of myth, legend, and nightmares. Hidden from the eyes of the Jedi, they could seek out the lost secrets of the dark side until its full power was theirs to command. Only then—once victory over their enemies was certain—would they tear aside the veil of shadows and reveal themselves.

The path ahead would be long and difficult. It might take years or

decades before they could strike at the light once more. Perhaps even centuries. But Bane was patient; he understood what was to come and what
must be done. Though he himself might not live to see the triumph of the
dark side, those who followed him would carry on his legacy. Someday in
the distant future, the Republic would fall and the Jedi would perish, and
the entire galaxy would bow down to a Dark Lord of the Sith. It was inevitable; it was the way of the dark side.

Satisfied that his work on Ruusan was done, he began the long hike to
where he had hidden his ship. He knew the remaining Jedi would come
looking for survivors, but by the time they arrived he would be long gone.

Still, one thing troubled him. In order for all this to come to pass he
had to find a suitable apprentice. One strong in the Force, but not yet
tainted by the teachings of the Jedi. Somewhere he needed to find a child
worthy of becoming heir to all the power of the dark side.

EPILOGUE

Rain stirred in her sleep, yet didn't wake. Someone was calling to her, but she didn't want to answer. In her dreams she could imagine she was still back home with her cousins, enjoying a simple but happy life. If she woke, she knew she'd have to face the truth: that life was gone forever.

Wake, Rain . . .

It had vanished the moment that the Jedi—Master Torr, his name had been—had recruited them to join the Army of Light. She hadn't even really wanted to join. But Bug and Tomcat, her cousins, were both going. They were her only family, and she didn't want to be left behind. She was young—only ten—but she was strong in the Force. And so Master Torr had let her come, too.

He had told them he was taking them to Ruusan, where they would become Jedi. Only that never happened. Their shuttle had been attacked as soon as they entered the atmosphere. What occurred next was just a blur, but she remembered an explosion and screams. One wing of the ship had sheared away and suddenly she was falling. The smoking wreckage of the shuttle became a speck in the sky above her as it spiraled off out of control and she fell down, down, down until—

Rain, wake!

Laa! Laa had saved her, and it was Laa who was calling to her now. Slowly she opened her eyes and sat up, still groggy.

Rain slept long. Now Rain must wake.

"I'm up, Laa," she said to the bouncer hovering above her. Laa had saved her from that fall, catching her as she plummeted from hundreds of meters above Ruusan's surface.

Bad dreams, Rain.

"No," she replied. "Not bad dreams, Laa. I dreamed I was back home." Laa never actually spoke to her; she only heard the words inside her head. They communicated through the power of the Force, Laa had once explained to her. But whenever Rain answered, she always voiced the words aloud.

Bad dreams coming.

Rain frowned, trying to figure out exactly what Laa was trying to tell her. Sometimes when the bouncers talked about dreams they actually meant something else. Sometimes it was as if the bouncers had visions of the future. She remembered what Laa had said just before the entire forest had exploded in flames: *Bad dreams, Rain. Death dreams.*

The fires had killed most of the other bouncers. The survivors had all gone mad. All except Laa. Somehow Rain had saved her. She'd used the Force, shielding them both from the burning death and destruction, though she wasn't quite sure how she'd done it. It had just sort of . . . happened. Now she and Laa had nobody left but each other.

Bad dreams coming, the bouncer repeated.

A few hours earlier she had felt something strange: the ground rumbling beneath her feet as if something had exploded far, far away. Was this what Laa was talking about? Was this the bad dream? Or was her friend trying to warn her about something that hadn't happened yet?

"I don't understand," she said, looking around at the bushes surrounding the clearing where she had lain down to sleep. She didn't see anything out of the ordinary. Not yet, anyway.

Good-bye, Rain.

There was an aching sorrow in Laa's words that stabbed through Rain's heart like a knife, but she still didn't know what the bouncer was talking about.

Before she could ask, there was a sound from the bushes. She spun around to see two men come crashing into the clearing. She could tell right away they were Jedi: they wore the same brown robes as Master Torr, and she saw lightsabers dangling from their belts. Each one also carried a large blaster rifle.

"Bouncer!" one shouted. "Look out!"

They reacted so quickly their motions were nothing but a blur as they opened fire. By the time the scream left Rain's lips, her friend was already dead.

She was still screaming when the first Jedi ran up to her. "Are you okay, little one?" he asked, reaching down.

Instinctively, she lashed out at him. She didn't know how she did it; it wasn't even a conscious thought. She only knew he had shot her friend. He had killed Laa!

"What's the mat—" His voice was cut short as she snapped his neck with the Force. The eyes of his companion went wide in horror, but before he could do anything else she had broken his neck, too.

Only then did Rain stop screaming. Instead she began to cry, great heaving sobs that racked her body as she crawled over to press herself against the soft green fur of Laa's still-warm body where it had fallen to the ground.

———————

Bane found her there: a young human child weeping over the remains of one of Ruusan's native bouncers. The corpses of two young Jedi lay nearby, their heads twisted at obscene angles to their bodies. It took him only an instant to piece together what must have happened.

The girl looked up at him as he approached, her eyes puffy and red. He guessed she was nine, maybe ten at the most. He could feel the power of the Force burning in her, fueled by grief and rage and hatred. Even if he hadn't sensed it, the broken Jedi at her feet gave mute testament to her abilities.

He didn't speak, but stood silently. The girl's sobbing stopped. She sniffled and wiped her nose with the back of her hand. Then she rose to her feet and took a tentative step toward him.

"Who are you?" he demanded, his voice deep and threatening.

She didn't retreat or flee, though her reply was hesitant. "My name is

Rain . . . I mean Zannah. My cousins used to call me Rain, but they're dead now. Zannah's my real name."

Bane nodded, understanding completely. Rain: a nickname, a name of childhood and innocence. An innocence now lost.

"Do you know who I am?" he asked.

She nodded and took another step forward. "You're a Sith."

"You're not afraid of me?"

"No," she insisted with a shake of her head, though Bane knew she wasn't being completely honest. He could feel her fear, but it was buried beneath far stronger emotions: grief, anger, hatred, and the desire for revenge.

"I have killed many people," Bane warned her. "Men, women . . . even children."

She shuddered but held her ground. "I'm a killer, too."

Bane glanced over at the Jedi corpses, then turned his focus back to the little girl standing defiantly before him. Was she the one? Had the Force led him along this route back to his ship? Had it brought him here at this exact moment simply so he could find his apprentice?

He asked the final, most important question. "Do you know the ways of the Force? Do you understand the true nature of the dark side?"

"No," Rain admitted, never dropping her gaze from his own. "But you can teach me. I'm young. I will learn."

ABOUT THE AUTHOR

DREW KARPYSHYN is a fantasy and science fiction novelist and an award-winning writer/designer for the computer game company BioWare. He lives in Canada's hinterlands of the Great White North with his loving wife, Jen, and their cat.

ABOUT THE TYPE

This book was set in Minion, a 1990 Adobe Originals type-face by Robert Slimbach. Minion is inspired by classical, old style typefaces of the late Renaissance, a period of elegant, beautiful, and highly readable type designs. Created primarily for text setting, Minion combines the aesthetic and functional qualities that make text type highly readable with the versatility of digital technology.